LIFE
IN A
BOX

EINAT LIFSHITZ SHEM-TOV

D1715849

Life in a Box / Einat Lifshitz Shem-Tov

All rights reserved; No parts of this book may be reproduced or transmitted in any form or by any means, electronic or mechanical, including photocopying, recording, taping, or by any information retrieval system, without the permission, in writing, of the author.

Copyright © 2017 Einat Lifshitz Shem-Tov

Translated from the Hebrew: Pamela Gazit
Contact: einats58@gmail.com

ISBN: 9781546784456

In loving memory of my parents,
David and Ada, who left too soon.

To Jacob, my beloved husband,
and to my daughters Ortal and Reut:
You are my inspiration. And I love you so much.

1

The accident was unavoidable. It was one of the coldest days of the year. A thin layer of ice covered the streets, and the air itself was frozen, as if it was also suffering the cold. There were only a handful of cars on the road. Those who could avoid leaving home did so. It was nine o'clock in the evening. The stores along the street were closing and it was almost completely dark outside. I was later informed that my mother was still wearing her coat, while my father's coat was lying on the back seat. They were driving in a car my father borrowed from work.

My parents had been invited by a colleague to celebrate the birth of his first grandson. They rarely left the house together; usually my father went to this kind of event alone, leaving my mother at home. For some reason, she insisted on joining him that evening. I vaguely remember that before she left the house, she glanced back and her eyes settled on me for what seemed like a long time.

"The roads were slick and your father was driving too fast. The car swerved on a curve and went over the side of the road. It took two hours for someone to find them at the bottom of the cliff." This is what I was told by the policeman who came to my house.

My father was killed instantly. My mother fought for her life for one week.

Only a few people came to the funerals. My parents didn't have friends or family. There were about ten people at my father's funeral, all of them colleagues from work. Another group of people stood further away from the grave; I didn't know whether they knew him or were just at the cemetery by chance and decided to pay their respects to the stranger.

A week later, as I buried my mother, several of the neighbors came to the funeral, but only those who seemed to feel an obligation to come. To me, they looked like faceless shadows.

I am an only child and in the days following the tragedy, I functioned on autopilot. I slept alone the first night after my mother died. The days between my father's death and my mother's were spent at the hospital; upon coming home to shower and change clothes, I would find a bowl of some kind of food on the table. There was no taste in any of it, but each day the food was exchanged for something fresh and appetizing, albeit not to me.

During those difficult days, I didn't stop for a minute to wonder who was leaving the food on my table, or who was taking care of it afterward. My body moved completely on its own. I was awake but numb.

A small number of people came to my house to pay their condolences, among them Sarah, a neighbor and friend of my mother's. She suggested I stay at her house for a while, but I firmly refused. Some days she would knock on the door, and when I opened it she would walk in without being asked. Sometimes she would sit in the kitchen and ask questions about my life and my plans for the future; sometimes she would just sit quietly. It was at those times I felt the most uncomfortable.

***

The town I live in is a three-hour drive from Chicago. It is a suburb that looks like a lot of other suburbs in the United States. It has a quaint park at the center of town with wooden benches scattered along the pathways. On the weekends, families come out to walk along the paths and the sounds of young children on bicycles or roller skates echo in the air. Couples arm in arm wander around the park trying to avoid the children's reckless mischief.

The farmers live on the outskirts of town. Corn fields like endless tapestries surround the city, waving every which way in the wind. The farmers' broken-down homes stand like gravestones, a testament to the town's age.

Once there was a movie theater in town. It was replaced by a small shopping mall, providing the residents with the illusion of a big city: it has clothes shown in fashion magazines, modern electric appliances, and food stalls.

Up until the accident, my life passed by like scenery on a train. I never touched it and I left no footprints. I lived my life like a horse with blinders on. Apparently, it was my way of surviving, but my parents' deaths and the events that followed roused my sleeping demons; suddenly I was forced to look inside myself and deal with them.

The chain of events that followed the tragic accident began the night after I buried my mother.

I was very tired, without even the energy to take off my clothes and make up the bed. I lay down in my black mourning clothes, exhausted and spent, curled up in the fetal position as if trying to find shelter inside my newly orphaned self. All of a sudden a feeling came over me: I wasn't alone. A shadow seemed to cross the doorway, a sort of invisible wave that passed from one side of the door to the other and continued down the hallway. I froze, holding my breath. My heart began to race. My eyes opened and closed intermittently.

After several minutes of this, I suddenly remembered something my father told me at six or seven years old, one morning after a nightmare. I had woken up frightened and called out to him, but he hadn't heard me. To my surprise, he said in a commanding voice, "You must learn to deal with your fears by yourself. Trust only yourself!" My father represented the ultimate truth for me. He knew everything and I always turned to him. But at that moment, in addition to my panic, I felt a touch of despair; I had disappointed him, and that feeling was even worse than the fear.

I wanted to get up to peek into the hallway, to ask who was there. My body and my voice wouldn't comply. I continued to lie in my childhood bed, the only bed I ever knew, opening my eyes from time to time but seeing only darkness. Gradually the fear shifted to logic. *It was just my imagination playing tricks*, I thought. Little by little, the fatigue of the day washed over me and gave way to sleep.

I slept until the late afternoon—it felt like a week. The house was as quiet as a cemetery at night. *What am I going to do with myself now? I'm completely alone.* I had no idea where to go or what to do; should I go right back to my routine or allow myself to get sucked into the grief?

At seven o'clock that evening the doorbell rang. Sarah was standing there on my doorstep, holding an eggplant quiche. She made her way into the house and sat down in my father's armchair in the living room. Seeing her stumpy body sinking into my father's chair was more than I could handle. I asked her to change places, but she remained sitting where she was staring at me. She let out a sigh. After a few minutes, she finally got up and mumbled something to herself.

"What are you going to do now?" she asked.

"I don't know," I answered.

"What do you think?" she asked insistently.

I decided not to answer. But her eyes showed she was still waiting for an answer. She wasn't going to let me off the hook.

Her gaze broke down my defenses, bringing up the urge to retreat.

I think Sarah felt it too. She moved closer to me, sat down on the arm of my chair and put her hand on my shoulder. This small, unfamiliar gesture made a small crack in the dam that held back my tears—a crack that gradually grew until the waterworks locked inside my body broke through all at once. Yesterday's pent-up tears now burst forth, despite the inopportune moment. I wanted to weep alone, like always, but instead a stranger witnessed my sorrow.

Sarah's caressing my head together with her silence only served to increase my crying. It was her gentle touch—something that, to the best of my knowledge, I had never experienced before. A thought ran through my head that if my father was here, he would have put an immediate stop to this display of affection. My father was disgusted by physical contact. He always insisted that physical contact was a sign of weakness and that people should derive strength only from themselves. Once my mother came over to console me after a fall from my bicycle along the path in front of my house. The bicycle was new—a birthday present, only a week old. My father taught me to ride. He said that he would show me what to do and then I would have to practice on my own. After one of my falls, worse than all the others, my mother ran out the door to help me. But my father followed right after her so he could keep her away from me. He gave her a withering glare—eyes like daggers—and she immediately stepped back. She took her hands away from my body with a hidden caress, her slim body stood up straight and she dragged herself back to the house.

"I don't know. I really don't know what to do," I said, admitting it both to Sarah and myself.

At twenty years old, I felt like a little girl. Time was slipping through my fingers. There was nothing in my life to be proud of, nothing that was all mine. I had lived at home with my parents, in the bedroom I'd lived in since the age of three. My life had been enmeshed with my father's; all decisions went through him, and his opinion was given on a routine basis.

Even when I made a decision on my own, any signs of dissatisfaction from my father made me give in immediately. I had been completely dependent upon him. *Who would decide for me now? Who is going to explain how to do things?* Drowning in self-pity, I whispered, "Daddy, what am I going to do without you?"

During those days, sleep was my only comfort. Each day I'd promise myself, *Tomorrow I will start making decisions about the future.* In the meantime, I slept on the unmade bed, submerging myself into the inviting darkness. I was lost just like the Little Prince on his star—a tiny dot inside an infinite universe.

One night I woke up suddenly, sitting up in bed and looking out into the black space of my room, listening to a rustling sound. Perhaps it was just one of the sounds the house made every night—sounds that I had learned to accept as part of the house's nightly routine. Sometimes it would be the refrigerator letting out a sigh, or the television with its crackles and pops; sometimes there would be a shadow roaming across the wall of the room, or a demon that at daylight became a shirt on the chair or the gaping door of a closet.

But this time the rustling sound continued. I sat up in bed and waited. There was silence for a bit and then that sound again—like an object being dragged. I tried to give the sound a rational explanation and decided it must be the wind moving the branches of a tree under the window, scratching the walls of the house. Except there was no wind that day; autumn had yet to come.

The noise again! And this time it seems to be getting closer. I looked around and searched for something that could serve as a weapon, but the room contained only my familiar belongings: old dolls sitting lazily against the wall, some with missing limbs; on the floor in one of the corners, the baseball my father had bought me; on my writing table, books that had waited for me to read them for over a year; and in the corner across from the bed, my guitar, one of the only presents my mother ever bought me. The strings were loose and a layer of white dust gave it the appearance of an old woman's skin. I wondered for a moment why I had never played it.

The noise grew louder and I looked from my childhood toys to the door, where a transparent wave crossed the opening; it swayed from side to side for a few seconds in front of me and continued on its way toward the kitchen. *I must be going crazy!* I wrapped myself up in the blanket and covered my head with it like a frightened child. *Except I am no longer a child.* My father's words echoed again in my brain, and the disappointment he most certainly would feel if he saw me now prompted me to get up, stripping off the blanket and waiting, listening. The noise came again, only weaker this time.

I put one foot on the floor and then the other. I walked on silent bare feet, crouching as if an upright body might make a sound, to the door of my room. It seemed as if the rustling grew louder. I made it to the door, held on to the door frame and poked my head out. Only darkness—nothing out of place, no form to be seen. The kitchen was to my left, a few yards from my room, seemingly at rest. Nothing had changed since the accident. There were a couple of dishes in the sink and a few more drying on the old countertop. My father's coat had been draped across one of the chairs at the kitchen table since before the accident. My mother got angry when he left his coat in the kitchen, but she never pestered him about it. He always put it down there, and my mother immediately put it on the hanger on the kitchen door. It was a brazen gesture on his part, the reason for which was unknown to me.

I turned my head in the other direction. To the right of my room, a short distance away, was my parents' bedroom. Nothing out of the ordinary there either. I left my room and turned toward the kitchen. This time the noise sounded quite close. It was obvious that the sound was coming from the kitchen. Continuing my crouch-like walk, like an old man who was out of energy, one step after the other, my entire body tense and prepared to run, I followed the sound into the kitchen, approaching the pantry at the far end of the counter. The rustling became louder. It was obvious that it was coming from the pantry. Somebody was looking for something. *A mouse, or some other, larger animal?* The pantry was very small and the shelves overcrowded; a person couldn't possibly fit inside. I debated whether to wait till morning and ask one of the neighbors to help me or whether—as my father's doctrine commanded—to trust myself and not others.

I switched on the light, at first turning the door handle slowly and then yanking the door open all at once. My eyes looked straight into the eyes of a terrified little raccoon. He backed up as far as he could into one of the shelves. It looked like he was trying to decide what his next move should be; my body was blocking his only means of escape. We were both flustered. I wondered whether to let him run into the house or leave him in the pantry for now. Closing the pantry door and opening the front door of the house, I put sofa pillows in a kind of wall between the kitchen and the bedrooms to direct him to the front door.

I went back to the pantry and opened the door, then quickly moved to the side. He bolted in the direction of the living room, but the pillows blocked his way, and the dim light from the street drew him outside. He moved slowly out the door, crossed the street, and continued to destinations unknown. *Maybe he hoped to find his mother and siblings,* I thought to myself, assuming he must be alone and scared. I closed the door and returned to the kitchen to check the extent of the damage he had caused.

The shelves were in complete disarray. Leftover food was mixed together, boxes had fallen to the floor, and lids were separated from their containers. Only the top shelf remained intact with the tin cans still standing like soldiers in formation.

It was already two o'clock in the morning, but there was no way I would be able to sleep. I decided that this would be the perfect time to put the pantry back in order, throw out old food, and clean the mess made by the raccoon. As I was contemplating where to start, I noticed that, although he had made a terrible mess of things, the shelves were neatly organized. Each container was marked with a sticker indicating its contents and the expiration date of each product.

This was the first time I noticed how organized and meticulous my mother was. Her kitchen was unfamiliar to me, although she spent most of her day there. Only rarely would she sit in the living room to read a book or watch television. Her figure would all but disappear between the stove and the countertops, the kitchen table and the refrigerator. She moved quietly around the tiny kitchen, in total control, knowing exactly where everything was and what its purpose was. Suddenly her image became vivid in my head. It was strange, because I had never stopped to truly think about her. She was like a butterfly flitting around with delicate wings, her movement so faint that it was at first hardly noticeable, and then invisible. This is how I thought of her, and probably how my father probably did as well.

I began to open each container. Some of the lids were hard to open, but they were identical except for their stickers. As I looked into each box, I thought how ironic it was that the groceries she had saved would outlive her.

I reached the last container on the shelf and tried to open it, but the lid wouldn't budge. Pulling it closer, I saw a thick layer of adhesive tape wrapped around the lid. *How weird. One or two layers around the lid would have sufficed to seal the box.* My curiosity grew. I took out a knife from one of the drawers and cut through the layer of tape. The lid, like all the other lids, fit snugly. There was no need for tape in order to seal it. With a twist and a yank, the lid came free. The box didn't contain food at all. There was a piece of paper rolled up and tied with a ribbon.

I took out the paper and unrolled it onto the table under the light. It was a birth certificate with a name I didn't recognize: Ethel Weiss, date of birth 1974. Surprisingly, the place of birth was blank. Reading it again, hoping to elicit a long-lost memory that would shed light on the document, I turned it over, but there was nothing written on the other side. I looked in the box again, but the container was empty.

Who is this Ethel person, and why did my mother hide her existence inside a tightly sealed box in the pantry?

A knock on the door brought me back to reality. Sarah was standing at the door.

"I was worried," she said. "I've been knocking on the door for several minutes and you didn't answer."

"It's two o'clock in the morning," I protested.

"I saw the light on in the kitchen," she said.

I looked at her and waited. I didn't invite her in, but as usual she came in anyway, with me trailing behind her like a little puppy. She led me into the kitchen, sat down on one of the chairs, and began to look around. "The kitchen is quite neat," she said. Then she added, "You know, your mother and I were very close friends."

I didn't respond.

"She was a very, very smart woman."

"Thank you," I answered.

"I wasn't trying to compliment you," she said.

I looked at her with a puzzled expression.

"I don't think you really knew her at all," she said, to my surprise.

My anger welled up inside, but I kept myself in check.

"Your mother was a strong woman. Sometimes I think she would have preferred to be a little less strong." She mumbled this as if to herself, brushing an imaginary crumb from her dress.

I wanted to stop her, to tell her that she didn't know my mother at all. Nobody knew her; my mother was alienated from the world. She and I were as far apart as the moon and the sun.

"I think you are wrong about her," I said out loud.

She stretched her body and fixed her piercing eyes on mine.

I turned away from her gaze and continued speaking. "My mother was a weak woman—very weak. I think you got the wrong impression about her."

Her face became taut and her eyes narrowed to slits.

"She was like...like a rag doll. Anybody could do anything they wanted with her." The train had left the station and there was no way I could stop it. "Yes, that's who she was. She was like a bubble. She never offered her opinion or interfered with anything—she just existed. So don't tell me that she was a smart woman, because it's just not true!"

My venom had been aimed at Sarah, but it changed directions and headed back toward me. It was one of the only times I had expressed my thoughts about my mother out loud, and it felt sharply painful, like an enormous weight crushing my heart. My disappointment and frustration about my mother's personality were like dynamite that had begun to slowly detonate after her death. Up until that point, I hadn't been aware of my rage toward her. Her shapeless presence in my life, so taken for granted, had left a huge void.

I felt Sarah's hand on my shoulder; an unwelcome consoling hand. I forcefully shook my body and her hand fell into her lap.

"Eva, listen to me," she begged.

"Please leave," I told her.

Her face showed a mixture of emotions. I saw compassion, determination, great anger, and frustration. She slowly got up from the chair with a look of humiliation. Suddenly her gaze passed over the document that had been sitting on the table all this time. I snatched the piece of paper away, folded it and put it in my pocket.

It looked like she wanted to say something, but she must have decided against it. I looked at her again and was shocked to find that the mixture of emotions shown on her face beforehand had been replaced by an inexplicable smile.

The door closed after her.

Sarah's words about my mother and the realization of the amount of anger I felt toward her made me burst into tears that only intensified. Tears of self-pity and loneliness ran down my face. I trudged to my bedroom and lay down on the bed. My sobs wracked my body, but the shaking quieted down little by little, eventually becoming more of a rocking motion. I felt my body giving in to sleep and I let out a long sigh.

I fell into a fitful sleep. Objects, words, expressions, fuzzy faces, numbers, bits of memories, landscapes, travel, funerals, my father, recurring phrases that were annoying, names... Everything in my imagination was jumbled together into one big sticky mess.

I woke up early the next morning and was surprised to find myself in my parents' bed. I had never slept in their bedroom before. It felt as though I was in foreign territory, but something made me want to stay there. The strangeness aroused my curiosity. Even though I could do anything I wanted in the room, it didn't erase the fear that someone might come in and see me there.

2

A few weeks later, sitting by myself on the sofa wondering who might be thinking about me, I took inventory. *My mother—gone. Father—gone. Brothers and sisters—none. Family—none. Maybe some neighbors?* But then I thought to myself, *No, they don't know me.*

While I was wallowing in self-pity, I heard a familiar knock on my front door. I knew the sound of this particular knock. It had its own rhythm. One knock, a hesitation, and then, as if more decisive, four more knocks.

"Hi, Roy," I said, opening the door.

"You haven't been answering me," he complained.

"I'm not in the mood to answer you," I said.

"Why?"

"Because I just don't feel like it."

I saw his Adam's apple move up and down and knew his feelings were hurt. I knew him, though, and he would repress it and move on.

"I was worried about you," he said.

"I know," I answered. "I'm OK, though."

"You are not!" Roy decided.

"Roy, I don't have the energy for this," I sighed. "Please leave me alone."

Roy came in and sat down in my father's chair.

"Would you mind not sitting there?" I asked irritably.

Roy got up, sat down next to me, and took my hand in his. I angrily snatched it away; I couldn't bear anything touching my skin.

"I called you yesterday, but there was no answer. Where were you?" he returned angrily.

"I was home, but I didn't feel like answering," I said nonchalantly.

I saw his Adam's apple move up and down again, but this time I felt the need to apologize.

"I'm sorry," I said.

"I understand. I just want you to let me help you," he urged me.

"There's nothing to help." I was making it hard for him.

"Eva," he begged.

I said, "Roy, I know you want to help. I am just not able to let anyone help me right now. I need to be by myself and try to decide how to move forward."

"But it's always like that with you. You never allow me to help you."

He was right. We had met in high school. It was my second day at school. I was wandering around alone during recess; not knowing anyone, lacking the courage to introduce myself to a stranger, I passively waited for someone to address me first. I was sitting in the schoolyard, in a lonely corner in the shade. My head was buried in the Jane Austen book *Pride and Prejudice* in an effort to cut myself off from everything around me.

"Hi, I'm Roy," a boyish voice suddenly said, interrupting the meeting between Elizabeth Bennet and Mr. Darcy. I lifted my head reluctantly and saw a boy who was too tall for my tastes.

"Did you hear me?" he said insistently. "I said my name is Roy."

"Yeah, I heard you," I answered.

I wanted him to go away, to let me go back to the intricate exploits of Elizabeth, who had just gotten angry with the wrong person.

Instead of being offended and walking away, this boy sat down next to me and continued. "I saw you yesterday. You're new at school," he said decisively.

"Brand spanking new," I said, mustering up some cynicism for assistance.

His blue eyes met mine and stayed there until I looked down.

"So, what are you going to do, keep pushing people away and being mean to them?"

His words embarrassed me. I loosened up, saying, "I'm sorry. That's how I react under pressure."

"It's OK," he comforted me. "When I'm under pressure, I don't stop talking."

We became friends over time. I can't say we were close friends, since my father didn't approve of our relationship and I had to play it down. But Roy became a familiar landscape to me.

When Roy left my house that evening feeling disappointed, I continued to sit on the sofa and contemplate my life. The house was silent. The leaves on the branches danced around slowly on the walls of the house in a caressing motion. It was dusk; the sun had already retired and left this side of the world dimming in the fading light. The street was practically deserted. The clatter of dishes could be heard, indicating that dinner was being served to tables filled with families: giggling children, parents exchanging looks, a mother looking at everyone with love.

The loneliness I felt during the months following my parents' funerals grew stronger. It turned into a feeling of such total isolation that even my breathing became slow and difficult. *Is this the way it is going to be from now on?* I asked myself. *Will the house remain dark and empty forever?*

The silence and my loneliness opened the door to new thoughts. *Why didn't my mother ever join us? Why was she on the fringes of our world and not a part of it? Why did she choose such a narrow existence, bounded by the kitchen and her bedroom?* I tried to picture her in my memories, but it was difficult. My father's clear and dominant image didn't leave any room for her. Every time I struggled to ignore him and think of her, he closed the curtain on her and took over. I had probably thought about her more since her death than the entire time she was alive. I asked out loud, "Mom, who were you? What was I to you? Did you even love me?"

I was so absorbed in my own misery that I didn't notice what was happening outside. The calm weather had turned into a storm, making the tree branches thrash around. I leaped up from the sofa to check the windows; the window across from the sofa shattered, sending shards of glass flying everywhere. The tip of a tree branch jutted into the room. The floor was dotted with pieces of glass and the wind rushed in. If I hadn't gotten up from the sofa at that precise moment, I would have been injured. Turning on the light, I walked carefully toward the kitchen.

It was one o'clock in the morning by the time I finished cleaning up the splinters of glass. I hung a blanket over the open window and got into my still-unmade bed.

How lucky. What if I had gotten hurt? Who would have known? Nobody has even checked to see if I am all right. Nobody is worried about me. Up until my parents' deaths, I took my life for granted. My father took care of me and protected me; my home was my shelter. The loneliness that followed their deaths created a tiny crack in the vault that had thus far been locked tight.

3

Having woken up earlier than usual the next day, I decided to clean and organize the house. First, bed-making, with flowered sheets that hadn't been used in a while. Next, kitchen cleaning: I washed the dishes that had piled up in the sink, washed the counters, put the chairs up and washed the floor—trying to wash away the remnants of loneliness left in the kitchen last night. Afterward, vacuuming the sofas and the carpet in the living room, listening to the soft tinkle of the remaining glass shards being sucked up by the vacuum cleaner. My parents' bedroom remained untouched, but I opened the windows to introduce a bit of life into the house. I decided to go into town to order a new window for the living room after finishing up the cleaning.

I finished all my chores, took a shower and put on clean clothes. I brushed my hair, which had become an unruly mess of tangles, and left the house.

My father's yellow car was parked in the driveway like an obedient soldier. It was about ten years old but looked like it just rolled off the showroom floor. My father polished the seats by hand at the end of every day, and they looked brand new. The steering wheel had a leather covering that had been replaced once a year. The car floors were spotless—not a single speck of dirt. My father was very proud of his car and took care of it as if it were a rare diamond. Nobody was allowed to drive it except for him. I don't know if my mother even had a driver's license. But if she had, it would have been useless. I had only driven it a few times with my father sitting next to me. I was never allowed to drive it by myself.

I drove through the streets of the city as if it was my first time, passing the local pizzeria, which was crowded with hungry patrons, and slowing down a bit. The familiar smell of melted cheese and fresh dough wafted in through the open window. With uncharacteristic spontaneity, I decided to stop. I got out of the car, walked into the restaurant, ordered a pizza with my favorite toppings, sat down at a corner table to watch the people passing by.

"Eva, I don't believe it! You left the house!" Roy appeared out of nowhere.

"Yes, Roy, I am out," I answered with indifference.

He sat down next to me, moved his chair closer to mine, and said, "If I had known, I would have made a date with you in advance."

"It was spontaneous. I wasn't planning on coming here."

"Spontaneous? Since when are you and spontaneity on good terms?"

"OK, now you're just making fun of me."

"I am not! I'm just surprised."

I noticed lots of girls glancing over at Roy, but he ignored them. He was handsome though. He was a tall boy with eyes the color of sky on a clear day. When a rare smile spread across his face, tiny wrinkles appeared, giving him the appearance of someone older. For years, I had taken him for granted.

"What are you thinking about?" He snapped me out of my ruminations.

"About us," I answered without thinking. Roy said nothing, only smiled. I noticed his cheeks had slightly changed color. I also remained silent; I didn't usually give such direct answers.

"What were you thinking about us?" he finally asked.

I mumbled something, got up from my seat, and muttered "See you later." I left.

When I started the car, my cheeks were burning. My foot slammed down on the gas pedal. I didn't notice how fast the car was going until it was too late. Almost too late. Another car was coming in my direction and my car was racing toward it. Only about an inch before certain impact, my hands twisted the steering wheel and returned to my lane. I stopped the car on the side of the road with my whole body trembling, my stomach extremely nauseated. My rapid breathing refused to slow down; the vomit spewed out from my throat and defiled the shiny leather seats; people came up to me and spoke, but I couldn't understand them. I sat in the car in complete shock.

When I had calmed down a bit, I looked around and replayed what had just happened a few minutes earlier. *Something* happened—something beyond the near accident. It was clear as day that this accident was about to happen.

I returned home without ordering a new window.

The next day, I was still shaken up from my terrifying experience when the telephone rang. There was an unfamiliar woman's voice on the line. "Is this the home of Sonia Schwartz?" she asked.

"Who is this?" I asked, confused.

"This is Keren Tesser, from Golding Helman Investigations."

I kept quiet and she repeated the question. "Have I reached the home of Sonia Schwartz?"

"No," I answered.

There was a brief silence on the other end and then she asked, "Is your address 12 Marker Street?"

"Yes," I answered, "but there is no Sonia here."

Another silence, and then the woman said, "Excuse me, I must have made a mistake." She hung up.

I sat on the sofa in the living room, not really knowing what to do with myself. I wouldn't dare drive into the city again, there was no one for me to call, and I had no plans. I thought about the events of recent weeks and once again sank into self-pity.

The feelings of loneliness were like a ping-pong game between two different voices in my head. "I'm alone. I have nobody in this world," said one voice, whining in my ear. The other voice pushed me, saying, "Enough! Stop feeling sorry for yourself. Keep on living. You are a grown woman now." This is how my thoughts ran through my head, and I wavered between believing one voice and then the other—one minute, the first voice was convincing; immediately thereafter, the second voice made more sense.

***

In the two years before the accident, I worked as a secretary in a company that specialized in surveillance equipment. These were miniature devices that were used mostly by the army, but that were also available to the general public. Most of the employees were engineers, people in their thirties with families, who dropped whatever they were holding as soon as the clock struck five p.m. At five thirty the building was empty of its inhabitants; the secretaries would organize our desks and leave the building around six o'clock. It was my fallback job.

A year earlier, I had begun to study at an out-of-town college. My father convinced me to study engineering. I agreed, of course. I remember my mother trying to interfere during the conversation between us, suggesting that perhaps I would like to weigh other possibilities. But I didn't give her the chance—she didn't even warrant a glance.

After I was accepted to college, my father suggested I work at an engineering company to gain experience and knowledge as I studied. My father knew the company manager, and he agreed to hire me at my father's behest. I worked at the company three times a week.

But for the last two months, since the accident, school had been put on hold, and I decided to discontinue my studies. I couldn't drag myself to do even the most mundane routine things, or to concentrate on anything, not even to read a book. Instead, my efforts went into maintaining a dull routine. To keep myself from thinking too much, I spent most of my time cleaning the house, but since no one else ever walked through it, it was spotless. The house was immaculate, and I was stuck.

Roy would visit every once in a while, but at some point, it was clear that he was tired of my somber moods; his visits became more and more rare. Sarah, my neighbor, came over a few times a week with a cooked dish of some kind and left it on the kitchen table. During every visit, she repeated the same question: "So, Eva, are you going back to living now or next week?"

"Next week," was always my answer. I think, although I didn't admit it, her visits created a strange bond between us, and in time I began to get used to her, and even look forward to them.

When a whole week went by without my hearing from her, I considered going over to her house to see why. But that action might be construed as an admission of my need for her to visit me, and this thought prevented me from crossing the street. After another four days, I couldn't refrain any more. I walked across the street and gave a timid knock on the door. She opened the door, looking surprised, and invited me in.

"I just wanted to make sure you were OK," I said.

"Why?" she asked in feigned astonishment.

I got confused; I didn't know how to answer the question. I didn't say anything at first, and then said, "I was worried."

"Come on inside," Sarah said, opening the door wide.

"Never mind. I just wanted to check to see if everything was all right," I said hesitantly.

"Come in!" she commanded.

It was the first time I'd seen Sarah's house from the inside. The first thing I felt was the heat: the home radiated warmth and calm. The windows were covered with soft, light-colored curtains. The floor of the living room was covered with a peach-colored carpet. The furniture was covered with embroidered cloth, apparently made by her. There was a pitcher of tea and a glass half full on the table. A television was on somewhere.

"Sit down," she said gently.

She sat across from me and poured some tea into a glass that she brought from the kitchen. It looked good. Her cheeks were round and flushed; she was wearing a flowery shirt over black sweatpants; her hair was gathered on top of her head in a gray bun and she was wearing a light lipstick; her clothes were old, but her appearance was well maintained and aesthetically appealing, like the room we were sitting in.

She was silent. It seemed like she was letting me get used to the new setting.

"How do you feel?" I asked.

"Just fine," she answered. I could tell she wasn't going to help me out of my embarrassment.

"I thought you were sick. I hadn't seen you for a few days," I muttered.

"No, I'm completely healthy," she replied.

The embarrassment had not yet passed. We both sat quietly sipping our tea.

"How do you feel?" she asked.

"I'm also fine," I answered.

"Great," she said. Silence once again.

"I think I'll go," I said, trying to escape the awkward situation.

"Was it difficult for you to come over here?" Her question shot suddenly into the empty air and caught me unprepared. My answer also was unintentionally blurted out.

"Yes," I whispered.

"I'm very happy that you came," she said in a warm and sincere voice. I felt she really was happy that I had come, but why? We had never spoken before my mother's death. Like my mother, she had been invisible to me, but even so, I felt comfortable with her now. She looked at me with real affection on her face, which surprised me.

Little by little the tension I was feeling began to dissipate. My muscles began to gradually relax and the chair became more comfortable. Sarah went into the kitchen and came back with a plate of warm cookies.

"I just baked these," she said. "Have a taste."

The cookie tasted wonderful, and a warm pleasant feeling filled my body. Evening had fallen and shadows began to appear around the room. Sarah didn't bother to turn on the lights, so we both sat in the mellow dusk. We talked a bit and sat quietly as well. I had never felt so comfortable simply sitting quietly with another person. When Sarah became nothing more than a shadow herself, I got up to leave.

"Come back tomorrow," she said. It was an order, and she knew I would obey.

4

My visits with Sarah became a matter of routine. Sometimes I went to her house and sometimes she came to mine. She always brought some kind of cooked dish; she never came empty-handed. During the many conversations we had, it always seemed that she wanted to say something to me, but was stopping herself from doing so. I let it go.

Because of my odd upbringing, I was pretty detached from the world. My communication skills were undeveloped; my social life included mostly my father and sometimes Roy. I was uncomfortable around strangers. The only time I didn't feel foreign was when my father was present.

I remember one day my father and I were sitting on the rug in my bedroom. My father loved to build things. Occasionally he would buy me an assembly toy—usually some sort of vehicle, mostly airplanes—and we would sit together on the rug building it. This particular day, he came home from work with a big box in his hands, placed his coat on the back of the kitchen chair, and made his way to my room. I was on the phone with one of the girls from my class who had called to invite me over. This was a rare occurrence indeed, since I didn't really have any friends. When my father entered the room, she was just explaining how to get to her house. He sat down on the rug and began to open the box, excitement apparent on his face. He spread the pieces around and began to read the instruction manual, mumbling, "An F-15 airplane. I've never seen anything like it."

"Dad." I tried to draw his attention away, but he didn't hear me.

I raised my voice. "Dad, I can't stay. I made plans to meet with a girlfriend from class."

At first I thought he hadn't heard me, but after a few seconds he raised his sword-like eyes and glowered at me. He didn't say a word, only fixed me with a piercing glare. Our eyes met for a split second. I immediately lowered mine and, feeling defeated, went off to cancel the visit. There were other instances similar to this, but this particular one is engraved in my memory—maybe because the hope I had of building a relationship with someone at school was wiped away in that moment, erased by a glare.

My father was tall and built well. Even though he was almost fifty, he had a full head of black hair, clipped short at the temples and in back; his hair was a source of extreme pride for him. He was without a doubt a handsome man. When we went out to do errands in town, I noticed both women and men glancing over at him. He was someone with a presence you couldn't ignore, and he knew it. He loved these looks: loved to be the center of attention. His voice was loud and his laughter boomed like a lion's roar. He was always an expert on any topic, even those he knew nothing about. I think people were cautious of him—the respect they showed him seemed tempered with fear. As far as I know, he never raised a hand to anyone, but his physical appearance and demeanor caused others to be guarded.

I loved him very much. When we walked around town together, I felt a great sense of pride. I always hoped to run into kids from my class so they could also admire him; in my heart, I hoped they would turn their admiration toward me as well.

My father didn't know about my social status—I chose not to tell him. I was ashamed, and maybe even a bit afraid that he would give me advice

I couldn't possibly carry out.

I was once tempted to share an incident that happened at school with my mother, but I changed my mind at the last minute. I think she knew what was going on with me, because there were times, albeit rare, when she asked how school was and who I had played with at recess. Surprisingly she knew the names of the girls in my class, even though I never mentioned them.

***

It was a Sunday night in June, but despite the time of year, the skies opened up and a torrential rain assaulted the town. Rivers were close to overflowing and threatened to flood many areas; schools were closed and there were intermittent blackouts.

It was eight o'clock at night after one of my visits to Sarah; as usual, we had enjoyed a pleasant evening munching on cinnamon cookies and savoring the easygoing conversation. I was once again filled with the same sensation—the feeling that Sarah wanted to say something but was holding back. Despite the warm connection we now shared, it seemed that there were undercurrents, things that were not being said. Sometimes it showed in her look; sometimes she would say things I didn't understand, but when I would try to explore further, she would avoid a direct answer. We seemed to be playing a game. I didn't understand the rules but played along anyway.

Upon my return to the house, I threw my colorful scarf onto the sofa in the living room and went into the kitchen to fix myself some dinner. On my way to my bedroom, after washing the dishes, I remembered the scarf and retraced my steps to retrieve it. To my surprise, it wasn't there. I bent down to look under the sofa, looked all around, but the scarf was gone.

I don't like leaving my things lying around—it's nice to wake up in the morning and find the house in order—so I continued my search for the elusive scarf. I lifted everything from the floor, moved the coffee table, shook the yellow curtains hoping something would fall out, and moved the sofa so that the floor underneath was visible. But the scarf was nowhere to be found. *Perhaps I left it at Sarah's; it couldn't have disappeared just like that.*

I moved my father's brown velvet armchair. It was very heavy. It had one of those footrests that opens when you pull a handle. I had to use my feet in order to get it to budge. I pushed and pushed until it finally gave in to my efforts and moved. I discovered a square patch of dust that had accumulated with years of neglect. Curled dust balls covered a large part of the carpet underneath the chair and the darker color distinguished itself, like an unwanted child, from the rest.

I stooped down to collect the dust and my hand filled with tiny balls of wool mixed in with grains of sand. I went back to the kitchen, opened the lid of the garbage can and threw the dirt in. As the lid was closing, I noticed a white object tangled in with the dust. I pulled the object out and shook it. Upon closer examination, I found that it was a tiny plastic bracelet that newborn babies wore around their wrists and had the mother's name on it. Pulling the bracelet closer to be able to read the writing, I read the somewhat faded ink spelling out the name **Sonia Schwartz**. *The name from the strange telephone call!*

I sat down on a chair in the kitchen and stared at the object in my hand. Thoughts were running through my head. I thought about the last few weeks, and bubbles with question marks floated around me like butterflies. "Something is going on!" I announced out loud. Oddly enough, it felt like someone was listening.

I began to make a list of all the strange events that had happened since the death of my parents: the birth certificate in the storage container, the broken window, the car accident that was avoided at the last minute, and the bizarre telephone conversation, now connected to the tiny bracelet in my hand. *Is there an explanation for all of these, or is my sullen mood responsible for these unfounded imaginings?* I wondered.

It was now after midnight. I took the white bracelet to my room and placed it in the drawer of my desk. I went to bed with all the unsettling thoughts still nibbling at me. *Maybe everything that has happened to me is just a coincidence. But these coincidences are disturbing my sleep.* Nevertheless, I finally fell asleep with these thoughts.

I completely forgot about the scarf.

5

One night I returned from work more tired than usual, wanting only to get into the bath and scrub away my annoying day at work. Everything made me upset. The secretary sitting across from me hadn't stopped asking me questions until I politely but assertively told her to stop because of my terrible headache. This obviously hurt her feelings, but I didn't really care. The department manager, a guy around thirty, recently married, continued to flirt with me like he always had since I started working at the company— instead of his innuendos being funny, today they made me angry. Even the sandwich lady who comes every day received a tongue-lashing from me. It felt like everyone was staring at me.

At five thirty, it was finally time to arrange my desk and gather my things. Before the clock struck six, I was out the door. The journey home seemed endless. I passed the public library and continued on to the suburbs. On the way, I also passed Henry's Warehouse, and stopped on an impulse. I would finally buy glass for my window and replace the sheet that covered the opening left by the shattered glass.

The store manager, George, Henry's son, came up to me. He knew me from my visits to the store on behalf of my father.

"Eva, good to see you," he said in welcome.

"Thanks, George. Good to see you too," I answered.

"How can I help you?" he asked.

"I need a new window pane for a window that broke," I said.

"What are the dimensions of the window?" George was making it hard.

I stopped and cursed myself for not realizing I had to measure the window to order a new one.

"I forgot the note with the dimensions at home," I said apologetically.

George gave me a thoughtful look. "You know what?" he said. "I'll come over tomorrow and take measurements myself."

"I don't want to be a bother," I said, a little embarrassed.

"Tomorrow at this time I'll be at your house," he said. I thought I saw a thin smile creep across his face.

I hesitated a moment and then nodded in agreement.

George looked at me again, this time longer, and then turned away to go back to work.

He arrived exactly at the time he promised. He was a big man with not a hair on his head. His bald head was shiny. His walk and physical appearance reminded me a bit of my father. His movements were sharp and full of confidence.

He went straight to the broken window, took measurements with practiced ease, and went back to his car to cut the glass he brought with him to size. He worked in silence. After about an hour and a half, the window was in place. George gathered his tools and placed them in his toolbox. I took out my wallet and asked him how much I owed him.

"Never mind," he said, surprising me. "A cup of coffee will cover the cost."

I was a bit rattled; I was not used to entertaining people I didn't know.

"I have to go," I stammered.

"Sit down, sit down," he urged me as he sat down in my father's chair. His face was shiny with sweat, and he wiped it off with his sleeve, which was covered in glass dust.

I sat down awkwardly on the sofa. I wanted him to get up from my father's chair, but I didn't dare ask him to.

"So, Eva, how have you been handling things alone?" The word "alone" grated on my ears.

"Just fine," I muttered.

"So how about that cup of coffee?" he asked. Something in his voice made me uncomfortable.

I got up from the sofa and, like a robot, picked up a cup, opened the can of coffee, put a heaping spoonful of powder in the cup, and threw in a sugar cube. I poured in milk and served him the cup. I could feel his eyes watching my every movement. My body was tight as a guitar string.

"Sit with me a bit," he said. I saw glass dust sprinkle onto my father's chair. I wanted to ask him to change places, but my mouth refused to comply.

"I knew your father well," he said suddenly. "You could say we were friends." I didn't say anything. He continued, "We would meet every week."

He pinned me with a look that gave me the feeling he was trying to ascertain what I knew about those meetings. I don't remember his name ever coming up in our house.

"Yeah, every week for almost twenty years." His head was tilted to the side and his eyes wouldn't stop scrutinizing me.

"Did your father tell you about our meetings?" he asked as he watched my face.

"No," I answered in amazement.

"Your father was a leader. People obeyed him," he continued in his thick voice.

This I already know, I said to myself.

George got up from the chair and sat down next to me on the sofa. My sense of unease grew, so I straightened up and moved away from him somewhat.

He put his hand on my thigh and fixed me with a penetrating gaze. I tried to get up, but he caught my arm.

"You know, your father talked about you as if you were still a little girl. I had no idea you were such a beautiful woman. With beautiful thick blonde hair and blue eyes like the ocean, just right..."

He moved closer to me and I could smell the stink of his breath. His eyes suddenly looked huge and round and his mouth mumbled words I couldn't understand. My whole body was stiff as a statue. I couldn't move any part of my body, even though the danger became more and more tangible.

The sound of the doorbell was like a last-minute stay of execution for me. The ringing of the bell immediately relaxed my entire body, and I sailed over to the door. Sarah was standing there with a smile on her face and a plate of cookies in her hand. She came in without waiting for an invitation and turned toward the living room.

"George, how are you?" she asked innocently.

George looked somewhat embarrassed but recovered quickly. "Just great," he answered. "How are you, Sarah?"

Sarah nodded her head and said, "I see you were just about to leave."

"Yes," said George. He gathered his tools, gave a nod of his head and left the house.

Only then could I breathe easily. I sat down on the sofa shaking like a leaf. Sarah went into the kitchen and came back with a cup of hot tea. She held it out to me, but my hand was too shaky to hold it. I felt her hand hug my shoulder, and the fear I had just experienced burst out of me in the form of uncontrollable crying. Sarah rocked my body and made calming sounds, which only made me cry harder.

But the fear I had felt was now mixed with something else. The position we were in seemed totally natural. I unexpectedly felt love and contact—something I had received only sparingly during my life—for a brief moment.

"He's an idiot," I heard her whisper in my ear. "I always knew there was something devious about him."

"He was a friend of Father's?" I asked, my voice shaky from crying.

She hesitated before she answered, "Yes, in a manner of speaking."

"What do you mean?" I wondered.

She didn't answer immediately. She disengaged herself from me and increased the distance between us.

"Eva, there are things you're going to have to find out for yourself. There are things that I also don't know. What I do know was told to me by your mother."

"Oh!" I blurted.

Sarah understood the significance of my reaction. Everything related to my mother gave rise to doubt and mistrust.

She said quickly, "Sometimes, Eva, what we see with our eyes isn't necessarily real. You need to remember that. Sometimes the reality you see was created by a 'director' with his own interests at heart. You need to put on glasses of a different color in order to see an alternate truth, one that is hidden."

After she went home, I was left with my thoughts. I was like a page that had been erased—the imprints of the letters still remained. Now I would have to find out for myself what the traces of letters and words meant.

6

The night began as usual. I brushed my teeth, took a shower, and brushed my hair. Before getting into bed in my underwear, I made sure the doors were locked and the window locks were in place. Since I have been on my own, I've turned the locking of the doors into a routine.

My bed has been the same bed since childhood. Same with the sheets. My father believed that as long as an object fulfills its role, there is no reason to replace it with a new one.

As I had in my childhood, I left one light on. The death of my parents had caused me to regress to old habits. The books that prepared me for high school finals leaned tiredly on the shelf, their accumulated dust showing that they had outgrown their usefulness. The rug, once the color of cream, is now faded and gray with dirt. It fit in with the rest of the furniture in the room. The appearance of the room itself was confusing: it had signs both of a young girl and an adolescent. There were no signs of femininity. George had told me that my father talked about me as if I was still a girl. Perhaps he really did refuse to admit that I had grown up. Even after my college matriculation, he still invited me to sit with him on the rug and put airplanes together. Sometimes he would scold me like a little girl. And me? I went right along, never objecting, postponing my plans in order to comply with his whims. Up until his death, apathy and passivity were the main characters in my life. There was nothing in my life that I was proud of doing—nothing. A terrible sense of frustration engulfed me.

Suddenly I felt that I wasn't alone. Something moved across the door from right to left. Sitting down on my bed in a panic, I didn't know what to do or how to react—something was moving around the house, something whose presence I had no control over. I couldn't hear any noise, but the strange presence was making sounds inside my head.

I rocked back and forth in my bed, hoping the repetitive motion would calm me down. My eyes were fixed on the doorway, and once again it crossed, this time from left to right. A scream escaped me—"Daddy!" I grabbed the pillow and covered my face with it. I wanted him so badly right that second. *What am I going to do? Call for help? Get up and run from the house?* My body froze. It was completely silent all around me.

I took the pillow off my face and waited. Time passed, but nothing happened. The house was still quiet. Huddled in my bed with my legs tucked under, between the pillow and my body, I don't know how much time passed—but it was passing very slowly. Hours had gone by; my eyes wanted to close, but I fought the exhaustion. *Is that a sound coming from the living room?* I was afraid to get up. I was a scared little girl who needed a grownup to calm her down. But there was no grownup to be found.

The beginning signs of dawn crept through the slats in my bedroom shutters. The sun began to cast its rays signaling the dawn. Morning had arrived. My eyelids refused to open. With great effort, I opened my eyes and discovered it was already the middle of the day. I looked around. Every object was in its place. Everything looked familiar. I walked barefoot out of the room, slowly. My heart pounded at the memory of the night before. I checked the hallway, which was partly in darkness and partly lit; the lit part came from the direction of the living room. Nothing was out of place, and everything looked normal. Was I going crazy?

I wanted so badly to tell someone about what was going on, but nobody would believe me. I could imagine the reactions. "You are in mourning. You haven't returned to your old self yet. People who are grieving imagine all kinds of things." *And maybe I really am imagining it all. I mean, there is no logic in ghosts roaming my house. But still...*

I arrived at the office a bit late. I could feel Donna, my boss, staring at me. Everyone at work had been very considerate since the death of my parents, but I knew that it would end at some point. My mood encouraged people to keep their distance from me. In some way, this arrangement suited me just fine. I wasn't in the mood to speak to anyone, to explain or apologize for my behavior. But the distance also increased my feeling of loneliness and even perpetuated it.

"Are you through feeling sorry for yourself?" I suddenly heard someone say.

"What?" I answered, surprised.

"I asked if you were through feeling sorry for yourself, because if you aren't, maybe we could bring a bed into the office and you could be depressed and work at the same time," said Donna.

I didn't say a word. I didn't know if she was angry or just joking.

"Eva, you have to snap out of it. Not because of work—mostly for yourself. If you don't do something, you might sink into a deep depression, and your chances of pulling yourself out of it will be slim. If you don't smile a bit, then I guess I'll have to open up a psychiatric ward in the office. Your mood is affecting us all."

The shock was so great that I still couldn't speak.

"A different expression, please." That was a command.

I sat up straight in my chair.

"Take a deep breath," said Donna. "Good, now let it out in one long exhale. Great. Again. Now start moving the muscles in your face. Your mouth too. Stretch your lips. Good. Again. You see? It's not that hard.

Practice it at home in front of the mirror and you'll see that you're prettier when your mouth is stretched and your teeth peek through your lips." Slowly but surely, as she was talking, she walked away from my desk. Her butt moved defiantly from side to side and the heels of her shoes clicked steadily. The sound receded into the distance.

Upon reaching home that night, I went straight to the mirror in my bedroom and looked at myself, something I hadn't done in a long time—really looked at myself. My eyes began at the top of my head, covered with a mane of blonde hair, down to my large round blue eyes. A nose not too big and not too small graced the middle of my face and my pink lips were too full, in my opinion. The wide shirt I was wearing hid the outline of my body. I threw it on the floor, and my eyes took in my chest covered by an old-fashioned and unremarkable bra. My breasts were medium sized and pear-shaped. I removed the bra and let it fall like a leaf to the floor.

It was the first time I had ever examined my body like this. Embarrassment washed over me. I looked down at my toes and could feel my heart pounding. I felt like there were two Evas fighting each other inside me. One was embarrassed and terrified, and the other was bolder, pushing forward, wanting to discover, touch.

My hands lifted up of their own accord and touched my erect nipples. My body took on a life of its own. I became frightened, a new feeling for me. I unbuttoned my trousers and took them off. I stood in my too-large nude-colored underwear. My hips were narrow and grew wider at my thighs. The last item to remove proved too difficult for me. I also didn't see the point in taking off my panties. Standing there almost completely naked, my eyes scrutinized my body without restraint. A strange aroma spread across the room and mixed in with the presence of an unfamiliar body. My buttocks contracted instinctively and my thighs closed. Heat emanated from my groin area and shame clutched me like an armored plate.

My eyes never moved from the reflection. *Is that me standing there in my underwear?* I thought to myself, experiencing for the first time in my life—a girl over twenty years old—what girls experience years earlier. My hands flew to my panties and took them off. I now stood there completely naked, exposed and vulnerable, facing myself. I couldn't take my eyes off the mirror. I stood like that for a long time, introducing myself to my body that had, until then, been a mystery to me, until the room grew dark and my figure grew dim in the surrounding darkness.

That night I experienced the same feeling. I touched my body that was foreign to me. My hands felt every inch, touched, pinched, and rubbed until my body grew stiff with overwhelming pleasure. Something inside me let go, like liquid spraying out of an open bottle.

7

The next day, when I got to the office, I sat down in my chair. When I lifted my head, I caught Donna looking at me. She didn't say anything at first, just watched me closely. Then she asked, "What happened to you?"

"What happened to me?" I asked, somewhat puzzled.

"Something is different about you today," she said thoughtfully, looking directly into my eyes.

I gave her a penetrating look.

"OK," she said. "Duche wants us to send them the protocol from yesterday's meeting. Could you take care of it?"

I nodded my head. She turned away from me, her bottom wiggling as she walked away from my desk.

I drove home slowly. When I reached my street, I could see that the pleasant weather had drawn people out of their houses. The neighbor's children were playing in the yard, spraying water on each other from a sprinkler spinning slowly around the grass. I could see Sarah across the street sitting on her porch with a drink in her hand. When she saw me, she waved hello and sent me a warm smile.

I parked in the driveway and, as usual, went over to the mailbox to collect the letters. I waved back to Sarah and went inside the house. I hung the car keys on their usual place and casually tossed the mail down on the little table.

In one hand was my cup of hot coffee, and in the other, I scooped up the letters from the table. I sat down in our old rocking chair on the porch and began to go over the mail—the electric bill, the telephone bill (which was lower than normal), and a colorful flyer advertising a roofing service. The last envelope came from a company in Chicago whose name was unfamiliar to me. Turning the envelope over to see if it was intended for me, the name printed on the other side jumped out at me: **Sonia Schwartz**. I felt like I was suffocating. That name was haunting me.

With shaky hands, I tore open the envelope. Inside was a check for thirty dollars, together with a typed letter.

Dear Mrs. Schwartz,

We apologize for the delay in sending the reimbursement for your purchase of the single bed, Model OR2614.

Our company is closing its doors after thirty years of continuous service. We have always been proud of our loyalty to our customers and our professional integrity. As part of the closing process, we have reviewed our outstanding debts to our loyal customers. We found that you are entitled to a refund of thirty dollars.

We have enclosed this amount together with this letter.

Sincerely yours,
Shlomo Cohen
General Manager

Sonia Schwartz. Who is this woman who has invaded my life, and like a sly fox, found my home in strange and unusual ways? I decided to take action. I went inside and dialed information, asking the operator for a telephone number for Sonia Schwartz at our address. A few seconds passed before the operator said, in a businesslike voice, "I'm sorry, ma'am. I don't have that name at the address you indicated. You have a nice day."

I continued to hold the telephone for a long time—until I heard the dial tone. When I returned to the porch, Roy was sitting in the rocking chair holding the letter in his hands. I snatched it away from him. "What are you doing?" I asked in annoyance.

"I heard you were on the phone, so I waited patiently." Roy answered.

I sat down across from him.

"Did something happen?" he asked.

"Nothing happened," I answered angrily.

"Are you mad at me?"

"No. What are you talking about? Why would I be mad at you?"

"I don't know, but you sound angry."

"I'm not angry," I answered angrily.

"Eva..."

"WHAT!"

"What happened?"

"I don't know." Roy didn't react. "I really don't know," I sighed. Roy was still silent. "People are trying to find some woman here at my house, and I have no idea who she is." I told him the whole story from the beginning.

"That is strange," he said.

"Yeah," I answered.

Suddenly he got up from the rocking chair. "It must be someone who lived here before you," he said.

I looked at him for a moment, and a huge smile spread across my face. I said, "You're right. Why didn't I think of that? It's so obvious.

Although... I called to find out if she's listed at this address and was told she wasn't."

Roy continued to stand in front of me with his eyes locked onto mine. "She must have changed her address," he said. His hand brushed back his hair as it always did when he was thinking about something.

"How would you like to try and find her?" he asked finally.

"What for?" I asked.

"I don't know. Maybe so you can give her the money and the special bracelet you found... I don't know. Or maybe just to do something good... for the adventure..."

Life in our small town lacked any promise and was sometimes discouraging. We avoided thinking about the future because to us it looked exactly like the present. Those who dared to dream did so with the belief that they would leave one day. I never imagined myself anywhere else. In some strange way, I liked it here.

"You're completely crazy!" I said to Roy, but inside I knew that his offer excited me; it was something to put a little variety in these gray and boring days.

He didn't say anything, but his eyes were still locked on mine.

"Roy..."

"Eva..."

"OK, let's play detectives."

We made a date to meet after work. Roy worked at the regional prison, situated some fifteen miles north of the city. He belonged to the intelligence unit of the Prison Authority. If there was suspicion of illegal activities on the part of the prisoners or the staff, he went and stayed there to try to identify and expose these activities. I was among the few that knew about his real job. Other people thought he belonged to the rehabilitation unit of the prison and was responsible for initiating rehabilitation programs for the prisoners. His job description allowed him to wander the halls of the prison freely, talk with prisoners and staff, and to evaluate what was going on inside its walls. Sometimes he was sent to other prisons in the state, though these were usually located a few hours from the area.

Roy suggested we go to the municipality offices and find out who the previous owners of the house were. We only had an hour before the offices would close their doors for the day. We asked the information clerk where we should go regarding our matter and she suggested we go to the tax department. There was one clerk at the tax department; every few seconds she shot a glance at the clock on the wall in front of her. Silver rings covered most of her fingers and she had on red and yellow nail polish. A colorful handkerchief collected her dark hair. When we sat down in front of her, she let out a long sigh without lifting her head and asked, "How can I help?"

Roy cleared his throat and then she turned to look at us. Now we could see her black eyes, with no makeup but beautiful nonetheless.

"We're looking for someone who used to live at 12 Marker Street," I began.

"What for, if I may ask?" she asked.

"I live there now, and every once in a while, I receive letters for her... I want to send her these letters and this check that came yesterday."

The word "check" succeeded in raising some interest on her part.

"Ahh... Identification, please," she muttered.

"I don't know her ID number."

The haughty woman let out a long breath full of contempt and said, "Yours... *your* identification."

I held out the document.

"Are you Eva Brown, 12 Marker Street?" she asked in an official voice.

"Yes," I answered.

"Father John, mother Maria?"

"Yes...they passed away..."

She looked at me and went back to looking at the screen in front of her.

"What name are you looking for?"

"Sonia Schwartz," we answered together and smiled at each other.

"Sonia Schwartz... Sonia Schwartz," she murmured and her sharp nails clicked on the keyboard.

"No... no Sonia and no Schwartz ever lived at that house."

"Are you sure?" I asked.

The clerk lifted her eyes, looked me over, nodded her proud head, and said, "Yes, young lady, I am most certainly sure of what I just said. And now, if you'll excuse me, I need to close up the office and get myself out of here."

She got up, covered the computer, turned off the light in the room, and walked out. Roy and I got up quickly and hurried to leave before the door closed on us.

We sat on a bench outside the building, disappointed, and tried to figure out what to do. For a brief moment, we had been the stars of a movie that gave us hope for a bit of adventure.

We sat in silence.

Then Roy said, "Let's continue."

"Roy, come on, we're not detectives. We're just a couple of people who are bored and looking for some action in our lives."

"Exactly," he said. "We're looking for something interesting, and that something just came up."

"You're dreaming."

"Eva, this woman, whoever she is, is entitled to receive her mail. Maybe that phone call asking for her is really important to her; maybe she's going to inherit millions; maybe they wanted to inform her that someone important died, maybe...maybe... I don't know... Maybe you know her."

I sat quietly. What he said made sense, even if I had the feeling he wasn't telling the whole truth; behind the reasons he listed was another reason. But he was right that this adventure might put a little variety into our otherwise routine lives. *If searching for this previous owner keeps me busy and gets me out of the house, then why not.*

"OK, let's go for it." I gave in.

The kiss I received on my cheek, and Roy's shiny eyes, confirmed what I was thinking.

***

The next day we met again. We sat on the rocking chairs and rocked a steady rhythm.

"What do we do now?" he asked.

"You're the investigator, don't you have any ideas?"

"I've never had to locate people."

Suddenly, an idea came to me like fireworks. "The bracelet," I called out. I went inside the house, came back with the little plastic bracelet, and held it out to Roy. Roy brought it close to his eyes, trying to read what was written.

"It's a little blurred, but it definitely says Sonia Schwartz," he said with a smile.

We decided to start checking the hospitals in the area, even though it was obvious we were shooting in the dark; Sonia Schwartz could have had the child at any hospital in the state.

We called a number of hospitals, but they all gave the same answer: "We don't give out information about women who gave birth with us unless you have a power of attorney from the woman herself."

After a few days, I said, "Roy, it looks like we should forget the whole thing. We haven't gotten anywhere at all, and we have no idea how to continue."

"No!" I turned my head at the decisive tone of his voice. "I'm not giving up! There must be a way to locate people," he said with determination.

"I don't have any ideas," I replied.

"We could put an ad in the newspaper," he suggested.

"Roy, listen," I said, as if I were talking to a small child. "This futile search has led us nowhere, especially nowhere we want to be."

"Eva—"

"No! Hear me out. The search for this woman isn't going to change our lives. Even if we find her, that will be the end of it. We'll go back to our boring lives. So, what, are we going to look for another adventure then?" I asked condescendingly.

Roy kept his thoughts to himself. He got up from the rocking chair all at once—the movement was so sudden that I almost lost my balance—and turned and walked away from the house.

I couldn't sleep that night. I tossed and turned restlessly and sleep refused to rescue me from my misery. Some of the time was spent half-dreaming, and sometimes I nodded off for a short time, only to wake in a panic. Something was preventing me from sleeping despite my exhaustion. Thoughts were racing through me like ping-pong balls. One optimistic thought would be trampled by a pessimistic one—light crushed by darkness, desire canceled by desolation, the dream shut out by the bleak reality. Visions mixed together with thoughts and images came and went. I got out of bed defeated and weary.

I turned on the television in the living room just to feel less alone, and then made myself a cup of tea, sat down in the living room, and stared at the screen, not really seeing anything. The pictures vacillated at an uncontrollable pace, which only increased my dizziness. I was tired but couldn't sleep. And then it appeared again at the edge of my vision. It crossed by the kitchen and continued on toward the front door. Curled up on the sofa, with droplets of reddish tea dripping onto my white nightgown, I waited a moment and then turned my head in that direction. I was my father's daughter, and he should be proud of me even after his death.

I sat still and waited, but nothing happened. I fought the urge to get up and peek, but remained seated, staring in the general direction. Finally, gathering all my courage, I pushed myself up from the couch and slowly walked in the direction from which the something had come, looking behind me to be sure there was no one there. Taking tiny steps forward along the hallway leading to the front door, I kept close to the wall, my hands embracing it with each step. I hesitated for a moment, wondering whether to just let the whole thing go and return to my bedroom. Thoughts were swirling around my head like a kaleidoscope.

My legs began to shake more and more as I came closer to the hallway. The kitchen light lit a part of it, but I had to turn left, into the dark, to follow the thing. At the wide entrance to the living room. I wanted to thrust my head around all at once to see what was ahead, but feared that the sudden movement would affect something. Moving my head as slowly as possible, I twisted my neck in the direction of the door—nothing.

Standing anchored to my spot, holding my breath, I strained my eyes and waited, not knowing for what, but expecting to see something. But nothing happened. Taking small steps, I turned toward the front door. My hands held on to both sides of the wall, my body was tight as a drum, and my eyes stared straight ahead. Terror and the resolve to continue battled with each other fiercely. I continued slowly, one step followed by another. The rustling made by my legs sounded like a thunderstorm to me. I had almost reached the end of the hallway and nothing had happened. The house was quiet—too quiet; only the sound of my breathing could be heard.

At the end of the corridor, the front door was closed, as usual, as was the door to the basement. Everything looked normal. I tried to open the front door—locked. But the door to the basement opened with a soft groan. I looked into the darkness. *Should I go down or retreat to my bedroom?* My deliberations continued for a few seconds, and then my feet began to move involuntarily toward the basement. I put my hand out to turn on the light switch and a dim light filled the room. I went down step by step.

The scent of mildew was all around. *Have I ever been down to the basement before? Maybe when I was a little girl. I never had a reason to go down to this dark place.* I reached the last step and looked around, my eyes trying to adjust to the faint light coming from the top of the stairs.

The place was neatly organized. There were boxes on the right side of the basement and old furniture and junk on the other side. I noticed a baby crib that was probably mine before I graduated to a single bed. I also saw my old bicycle. I went over to where the furniture sat, looking like old men with no purpose. I looked behind some of the items and discovered other pieces of furniture.

The stench of mildew was more pronounced, as if to signal me that it was time to leave. I stayed where I was and looked in the other direction, where all the cardboard boxes were arranged like soldiers. I was planning to go over to them, but my body appeared to be against the idea; I stood and looked at them from afar, and my feet refused to go any further. The stairs to my right were tempting me to go up and close the door behind me. My body finally roused from its fixed position and my feet advanced in the opposite direction. Something was written on the boxes, but I didn't recognize it. I touched them, and a thick layer of dust came off on my fingers.

There were boxes of various sizes. The smaller ones were placed on top of each other and the larger ones sat beside them. They were carefully arranged, with not an inch between them. It was obvious that my father was responsible for the arrangement. He loved everything to be in its place. He always said that the world is an organized place with a distinct order. The temptation to open the boxes and discover their contents was enormous, but the dim light in the basement would never be enough to see clearly. *Tomorrow, at daylight, I will return and find out what is hidden inside the boxes.*

When I reached my bedroom, I couldn't get to sleep, instead going over what had transpired in the last hour: the uncertain something seen from the corner of my eye, and my feeling that someone is here, watching over me—someone who wants me to know it. I smiled to myself. The panic that had taken hold of me earlier was gone, and in its place was an inexplicable feeling of relief.

A pleasant warmth spread throughout my body, acting as a kind of shield from the fears I had been experiencing lately. A peculiar feeling of security now took their place. I murmured into the pillow, "Dad, I know... I feel you..."

From that night on, I was no longer afraid. On the contrary, I even became friendly with the something. When it didn't appear for a long time, the fear inside me would stir. I became dependent on its presence. I wanted it to come; it chased away my loneliness. I called it "Dad." It seemed that my strong and confident father was able to deceive even the heavens above to return to me—in his death, as in life, he controlled everything around him.

8

"Brown, you came back to us... Is your journey of self-involvement finally over?" Donna rejoiced when I got to the office, shooting an inquiring look at me. Her pencil-drawn eyebrows were raised and her pointed heels made her tower over my desk. She bent down toward me and her eyes focused on mine.

"Just a minute, Brown, don't look away. I want to see if there's any life in those eyes," she continued.

"I finished that report you asked for," I said humbly.

"Oh... So now we're efficient too," she said with her usual sarcasm.

I didn't respond.

"And very serious," she said in mock seriousness.

I couldn't hold back anymore and smiled.

"Yes...we are definitely back among the living," she exclaimed.

I received the same reaction from Roy when I called him and asked him to come over. It was one of the first times that I had initiated a meeting with him. In our many years of friendship, he had always been the one to call or suggest we get together. He was so surprised at my call that he said he would be over within the hour.

"I think we should continue to try and find the mystery tenant," I said as we sat down on the porch with a cold drink. Roy waited for me to continue. "You were right. It's possible that the phone call or the check was very important to her. Probably more letters will come... I think we should continue."

Roy looked down at the drink in his hand, and then lifted his hand to my face, the tips of his fingers brushing my cheek almost imperceptibly. Finally, he said in a quiet voice, "OK, let's go for it."

***

One week after that conversation, Roy told me that something had changed in me lately.

"Yeah, I feel it too," I answered.

"Did something happen?" he asked.

"Yes... no... I don't know. I'm now more than twenty years old. Until now, I haven't done anything significant with my life. It's bothering me. It would be terrible to look back as a fifty-year-old and not have done anything with myself—to come and go and never even be noticed. I want someone to miss me, to think about me... Oh, I'm just babbling..."

Roy moved closer, put his arms around me, and whispered in my ear. "I'm here." I could feel his breath on me. I leaned my ear against his chest, which rose gently with each breath. We stayed like this for several minutes. I avoided raising my eyes, afraid of what I might see in his face. His rapid breathing was calming.

We met again the next day. Neither of us mentioned the intimate moment we shared the day before; we just exchanged ideas about how to go about looking for Sonia. We had begun calling her by her first name, as if she were an old acquaintance.

"I think we should go to Chicago and show the bracelet at hospitals in the area. Maybe every hospital has its own kind of bracelet, or different colors..." I said, drawing out my words. "It would really help if you wore your uniform and clipped on your police ID badge."

Roy didn't like the suggestion, but two days later, he arrived dressed in his police uniform—one of the rare times I'd seen him in it. During most of the time he had worked for the police, he hadn't had to wear uniform.

"It suits you." I smiled.

"I'm not comfortable at all," he answered self-consciously.

The truth is the uniform made him look terrific. Suddenly he looked older, more serious, attractive.

I looked down and said, "Let's get going."

Chicago is blessed with over a hundred hospitals. We focused on those that had a maternity ward. The first one we visited was in a relatively new building, but despite its young age, the walls were already sullied with dark stains. The structure was plain in design—straight lines, narrow windows and square entrances.

Roy cleared his throat and the nurse raised her head to look at us with inquisitive eyes. On our way to Chicago, we had improved our story regarding Sonia Schwartz. I knew that if we told it the way it was, we would never get help, so we told the nurse that we were looking for Roy's biological mother. We told her that his mother disappeared when he was a baby and that he recently found this bracelet, which he was hoping would lead us to her. Roy put on the face of a lost child. The nurse looked at his face, and because of his pitiable and yet impressive appearance, she gave him her full attention.

"Show me the bracelet," she requested. I gave Roy the bracelet and he placed it in the nurse's hand. She turned it over in her hands, then let out a sigh and said, "I'm sorry. We've never produced this type of bracelet. Every hospital has a different type of bracelet to identify the newborn baby."

"Could you have had this type of bracelet in the past?"

"No, dear, this hospital has only been around for ten years, and nothing has changed much since then."

We thanked her and went on to the next hospital on the list.

The next hospital looked more pleasant. The walls were painted in joyful colors; characters from Disney cartoons were drawn on the walls, and each room was named after a character; there were colorful flowers in vases on the chest of drawers in each new mother's room; and green and white balloons tied with a ribbon swayed happily at the nurses' station.

One of the nurses came up to us and asked if she could help us in any way. I explained the reason for our visit. The smiling nurse politely asked us to follow her, and led us into the Winnie the Pooh room. She sat on a ball-shaped chair, crossed her long legs, and looked at us with her complete attention. She said, "Look, you seem like nice people, and I would love to help you, but you are looking for a needle in a haystack. Are you planning on checking every hospital in Chicago? I mean, there are more than a hundred hospitals in Chicago alone, and even more in the outlying areas."

Roy and I looked at each other. The nice nurse said that in any case, they didn't use this type of bracelet. "This is a very old bracelet," she said. "How old are you?" she asked suddenly, turning to Roy.

"I'll be twenty-two soon."

"I would exclude hospitals that didn't exist before twenty years ago, then."

When we left the hospital, we felt very stupid. We were so excited to begin the mission that we didn't think of all the important details. Actually, we didn't think at all. We didn't plan anything, we just went on our way, thinking our lives would take an interesting turn.

We sat silent and ashamed. Neither one of us wanted to bring up the obvious. Finally, Roy said, "Look, it would be really easy to decide to just stop, but I think we should continue."

I also wanted to continue, but it was clear that we were deluding ourselves. We were chasing after a ghost, convinced that finding it would change our lives. I said, "Let's go on, but let's be smarter about it. You have to think like a policeman. You need to use your friends on the police force. We can't do this alone."

He said, "OK, I'll ask someone from Missing Persons what we should do." Roy started the car, turned it around, and began driving us out of the city. We sat in silence the entire way, each one lost in his or her thoughts.

That night, I decided it was time to take action. I turned on every light in the house, opened the windows, and went down to the basement with a new light bulb in hand.

This time I was sure of my steps, going straight up to the empty light socket and screwing in the new light bulb. I went over to the boxes—the small ones first—and, using a knife I brought with me, opened one. A cloud of dust erupted from it and caused me to choke.

The box was full of notebooks—my math notebooks from the first grade. Farther down the pile were other notebooks from elementary school, containing the first letters I had ever written. Some of the covers were torn; my father must have taken the time to fix them. Flipping through the notebooks, my imagination took me back to when I wrote in them. Even though hardship was my lot in life, I had been very neat. Letters that were printed crookedly rested on the guidelines and my name was on every page. I took the notebooks and the workbooks out of the box one by one until I found the sheets of paper lying at the bottom.

I took one of the pages in my hand. My school logo was printed on the right side of the page. It was a letter. "Dear Mr. and Mrs. Brown: I would like to set up a meeting with you regarding your daughter's grades. For the last several weeks, Eva has been showing up without the required homework, and we need to discover the reason for this behavior. I can meet with you on Monday at noon. Sincerely, Mrs. Prewitt, Homeroom Teacher."

The next page I took out of the box used the same wording and was sent one week later. It said, "Dear Mr. and Mrs. Brown: Since you were unable to attend the previous meeting, please meet with me in one week, Tuesday at one o'clock. If this is not convenient for you, please let me know in advance. Sincerely, Mrs. Prewitt, Homeroom Teacher."

The third letter, sent by the school principal, contained an urgent request to meet with him. My parents were again required to let him know in advance if they were unable to attend the meeting.

There was another stack of letters containing the same message. In each letter, a new meeting was set up.

In the last letter, at the bottom of the box, the principal notified my parents that it was he, the homeroom teacher, and the school counselor intended to come for a home visit. His signature at the bottom of the page looked extremely angry.

The page in my lap was stained with my tears.

I couldn't stay in the basement any longer. The weight of my emotions was so heavy that my legs could barely carry me up the stairs.

The brightly lit house did not help the feeling of shame I carried with me from the basement. I could see myself as a young girl at school, whose parents couldn't find the time to deal with her learning difficulties.

I sat in my bed for a long time, hoping that the something would come. I wanted to ask him why he ignored the letters, why he never came to school, why he didn't deal with my learning problems. Surely the feelings that had overcome me now were the same ones I felt as a girl, except then I wouldn't have dared to ask my father to take care of me. Back then, as a young girl of seven or eight, it wasn't in my nature to tell him that I was full of shame and embarrassment every time the teacher looked at me with pity.

I do remember one time where my father came to school, but after that I prayed he wouldn't ever come again. I was in middle school then. The teacher asked that one of my parents come to a meeting regarding my studies and my social status. After three letters, my father decided to meet with her. He insisted that I also be present, even though the teacher suggested that the meeting be held without me.

The teacher began by describing the state of my studies. She said that, despite my efforts—and she was aware of them—there were difficulties I couldn't overcome by myself. She added that my learning problems were affecting my social status, and that many times she would find me reading a book in one of the corners of the school yard. "It is very important for children to have social interactions at this age," she emphasized. "This will influence her ability to interact with others in the future."

My father sat the entire time in silence. His jaws were tense and his hands held tightly to the arm rests. There was a look on his face I didn't understand. It was a combination of anger and sadness. I saw him swallow, but no words came out of his mouth. After the teacher finished speaking, she waited for his reaction, but it never came. Finally, he asked, "Is that it?" The teacher nodded and then he got up from his place, patted my back and ushered me out of the room. I couldn't raise my eyes. Out of the corner of my eye, I remember seeing the teacher still sitting, not moving, until she disappeared from view with the closing of the door behind us.

We were silent the entire way home—me because of my deep shame, and him (it seemed) because of anger. I expected a harsh lecture when we got home, but this never happened. When he stopped the car in the driveway, he turned to me with a strange look on his face. His eyes looked at me with warmth and his hand left the steering wheel, took mine, and softly squeezed it. For a split second, I could see that a crack had been formed. This unfamiliar gesture both scared me and calmed me at the same time. It was only for a second, but in that moment, I suddenly realized that underneath his rigid shell, there was also something soft.

Life after that day went on as usual and this special moment was covered with layers of other memories.

9

The day after I found the contents of the basement, my life was saved once again.

I arrived at the office a little before nine o'clock. Most of the secretaries hadn't yet arrived, and the computers with their covers looked like a museum display. I turned on the lights over my space and went into the little room with the coffee machine. I went back to my desk, hot drink in hand, and found Donna waiting, fresh and stylish, like it was already the middle of the day. Her hair was adorned with a colorful comb and her flowery blouse perfectly matched her pink skirt. She wore pointed high heels and her nails were painted pink, completing her curvaceous but distinguished appearance.

Donna was about thirty years old and boasted the title of Head Secretary. She was very attractive and well-groomed and always left an enticing aroma in her wake. The men in the office, even those in top positions, would change their tone of voice when addressing her and it seemed like their bodies were slightly bowing as they spoke.

The day began with the monotonous melody of clicking computer keyboards. Phones rang, orders were shouted into the air, and looks were exchanged. Definitely a normal day. At 11:30, Donna buzzed me and asked me to come to her office. Her office was located at the end of a long corridor where she could look out over everything that was going on.

"Sit down," she ordered me as I entered. The office, like Donna, was full of bright colors. The shelves behind her were each a different color and jam-packed with different colored binders and other little colorful objects—little angels, a miniature can of Coca-Cola, the figure of an Indian woman with feathers in her hair, cubes in red, yellow and blue. Two pictures were hanging on the opposite wall: one of a clown and the second one of a golden wheat field. Donna completed the atmosphere with her colorful personality and appearance.

When I was about to sit down in the chair across from her, she stood up and offered me her chair. I looked at her in confusion, smiled, and sat down in the chair across from her, but she said, "No, Eva, sit in my chair."

"I don't understand," I said.

"Sit in my chair," she reiterated.

I walked around the desk and warily sat down in her chair.

"How do you feel?" she asked.

"I don't understand," I repeated.

"I asked how you felt," she said.

"Strange," I answered.

"Well, get used to it."

Donna left the room and left me alone. I didn't understand her actions and felt uncomfortable in her chair—I wanted to get up. It wasn't my place. It wasn't my chair or my office. Donna wasn't very talkative. She chose her words carefully, and they were just enough to convey the necessary message. Not everybody liked her—some of the other secretaries gossiped disapprovingly about her appearance—but we all knew that she was extremely professional in her work. I liked her, although I didn't really know her.

All this flashed through my head as I was sitting in her chair. My hands

LIFE IN A BOX | 65

played with a pen with a tiny wide-brimmed hat on the end. Under the glass on her desk, there were pictures spread around, most of them of little children. On second glance, I saw that they were pictures cut out from magazines. I didn't know anything about her personal life—whether she was married or not, or if she had any children. Yet I was sitting in her office, in her domain, and getting used to it. Used to what exactly, I didn't know.

I decided to go back to my desk and wait for her to return and explain her actions. I put the pen with the hat down on the desk and gave a last glance around the room. Just as I got up from the chair, there was a dull screech. Everything happened too fast. I pushed the chair on wheels back and jumped to the side. My leg hit the corner of the desk and a stream of blood spurted out. I fell and hit my head hard on the floor. The entire shelf collapsed onto the place where her chair had stood. Binders were scattered everywhere and the papers that were inside flew around like kites until reaching the floor.

In seconds, the room filled with people. The noise made by the falling shelf could be heard all the way down the hall where the secretaries worked and even to other rooms. My colleagues grouped around me with concern. I was more shaken by the commotion than by the shelf. They called for an ambulance; somebody pushed me gently to the floor and put a pillow under my head; someone else brought me a glass of water. All I wanted to do was run away and hide.

When things died down, people began to return to their offices. Only a few people remained in the room, among them Richard, the company's owner. Richard hadn't seen me since my parents died. Between my first day at the office, when he wished me good luck, and today, I hadn't seen him. His office was on the second floor, away from the secretaries. Now he stood over me, worry etched on his face.

How do you feel?" he asked.

"I'm OK," I answered with effort.

"I'd like you to take a few days' vacation and rest; the company will pay for any expenses you may have. Are you sure you're all right?"

"I'm fine," I assured him.

He touched my forehead with his hand and looked into my eyes for a number of seconds. "You sure are a Brown, no doubt about it," he said, and he turned around and left the room.

The clicking of high heels announced Donna's arrival. "What happened?" she asked, her chest rising with each word. She must have run with all her strength. Her hair, normally flawless, was draped over her face with a barrette hanging on the end of a strand that had come loose.

"I'm OK," I reassured her. "Everything is fine."

Donna looked around and slowly began to understand what had happened just minutes earlier.

"I don't believe it," she mumbled. "I don't believe it." She was on the verge of tears. It was the first time I had ever seen her lose her composure. Her face showed honest concern.

"I am so sorry," she continued. "I should have been sitting there, not you."

"Donna, I'm fine, really. Actually, I can get up and continue working," I said, trying to calm her down.

"Absolutely not," she said decisively. "I'm taking you home right now!"

It was obvious that there was no point in arguing with her. I lifted myself up with her help, but once upright, I felt dizzy. Donna held on to me firmly and led me to the red sofa underneath the pictures. She sat me down, gave me a glass of water, and ordered me to drink. I did as she said and waited for the dizziness to pass. In another few minutes, I felt better and asked her to take me home. She led me outside slowly, supporting me.

The ride passed mostly in silence. Every once in a while, Donna would inquire how I was feeling and if everything was OK. When we arrived at my house, she poked around in my purse in search of the key and put both purses on her shoulder, one arm hugging my back as we walked slowly to the front door.

"Thanks, Donna. It's OK, you can go. I'll just lie down a bit," I said.

Donna didn't answer—I thought she didn't hear me. We went inside. I saw her quickly take in the surroundings, and then she continued to lug me toward the living room. She gently sat me down on the sofa, helped me lie down, and brought me a pillow for under my legs.

"Where's your bedroom?" she asked. I pointed back toward the hallway. Donna came back holding my blanket and a pillow.

"Kitchen?"

"Behind you," I answered.

A few minutes later, she came back with a cup of tea. "Drink," she ordered.

I sat up. She sat some distance from me.

"I am so sorry," she apologized again.

"It's not your fault," I reassured her.

"It is my fault. I shouldn't have crammed so many binders on the shelf," she said.

"But it could have happened to you too," I said, trying to comfort her without success.

"Yes, but it happened to you," she said. "I should have been more careful, less complacent."

"Donna, stop it. It happened by chance; I just happened to be sitting there. By the way, why did you want me to get used to sitting in your place?"

"I'm getting a new job. I'm going up to the second floor—Rachel's floor."

"Rachel, Richard's secretary?"

"Yes, she's retiring. Actually, Richard asked her to retire."

"I see..." I said, but my mind began to concoct different scenarios.

Donna saw me looking pensive, and I lowered my gaze. She said quietly, "You think I'm having an affair with him and that's why he's giving me the job."

"It's none of my business," I said.

"You're right; it isn't any of your business. But it's insulting! I'm good at what I do. I'm a professional, and that's the only reason I was offered the position."

I could tell she was angry. I immediately apologized. "I'm sorry. The truth is, we don't know each other very well, and I thought that... I'm sorry."

"You're forgiven," she said. "And you are not getting out of bed till tomorrow. You're not coming to work. I'll be back at the end of the day."

She helped me to my room, made me another cup of tea, set it down on the nightstand by my bed, and covered me with the blanket.

"I'm taking the key to the house with me so I can come in without you getting up."

I nodded. I didn't have the energy to resist or argue.

I heard the front door close and remembered that Donna had never explained to me why she wanted me to get used to her chair. Exhaustion drew me into a deep dreamless sleep.

I woke up with the house beginning to darken. *Is it early or late, night or day?* It took me a number of minutes to remember the events of the morning. My body was heavy. I could have continued sleeping, but if I went back to sleep, I would wake up in the middle of the night.

When I dragged myself out of bed, dizziness overwhelmed me; I steadied myself until my confidence returned. After washing my face and changing clothes, I took the cold cup of tea from the nightstand, trudged to the kitchen, and made myself a cup of black coffee, needing something strong to wake me up.

I sat down at the table, put my elbows up, and held my head in my hands. The day's events flew in front of my eyes like a speeding train. I saw myself sitting in Donna's chair, wondering why she put pictures of children cut out from magazines under the glass. I remembered lifting my gaze and looking at the paintings on the wall across from me. I distinctly remembered the second when the dull, almost imperceptible creaking, like the footsteps of a cat on sand, started—and the way my body was suddenly pushed aside, as if on its own, away from danger.

I ran those few seconds through my mind again and again and tried to understand what made me jump away from the source of danger; I had had no idea the shelf above me was unstable, and I was not worried that it would collapse under the weight. Slowly, my thoughts turned to another place and time—to the car accident that should have occurred but didn't. The two incidents were connected. This aroused a strange feeling in me. There was no logical explanation for what took place in either incident. I certainly should have been injured in both of them—it ought to have happened, and yet it didn't. Something or someone saved me. Something or someone protected me again.

My body flushed with warmth, and a gentle smile appeared on my lips. This enormous feeling of security was filling me up, and new energy surged through my body, filling me with vitality. I wanted to share my feelings with someone, but it still wasn't the right time. How could I tell someone about my certainty that my father was still by my side? How could I describe the shapeless creatures that were hovering around my house and leading me to all kinds of places? How could I convince someone that I was protected from accidents—not by chance, but by a guiding hand?

With a smile on my face, I got up and walked confidently to the basement. This time my steps were less hesitant. Sitting down again, in the same place as before, I eagerly opened another box. It was brimming with my childhood games and toys. As I began to take them out one by one, nostalgia overcame me. The first object was a board game that contained plastic soldiers. The board had pictures of planes, bridges and tanks, and the player had to plan phases of war and bring his soldiers to victory. The game wasn't that much fun, but my father gave it to me as a present, and I couldn't refuse to play it with him. I used to wonder why he liked playing games with me that were considered masculine; he never bought me dolls or other feminine things.

Underneath this game were other boxes of games, mostly war games. At the bottom of the pile there were boxes still closed in their original packaging; boxes that had never been opened. There were art and craft kits, works in plaster, tons of coloring books without a mark on them, and crossword puzzles. There was also a heap of crayons and markers. I didn't recognize any of these objects. They didn't arouse any memory. I wondered who they belonged to.

I went to another nearby box. It opened easily, and surprisingly, there were dolls of various sizes inside, as well as a doll's bed and a doll-sized folding stroller. There were also other things that were completely foreign to me: tiny kitchen utensils, such as pots, cutlery, and plates, and a pouch containing different kinds of plastic makeup. I thought, *it's possible that these things belong to someone else who asked my parents to store them in our basement.* I returned the toys to the box and turned it around to see if something was written on it. I turned it in each direction until I finally found it. On one of the sides, written in large letters with a dark-colored marker, it said "Ethel."

The sound of a key turning in the lock snapped me out of my reverie. Donna was calling me from upstairs. I could hear her hands groping the wall in search of the light switch.

I got up, turned out the light, and walked up the stairs, where I met a face full of concern.

"How do you feel?" she immediately fired at me.

"I'm fine," I answered.

"Did you rest?" she asked.

I nodded.

"Did something happen? Is everything OK with you?"

"I'm fine," I said, pacifying her.

"Come to the kitchen. I brought you something you can't refuse."

Donna took some muffins out of a bag, filling the kitchen with a strong aroma of cinnamon. She found a plate and set them down on it. In another minute, the table was set with two cups of tea as well. Donna moved about with efficiency, and even though she had only been in the house a short time, she seemed as natural as if it were her own home.

How strange that Donna was the one in whom I chose to confide my experiences since my parents' deaths. But something about her made me trust her and want to confide in her. Maybe it was her true concern for my welfare, or maybe it was the fact that she was a stranger. In any case, she listened to me patiently. Every once in a while, she asked a question to clarify something for herself, but most of the time her eyes rested curiously on my mouth. When I finished speaking, my clothes were drenched in sweat. My hands were forcibly stuck to my body and I could hardly breathe. I waited for her reaction. Like a defenseless animal in a dark forest, I had no idea where the predator would come from.

"Ghosts, huh?"

I was immediately inundated with shame and regretted my candor. After all, Donna was my boss. *What was I thinking, telling her, of all people, my strange story of ghosts hanging around my house?* I waited for her to clear her throat and suggest my taking an extended vacation from work, but she just said, "You know, Eva, you just told my story."

"What?" I was shocked.

"I listened to you and felt as if your words came out of my mouth."

"I don't understand."

"My parents were divorced when I was three years old. My father kept in touch for about a year and then completely disappeared. To this day I don't know if he's alive somewhere or dead. My mother was very young and couldn't take care of me. At first, we lived in a trailer park, but then we had to move out because my mother couldn't even make the meager payments. I lived on the neighbors' pity. There was never any hot food at home. We never tasted meat.

"My mother looked for a job during the day and I stayed with the neighbors, each day with a different neighbor. I grew up extremely lonely, feeling like a burden. As a child of three or four, I couldn't do anything. I was neglected and hungry most of the time. One day, a social worker came to visit—one of the neighbors must have called her. She came into our trailer and immediately saw that nobody was caring for me properly. It took another six months until they took me out of my mother's custody. At first, she tried to fight for me, promised to change, said that she would make an effort, but it was too late. I was taken from her and began to make the rounds among the orphanages and foster families. Feeling unwanted, like a burden, became an integral part of me."

Donna stopped for a moment and let out a long, deep sigh. We were silent for a few minutes, each of us consumed with our own stories. The kitchen was dark, but neither of us got up to turn on the light. The darkness helped us hide the pain, the shame.

"When I was seven, a family took me home for a trial period. I wanted to stay with them so badly. I was quiet most of the time so as not to say the wrong thing and make them angry or do the wrong thing and make them not want me. So, I sat in my room and played by myself. I was the perfect little girl. Didn't annoy anyone, didn't get in the way, didn't ask for a thing and never made demands. And it helped.

"My room had all the accessories. The shelves were packed with books; the furniture was shiny and new. The room was cheerful and perfect, and I was lonely—so lonely that one day I began to see creatures. They would appear at will and disappear at whim. At first, it was frightening. I couldn't tell my foster parents about it—they would think I'd lost my mind and send me back to the orphanage. Little by little, I began to get used to the creatures. When they stayed away, the figures on the shelf were my friends.

"Suddenly my loneliness was gone. I felt lucky to have so many friends (even though they were imaginary). My parents were satisfied. I was grateful for everything they did for me. Especially when they would add to my collection of figures and other objects. Over time, I developed a dependence on these entities. For me, they were real and wonderful friends—they didn't ask anything of me, didn't judge me for my actions, accepted me as I was. From my point of view, it was the ultimate kind of love. And that's how I came to live in two worlds: the narrow world outside and the vast world in my bedroom."

Donna stopped her story. I waited for a moment to allow her to collect her thoughts and return to the story, but the silence continued until it became uncomfortable.

Finally, when I couldn't take the quiet any longer, I whispered, "And then what happened?"

A long time seemed to pass until she said, "Nothing happened. My foster father died and my mother went into a deep depression. She was hospitalized over and over again in different hospitals. At first, I visited her, but over time I realized that she wasn't interested in my visits, so I stopped going. About five years ago, I was notified that she had died. And now let's make you dinner." She got up from her chair, turned on the light and the kitchen was infused with a bright light that immediately wiped away the intimacy that had just been there.

After she left, I sat a little while longer and tried to digest what I had heard.

10

Roy came over to visit the next day. It was a calm afternoon. There was an almost undetectable breeze gently blowing the leaves on their branches. The sun was exactly the right temperature. Infrequently, a car moved by slowly, as if the purpose of their trip was the driving itself, not to actually go anywhere. A mother was crossing the street dragging a boy of about four. One of his hands held hers and the other a dripping ice cream cone. A sprinkler ticked rhythmically on the lawn of the house on the right. I saw a man sitting on the porch in one of the houses across the street reading the newspaper. The air seemed to be cloaked in a light fabric of serenity.

Roy shattered the idyllic scene all at once. He sat down on the bench of the rocking chair, which creaked under his weight, and announced with a smile, "There's a new direction."

I waited for him to continue.

"I went to the intelligence unit of the police and asked for help from someone I know." Roy stopped talking; anticipation had taken hold of me and was gradually increasing. "He suggested we try to think about all types of routine contacts people have: the library, church, courses, bill paying. He also suggested we put an ad in the local paper that we're looking for her. He said that even if she doesn't answer the ad herself, maybe somebody who knows her will contact us."

"And that's it?" I was disappointed.

Roy raised his puzzled eyes to me.

"We could have thought of that all by ourselves," I said. "We didn't need an intelligence guy for that."

Roy looked frustrated by my reaction.

"How about, for example, looking for her through the police computer program?" I asked condescendingly. "Maybe one of your police friends could take over the search."

I don't know why I was so mean right then. His naïvety made me angry. I thought to myself, *How could a person so talented, with a job that demands that he work undercover, perform interrogations, and talk with dangerous inmates, still be so naïve?*

He leaned back and looked forward, staring. I knew he was hurt.

"So, what now?" I asked.

My desire to continue the adventure fluctuated like the ebb and tide of an ocean. One day I was full of energy and willingness to invest time in the search, and the next day I despised myself for getting involved in this childish game. Finally, we decided to do two things simultaneously: put a personal ad in the local newspaper and ask around town a bit. Roy would take care of placing the personal ad. The following day, we went to the municipal library. The librarian, Ira, who has been running it for several decades, seemed to have aged at the same pace as the library without taking any steps to adapt the literature to the times. New books were hardly ever introduced; the computers were outdated and the heavy and bulky printers stood like archeological exhibits. Civic leaders were waiting for Ira to decide to retire. They couldn't bear to force the retirement of someone who had given service to the residents of the city for so long.

When we arrived at the library, there were only a few people there. Ira, who sat behind the counter, looked like a sticker that had been stuck there for many years. I remember her from when I was a little girl. She must have been pretty once. Today her gray hair was spread over her shoulders like the halo of a moon. Rivulets of protruding veins crisscrossed over her bony hands. Her skin looked purplish and loose. Only her eyes remained young as always, brown eyes that looked at you with great attention and knew exactly what you came for and what you needed.

"Hello, Roy." She lifted her gaze to him and then turned her head toward me. She squinted her eyes for a moment and then said, "Eva, it's been years since I've seen you here."

I nodded sheepishly. She rested her eyes on mine and asked what she could do for us.

Roy told her about the anonymous tenant and said that a large check had arrived for her and we needed to find her so we could hand it over to her. (It was obvious that good citizenship would grant us an especially warm response.)

Ira looked at Roy and me tenderly and promised that God would reward us for our good deed. "Come back again on Wednesday," she said. "By then I will have gone over the list of cardholders in recent years."

"Eva has lived there for the past seventeen years, so you would need to check the years before that," said Roy.

"I understand," she said.

Our next stop was the church. We hoped that the priest was in. Sometimes he would visit residents at their homes, mostly at old age homes where they weren't able to make it to church on their own; at those times, he would leave the door to the church open for any occasional visitors.

Father Peter welcomed us with a big smile. I think we were the only visitors during the week. It wasn't clear how he spent his days and what he did with himself, but it was obvious that he loved his job and saw it as a true calling. His chubby figure came toward us with a warm and inviting smile. He invited us to come in and called Roy by name. He didn't recognize me—with good reason. My family didn't come to pray, as my father despised religion and faith and my mother rarely left the house.

We sat in one of the pews in the large empty church hall. There was a faint scent of forgotten fruit in the air. Actually, the odor gave me a feeling of warmth; there was something homey about it. I was comfortable in this place, even though I had never visited it before. Roy sat between me and Father Peter, who leaned against the pew in front of us so he could look at me too.

"Roy, introduce me to this beautiful girl you have with you," he said.

"I'm sorry, Father, this is Eva, she's—"

"Maria's Eva," the priest finished his sentence. "Of course, how could I have not recognized you right away? You are an exact copy of your mother. I should have seen it straightaway."

I was in complete shock. There was a look on Father Peter's smiling face that I didn't understand.

"The last time I saw you, I think you weren't quite five years old, but there's no mistake. You are definitely Maria's daughter."

I was surprised by his words; I didn't remember ever setting foot in this place.

Roy broke the silence and explained our reason for coming. I remained silent and let Roy do the talking. The priest listened patiently and finally shook his head from side to side.

"I don't remember a name like that, and that's strange," he said, pondering out loud.

"How long did this woman live at the house?" he asked.

"We don't exactly know," Roy answered. "To us it looks like a pretty long time."

"Very strange. I know all the residents here," he said apologetically. "I have to check... I have to check..." he muttered to himself. "Come back next week. Until then I will look for this woman for you. If she lived in town,

I'll find out about it and can give you the information you're looking for."

Roy turned to me and with a small nod of my head, gave him the sign to end our visit.

"We thank you very much, Father Peter," Roy said politely.

Father Peter nodded, turned to me, and said, "I would be very happy if you would come to visit me some time, Eva."

When we left the church, Roy was deep in thought and I was distraught. *My mother met with the priest, my mother went to church, I look like her? What else will I find out about her? Did my mother lead a secret life that we knew nothing about? Did my father know about her connection to Father Peter? I didn't think so—I'm sure he would have forbidden her to go. Was my mother afraid of him? Was that why she didn't talk about her visits? Did she take me with her during these visits? And if so, why?*

11

It was a Wednesday in the month of April. The sky was clear, but the cold still chilled to the bone. The sun was strong but wasn't able to chase away the chill. People were getting up and going to work just like every morning, trying to shake off the cobwebs still remaining from the night's sleep. Everyday routines were being carried out automatically: taking the mail out of the mailbox, bringing the newspaper inside the house, sipping coffee while tying a tie. The routines swept me up in them too. I reluctantly threw the warm bed covers off and shuffled barefoot into the bathroom—it was freezing. I brushed my teeth rapidly with my eyes closed, made the bed, and chose some clothes for myself—my old orange blouse and a brown wool skirt. I hadn't bought myself new clothes in a long time. My father usually brought home clothes for me. He knew my exact size, and every once in a while, he would come home from work with a shopping bag. Most of the time I liked what he bought, but not always. I kept the clothes anyway and never asked him to exchange them.

Suddenly I remembered the only time my mother took me to the shopping mall to buy some new clothes. She was wearing a green dress with a silver belt that wrapped around her hips. Her hair was brushed back and clipped to her temples with two brown hairpins, and I remember being in awe of her full and luxuriant hair. Her lips shone in a light shade of pink and her eyes were emphasized by dark mascara, giving her gaze an unfamiliar depth. Up until that time, I never noticed that her eyes were really green. Her dress accentuated her slim figure and she looked beautiful and foreign. It was the first time, maybe the only time, where I saw her as an entity unto herself. As a woman.

My feet walked by themselves to my parents' bedroom, to their closet. On the right side were his clothes and on the left, hers. I slid the hangers aside until I found the dress. I slipped it over my head, straightened out the wrinkles of the dress and fastened the belt around my hips. I sat down in front of the mirror of the dressing table and opened one of the drawers. It was neatly arranged and organized. I rummaged around with my fingers, opening tubes of lipstick. The last one was the right one, and I colored my lips. In another drawer was the mascara, a bit dry but still usable. With a shaking hand, I brushed the tips of my eyelashes with a long stroke that reached the corner of each eye.

Still not pleased, I opened the bottom drawer and found a hairbrush, a comb, and hairpins. The brown hairpins went into my hair, clipping it to the sides of my ears. The hairbrush still had her hair in it. I touched the hairs with my fingers and pulled out a handful, pressing it to my cheek, moving my fingers up and down, feeling the delicate hair caress my face. I had never felt so close to her, as if she were standing next to me caressing my cheeks. I stood up from the chair and straightened myself in front of the mirror. The vision that stood before me paralyzed me. My mother stood there, with her blue eyes, her high cheekbones, and her hair gathered high. My face was her face, and my body her body. Tears flowed from my eyes nonstop, like a dam that had burst. They dampened the dress and smeared the black mascara all over my face.

Still crying, the rest of the memory came to me. When we arrived at the shopping mall, my father was waiting for us with a look of victory on his face. I remember very clearly that I turned to look at her and saw the familiar look of defeat etched her face.

***

"What happened? Did you try putting on makeup?" Donna met me as I walked into the office. "Come here, let me fix you up." I went into her office and she sat me down on the red sofa, went over to her pink purse, and took out her makeup kit. I sat like a little girl whose mother is cleaning her face after playing with her friends outside.

"There, now you look human," she said. I nodded feebly. She took my chin with two fingers and said, "I want a smile, not bursts of laughter. A smile will do for today."

I stayed serious, but she wouldn't give up. Her fingers pinched my chin harder until I groaned in pain.

"That's right," she said. "And it will hurt even more if you don't smile at me."

A feeling of anguish stayed with me for the rest of that day. What happened this morning at home really bothered me—my sadness was inexplicable, and the overwhelming feelings the memory had triggered troubled me a great deal. The anguish became an actual stomachache. I replayed the sequence of events over and over: my mother's beautiful appearance and the happiness showing on her face as we walked to the bus stop on our way to a rare afternoon outing. Her hand holding mine—the sound of her shoes clicking on the pavement, as if she wanted the whole world to see her with me. Her making room for me to board the steps of the bus ahead of her and making sure I didn't lose my balance when the bus driver began to drive. Details that at the time seemed unimportant popped up like clues to a game. Now I remember sitting on the bus. Even then, she wouldn't let go of my hand. She didn't talk; only her hand holding mine connected us. When we got off the bus, she went down before me and helped me navigate the high steps of the bus. We walked through the mall, still hand in hand, to the escalators for the clothes stores. We ascended slowly. I leaned my head against the moving rail and she lifted me up gently and rested me on her hip. We reached the top of the escalator, began walking, and suddenly saw my father. She saw him before me. In one moment, everything changed. She dropped my hand, her steps halted and her face turned ashen as if it had aged decades in that flash of a second.

I looked in the direction of her eyes and met my father's glare. He had the look of victory in his eyes. Only now I knew that in addition to the look of victory, there was a look of defiance. His eyes shone and his hand was outstretched, expecting my hand to take hold of it. The last picture tacked on to the bulletin board of my memory was her face. A face etched with defeat. The makeup seemed out of place now and her dress suddenly looked like the apron she wore every day. And then, like a mask replaced by another, a look of acceptance took its place on her face.

And me? I took my father's hand and moved away from her. When I turned to look back, I saw her green back disappear as she went down the escalator.

An unfamiliar feeling crept into my stomach. I was afraid to give it a name. I preferred to ignore it, as I had ignored many other things in my life. I now knew exactly how to define the discomfort that had been with me; it's the discomfort of the memory. Not the memory of walking together, nor the fact that she held me on her hip, nor her special appearance. But the memory of his face. The look of contempt; the look of victory. *Why did he wait for us at the mall and not let us spend the afternoon together? Why did he feel victorious? Victory over what? Over whom?* There were a lot of clues there, words and facial expressions that formed a story, but the story's significance still evaded me.

"We didn't get very much done today, did we?" Donna's voice brought me back to the reality of the office.

I tried to apologize, but she stopped me and invited me to have a drink with her. We went into one of the only places in town that could be called, if even barely, a pub. Tom was the bartender and also the owner. Even though it was still light out, it was dark inside. We sat across from one another and Tom came over and cheerfully asked us what we would like to drink. Donna answered for the both of us and ordered vodka with orange juice. "But it's only afternoon!" I tried to protest, but she ignored me completely and nodded to Tom, assuring him that this was indeed our order.

"I'm not going to ask you what happened today," she said. "It must be one of your moods regarding your parents or something else, God knows what. In any case, I want to know how we can continue looking for this woman."

For a moment, I didn't know what she was talking about, but then I remembered that I had promised she could be part of the search team.

"The truth is that I don't know," I answered. I hoped that answer would mollify her for now, or at least postpone the conversation on the subject to another time. But Donna said, "There's no way you're going to put me off with your nonsense. I want us to think together how we can continue what you both started. Now tell me everything you know about this woman. Don't leave out any details, even if you think they're insignificant... Everything."

I told her about the bracelet I found at home, about the phone conversation from the detective agency, about my and Roy's visit to hospitals in Chicago, about the conversation I had with the priest, about the advertisement we placed that hadn't generated a thing, and about our visit to the city library. I emphasized that everywhere we went, we reached a dead end.

"I think it's just a waste of time," I said.

"Have you told me everything? Think hard. There's nothing else? I don't know—anything." Donna was unquestionably blessed with determination.

When I told Donna about the check that came to the house, she wisely suggested that we try to locate the store that sent the check to see if they could dig up details that would help us locate Sonia Schwartz.

When Tom arrived with the drinks, Donna gave me the narrow glass and ordered me to drink it down all in one gulp.

"But it's too strong for me," I complained.

"All at once," she insisted.

I tipped my head back and tossed the drink down my throat in one gulp. I immediately felt the warmth radiating throughout my entire body. My throat burned, but a pleasant feeling had taken over. I said, "OK, let's go for it. We'll tell Roy that you're joining us and together we'll devise our adventure."

"Oh, my God, what one glass of vodka can do," Donna said with a smile. "I wonder what would happen after a few more of those."

12

We met two days later—Donna, Roy and me. We sat in the wicker chairs on the porch and began to plan our next steps. Roy tried to object to Donna's suggestion that we find the store where the check was sent from, claiming we should wait for results from the priest and the librarian first. He said he would prefer to check at home rather than travel somewhere far away.

It seemed to me that Roy was quieter than usual. Most of the time he listened to the conversation between Donna and me and almost never intervened. Every once in a while, he would throw in a word, but did not really contribute ideas. I was a bit surprised but didn't say anything. Donna was against his idea of waiting and insisted we check things simultaneously. She won, of course. I brought the envelope with the check and together we examined its details. The letter was signed by somebody named Shlomo Cohen, and it gave a telephone number and exact address. We tried to call the number, but a recording answered saying that the number had been disconnected. The only other possibility would be to go the address on the letterhead.

We drove to Chicago the following day. The name of the company was Cohen and Sons. The address on the letter was located in the center of the city. We found the address fairly easily. Cars passed by us in a constant buzz, horns honked, and people crossed in front of us, caught up in their own lives. I felt slightly uncomfortable. Big cities made me shrink. I felt lost in them. The fast pace, the blasting car horns, the smoke, smog, and people hurrying about. All of these things exacerbated my feelings of loneliness, of not belonging. I let Donna and Roy lead the way. They were holding a map that they used to navigate. Above our heads, there was a sign with its lights turned off. It read, "Cohen and Sons Ltd." Underneath the sign, there was another one that read, "Unsurpassed Quality and Attention Since 1947." Both signs looked very old. Underneath those were two glass doors locked with a large iron padlock. We knocked on the glass doors but didn't get an answer. We tried to look through the glass. It was dark inside, but we could see that the place was empty and abandoned. There were a few boards, some lying on the floor and others leaning against the wall. Papers were strewn all over.

"I'm going to look around back," said Roy. Several minutes later he came back and asked us to join him. We arrived at the back of the store, which faced a narrow alley lined with huge dumpsters.

"Where are you taking us?" Donna asked, obviously irritated.

Roy didn't answer, but suddenly opened a door and invited us to go in. It was a small room, not more than two hundred square feet. In the middle of the room was a table, and sitting on a chair next to it was a man in his early thirties. When we walked in, he stood up and his face was pleasant and inviting. He held out his hand and said, "Michael—Mickey. Nice to meet you, Eva."

Mickey was a very handsome guy. His body was slim and long and he had a healthy head of brown hair. His clothes were fashionable and suited his figure. When he introduced himself, he had a warm smile, despite the air of sorrow that touched his eyes like a thin, almost imperceptible thread.

I looked around. Aside from the table and chair, there was also a brown chest of drawers, old but in good shape. Pictures were hanging on the walls, most of them black and white. Under the pictures was a shelf that held a number of medals. When I got closer, I read on one of the medals that it was given for excellence in business; another was awarded for huge sales in 1982; and one personal one was awarded by the City of Chicago honoring the generous contribution of Mr. Shlomo Cohen to the city. On the opposite wall were paintings in various shades of turquoise, red, blue and yellow. There was one painting that drew my eye in particular. The brush strokes were circular and soft and the colors blended together in beautiful harmony.

"My father made that painting even before the business was established," said Mickey. He stood beside me and looked at the painting as if for the first time. I turned to look at him and met a pair of green eyes, deeply recessed in their sockets but full of warmth. I smiled at him and told him that I loved the painting.

"Why?" he asked.

"I'm not sure, but I feel like in spite of the colors used, there is something sad about it. Some kind of secret. As if underneath the happy circles, there's something that the painter doesn't want known or seen and therefore it's trying very hard to hide it in the vibrant cheerful colors... Too cheerful."

Mickey looked at me and nodded.

"I'm sorry," I said, embarrassed. "I don't understand art very well. I'm just babbling."

"You're not babbling," he said. "It's your powerful intuition."

In answer to my questioning face, he began to talk about his father, who was a young boy when World War II broke out. As soon as they took the Jews to the camps, they separated him from his parents. They were both killed and he was the only one lucky enough to survive.

"And the painting?" I asked.

"The painting covers everything he went through back then."

"And..." I wanted him to continue talking.

"Mr. Cohen, we wondered if you could help us with something," Donna said in a pragmatic voice.

"Yes, of course, how can I help?" His voice became official and the warm and humorous look in his eye turned serious and businesslike.

"We're looking for a woman named Sonia Schwartz."

"I'm sorry, I don't know—"

Donna cut him off. "A little while ago, you sent her a check in the amount of thirty dollars..." She continued to lay out the facts before him, explaining how important it was to us to find this woman and pass the money on to her. "We ask that you please check your records and see if this woman is living at another address, so that we can send her the check."

Mickey asked to see the check and went straight to the task at hand. He sat down in front of the computer and got to work. Every once in a while, he asked a question, but beyond the information we had already given him, we didn't have any answers.

"Interesting," he muttered to himself. "I can't find this name in the computer."

"That's impossible," Donna insisted. "You're the ones who sent the check to her. Why did you send this check out after such a long time?"

"That's who we are," he answered immediately. "My father brought us up to be fair. We never left debts unpaid. If someone is entitled to something from us, he will receive it even after thirty years." Mickey got up from his chair, went over to an old filing cabinet standing next to the wall across from the table, took out a box and began to go through the papers inside.

"I knew it," he shouted. "My mother was our bookkeeper. Even after we introduced computers to the business, she refused to use one and continued to do her work by hand. Besides, I see that this was something that was purchased more than ten years ago."

He put an old, foul-smelling yellow index card in Donna's hand. Roy and I moved closer and saw the name "Sonia Schwartz" written in blue

LIFE IN A BOX | 89

ink on the card. We saw that on November 10, 1983, she had purchased a single bed made of maple with a matching mattress. On the next line was my home address. We looked at the writing over and over again as if it would tell us something more about the woman.

"What now?" I asked disappointedly. The truth is, as usual, we didn't think ahead. We didn't plan what we would do if we received proof that the woman really existed.

"Give me the card," Roy ordered. Up until now, he had kept his distance and not interfered in the conversation.

Donna held out the card and Roy moved it closer to his eyes. Every so often he turned it over and around and looked at it for a long time.

"What?" asked Donna with obvious impatience.

Roy came over to me and said, "Somebody erased something here."

Mickey also moved closer and asked to see the card. He also turned it over, moved it under the ceiling light, and turned it around and around. He finally said that it was impossible to read the writing.

"Do you think your mother could have erased something here?" Roy asked Michael.

"Of course not," he said adamantly. "My mother never did anything like that. If she made a mistake, she would white it out with correction fluid and write over it in clean and clear writing. This was not her work."

"Strange," Roy mumbled to himself.

"Do you think we could have this card?"

"I don't think..." he began. Then, seeing our disappointed faces, he said instead, "You know what, I'll make a photocopy of the card and let you have it, just for good measure."

We left the building and took deep breaths. Even though the room was neat and orderly, we felt suffocated inside.

Donna suggested that since we were already in Chicago, we should sightsee for a while and then get a bite to eat. Roy agreed right away. I didn't answer. They both turned to me with puzzled looks. They were surprised by my silence.

"You both go ahead," I said finally.

I saw Roy's questioning glance. Donna nodded her head in agreement.

We agreed to meet in two hours. I went back to the alley and walked into the room. Mickey smiled at me. "I knew you'd be back," he said. He pointed to a chair at the end of the room and asked me to move it closer. He took a photo out of a drawer in the table, held it out to me, and said, "This is my grandfather, Yakov."

In the picture, faded with age, was a man about forty years old, with the same warmth in his eyes possessed by his grandson. He had a black beard whose ends were rounded and every hair was tucked into place. His image was of a man who commanded respect. His dark suit afforded him the look of a wise and self-confident man. Mickey took the photo from my hand and looked at it for a long moment. "My father says that he was a very wise man," he muttered to himself. "There was not a soul who didn't respect and love him."

"He looks like it," I agreed.

He began to talk. "My grandfather and grandmother were born in Ukraine, in a city called Yelizavetgrad. During the early 1920s, riots broke out in the city. My father told me that most of the Jews in the city were killed in a pogrom, and that his parents survived by luck. Many of the women were raped and injured, and many people lost all of their property. They escaped from there and arrived in Poland. When Hitler took over, my grandfather was already a wealthy man. He was in the coal mining business, and the company he founded employed dozens of people. Hitler's being elected didn't raise any special concern for him. Nobody imagined that Hitler's rise to power would be the first step toward the atrocities that would take place in the future. My grandfather continued to work at the company. They lived in the city of Katowice, southwest of

Warsaw. There were Jews, Germans, Poles, and Silesians living in the city, and my grandfather lived in peace with all of them. My father told me that even though my grandfather was a very busy man, he always found time for my father. Grandfather would tell him that the company was Father's, that Grandfather was only taking care of it until my father decided he was ready to manage it on his own. My father always said that he aimed to be admired the way his father was." Mickey stopped talking. For a minute I thought he had fallen asleep, but suddenly I heard him mumble, "They had a special bond..."

His monologue began to make me feel uncomfortable, as if someone was loading especially heavy bricks upon my shoulders. Mickey seemed to have completely forgotten I was there. I cleared my throat in order to get his attention, but he continued talking, ignoring me entirely, sitting on his chair and staring into space. I decided to get out of there. I took a piece of paper from the table and wrote down my phone number. He didn't notice me leave. Even as I closed the door behind me, I could still hear the sound of his voice.

The light outside blinded me—it was less than half an hour until my meeting with Roy and Donna. Walking toward the busy street, I felt confused. Something undefinable was stirring inside me. Mickey was a complete stranger to me—we had never met before, I had never been in his store or on this street. The story he told me had nothing to do with me at all. It was the story of a family I don't even know. But still inside my stomach, deep inside, something bounced like a small ball, and every bounce shook its sides. I had to hear the whole story—clearly, there was a lot more to it. I decided to wait two weeks and then call Mickey, if he didn't call me first.

Donna was very cheerful and satisfied when we met up with them. Roy was restrained. I could feel him looking at me and I avoided his eyes. He was quiet the entire way back. Donna filled the void of the car with cheerful chatter, and I murmured every once in a while in response.

13

The house wasn't calm that night. As soon as my head hit the pillow, I heard noises. The window in the bedroom was creaking; a popping sound rose up from the television in the guest room; the coffee maker in the kitchen made noise. Each time I got up and went to check the source of the noise, silence filled the house. But as soon as I got back into bed, the noises returned. Sleep was fitful, and at five a.m., it fled for good. I sat in the living room and turned on the television. I flipped through the stations but couldn't find anything interesting on any of the programs.

Suddenly, as I was changing stations, I heard a familiar name and went back to the previous channel. Filling the entire screen was a figure whom I had only learned about several hours earlier: Mickey's grandfather, with the shortened beard and brown eyes, smiling at me from the screen. The narrator's voice could be heard in the background:

"This is a story about people who are deeply scarred from the atrocities they suffered and the inhuman situations they were forced to contend with. Those of us who didn't endure the tragedy grapple with questions that we will probably never be able to answer. Despite this, they raised families, built businesses and contributed a great deal to society. Shlomo Cohen was one of many that experienced and survived one of the greatest abominations in the history of humanity. The determination of these people to continue living, despite the horrors they experienced, is an example for the entire world in general, and the Jewish people in particular."

The program had finished and the credits were rolling quickly on the screen, accompanied by an unfamiliar melody.

I sat completely rigid. "That can't be. It just can't be," I muttered. "This isn't a coincidence any more, this is a guiding hand." It seemed totally absurd that I would get up in the middle of the night, turn on the television, and find Shlomo Cohen on TV.

What to do? Going back to sleep was out of the question. There was no one to talk to—it was way too early. I was alone, and these thoughts were disturbing my peace of mind. And then, completely naturally, I began to speak to my father out loud.

"What do these incidents mean? I know you're steering me toward something, but I don't understand the significance of your actions. I miss you; I don't know how to deal with things like this by myself; I need you to show me the way, to solve all these questions that have arisen throughout the last year for me."

The house stayed quiet. Pictures flickered across the television set. The first rays of sunlight snuck in through the shutters and tiny dots of light could be seen on the living room table. It was a few minutes after six o'clock a.m. Roy usually gets up around this time. I wanted him next to me—to talk to him. I walked hesitantly toward the telephone, picked up the handset, and dialed. After two rings I heard his voice, surprised and tense.

"Roy, it's me."

"What happened?" he asked with concern.

I was silent for a moment, the words stuck in my throat.

"Eva, what happened?" There was definite anxiety in his voice.

"Everything is fine." I tried to calm him down. "I just thought maybe you could come over for a few minutes."

There were several seconds of silence and then, "I'll be right there." And the line disconnected.

Time crept by at a snail's pace. I sat on the sofa and waited. My eyes rested occasionally on the television that was still on, but I didn't see a thing. Finally, I heard Roy's car in the driveway. When I opened the door, I saw a look on his face that I had never seen before. It was complete panic. He came inside and quickly scanned the room.

"What's going on, Eva?" he asked. I think he saw something in my face, because in an instant, he took me in both his arms, and in a softer voice, he asked for the third time, "What happened?"

I don't know if it was his soothing voice, the touch of his arms on my skin, or maybe the tension that had built up inside me, but I burst into tears. Roy held me close. My head was on his chest while his hand caressed my hair. He tried to hush my sobbing, but that only served to increase my tears. We stood there for several long minutes before I finally began to calm down a bit. Roy led me into the living room and gently sat me down on the sofa. His arms continued to hold me, and I silently thanked him for that. It was nice to feel him close. I put my head on his shoulder and absorbed the heat that radiated from it. The sun had already lit up the sky, but the house was still dim. Roy was quiet, waiting for me to speak.

"Yesterday, when we were in Mickey's store, I felt like something happened to me. I can't explain exactly what, but it felt like I had to get to know him better. That's the reason I went back inside. Do you remember the painting that was hanging on the wall? His father painted it."

I thought I could feel his body grow a bit stiff, but he didn't say a word and continued to hold me.

"He told me that his father was a boy when World War II broke out. The Germans caught his parents and imprisoned them in a work camp. What is so strange to me is that he talked as if he himself had been there.

He stammered, and I could hardly hear what he was saying. At one point, he even began to cry. He didn't hear me anymore; he forgot I was there. Last night, I couldn't fall asleep and was watching television—a program about people who had been through the Holocaust. They showed a picture of Mickey's grandfather and mentioned his father. Roy, don't you think that's weird?" I pulled away from his embrace and turned to him. I couldn't read the look on his face.

"I don't know. What do you think?"

I was hesitant to share the chain of coincidences that had befallen me lately. I didn't know how he would react. Roy was a man of facts. Even at his job, he gathered evidence, analyzed it, and drew conclusions. If I told him about the creatures hanging around my house or about my unfounded feelings, he would ridicule me or maybe even distance himself from me, and I couldn't bear that thought.

"I don't know either. Maybe I'm just imagining things." I tried to make the tone of my voice cheerful. Roy noticed the difference in my mood and moved away from me a little.

"Would you like something to drink?" I asked, trying to break the ice that had begun to form between us.

"No," he answered. "I have to get to work."

He began to make his way toward the door. Before he left, I asked him what he was doing with the index card he took from Mickey.

"I'm working on it," he answered and closed the door behind him.

For the rest of the day, I couldn't stop thinking about Roy—his hug, how safe I felt in his arms, how he came when I needed him, how he caressed my hair and calmed me down with his low voice. My hand reached for the telephone at the end of the table and punched in Roy's familiar number. After the first ring I hung up—perhaps I was confusing Roy's friendly hug with thoughts of a different nature.

At the end of the work day, I arranged my desk and gathered up my things. Donna walked by my desk and suggested we meet to decide our next steps, but I was tired from the sleepless night and declined her offer.

I got home and collapsed onto the bed, completely exhausted. The knock on the door fished me out of the depths of slumber. I dragged myself to the door and opened it right before Sarah was about to knock again.

"You disappeared on me," she declared.

"I didn't mean to, I've been really busy," I said apologetically.

She went ahead and went to sit on one of the chairs in the kitchen, but not before she placed a plate of cookies on the table.

"I came to visit you the day before yesterday, but you weren't home."

"I was in Chicago." She was quiet, waiting for me to continue. "Roy and I are looking for the tenant who lived here before us. A check arrived for her and we want to give it to her."

"That's why you went to Chicago?"

"It turns out that the check came from a company in Chicago, so we went there to investigate."

"And what's the name of this woman you're looking for?"

"Sonia—Sonia Schwartz."

Sarah got up from her chair.

"Are you going?" I asked, disappointed.

"Yes."

As she left, again I thought I saw a hidden smile creep over her face.

14

It was now August, the height of summer. The air was dense and stifling. The weather forecaster said it hadn't been this hot for twenty years. There was no escaping it. Even the air conditioners didn't help. The electric companies were so overloaded that there were blackouts from time to time, during which it was impossible to work. People walked around the office in a daze; there was little conversation. The work rate dropped and everything basically crept along slowly. People shut themselves up in their houses seeking any source of shade and respite from the heat. I also preferred to stay at home. I was upset, I couldn't seem to relax. It was difficult to drag myself to work in the morning, and in the evenings I came home tired and worn out, not speaking to a soul until the next morning. Sometimes the sound of the neighbors' sprinklers in their yard and the kids playing penetrated my walls. Sarah called every once in a while and invited me over to her house, but it seemed like she was relieved to be turned down. Donna completely disappeared—we didn't speak outside of work. On television, they promised that there would be relief from the hot spell next month.

I hadn't heard a thing from Roy. In the weeks following the trip to Chicago, it felt like he was avoiding me. He didn't return my phone calls, and after several failed attempts to make contact with him, I decided to give up. Spending long periods of time at home didn't make matters any easier. The feel of his hug was evaporating, although it was still fresh in my memory. *Why did he run away from me? We've been friends for nearly a decade and this is the first time he's cut off all contact with me for so long. Maybe I hurt him somehow—maybe something scared him.* I panned through my memory, but couldn't find any justification for his behavior. Finally, I couldn't hold back any longer.

It was early evening, and I knew that Roy usually tried to make it home in time to have dinner with his family. I called his home phone number. My heart was beating so fast I almost hung up. I heard Barbara's voice, his mother, on the other end of the line. A slow and firm voice.

"Barbara, it's Eva." My voice shook.

"Eva." Her voice was cold.

"Is Roy home?"

I don't know why, but Roy's mother never particularly liked me. She was always polite and courteous, never hurt my feelings, but when our eyes met her look was cold and distant.

"Oh. How are you, Eva?" she said. Before I could answer, she called out to Roy and told him I was on the phone.

It seemed like an eternity passed before I heard his voice. Like he was trying to put off the conversation for as long as possible.

"Hi, Eva. How are you?" he asked with a serious voice that made me want to hang up right then.

"I'm OK," I answered. "And you?"

"Everything is fine," he answered.

There was an uncomfortable silence. In the background, I could hear the rattling of plates and his mother announcing that dinner was ready.

"I understand you have to go," I said, breaking the silence.

"Yeah." He answered, but he didn't make any effort to rescue us from the lagging conversation.

"I hadn't heard from you in a while, and I got worried," I said carefully.

"Everything is fine. I've been under a lot of pressure at work and haven't had time for anything else."

"Are you mad at me?" I tried.

"No," he answered immediately. He didn't volunteer anything else.

"Listen, Roy, I understand that something happened, but I don't know what." I was on the verge of tears, my voice shaking, and I couldn't continue.

"I'll come over after dinner, OK?" Roy said in a low voice. "In about an hour."

"OK, see you then."

It was almost two hours before I heard the rattle of his car's engine. I opened the door even before he knocked. He had to duck down a bit in order to get through the front door. He filled the entire entrance. He was wearing a blue shirt and jeans, and when he turned toward the living room, his steps were hesitant. He avoided looking at me directly, and I was surprised. Usually, when we met, he would smile his familiar smile and make some kind of movement with his hand—sometimes ruffling his hair, other times stroking my cheek with his fingers. These were gestures that became a kind of ritual every time we met, until we barely even noticed them.

Roy held a brown envelope in his hand. He sat down on the sofa, gave me a quick blue-eyed glance, and told me to sit down next to him.

I sat down in my father's easy chair, some distance away from him. The collar of his shirt was turned inside, and I was almost tempted to fix it. His hair was unkempt, and I could tell that it was his own hand that made it so. When he was embarrassed or felt uncomfortable he would use his hand to mess up his hair. I waited for him to begin speaking.

He was quiet for a couple of minutes and then said, "I'm sorry I haven't spoken to you for so long, but there was a reason for it."

I waited for him to continue. His hand incessantly fiddled with the envelope, crumpling it between his fingers. His continuing silence began to alarm me. Roy was not himself; he was tense and uncertain.

"Listen, Eva, I want you to hear me out."

It was obvious what I was about to hear. It had always been a fear of mine, but this time my fear became real panic. I always took Roy for granted, couldn't picture my life without him. My moods, my demands for time away—all these never put any distance between us. He couldn't be anyone else's boyfriend. He was always available for me any time—he was the one thing that gave me security and kept me balanced. Now I didn't want to hear what he had to say. I was sorry to have called him. I was like the defendant who wishes the trial to continue so he doesn't hear the verdict that would clearly announce his guilt.

Roy opened the envelope and took out the yellow index card. The next words he said completely surprised me and proved me wrong.

"This is the card we took from the store," he stated.

"Yes, I know."

"Do you remember that something had been erased and Michael didn't know why?"

"I remember."

"Well, I examined the card."

I still didn't know where he was going with this.

"At first I tried to scratch off the dark part with a file, but whoever erased it was trying very hard to hide what was written. When I saw that this was unsuccessful, I asked a friend of mine for help. He works at the lab and has a modern device that can identify the original even if it was erased or blurred. In any case, I got the answer two weeks ago."

His voice got softer. His body moved on the couch as if he was about to bolt. His hand shot out to his hair and messed it up.

"Can I have a glass of water?" he asked.

I came back from the kitchen and held out the glass of cold water. Roy drank the entire glass in one gulp. He then got up from the sofa and began to walk around the room. I watched him in amazement as he touched this object or another. Finally, he came back and sat down again on the sofa. He held out the yellow card to me. I took it from him and brought it closer to the light to read the writing clearly. In an unfamiliar handwriting, under the line that had been erased, someone had written the name "Maria Brown." Looking at the writing, reading it again and again, I didn't know what to deduce from it. I held the card out to Roy and said, "I don't understand."

Roy moved closer to me, took my hand in his, and said, "Eva, I think Sonia Schwartz is your mother."

The laughter that shot out of me was like lava erupting from a volcano.

15

I dreamt about my father that night. His image was so clear and alive that when I woke up, I expected to see him standing next to me.

In the dream, I saw him on one of the nights he went to the weekly men's meeting. George came to pick him up in his car. When George came into our house, he had short horns on the top of his head, and his teeth protruded out of his mouth when he spoke. He looked at my mother, who was standing in the kitchen cooking. In the dream, he had bulging black eyes and his lips were stretched into a smirk. He moved closer to my mother, who was standing with her back to him, and reached out to her hair. My mother didn't move, remaining with her back to him. His hand continued from her hair to her back, and his smile grew into a roar of laughter. Suddenly, he grabbed her shoulder and spun her around to face him. A scream escaped me when I saw my mother's face. It was black and gaunt. Her cheeks were elongated and she had sprouted rounded horns. Her smile was wider than George's and the laughter that spewed out of her mouth was deep and slow. My shocked expression moved to my father, begging for his help, but he remained standing without moving, just staring as the actions played out before him. I shouted, "Dad! Dad!" but my voice wasn't heard. He continued to stand still. I ran to him, scared, my whole body shaking, and hugged him, but his body was transparent and I found myself hugging my own body. I ran out of the house and saw my father's shiny car pulling out of the driveway, leaving George's car behind.

I woke up all at once. My body was drenched in sweat. My breathing was rapid and my chest rose up and down at an accelerated rate. I sat up in bed and looked for my father, but all I saw were the familiar objects in my room—the clothes on the chair, books aslant on the shelf, and the dusty guitar leaning against the wall. At that moment, my yearning for my father was so acute it was painful.

Our relationship had always alternated between closeness and distance. We were connected by thick flexible cords that could neither be detached nor ripped apart. Sometimes we were close and sometimes distant. Sometimes I felt safe and loved, and sometimes he pushed me away with a glance or a look. All this created the expectation and hope that one day the distance would disappear, and I would be secure in the knowledge that his love wasn't dependent on anything.

The morning after the dream, I felt weak. Donna asked me what was going on, but I avoided her. I also kept my distance from Roy. I was mad at him; his behavior that night outraged me. In my opinion, he was patronizing me. How did he reach the conclusion that the woman who lived in the house before us was my mother? It didn't make any sense. There had to be a more reasonable explanation for the coincidence of the two names on the index card, and I decided to check it out for myself. In any event, I planned to contact Mickey. For some strange reason, a stirring inside me made me want to hear more stories about his family.

I set up a time to go see Mickey at the end of that week without telling Roy or Donna about my trip. This would be the first time I would drive such a great distance alone. There were moments when I debated inviting one of them to join me, but I felt the need to keep Mickey's story to myself; I felt that it was something related only to me.

Mickey gave me a warm reception. He planted a kiss on my cheek and sat me down on an easy chair I don't remember being there last time. He served me a glass of water and apologized that he couldn't offer me something hot to drink. He pulled some cookies out of a tin that was sitting on the brown bureau and told me that his mother heard that I was coming and baked these *kichalach*. He explained that *kichalach* means cookies in Yiddish.

The cookies were delicious, crunchy, with just the right sweetness. I was at ease. The atmosphere was pleasant even though the place was small. The pile of papers that was on the table had grown smaller, and now there were only a few sheets.

"I apologize for the way I acted before," he said. "Sometimes I get too deep into the story."

"Why?" I asked.

"I don't know. Maybe it's because I still don't know the whole of it. My father didn't really like to talk about what happened there."

"So then where did you hear the story you told me?" I was interested.

"Some of it I heard from my mother and some he talked about, but as soon as I asked him a question about what he went through in the camp, he immediately shut down and said that he doesn't remember any more."

"What do you think happened?" I continued probing.

"I don't know, but it's clear to me that horrible things happened to him."

I decided to change the subject and asked when he expected to finish work and close the company for good.

"I believe within a week," he answered.

"And then?" I asked.

"And then the doors will be permanently closed," he said, his voice sounding a bit hoarse.

"Does that make you sad?"

He thought about it for a while and then he answered, "Yes and no."

I waited for him to continue.

"You see, this company was like a living organ in our family. We grew up with it, lived with it. It was like the daughter of close relative. If a customer complained, we would all take it as a personal assault. That's how my father raised us. It was important that people were satisfied and not get angry at him. If someone complained, he immediately compensated him. That was the reason we sent out the check. If we made a mistake, we would rectify it even if a long time had passed. It was a very emotional business. Things are different today. Business is business. Suppliers aren't willing to take our word any more—they want guarantees. We used to seal a deal with a handshake; there's no such thing today."

Then there was silence. Not an uncomfortable silence; it felt relaxed. *Strange*, I thought, *it is only the second time I have met him, but already I feel as if we had known each other for a long time.*

Finally, he said, "Would you like me to check the card again? Did you bring it?"

"Yes," I answered.

All of the sudden I felt cold. My whole body began to shake. I crossed my arms over my chest to hide my shivering. I took a sip of the water he gave me earlier and placed it on the bureau. My body was tense. Mickey's eyes were fixed on the painting; he didn't speak, and his breathing could barely be heard. It appeared as if he was traveling back in time, as if he wasn't in the little room in the back alley in the center of the city. Not knowing where he was at that moment, I kept quiet and waited for him to begin speaking.

Then the telephone on the table began to ring. Mickey picked up the receiver and I could only hear the impatience in his voice.

When he finished the conversation, he explained, "That was my mother. She wants you to take the cookies that are left."

"Thank you," I said. Then, with uncharacteristic bravado, I asked, "Did she say anything else about me?"

He hesitated for a moment before answering, and then he said, "Yes, she wants me to invite you to our home."

"Why?" I wondered.

"I don't know," he replied.

"I mean, she doesn't even know me." I tried to understand.

"You're right, but she tries to fix me up with every Jewish girl I talk about," he said with an apologetic smile.

"But I'm not Jewish!" I exclaimed.

"Oh, I'm sorry. I don't know why I thought you were. Maybe because of your interest in my father's story. I just assumed that... I'm sorry..."

"It's OK," I consoled him. "It doesn't matter, I still want to hear the story."

"On September 1, 1939, Hitler invaded Poland and demolished the Polish army," he began. "It was a Friday, the day when Jews prepare for the Sabbath and therefore their work day is shorter than usual. When rumors of the invasion reached him, my grandfather asked his employees to go home and look after their families. After he locked up the factory, he hurried home. The family packed one suitcase and fled. Two weeks later, the Jews in the city were all rounded up and deported to the General Government Zone.

"My father and his parents boarded the first train that came their way. It took them southward to the city of Krakow. From there, they traveled to a city adjacent to the Slovakian border. I don't remember the name. My grandfather hoped that the further away from the center they got, the safer they would be. With the money he took with him, he rented a small room in a crowded, poor neighborhood. He thought it would help them assimilate among the residents. But my grandfather didn't take into consideration the fact that some make their peace with poverty and some try to escape it. One of the neighbors suspected that his new tenants were Jewish, so he turned them in to the Germans for money.

"At five in the morning, there was a knock on the door. My grandfather woke up in a panic—he knew exactly what was happening. He went to my father and begged him to hide in the closet. At first, he refused, but after my grandfather pleaded with him, he climbed into the closet. The bedroom door opened and there were three Germans standing in the doorway. They beat my grandfather with a club. One of the soldiers grabbed my grandfather and dragged him to the car waiting outside.

"This is how my father was torn away from his parents. He swore to himself that he would not rest until he was reunited with them. He couldn't imagine his life without them."

Mickey suddenly stood up, opened the door, and went outside, leaving me alone inside, stunned by his story. The air in the room was dense. It was dim inside, and only the small amount of light that came in through the open door reminded me that there was still a long trip home ahead of me. I got up and went outside. Mickey was leaning against the wall, his hands hiding his face. He was crying, but when he felt my presence, he quickly wiped his face. "I'm sorry," he said. "Every time I talk about that period, it feels as if I was there myself. Maybe if my father would tell me what happened, that would give me some relief. But you came here to check out the card and here I am yammering on and on about horrible things."

"Don't say that," I said, becoming angry. "I was the one who asked you to tell me."

Mickey smiled. We were both quiet.

I finally said, "OK, I have to go. It will be dark soon, and I don't like driving in the dark."

"How about spending the night with us?" he said surprisingly.

His offer caught me off guard. I didn't know how to refuse without sounding like I was trying to get out of it. I said, "I don't want to be any trouble. Your parents don't know me and I don't want to make them uncomfortable."

"Ridiculous," he said. "My mother will be happy. She loves having guests over, and there is always enough food for the occasional visitor."

"You have that many random guests?"

Mickey smiled and I saw his shiny white teeth in the gloom. "The truth is, we have a spare room for potential Jewish brides," he said.

"But I'm not Jewish," I insisted.

"So, you will sleep in the room for nice gentiles who aren't potential brides."

After an answer like that, I couldn't refuse. I nodded and Mickey began to organize the table and pack up his things. He opened the door for me and took a last look around the room, his eyes lingering a bit on the colorful painting. I left my car next to the office and we drove in his car. The landscape slowly changed. The tall buildings were replaced by one-story houses. The foliage became lush and the air clearer as we left the noisy city behind and drove to a rural area. I opened the window on my side and let the wind caress my face, comfortable in my silence, wanting to completely succumb to the landscape. Wide expanses of green stretched out like a tapestry on either side, hidden every now and again by tall trees that allowed the setting sun to peek through their branches, swaying in the wind. The sky painted in purple and orange hinted at the sun's transient nature. Very soon it will disappear only to bring light to another place.

I closed my eyes and became completely addicted to the feeling of calm that washed over me. My hair was fluttering in the wind annoying me, but I didn't make a move. Mickey was quiet next to me. His driving was relaxed and confident and complemented my own tranquility.

He suddenly stopped the car.

"What happened?" I asked.

"We're here," he answered with a smile. "You fell asleep."

"Really? I was sure that I was totally awake."

"I didn't want to wake you," he said. "You looked so calm and relaxed."

I smiled at him in appreciation.

"Come, let's go inside."

Only when he said that did I raise my eyes. A huge beautiful house with three separate sections stood before me. The central wing jutted forward and the side wings were placed further back. I couldn't discern the color of the house since it was already dark. Lanterns had been lit all around me and cast tiny stars everywhere. The door opened and light poured out from inside the house.

"Michael," said a voice.

"This is my mother," he said.

We moved toward the entrance; the gravel crunched under our feet. Before I knew what was happening, big fat arms encircled me and pulled me to an ample chest in a hug that choked the breath out of me for a moment.

"Eva, I'm so happy you came," said the woman.

"Thank you, I am too," I said.

She pushed me away a little bit, looked at my face and said, "Beautiful."

Mickey planted a kiss on her check, pulled me out of her embrace and pulled me inside.

"I didn't hear her name," I whispered to Mickey.

"Rivka," he answered, also in a whisper. "Like Yitzhak's wife from the Torah."

I nodded.

Mickey closed the door behind us. His mother disappeared somewhere in the house and I was captivated by the strong aromas that filled the air.

"What are those smells?" I asked Mickey.

"Shabbat home cooking."

"I can smell chicken soup," I mumbled and inhaled the odors.

"That's right," Mickey confirmed with a smile. "What else?"

I inhaled through my nose once again and said, "Meat—roast beef with gravy."

"Good," he said with a chuckle. "Go on."

"Noodles with raisins."

This time he laughed out loud and stated, "Your sense of smell is quite developed. What else?"

"Fish. Carp?" I asked it as a question, even though I was certain I knew the answer.

Mickey roared with laughter. "I didn't know you were such a good cook," he said.

"I'm not in the least, but the smells remind me of the dishes my mother used to prepare."

Mickey looked at me, and it seemed as if he wanted to say something, but he decided against it. He just smiled, took me by the hand, and led me to the room selected for me.

We went up the stairs to the second floor. The living room was underneath us. An enormous crimson- and cream-colored carpet was on the floor. Two brown sofas sat across from each other. There was a coffee table between them, holding a fresh vase of flowers. A chandelier hung from the ceiling with arms curved upward; it formed silhouettes of flowers on the ceiling. A long bureau next to the adjacent wall had many photos crowding for space. There were a number of paintings hanging on the wall. The room radiated warmth.

We reached the top of the stairs, from which a long corridor with doors on either side of it stretched. Mickey still held my hand when he opened one of the doors for me. "We have reached the Room for Nice Gentiles," he said with a smile.

I went inside and a feeling of warmth enveloped me all at once. The light wood floor was partially covered by a shaggy carpet and there was a bed with a colorful quilt with two white nightstands on either side; on each of them stood a lamp with a lampshade with colors that matched the quilt. On the wall across from the bed hung a picture of a ballerina.

"This was my younger sister's room," he explained before I could ask. "She was married a few years ago and lives in New York. They are supposed to come for dinner."

"Do you have one sister?"

"No, two. My big sister lives in San Francisco. She moved there a couple of years ago. She's a partner in a law firm, married to a doctor, and they have two children. Typical Jewish family," he added cynically. "OK, I'll leave you alone. Oh, there are clothes in the closet my sister left behind. You can use anything you want."

Mickey left and closed the door behind him.

Lying down on the bed with my feet dangling, I took a deep breath and tried to digest the last several hours. *Me, a friendless girl who doesn't know how to make contacts—I am in a total stranger's house and... And it doesn't feel so bad.* I got up from the bed, stood in front of the mirror and looked at myself. For a minute, I didn't recognize my own reflection. *What are you doing in this house?* I asked myself.

Suddenly there was a knock on the door. "Eva, are you ready?" Mickey called out.

I looked at the clock and was surprised to see that almost a whole hour had passed. I hadn't taken a shower or gotten ready. "I'll be down soon," I yelled.

I washed my face in the bathroom, sprinkled some perfume from an almost empty bottle on the shelf, brushed my hair with my fingers, put on some lipstick I brought with me, and went downstairs. Mickey was waiting at the bottom of the stairs to lead me into the dining room where the rest of the family had gathered. He introduced me to his younger sister Naomi and her husband Jerry, and then to his father, Shlomo, who shook my hand with indifference. That's when I saw how much Mickey looks like him: the same lips, the same big eyes, and the same facial features, but the mouth was different. Mickey's mouth had a wide, warm smile, while his father's remained clenched shut.

"Time for candle lighting!" Everyone turned around to face the mother, who had a clean white handkerchief on her head. She stood in front of two tall candlesticks made of silver. She lit the candles, lifted her arms up and then down to cover her face. Everyone stood and watched her. A murmuring could be heard from behind her hands and everyone around her was quiet, waiting for the prayer to end. All of the sudden I broke out in a cold sweat, my head so dizzy that I had to hold on to the end of the table to stop myself from falling. The room was spinning and with it the mother's praying figure. Mickey could feel my distress and hurried to bring me a glass of water. "Are you OK?" he asked with concern.

"I'll feel better in a little while." I could barely answer.

"Do you want to sit down?"

"No, no. I'll be fine in a minute."

The dizziness began to dissipate slowly and I was able to stabilize myself again. Except for Mickey, nobody noticed what was happening. Rivka finished the prayer and everyone turned back to sit around the table. They sat me between Mickey and his younger sister, Naomi. Shlomo, who sat at the head of the table, stood up. In one hand he held a cup of wine, and in the other a small prayer book. Everyone stood up from their chairs and listened to his words. He said the blessing for the Sabbath and finally blessed the wine and everyone answered, "Amen." At the end, he said, "*Shabbat Shalom*," and we all sat down.

Naomi and her mother went to the kitchen. They came back with the first courses and placed them in the center of the table. Mickey asked what I would like, and I asked for the familiar fish patties that my mother used to prepare. They were delicious. Just the right amount of sweetness. Suddenly

I saw my mother leaning over the counter in the kitchen cleaning the scales off the fish, and my father's look when she served them to his plate. A look of loathing. He ate what she prepared but never missed an opportunity to express his disgust. I, on the other hand, loved her cooking—and the realization hit me that I never told her so. Eating the fish with the sauce, every bite was a memory mixed with pleasure and guilt. The second course was a clear broth with a greasy bone floating in the yellowish liquid, like a monument to the tastes of the evening but also to the loud sucking sounds made by my father. The main course included roast beef and baked chicken with potatoes. Next to this, she placed a sweet noodle quiche (which I loved) and sweet carrots topped with dark raisins.

I couldn't stop refilling my plate. Mickey's mother looked at me with satisfaction. Between each course, casual conversation was made. Naomi talked about her new job that is supposed to begin in two weeks' time. Her husband, Jerry, talked with Shlomo about business. I noticed that Shlomo was listening to him, but, although he nodded his head, he didn't say a word. Rivka asked me about myself and my parents, but as soon as I told them they were dead, she stopped talking about them. I guess she didn't want to hurt me.

Dessert was served to the table and for me it was a great surprise. It was dried fruit compote. The water had absorbed the sweetness of the fruit and it tasted like heaven. My mother made this exact same compote.

When I told Rivka that every dish she served stirred a childhood memory, she gave me a strange look and smiled, and I relished all the flavors that reminded me of a home in a place that was completely foreign to me.

When dinner was over, the men remained at the table and read from one of the prayer books. Mickey explained that this prayer was called "Blessing of the Food," where the Jews thank God for the food He has given them.

"But you said your parents aren't religious at all," I said.

"That's true, but my father carries out some of the Mitzvahs. He goes to synagogue on the holidays and says certain prayers. Apparently, this is his way of dealing with the experiences of the Holocaust and the death of his parents."

When the men sat back down at the table, we—the women—got up and cleared the dishes and the food. Naomi washed the big dishes and put the rest into the dishwasher. Rivka and I brought her the empty dishes. Once the table was clean, we three stood in the kitchen. Rivka handed me a towel and I dried the washed dishes while she arranged them in the cupboards.

This situation, seemingly so routine, brought tears to my eyes. There was never this kind of togetherness at my house. My mother was responsible for the kitchen and no one was a part of what she did there. Not because she forbade it—ever since I could remember, the kitchen had been her kingdom, and I believed she wanted it like that. I never offered my help and neither did my father. I don't remember ever doing things together; we definitely never had casual and relaxed conversation. Each of us had his own place and his own role and nobody interfered with anyone. *Now I'm standing in a strange kitchen, with a family I only met several hours ago, and feeling so comfortable and so at home.*

Rivka could feel me becoming melancholy and caressed my face with her hand. I felt like an open book to her. Every once in a while, during the meal, she looked over at me. An understanding look. A mother's look.

After we finished, we joined the men, who were already sitting in the living room. Rivka sat down next to me on the sofa and said, "Michael tells me that you have a question regarding a specific card."

Her question brought me back to reality, to the reason I was in their home.

"Yes," I answered. "Do you remember anything about it?"

"Perhaps," was her evasive answer. "Tell me the whole story."

I told her about the letter, about the check that arrived and about the name on it. I told her that it must have been a previous tenant living in our house and that I had run into her name on several occasions. I also told her about my friends' and my decision to find her.

"I see," said Rivka.

I waited for her to continue, but she just said, "We'll talk about it tomorrow."

I wanted to tell her that I was leaving tomorrow, but decided to keep quiet.

The evening passed pleasantly. It was the beginning of September. The days were fairly warm, but the nights were already cool. A slight breeze was blowing that swayed the leaves and branches. The atmosphere in the room was relaxed and the conversation among the men focused on the Olympics. Rivka and Naomi talked about personal things and I let myself sink into the comfortable sofa, listening to the voices around me and absorbing the serenity and the security that each one of them felt in his home surrounded by his family.

Naomi's voice said, "OK, we're going to bed. Tomorrow we're getting up early. We made plans with friends to go on a short trip."

Jerry got up from his seat, and Mickey followed suit. The men shook hands and the women gave hugs and received hugs, including me in the exchange.

"I really am happy to have met you," Naomi said to me, and I believed her.

"She'll be back," Rivka said suddenly. I looked at her and felt flustered.

"Great," said Naomi.

After they went upstairs, the sounds of the house had quieted. Rivka and Shlomo went up to their room a few minutes later, and Mickey and I remained alone. Mickey sat down next to me on the sofa with a smile on his face.

"Why are you smiling?" I asked.

"Just because," he answered.

"No, really, why?" I insisted.

"Because I'm just happy that you're here," he answered. I felt myself blushing. "How did you enjoy the evening?" he asked.

"It was fine." Mickey wasn't satisfied with the answer. He kept his eyes on my face, waiting. "Actually, I felt very comfortable. You have a wonderful family."

"And..."

"And it's strange, because I've never been a guest at a home where I don't know the people. I thought it would be uncomfortable, but your family—especially your mother—made me feel as if I belong here, even though she only met me today."

"What do you mean, you've never been a guest?"

I thought for a minute before answering. *I don't know how to present my family to him. Lately, a lot of questions about them have come up. The only life I knew is suddenly being shown in a different light.*

"It's hard for me to answer that question. It isn't that simple."

Mickey waited for me to continue.

"Life at my house was totally different than the life you know. Up until recently, I thought my life was normal, but since my parents died, I've begun to understand that it wasn't."

"In what way?"

"I didn't have the kind of relationship with my parents that you have with yours. I had a very flimsy connection to my mother. But I had an especially strong relationship with my father. I idolized him. He was everything to me. Everything he did was right and just in my eyes. And my mother, my mother didn't even count."

Mickey moved closer to me, took my hand in his, and rested our joined hands on his thigh.

"Go on," he said.

"My father's life was very organized. Every day he would get up for work, come home in the afternoon, sit down at the table, and wait for mother to serve him his food. I don't remember him ever showing any affection for her. Once a week he would meet with friends. He never missed these meetings. He would come back from them full of energy. Every time he came home, he had something bad to say about my mother. Sometimes he would send me to my room, and then I would hear his severe voice coming from there. Many times I heard him complain about something related to her: the food, how she looked, that she embarrassed him. Not once did she ever react, except for one time when he threatened to take me and leave the house. Then she yelled 'Never!' We were both surprised by her reaction. That time, he stayed quiet. He sat down in his chair and pretended to read.

"You know, lately I've been remembering all kinds of things that went on in my house—incidents I thought I had forgotten. They are coming up and making me angry at myself."

"Angry at yourself? Why?"

"Because I acted exactly like my father and rejected her. I didn't allow her to be a mother. Today I regret it. I needed her—I needed a mother."

"So why didn't you say anything when you were older?"

"I don't know. I think my father wouldn't have liked it."

"I don't understand."

"I think I knew deep inside that this was the way he wanted things to be. If I had tried to get closer to her, I'm sure he would have prevented it somehow."

"Why wouldn't he want you to be close?"

"I don't know, but that's how I felt, and it was important for me to please him."

"You think that if you had acted differently, he would've been angry with you?"

"Maybe," I said, thinking to myself. Then the words shot out of my mouth like a geyser. I said with confidence, "I would have lost him, and he never would have said a word to me. I know that from his point of view, it was her or him. There wasn't room for a relationship with both of them."

"That's too bad," I heard him say.

I realized I was crying only when Mickey wiped away the tears streaming down my face.

"Lately I've been wasting a lot of tears." I said with an apologetic smile.

"Come here." Mickey brought me closer to him, leaned my head on his shoulder, and stroked my hair. We sat for many long minutes quietly. I didn't feel embarrassed or that I needed to run away. I felt that, at that moment, I was in the best possible place for me.

Then I asked, "And you?"

"I what?" he asked and moved away from me a bit.

"How come you still live here, with your parents?"

He moved further away from me and said, "It's complicated. I can't leave them alone."

"Because of him—to protect him?"

"Every so often I decide I'm going to leave, but then something happens and I stay. And now enough with the questions, let's go to sleep."

A little while after, we went upstairs, each to our own rooms. I remembered how he smiled when he invited me to sleep in the room for nice gentiles who aren't potential brides.

I woke up late the next day, shocked to see that it was after ten o'clock. I quickly packed up what little stuff I had, straightened the bed linens, and went downstairs to see the family that was already sitting around the dining table.

"Come, join us," Rivka said. She got up from her chair and went into the kitchen. After a minute, she came back and served me a cup of hot chocolate.

Shlomo was engrossed in the newspaper, lifted his head to me, wished me a good morning and dropped his eyes back down. Mickey looked at me with big eyes and gave me a warm smile. "Did you sleep well?" he asked.

"Very well," I answered.

"Would you like to go for a walk later?"

"I think I'll go home."

"Absolutely not!" said Rivka emphatically. "You're staying for lunch."

I didn't know what to say. I noticed that food was the main theme in the lives of this family.

Less than an hour later we were outside. I looked at Mickey's profile while he drove. He had the nose of a Greek god—long and straight. His wavy hair came over his ears a bit and covered the back of his neck. One hand held the steering wheel while the other rested on the open window. Every once in a while, we spoke, but most of the time we were quiet, enjoying the closeness that had developed between us.

It was the weekend. Traffic was light, and the car glided down the road like a boat on still waters. Soft music filled the interior of the car.

"Let's stop here," he said suddenly.

I lifted my head and saw that we had parked across from a lake with smooth waters and banks lush with low-growing vegetation. I got out of the car and took a deep breath of the crisp fresh air. The sun was reflected in the lake's surface, and its rays shimmered like an endless dance. Mickey took my hand and said, "Let's go for a walk."

We walked for several minutes in silence and then he said, "I'm really glad you stayed."

"Me too."

"Why don't you stay tomorrow too?"

"No," I answered, too quickly.

Mickey wanted to ask something but didn't.

"I need to get back," I explained.

"I understand."

I didn't have anything special to do at home, but I felt that it wasn't appropriate to spend another night with them. Even though their hospitality was warm, they were still strangers to me. The only thing that connected us was the yellow card, about which I hadn't yet discovered a thing.

I said, "Mickey, I want to talk to your mother about the card."

"Of course," he answered. "Show it to her when we get home and see if she remembers anything about it."

"Thanks."

"But until then, let's enjoy this beautiful Saturday."

We walked alongside the lake and then turned slightly inland. We walked along a path that led into the woods. The sagging tips of the tree branches provided shade and the sun flickered among them. The air was cooler and less humid. There were fragments of boulders scattered on the forest floor, and we were forced to skip around them every now and then. Once, I tripped on a stone and almost fell. Mickey caught me at the last minute and prevented me from falling.

I asked him how his parents took the closing of the company.

"The truth is, my father lost the motivation to hang on to the company," he answered. "It was like the motor that was driving him at work became worn down. He would barely show up at the store during the last few years; he preferred to stay home."

"So why don't you keep the business going? Why close it down?"

His expression became serious. He answered, "Because this was an opportunity for me to leave something I didn't really want to do."

"I don't understand," I said, looking at him.

Mickey let out a sigh. I could see that he was debating whether to say something. In the end, he just said, "He wanted me in the business with him, and I couldn't refuse him. The truth is, I admire him." He looked ahead at the forest. "To survive the hell he went through as a young man and then raise a family and establish a company—well, he needed a lot of courage to do all that."

"So, what will you do now?" I continued to show interest.

"I'm still dealing with the company's paperwork and final accounts, so I don't really have time to look for something else."

"I understand that your sisters didn't want to take part in the company," I said.

"No, they preferred to go in other directions."

"And how did your parents take that?"

"It's complicated," he said vaguely.

"I'm sorry. I didn't mean to pry." I pulled back.

"It's OK," he reassured me.

When we got back to the house, the table was already set. Mickey's father washed his hands and sat in his place at the head of the table. Rivka darted between the kitchen and the dining room. The meal passed by pleasantly. Toward the end, Mickey turned to his mother and told her that I wanted to talk to her about the card we found at the office.

"Let's clear the table. Then we'll talk about it."

We finished eating and Mickey got up and went into the kitchen. Rivka and I brought him the dishes and he put them into the dishwasher. Rivka cleaned the table with a cloth and once it was sparkling she covered it with a crimson-colored tablecloth. On one side of the table she placed a large bowl of fruit and on the other, a pair of silver candlesticks stood guard. Shlomo claimed to be tired and went upstairs to his room. We went into the living room and sat down. Mickey made space for me beside his mother and suggested I show her the card. I took the card out of my purse and presented it to her. I pointed out the place where the original name had been erased and the new name written over it. Rivka took the card, looked at it for a long time, and said, "I remember the woman."

My heart began to pound. Heat spread throughout my body, and I could feel my hands shaking. I put them on my knees, hoping that Mickey and Rivka didn't notice my nervousness. Rivka turned the card over again and said again, "Yes, I definitely remember her."

I held my breath and waited for her to continue.

"She bought a bed, like it says here. It was very important to her that the bed be pretty and suitable for a girl—that's what she said to me. She asked for the most beautiful bed we had. She was an attractive woman. Very thin, I remember, and impressive. I asked for identification in order to fill out the order form. I copied the name as it was written on her ID and filled out the rest of the necessary details. When I gave her the card to sign, she read what I had written and she used a pen to scratch out the name written on her ID and replaced it with the name written here, Sonia Schwartz."

Rivka was quiet for a moment and continued to look at the card.

"But didn't you ask her why she changed the name?" I asked.

"Actually, yes, I did ask her," answered Rivka, still thoughtful.

"And?"

"She said that this was her name."

"I don't understand," I said.

"She said that she had two names, but her real name was this one. And then she pointed to the name I told you, Sonia—Sonia Schwartz."

"But what kind of name is that?" I asked.

"It's a Jewish name!" they both answered.

I could feel the blood surging through my veins. It felt like it was about to flow right out of my body. The dizziness I had felt before, by the table, came back. Images and parts of images were swirling around me. I put my hands down at my side and used them like crutches. I had to ask one final question, but my throat was hoarse and not a word came out of my mouth. I cleared my throat and let my body sink into the sofa, and I was finally able to ask my last question.

"What was the name she erased?"

"Maria Brown," said Rivka. "Yes, I definitely remember the name. Maria Brown."

My body felt crushed by the knowledge and couldn't hold me up any longer. I fell and Rivka caught me in her arms. I don't remember anything else. When I woke up, I found myself lying on the sofa. My head rested in Mickey's lap and Rivka held a wet cloth to my forehead.

"Poor thing," I heard Rivka mutter.

"You knew," I whispered. She nodded.

"The food?" I asked.

She answered, "Yes, typical Jewish food."

"The candlesticks—lighting the candles," I said to myself. Now I understood. I once saw her lighting the candles and praying. My father wasn't home that evening. I came out of my room for a minute and saw her with a handkerchief on her head and her palms covering her eyes. She didn't see me. I looked at her with wonder, as if she was a figure in a theatrical play. Her prayer was long. She seemed to be crying—there were faint sounds coming from her covered mouth. When her hands dropped from her face, I slipped back into my room without her noticing. When my father came home, the candles were already out and the candlesticks were completely devoid of any remaining wax.

Suddenly the partial images became a whole picture. The ends of the rope were joined together and became one.

16

It felt like time wasn't passing whatsoever during the drive home. It was a miracle that nothing happened to me. Disjointed thoughts were rattling around in my head. When Roy told me that my mother was Sonia Schwartz, I hadn't believed him at all—he had to be wrong. But Rivka's words didn't leave room for doubt. My actions became automatic and it was as if the car drove itself. Arriving home late in the evening, I didn't notice the flashing light on the answering machine. I just wanted to get into bed and disappear. I threw my clothes every which way and got into bed, completely exhausted. I fell asleep before my head hit the pillow and slept until Sunday afternoon, when I got up to put some food in my mouth and went right back to sleep.

They say that morning brings with it new hope. I landed back in reality on Monday morning. As soon as went into the office, I ran into Donna. She took my arm and led me into her office.

"Are you out of your mind?" she yelled as she closed the door to her office. "I've been calling you for two days at all hours and you didn't answer. I went to your house. It was dark, locked up tight, with no sign of you. Where were you? Why didn't you call?"

"Stop it, Donna. I have a headache. Don't yell," I pleaded.

"You have a headache? My whole body hurts from worry. Did you know that I almost called the police to break down the door? Did you know that if Roy hadn't said to wait until the beginning of the week, I would have reported you missing? Do you have any idea how worried Roy and I were?"

"I'm sorry," I apologized.

"You're sorry—that's it?" Donna turned around to face her desk. It looked like her shoulders were shaking. Maybe she was crying.

"I'm really sorry. I didn't think you would worry so much."

"You didn't think we would worry so much." She repeated my words with her back still to me. "Get out of my office. Go to work."

"What?"

"Get to work—go to your desk."

I got up and left her office. When I turned around she was still standing with her back to me.

She didn't speak to me the entire day. She passed by me and completely ignored me. I wanted to go to her, to try and explain, but I didn't have the energy to raise the subject—if I talked about it with her, it would be impossible to continue ignoring it. At the end of the day, on the way out, I passed by her office, but it was empty.

When I got home, the refrigerator was empty of fresh food, and some dishes were growing mold. The milk had expired—I couldn't even make myself a cup of coffee. I went out and crossed the street. Sarah's door opened as soon as I knocked, like she knew I was coming.

"Come in," she said and hugged me to her. "Are you hungry?" she asked.

"Yes," I admitted.

"Come into the kitchen."

I sat at the table and watched her move between the fridge and the stove, to the counter and back to the fridge and once again to the stove. In a matter of minutes there was a dish sitting before me with hot, appetizing food.

I devoured the food like I was breaking a long fast. She sat in front of me with a look of satisfaction. When I finished, she collected the dishes, put them in the sink, and invited me into the living room.

I knew I couldn't hide what I had discovered from her. Her sharp eyes penetrated my mask and I had no choice but to confess. It had happened before when I tried to hide things from her—with her direct questions and penetrating stare, she knew how to get the truth out of me.

"I haven't seen you lately."

"Yes. Lots of things have happened, and I've been busy," I answered.

She waited for me to continue, knowing that I couldn't bear any long silences. When I could tell she wasn't going to talk, I broke the silence myself.

"I'm Jewish!" I declared. I wanted to shock her, but she remained silent.

I told her about my journey to Chicago, about Mickey and his family, and about everything I found out through them. She was silent the entire time, her eyes never leaving me, and she listened to everything I said until the very end. Suddenly she got up and disappeared into the kitchen. When she came back, she put a dish with brown cookies and two cups of tea on the table, sat down in her chair, and asked, "How do you feel today?"

I thought for a few seconds and then answered, "I don't know. On the one hand, nothing has changed, but on the other, everything has changed. I feel strange. I don't know how to define what I am, how I feel, or even what to think... Did you know about this?"

She put down her cup of tea, folded her hands in her lap, and said, "Your mother was a very private person. There were a lot of things that nobody knew about her—things that she kept to herself."

"But you knew? She told you? After all, you were friends."

"What does it matter, Eva? What's important is that you need to know what to do after you have the knowledge. Now I have to go out. Come visit me again."

She got up from her chair and put her hand on my shoulder with a slight push. I had no choice but to walk toward the door, leaving behind my full cup of hot tea. The door closed behind me, gently but with resolve. I crossed the street to my house. It felt like I had been thrown out.

When I got home, the red light was flashing on my answering machine; the machine's metallic voice announced that there were twenty-two messages waiting. Most of them were from Donna, some from Roy, one from Mickey asking if I got home all right, and one from the priest asking me to contact him. It was already after eight o'clock in the evening. I erased all the messages and decided to deal with them tomorrow. I didn't feel like talking to Donna or Roy; I still didn't want to admit to Roy that he had been right.

When I got to the office the next day, I called the church, but there was no answer. I tried again after an hour and heard the soft voice of the priest on the other end of the phone.

"Good morning, Father. This is Eva Brown. You left me a message—"

"Yes, yes," he interrupted me. "How are you?"

"I'm just fine," I answered.

"Good," he answered and then there was silence.

"Father Peter?" I asked with trepidation.

"Yes, my child," he answered.

"What did you want?"

"I am so confused. Edna, my secretary, has been ill for several days, and I can't seem to manage things here. Suddenly I realize how helpless I am without others by my side."

I nodded in agreement.

"What can I do for you, child?"

I felt like I was about to lose my patience. I said, "Father, you called me and left me a message telling me to get in touch with you, so here I am calling to ask what you wanted... Maybe it has to do with the woman we asked you about?"

"Ahh... Yes, yes... Right, someone was here asking about your father."

"About my father?"

"Yes, I told him he had passed away, and then he left very quickly."

"Did you know him? Did he leave an address? Telephone number?"

"No, no, as I said, he ran out of here without letting me talk to him at all."

"I don't understand, Father," I said. Then, resolved in my decision, I asked, "Can I come over now to speak with you?"

"Yes... Yes, of course. I'll tell Edna to write...oh, but Edna is ill and won't be here today."

"I'll be there in fifteen minutes." I put down the phone, grabbed my purse and left the office. I thought I saw Donna lift her head from her desk, but I just continued on my way.

Driving to the outskirts of town usually took more than twenty minutes, but this time I arrived at the church in fifteen. I found Father Peter leaning over his desk, his glasses perched at the end of his nose. He didn't hear me come in because he was immersed in a large book whose pages had yellowed due to its advanced age. I cleared my throat, but his head remained in the same position. I moved the chair in front of him. It screeched. Only then did he raise his head, and I could see that his eyes were looking in my direction, but he was somewhere else entirely.

I said, "Father, I'm Eva, Eva Brown. I spoke to you on the phone."

Like a blurry picture gradually coming into focus, his hollow eyes made their way from where they had been to the room crowded with books where we were now.

"Sit, sit, my child. I'm sorry. You must think I'm a bothersome old man. But when Edna is away, it is as if both my hands have been cut off. I can't find anything and I'm confused and forgetful. But I do remember why you came."

I gave him a warm smile. He was a good man. The community was his family. He had never married and didn't have any children.

"A few days ago—I think it was on Friday—a pleasant man came to see me. I don't remember his name, but he asked me about John Jos...

"Brown," I corrected him.

"Absolutely right, Brown. I think he said he was family and that he was checking to see whether John lived in our town. The name sounded familiar, but I couldn't remember why. After all, your father never came to church—perhaps I never saw him. I asked Edna, and she, of course, knew exactly who I was talking about. You see, Edna knows everyone in this city; even at her age, her memory is better than mine, and when she's gone..."

I cleared my throat.

He stopped for a moment, and then continued, "I went back to the man, who was sitting outside the church, and told him that, sadly, the person he was looking for passed away. I didn't have a chance to say one more word. The man turned around and bolted from the place. I tried to follow him, but, you see, my legs are not as young as they used to be. He disappeared as if the earth swallowed him up without leaving a trace. The next day, Edna cleaned my desk, as she does every weekend. She found the note with your name and telephone number written on it from when you were here asking me about that woman."

I let out a heavy sigh.

"I see you're very disappointed."

"Yes," I said.

"Well, then, if he comes again, I'll send him directly to you."

"Thank you, Father. Thank you."

I left there disappointed and frustrated—it seemed like I had reached a dead end, like I was trapped in a room with a locked door that was preventing me from going out and discovering the world beyond. My uneasy new knowledge that I was Jewish didn't give me any rest. *What should I do with this news—change my way of life? Think differently? Act differently? Should I keep it bottled up and ignore it?*

I didn't know anything about Jews or Judaism. Of course, I knew about the Holocaust. I don't remember if there were any Jewish kids in my class. Actually, the subject was never raised except for one time that I remember clearly. A group of young neo-Nazis marched down the streets of Chicago. They were waving the swastika flag, marching with their hands raised in the Nazi salute, chanting Hitler's name. Some of them were carrying signs that read, "Hitler should have finished the job."

I was fourteen at the time. The television nightly news was broadcasting the event. The parade quickly deteriorated into a brawl between the demonstrators and a group of Jews and others that protested the anti-Semitic parade. The police tried to separate the groups; during the altercation, a police officer was killed and a number of protestors injured.

I wouldn't have remembered the incident if it wasn't for the portrait engraved in my memory. My father was sitting in his chair, smiling, while my mother was leaning tiredly against the kitchen doorpost with a sad expression, staring blankly at my father's face.

17

I got together with Roy a week later. Since I had returned from Chicago, we hadn't seen or spoken with each other. I finally called him. The conversation was brief. He asked where I had been and when I told him I had spent the weekend at Mickey's, he cut the conversation short.

He came over the next day without advance warning. I had come home from work and, after a short rest, was getting ready to get into the shower when I heard the knock on the door. He did not look good at all. Tired and disheveled. It looked like he hadn't shaved in days—his prickly stubble had grown, giving his face a different look.

I made coffee for the two of us and we sat down in the kitchen.

"Everything OK?" I asked with genuine concern.

He nodded and sipped the coffee. His head remained down, and he was staring into the brown liquid in the cup.

"Roy, you're worrying me. Did something happen?"

"Nothing happened. How did you like Chicago, at Mickey's?"

"It was good; they were really nice to me."

"They?"

"Rivka and Shlomo and his sister."

"Rivka and Shlomo..." he repeated after me, drawing out each word.

"Yes, his parents. We had dinner together, and his sister and husband were also there. The truth is, I wanted to come home a day earlier, but they convinced me to stay."

"I see."

"Roy, look at me,]. Is there something you want to tell me?"

He lifted his head and looked at me for several long minutes, but didn't say a thing.

I raised my voice. "Roy, why are you so distant?"

"You don't understand anything, do you?"

"I don't understand why you're talking to me like that and why you look like you do."

He looked at me again, then suddenly got up and said that he had to leave. He moved his cup to the center of the table, dragged the chair under the table, turned around, and began to walk toward the door. I went after him and stood with my back to the front door, preventing him from opening it.

"I want you to tell me what happened."

"Eva, I have to go."

"Roy, you are not leaving until I know what's going on."

He moved closer to me, his face inches from my own. His eyes were tired and he suddenly looked much older. I felt uncomfortable and tried to break away from his gaze, but his hands caught my arms and didn't let me move. He didn't say a word the entire time; he continued to look at me as if he wanted to infer something from my eyes. His grasp tightened and began to hurt me. I must have wrinkled my face in pain, because he let go of my arms all at once, moved me aside, opened the door, and was swallowed by the darkness outside. I knew that something had changed between us.

In the following days, I tried to comprehend what had happened, but I gave up in the end and decided to put my thoughts aside for the time being.

The knowledge of my being Jewish began to slowly get buried under layers of denial and repression. I convinced myself that everyone was wrong and they were reaching illogical conclusions. I wanted to go back to the life I knew: dull, soporific and safe.

Two weeks after my meeting with Roy, Mickey called. He had left me two messages on my answering machine in the last month, but I hadn't called him back. I was afraid that contact with him would awaken the need to deal with what Rivka told me about my mother. It's possible that his being Jewish deterred me. I didn't want any connection to that religion. When I heard the phone ring, I picked up the receiver and immediately recognized his voice.

"Eva, how are you?" he asked. He didn't bring up the messages on the answering machine.

"I'm fine, and you?" I answered calmly.

"Just fine. I finished the work at the office and yesterday the company officially closed."

"And how do you feel?" I probed.

"Bittersweet relief." He chuckled.

"I understand. And how are Rivka and Shlomo?"

"They're fine. My father reads a lot."

"And your mother?"

"She's always busy. She cooks a lot. Lately she's also been volunteering at the Jewish Center in our neighborhood. Aside from that, she also tutors, sometimes cooks for special events, does paperwork…"

"Great."

They both were silent.

"Eva, I was thinking of coming to visit you," he said finally. When I didn't respond, he said, "How about next week?"

"The weekend is good for me."

"So, Friday?"

I gave him directions to my house and we hung up.

From that conversation until he arrived almost a week later, I walked around in a daze. There were times when I picked up the telephone to cancel his visit, but then hung up at the last minute. I didn't know how to entertain anyone. We never had guests stay for very long at our house. *Does he intend to stay? Should I invite him to spend the night or let him go back to Chicago? The house is embarrassing—old on the outside and on the inside. Maybe when he sees it he will want to run away. What am I supposed to do with him for that many hours? Will I have to cook? My cooking repertoire is extremely limited.* I was totally confused.

On Thursday I decided that I had to do something. I crossed the street and knocked on Sarah's door. She welcomed me with a big smile. As soon as I set foot in her home, comforting thoughts took over. This was the impact she had on me. I sat on the sofa and was careful not to wrinkle the embroidered napkin that decorated the armrest. Sarah went straight to the kitchen.

"Tea?" I wasn't sure if it was a question or a decision.

"Yes," I answered.

She returned in one minute with a small painted tray carrying two cups of tea and a plate of warm cookies. *Every time I come over, there are always warm cookies, like she knows I'm coming.* Her gaze caressed me, and my body relaxed as though it had slipped in a hot bath with bubbles. My muscles relaxed, and I sank deep into the dent my body made in the sofa.

"I need your help," I announced as soon as I finished my first sesame cookie. Sarah raised her eyebrows in surprise.

"I need to cook tomorrow, and I don't know what to make or how."

The one thing I had learned about Sarah over time was that she didn't ask too many questions. I was sure she was surprised by my showing up and my announcement, but she suppressed her curiosity and didn't ask a thing.

"For how many?" she asked.

"Two," I answered, feeling my cheeks redden.

"Have you been to the market yet?" she asked.

I shook my head.

"What do you want to make?"

"Something tasty," I said with a smile.

"OK, come with me into the kitchen."

I followed her. She pulled out a cookbook covered in stains, witnesses to the many times she had used it.

"I suggest a meal that is simple and nutritious," she said.

"No meal will be simple for me," I said.

She didn't reply. She continued to flip through the pages of the book until she stopped and said, "Oh, here we go: broccoli and cauliflower pie and mushroom quiche. I recommend a fresh green salad on the side and coleslaw or another salad that you like."

"That sounds OK," I mumbled, thinking to myself that the foods she mentioned sounded difficult and complicated for me to prepare.

"Here, take a piece of paper and write this down," she commanded. She read me the list of ingredients I needed to buy and added also bread and butter. But then she changed her mind and said, "Actually, I suggest one quiche and honey-baked ham. That's very easy to make, but it makes an impression of being complicated, and it's delicious."

When she finished dictating the long list, she said I should go grocery shopping today in order to have enough time tomorrow to prepare the meal. "Are you free tomorrow morning?" she asked.

"Yes," I answered. "I took the day off."

"Great. Then I'll come over around nine o'clock and we'll cook together."

Like a block of ice that melted the second it touched heat, the tension built up inside me melted. Suddenly I was encouraged. I told myself that the meal would be good and therefore the time with him would be pleasant.

Sarah arrived at exactly nine o'clock a.m. She moved around the kitchen as if it were her own. She knew where everything was, opening cupboards, taking out containers, spreading out different utensils on the counter, and giving me orders as if it were her kitchen. If she had prepared the meal on her own, we would have been finished within the hour, but she wanted me to learn, so she allowed me to try my hand at cooking. When I made a mistake, she pointed it out. When I didn't stir enough, she told me to continue. The meal was ready by the afternoon. She left me with instructions on how to warm up the meat before serving the meal and even helped me set the table. The table was tastefully arranged, and flowers in the vase I placed at the center gave it a relaxed atmosphere. Now all that was left was to wait.

At five o'clock, I went upstairs to my bedroom to get dressed. On my way back from the supermarket, I stopped at Laurie's—a tiny but well-known clothes shop in town—and bought a dark green skirt and a white knitted blouse that had a small green bow sewn into its right side. Looking back at me from the mirror at the store was a different Eva. I had never worn a skirt so short. I felt naked, but Laurie—the boutique owner—insisted on my wearing it to show off my beautiful legs. I hoped I wouldn't change my mind that evening and wear some of my old clothes.

Mickey arrived at six o'clock.

He looked good. He was wearing an elegant white shirt and gray trousers; his wavy hair rested on his shoulders and his white teeth were exposed when he smiled. He kissed me on each cheek, held out a box, and said, "My mother sent you this Rose Cake—that's what she calls it. She said she's sure you'll like it. She sends you warm greetings and asked me to tell you that she's waiting for you to come again."

I smiled and thanked him.

"You look wonderful," he said. I saw his eyes scan me up and down. I had put my hair back with two combs so that my face was completely uncovered. It was obvious he saw my flushed cheeks.

"Would you like something to drink?" I asked.

"What do you have?" he asked.

"White wine, dry red wine...and..."

"Red wine would be fine."

I poured each of us a glass of wine and we sat down in the living room. After a few sips, I began to feel the tension slip away. I felt relaxed.

Mickey asked me about the days following my discovery that my mother was Jewish. After a moment's pondering, I said, "At first it was very confusing. I didn't know if I needed to change anything in my life. These were not simple days. But later on, I decided to continue with the life that was familiar to me. Religion is not significant to me. I am who I am regardless of my religion... So right now, nothing has changed and I'm continuing with my life more or less the way it was before."

"You're right," he said after a brief silence. "You are who you are, regardless of the connection to your religion." Then he added, a bit softer, "And I really like who you are."

His words embarrassed me, so I immediately suggested we sit down at the table. The meat and quiche were already in the oven; the potatoes (a bit burnt) had come out of the oven earlier. I took the salads out of the refrigerator and placed them on the table. The meat and gravy looked appetizing. My heart was full of pride at seeing the festive table. The shades of the tablecloth and the dishes made it look meticulous but also soft and romantic. I invited Mickey to sit down, but he gestured for me to wait a moment and took a yarmulke out of his pocket. He placed it on his head, took the glass of wine, and said the familiar blessing from the family dinner at his home. When he finished, he signaled me to take a sip of wine and sat down.

The meal went by pleasantly. The conversation was smooth. He told me a bit about the company when it was still active. Every once in a while, he mentioned his grandmother and grandfather and also talked about his sisters. I could see a sparkle in his eyes when he spoke about them He loved them very much, and even though he didn't see them very often, they had a very close and warm relationship.

"But enough of me going on about my family," he said. "Tell me more about yourself. How do you spend your days? Tell me about your job, your ambitions... I want to get to know you better."

While he was speaking, I noticed he hadn't tasted the meat. "Don't you like the meat?" I asked.

"I'm sorry, I don't eat pig meat," he said awkwardly.

"Oh, I'm sorry. I didn't know." I was also embarrassed.

"There are a lot of Jews that do eat this kind of meat, but even though we're not really religious, there are some mitzvahs that we keep. Don't apologize. The meal was wonderful. I'm full."

We got up from the table and cleared the dishes together. I washed and he dried. Every once in a while, his arm touched my hand. Sometimes I felt his eyes checking me out, but I wouldn't dare look at him. When we finished, we went into the living room, and I placed a bowl of fruit on the table. I sat a small distance from him and turned my face to him.

"Would you like to continue your story about your father?" I asked.

"Yes, but not right now. I want to hear about you," he said. His hand reached up to brush away an imaginary hair from my cheek. I could feel the heat spread throughout my body. The dim light, the quiet all around us, our being alone—all these created an atmosphere of tension. It seemed like Mickey felt much more comfortable than I did on my sofa, in my house. I wanted to say something, but I couldn't think of anything.

He moved closer to me and pulled my chin toward him until our eyes met. His face drew closer to mine and his lips rested on mine in a soft kiss that for a moment connected his stable world to my unsteady and confused one.

The doorbell cut through the special moment. It was after ten o'clock and completely dark outside. I stayed seated, unsure if I had heard anything. Mickey's eyes asked a silent question and my raised eyebrows answered that I didn't know. Panic took hold of me. George's hand slithering on my legs suddenly appeared before me, and I was afraid that now he was waiting at my door. Mickey noticed the panic on my face.

"I'll open it," he said. He got up from the sofa.

I heard him open the door and then his voice, a bit high, exchanging words with someone. I got up from the sofa and went to the door. Roy's eyes met mine. I felt the blood rushing through my veins. Roy looked at me and then looked inside the house. In the dim light of the porch I could see, like in a movie, the wheels turning in his mind. Creating a story. His eyes roamed from my face to Mickey's.

"I'm interrupting you," he said finally. Mickey didn't say anything and turned to look at me. An unexplainable feeling of guilt and shame prevented me from speaking. Seconds passed and the silence became deafening. Mickey eventually asked Roy if he would like to come in.

"No, I'll leave you two alone," he said. It seemed like he spat the word "alone" like he couldn't wait to get rid of it.

Mickey stayed overnight. We never spoke about it and he didn't ask. We continued the evening and eventually made arrangements for sleep. My mood was ruined. The feelings of tension and expectation were replaced by the desire for the weekend to be over. Lying awake in my bed, I couldn't fall asleep. I was angry at Roy for showing up at my door without warning, putting me in such an uncomfortable situation, and I was angry at Mickey for acting like the master of the house.

Mickey left the next day, after we had breakfast together. He noticed the change in my mood and avoided asking me questions. He only said, "I can tell you'd rather be alone, so I'll go."

"I'm sorry," I said.

"Don't be."

"I'll call you," I said before the door closed after him.

"I'll be waiting," I heard him say.

I spent the next few hours doing nothing. The morning light turned into the yellow of afternoon and then the gray of evening. A blanket of shadows played on the living room walls, interspersed with streaks of sunlight that occasionally made their way through the branches of the tree swaying in the garden. I was sitting in the living room, my body on the sofa and my legs on the coffee table; the television was on, but there were no programs interesting enough to watch, so the sound was muted. The intermittent sunspots disappeared and the walls of the living room grew dark. I went into the kitchen, opened and closed the cupboards, and washed the sole glass sitting in the sink. I opened the fridge, looking for something tasty to eat, but just closed the door. Instead, I grabbed my car keys and the blue sweater hanging next to the front door and went out.

The road to Roy's house passed through one of the richest neighborhoods in town. As I was driving, I pictured Roy refusing to open the door, or opening the door but refusing to speak to me, or simply telling me that it was over and that he didn't want anything to do with me ever again. I didn't notice that I had left the main road and entered a side street by accident.

Lights were twinkling in the windows of most of the houses. It was prime time for television viewing—after dinner, just before the end of the day. Somebody had stopped his car by the sidewalk and was walking inside a house. A sloppily dressed woman with a handkerchief on her head was throwing a bag of garbage into the garbage can. A cat crossed the street with hesitant steps, shooting petrified looks to each side.

I slowed the car down as it approached the end of the street, where I stopped at the stop sign and looked both ways to make sure no cars were coming. That's when I saw him. George's heavy, thick body was slightly bent over trying to open his car door. The streetlight above him left no doubt in my mind. His sharp and confident movements when he rested his heavy body behind the steering wheel caused me to tremble. My hands broke out in a sweat and my breath caught. He couldn't see me, but I saw him clearly. He started the car and made a U-turn, his tires burning the asphalt as he passed by me quickly and turned left without stopping at the stop sign.

I turned the car around—my hands and feet moving automatically—and followed the black car. There were no thoughts or decisions in my head. I was on autopilot. My foot pressed gently on the gas pedal and kept a steady distance from the car ahead of me. Traffic was light. A car passed me every so often. A motorcycle rumbled behind me and then passed on the left. My gaze was forward and my eyes concentrated on the car ahead. Suddenly he turned right, and at the last minute I turned as well. The streets became darker and the cars almost nonexistent.

The car ahead slowed down and turned into an alley in a completely unfamiliar part of town. I had no idea where I was. Slowing down and stopping my car at the entrance to the alley, I heard a door slam shut and then silence. Waiting in the car, I slowly realized what I had done and was overcome by weakness, my body paralyzed. The desire to run away from this place and curiosity fought each other inside me. A car passed by me slowly and its driver turned his head toward me. I didn't know if he saw me or not. He continued on and turned into the same place the car before him turned.

I scooched down in the seat. Every once in a while, a car would pass me, turn right like the one before it, and a few seconds later a door would slam, then it would once again get quiet. I sat in my car for almost twenty minutes. During the last five minutes, no other cars passed by. I waited another few minutes and then got out of my car, walking with small and noiseless steps to the end of the alley. A cat was howling in the distance and a garbage lid crashed down. To the right, where the cars were turning, there was a line of neatly parked cars next to the wall of a building. There was no one outside.

I moved along the wall, looking back every now and then. The street was quiet and deserted. *Where had all the car owners disappeared to?* I reached the end of the row, where the first car was parked; slightly ahead of it there was a metal door with an open lock hanging on it. Suddenly I heard a deafening noise, but I saw nothing unusual. The street was still dark and silent. It was the pounding of my heart, trying its hardest to make itself heard! My body was divided into two parts. My head and upper body moved forward, but the lower half of my body stayed where it was. My body was fighting against itself. Curiosity fought against caution, the memory of his hand on my thigh fighting with a different memory, hazy, almost nonexistent. Then the autopilot conquered all the rest. My hand reached out and pushed the door open a little bit.

There was a thin scraping sound, and in one step, I pushed myself through the door, finding myself in a dark corridor with only one light faintly lighting a staircase. My heart practically jumped out of my skin. I tried to control my breathing but couldn't. I was someone else. Eva wasn't here at all. Eva was now in a house with four familiar walls. Somebody like her was standing at the bottom of a staircase taking a step onto the first stair. And then another.

Faint voices could be heard. I reached the top of the stairs. There were locked doors on either side. Only one door was slightly open with a bright light beaming into the darkness where I stood. Suddenly, without warning, the door opened wide. The suddenness of the light and the surprise hit me. I heard "*Sieg Heil.*" Strong, rough hands pushed me from behind into the room. Dozens of eyes stared at me. The hands behind my back continued to push me until they stopped. In front of me was a stage with a man standing on it. His hair was black as coal and he was wearing a brown army uniform. Behind him hung a giant flag with a large swastika in the middle.

I heard him say, "My dear friends, I'd like to introduce you to Hans' daughter."

I couldn't understand what the voice was saying.

"Come closer, child. It is our honor to have you here as our guest."

I felt like I had landed on another planet. Behind me was a group of three men; in front of me stood a man in an army uniform, and all of them were claiming that I was the daughter of Hans. *Speak*, I told myself. *Speak*. I tried to talk, but no sound came out of my mouth. My throat was hoarse. My heart slowed down a bit but still interfered with my thoughts.

"I'm not Hans' daughter," I was finally able to say.

"Excuse me, child, what did you say?" asked the voices.

"You are wrong. I'm not who you think I am." My voice began to be heard.

"Speak louder, child, so we can all hear," the voices said.

This time my voice was loud with anger. "I said that I'm not Hans' daughter. My father's name was not Hans."

Before I even finished the sentence, thunderous laughter broke out among those present. I lost my nerve. I wanted to run away from there. The atmosphere was intimidating. The laughter was hiding something. I felt like I was in danger and turned my body around toward the door. The hands that pushed me earlier came back to turn me back around toward the stage.

The man said, in a voice that was unnecessarily high, "My dear child, do you know where you are?" Without waiting for an answer, he roared, "You are at a meeting of the Brothers of our Holy Church. Up until his death, Hans was the head of the church in this county. He was a very important man who furthered our cause in the area and brought great honor to us."

"But my father's name wasn't Hans," I screamed.

"Dear child, each of us has two names. One is the name given to us by our parents and the other is one we choose for ourselves. Your father chose this name for himself."

"I don't understand," I mumbled.

The man on the stage smiled an all-knowing fatherly smile.

"You are welcome to join us whenever you wish. George can bring you with him."

Turning my head around, my gaze caught George's smiling face. I wanted to scream and tell them that they were making a huge mistake, that my father had no connection whatsoever to them, that I never wanted to see George ever again, but my mouth stayed shut. I turned back to the man on the stage. His face was serious now, lacking any hint of kindness. The room was silent and all eyes were on him. He began to speak, but it was as though my ears were stopped—I could only see his mouth moving and twisting. Every once in a while, he paused, his silence giving more weight to his words, and then continued, his cheeks moving up and down. Here and there I heard a few words: "Our eternal leader... Clean up the world..."

The crowd forgot about me; their eyes were focused on the speaker, and his words seemed to magnetize them. Not a sound could be heard in the room. The hands left me alone, and I walked slowly backward to the door and out until I was swallowed by the darkness in the corridor. I ran down the stairs. My feet took me outside of the building to my car. I started the car and drove out of the alley. After a few wrong turns, the area became familiar, and from there I knew the way.

It was after eleven o'clock at night. The house was dark and the shutters were closed. Only the lights in the garden shone on the manicured plants that decorated the front. I didn't think twice—I rang the doorbell. After I knocked on the door as well, it opened, and Roy's head peeked out of the narrow opening. When he saw me, the look of surprise on his face changed to worry. "What happened?" he asked and opened the door wide. His mother appeared behind him. When she saw it was me, she said with indifference tinged with restrained anger, "Oh, Eva, it's you."

"It's OK, Mother, go back to sleep," Roy reassured her and led me into his room, closing the door behind him. His bed was still warm and messy. I needed his warmth. My body was frozen, and not from the cold. I was shaking all over, and Roy wrapped me in his arms. His gesture released the lid on my tears, and they flowed in streams down my face and onto my clothes.

"I'm sorry," I muttered. Roy didn't respond and continued to hold me. When he saw my sobbing begin to subside, he asked, "What happened?"

"What day is today?" I asked.

"Saturday," he answered.

"Yes... This is the day he used to go out," I said out loud.

"I don't understand," said Roy.

"He used to go out every Saturday to meet with friends—that's what he used to say."

"Eva?"

"My father, he would be with the 'brothers' every Saturday."

"I don't understand what you're talking about."

"About my father."

"Yes, but what about him?"

"He was a Nazi. Did you know?" I threw at him.

No reaction came. My head was tucked into his chest, but it seemed that his muscles tensed up. I avoided his eyes. The shame was so great that I wanted to get out of his house without having to meet his gaze. Eventually I disengaged myself from his grasp and walked out of his room without lifting my head. He called my name, but he stayed sitting and didn't try to stop me.

At home, drowning myself in the darkness, I curled up like a fetus in my bed and stayed like that until the next evening. Perhaps there was a knock on the door, but my consciousness was so foggy that it could have been my imagination. I got up from bed that evening, still dressed in the clothes from the previous day, and washed my face and poured myself a glass of water. I had absolutely no appetite.

What to do with myself? Leaving the house was out of the question. I walked among the rooms before finally getting back into bed, where I spent a sleepless night, tossing and turning, but not finding peace. "Nazi, Nazi, Nazi," the word spun around in my head. *I'm the daughter of a Nazi.* The understanding began to seep in and wound me. It seemed that my body was bleeding, rivers of blood flowing out of me, emptying me. I wanted to become nothing, to be transparent, so that nobody could see me—not even myself. *It was my fault—my childish naïvety and blindness. How could I have not seen it?* I hated myself for loving him blindly, for idolizing him. *How did I miss the signs?*

The guilt was too much—I escaped into sleep. I didn't leave the house the next day either—didn't even call to notify work of my absence. Even the simplest of movements was becoming difficult. I stayed in bed on Monday, Tuesday, and Wednesday, not changing my clothes, not answering the telephone when it rang or the door when people knocked. I suspected Roy was looking for me, but I couldn't look him in the eye. My blanket hid me from the world, and sleep prevented me from dealing with the facts.

On Thursday morning, I heard Donna's voice calling me from the other side of the door, "Eva, I know you can hear me. Open the door."

I didn't answer.

"Eva, I'm warning you... Open the door right now."

I covered my face with the blanket and turned my head to the wall.

Several minutes went by and then I heard strong pounding. I jumped from bed in a panic. The door was hanging askew on only one hinge, and glass was strewn all over the floor. Roy stood at the entrance, and Donna stood behind him. She pushed him aside and stood in front of me.

"Oh, my God, look at you," she said in profound shock.

I turned my back to them and walked back to my bedroom.

"No, no, no. No way," she grabbed my arm firmly and led me straight into the bathroom. I didn't see Roy—didn't want to see him. Donna undressed me and stood me under the shower. My body was so weak that I let her do anything she wanted. When I felt dizzy, she held me upright. Several minutes later I was sitting in the living room, wearing clean clothes that Donna chose from the closet. The fast I had inflicted on myself and my lack of movement during the last few days had taken their toll. My vision was blurred and my head was spinning like a carousel.

"Don't move," she ordered me.

Roy came out of the kitchen holding a plate with a piece of bread spread with cheese. I turned my face away in disgust. I couldn't even think about eating. Donna caught my chin in her hand and said in a voice that could not be misunderstood, "Eat this now!" She cut the bread into tiny pieces and put piece after piece in my mouth. My hands were as heavy as lead, hanging lifeless by my side. I felt Roy's presence, but I didn't turn my head to look at him. I leaned back on the sofa, my head tilted back and my mouth receiving the pieces of bread fed to me by Donna. A glass of water appeared out of nowhere, and Donna made me drink.

"Start eating gradually. That's enough for today," she said in an authoritative voice.

I felt the sofa sink next to me and I knew Roy was sitting down on the other side of me.

"Eva, look at me," he said in a gentle voice that was unfamiliar to me.

"I can't," I answered, my voice choked with tears.

Roy took my face in his hand, turned it toward him and said, "Open your eyes."

"I'm so ashamed," I said.

"I know, but you have nothing to be ashamed of."

"How come I didn't know about it?" I cried. "How could I not have seen?"

"You were too young to know."

"Young, ignorant, and blind."

"OK," said Donna's decisive voice. "I think that's enough for today. You're coming home with me until Roy fixes the door he broke." She looked at Roy, and they exchanged a smile that sent an inexplicable pain to my heart.

Donna packed a few clothes for me and within twenty minutes we arrived at her home. This was the first time I had been to her house. The only thing I wanted was to feel a mattress beneath me. She led me into a bedroom, helped me lie down on the bed, and covered me with a thin blanket. I fell asleep before she even left the room and slept continuously for more than twelve hours. When I woke up, it was already afternoon. The house was cool and quiet and only small streams of light filtered in through the slits in the blinds. I got up and waited for the dizziness to pass, then left the room, passing into a small corridor and from there to the living room. Light was coming from the kitchen, where I found her sitting and reading a magazine.

"So, are you back with us?"

I nodded and smiled at her. I said, "Don't you have to be at the office?"

"Yeah, so what?"

I took a sip of the hot chocolate she gave me. I felt the liquid flow through my veins and little by little I began to feel my organs working. My body began to fill up and my skin once again became a type of thin protection.

18

I went home in the afternoon, thanking Donna and politely refusing her offer to stay another day. The door had been fixed. I went inside, and a pleasant coolness enveloped me. It was warm outside, but the shutters had been closed, and there was a chill to the house. I went into the kitchen and made myself a cup of coffee; when I sat down in my regular chair, I saw the note with Roy's name and number on it—numbers that were etched into my memory.

I returned to work the next day, trying with all my heart to get back into my routine. Donna greeted me with a smile. She suggested that I work only half a day, but I insisted on returning to my regular hours.

"We're going out tonight," she said. I asked if we could postpone till next week.

"You're not planning on doing your vanishing act again, are you?" she asked with a smile, which I returned.

"No," I promised.

Roy showed up that evening. It was as if the embarrassing episode with Mickey never happened, and the conversation flowed easily between us.

Autumn was at its peak. Leaves of red and yellow adorned the trees and dangled like earrings on the branches; from time to time they dropped, adding to the vibrant carpet on the ground. People on the streets were wrapped in warm jackets and became more and more scarce. Autumn quickly turned into winter; strong winds began to blow and angrily broke tree branches and twigs. Stores closed early, affected by the early darkness of nightfall.

Mickey and I spoke occasionally on the telephone. He told me he was very busy, although he never explained with what. One day he invited me to spend the weekend with them, but I dodged the offer, saying that it had been a very strenuous week at work. Two weeks later, he invited me to their home again, and I found yet another reason not to accept the invitation. I couldn't face Mickey and his parents knowing who my father was. I would not be able to keep it to myself when we saw each other. When he asked me for the third time to come visit, he would not accept my excuses.

"Eva, is there something you want to tell me?" he asked.

"What do you mean?" I answered.

"Eva, this is the third time I've invited you to our home and you've refused to come. Is there something I need to know?"

"No, it's just that..."

"Eva, please be direct with me."

"I'm sorry."

"Did something happen?"

"Yes... No... It's just that I discovered something that's very hard for me to talk about."

"I see. Would you like me to come to you?"

"'Yes... But not yet."

"OK. Then I'll call you soon and we'll decide, all right?"

"OK, thanks. I'm sorry."

I didn't know if there would ever be an appropriate time to tell him, but I delayed any thought on the subject for the time being.

Donna promised to come over and make dinner with me over the weekend. We invited Roy, but he said that he couldn't make it. She arrived at five o'clock on Saturday afternoon, carrying a large basket of groceries. It was freezing outside. Most people preferred to stay in their homes. Snow began to pile up on the sidewalks, covering them in a white shroud. Donna quickly took control of the kitchen, and I stood next to her obeying her every order.

"Wash the vegetables. Put them in the refrigerator for now. Mix this until it becomes a smooth batter; keep mixing until I tell you to stop. Bring over that baking dish, pour the batter into it, and put it in the oven. Slice five tomatoes and two onions..."

We continued like this for two hours. Donna was extremely efficient and focused. I watched her meticulous movements. It was the same way she worked at the office. She would be leaving in a few weeks. I would have to get used to the idea that I wouldn't see her every time I raised my eyes.

Suddenly she saw me watching her.

"What?" she asked.

"Nothing... You're so efficient and know what to do that I'm jealous."

"Don't be jealous of me," she answered. "I wasn't always like this. Life forced me to learn to take care of myself. I had to trust someone, and the only person I could believe in was myself."

"I'm sorry."

"You have no reason to be sorry. It's all behind me. In some ways, I'm even grateful to them," she said, deep in thought. "They made me who I am."

"And love—did you have it?" I asked without thinking.

Donna didn't answer right away. Her hands stopped moving for a moment and she stared at them in contemplation. She stood that way for a few seconds, and then said, "I did."

"Can I ask you about it?"

"Well, it's a very short story. There were two loves. One decided he wasn't going to leave his home for me, and the second one insisted on children. So, we broke up, and that's it."

"Don't you want children?" I asked cautiously.

"No!" she answered quickly and said no more. I understood that she didn't want to talk about it, so I let it go. My mind was spinning with questions, but I felt it wasn't the right time to continue the discussion. *Maybe one day she'll tell me more, and maybe not.*

Donna continued to cut vegetables and went to the refrigerator to remove something. Then she went over to the stove, turned down the heat, and licked her finger, and just like that, her tragic story was swallowed up by the routine of her actions.

"And what about the guy?" I whispered.

"Oh, he was killed in a car accident two years later," she answered.

I was speechless. I spread the white tablecloth on the table and put two plates down. Donna took a bottle of wine out of her grocery basket and put it in the center of the table. "Glasses," she commanded. She took out a pair of candles from somewhere, lit them, and placed them in the center of the table. The kitchen was fragrant with enticing aromas, and the table was set and inviting. We sat down and she poured wine into our glasses. She lifted her glass, and I followed suit.

"To true friendship and changes for the better," she toasted.

I replied with, "To a good friend." We touched glasses and Donna ladled the soup into our bowls. Steam swirled upward from the hot soup and its smell was appealing. Before I could swallow my first spoonful of soup, a loud knock sounded on my door. Donna looked at me, and in response to her silent question, I made it clear that I wasn't expecting anyone. The insistent knocking came again, this time even louder. It was eight o'clock and extremely dark outside. I got up from my place at the table and went to the door. There was heavy breathing on the other side. I attached the safety chain and slowly opened the door.

I was not prepared for what happened next. The door was forced open and hit the back wall. The chain was torn off like it was just a thin string. An intense stench of alcohol filled my nostrils and I became dizzy. George's full and solid body stood before me with a drunken smile on his face. His eyes were shiny and saliva dripped from his mouth when he opened it in his malicious grin.

He copied the words of his leader. "My dear child, I came to take you with me." I was paralyzed with panic. His hand shot out and caressed my face. The touch of his fat fingers felt like sandpaper. I took a step backward, and he came toward me. I feared my body would collapse at his feet, but it kept moving backward until it hit the wall. That was a mistake. He came toward me, and his hands took hold of me on either side. His breath smelled putrid, and his teeth, yellow from nicotine, looked like demented fangs. His face drew close to mine, his body touching mine. My hands pushed against his chest, making him snigger like a saw on metal. His body was on mine and his breath was in my face.

Suddenly it was all over. I heard him scream like an injured animal. His body fell all at once onto the floor, and his hands covered his face. He was screaming and swearing. His body was writhing left and right on the floor in an effort to relieve his pain. He tried for a moment to get up but fell down once again. A hand pulled me toward the living room. I began to feel nauseous and vomit spewed out of me uncontrollably. Donna came and went periodically. A lifetime seemed to pass before I heard her speaking with someone. Everything was foggy. Unidentifiable shadows were moving around me. Finally, the house grew silent. I sat in my own vomit until a hand lifted me up and led me to stand under the shower, dressed me, and seated me like a doll. Several minutes passed, maybe an hour, before I found myself sitting on the couch with Donna next to me.

"What happened?" I asked.

"The police took him."

"How... How..." I couldn't finish the sentence.

"I poured the boiling soup on him," she said. Her mouth twisted into a sliver of a smile.

"No more soup," I mumbled. She exploded with laughter that echoed around the room and sparked my own irrepressible laughter.

We sat there next to each other, our arms intertwined. We laughed and cried and laughed again.

19

The police called on Monday. They asked me to come in and file a complaint. Immediately afterward, the phone rang again. A familiar voice that I couldn't place said, "Hello, am I speaking with Eva Brown?"

"Yes," I answered hesitantly.

"This is Gerard speaking. I understand there was an unpleasant incident on Saturday." I didn't react, just waited for him to continue. "You know, George's actions were very severe. We must punish him. We already thought of an appropriate punishment."

I said, "Yes...?"

"I believe the punishment he will get from us will be more severe than whatever the courts may decide," the voice said. It was silent again.

"Sir, what do you want from me?" I asked with dread.

"My dear child—" As soon as he said "dear child," I knew who he was. "—I am asking that you let us handle the matter."

His voice was firm, and it was clear that he wasn't used to being refused.

Thoughts were running around in my head. My first impulse was to agree to his request. He scared me. His voice rekindled the image of him standing on the stage: tough, scary and dangerous. The words "dear child" contained a threat, both then and now, and I was afraid with every bit of my being. I wanted to say OK and hang up, but I didn't. Something about this conversation was connected to the load I had been carrying on my back for many years—a load related to the life I had and my relationship with my father.

I said, "Sir, I suggest you address the police on the matter, and I ask that you not call me ever again!" I put the receiver in its place. My entire body was shaking. The words may have sounded brave, but my body recognized my fear. I sat down and couldn't stop shaking. This story wasn't over.

Roy came over later. Genuine worry was written on his face. "Did he do anything to you? Did he hurt you?" he asked concerned.

"No," I answered.

"I'm adding more locks to your door," he said.

I didn't argue with him. His concern warmed my heart.

"Where were you?"

"I had to work out of town. I was there all weekend. When I got back, Donna told me what happened."

I felt a small pinch in my chest knowing that he and Donna were speaking to each other without me.

"Come into the kitchen. I'll make us something to drink."

I told him about the conversation I had with "dear child." I saw his body tense up, but he was silent.

"What do you think?" I asked.

"That you need to be careful."

"Do you think I shouldn't file charges?"

"I don't think so. These people are very dangerous."

"I'm surprised at you, Roy. A policeman willing to back down from punishing a rapist? You want me to ignore his actions?"

He was quiet for a moment, and then said, "I'm worried about you. You're in this house alone. These people are capable of anything."

The more he spoke, the more I felt a decision forming in my heart. *I owe it to myself*, I said to myself. *Yes, I owe myself.*

"I'm going to file charges for attempted rape tomorrow!" I declared out loud.

Roy must have read the determination on my face, because he didn't say a word, just nodded.

When I got to the police station, there were other people there, including "dear child" and two other men with him. I tried to ignore his stare, but he made sure I didn't miss him. Going up to the desk where the duty officer sat, I informed him that I had come to file charges for attempted rape. He looked at me for a moment and sent me to the room to his right with a nod of his head, yelling out, "Don, filing a complaint."

I went into the room, which was smaller than my bedroom. The room was gray and no one had tried to improve its appearance. The walls were completely exposed and the grayness from outside had made its way inside. Across the desk, overflowing with files, sat a man about thirty years old. When I entered, he lifted his head and invited me to sit down in the chair across from him.

Suddenly the room darkened. In the doorway stood "dear child," his wide frame blocking almost all the light coming from the corridor. The policeman across from me didn't say a word, but I got up and, with uncharacteristic bravado, shut the door in his menacing face. I think the policeman himself was surprised by my action. His expression showed amazement, and I think a little bit of admiration. He presented his hand and said, "Don."

"Nice to meet you. I'm Eva," I said.

"Yes, Eva, what can I do for you?"

"I would like to file a complaint for attempted rape," I said in a steady voice.

Don raised his head, a question forming in his eyes.

"Against George Lucas," I stated.

Everyone knew George. He owned the largest hardware and home appliance store in town. Everyone in town must have visited his store at least once. His family was also well known. His father established the business and managed it himself until he became too old. Then George took his place. The officer squirmed in his chair and the pen in his hand shook. He lifted his head again and looked me squarely in the eyes.

"Please describe the incident," he said. I could hear a change in his voice.

I described the entire incident, from the knock on the door until the policeman arrived at my house.

"Were there any witnesses to the incident?" he asked skeptically.

"Yes," I answered.

"I will have to question them as well."

He asked me to sign the form, then got up and told me to go home, that he would be in touch. Leaving the station, the same group of burly men was still there, waiting to terrorize me. I walked between them, my eyes straight ahead. It felt like someone touched my arm, but I kept walking out the station door. Standing outside, I could feel the immense tension that had built up in me; my balance wobbled slightly, making me grab the banister next to the stairs. Walking to my car, worried that the gang would follow me, my legs were unsteady. I got into the car, closed the door, and rested my head on the steering wheel for a minute, waiting for my breathing to stabilize. When I looked up, there were the three men, one in front of the car and the other two on either side. They didn't do anything, just stood there looking at me. It seemed like it took an eternity for me to get the car started and inch it past them.

In the rearview mirror, I saw them standing in a row watching me and knew at that moment that my life was in danger. For a split second, I thought about turning the car around and calling the whole thing off, but it was a moment that was almost imperceptible. My foot pressed down on the gas pedal and the car moved forward at a normal speed toward my house. I wanted to be inside the four familiar walls at home, to regain some of the confidence I had felt when deciding not to keep silent any longer.

Evening came quickly. Darkness covered the world, casting doubt on what had seemed so certain in daylight. A loud voice thundered in my head, trying to convince me to let the whole thing go. It was completely illogical to fight with men that would stop at nothing to get what they wanted. These men were motivated by a sense of power drawn from the fact that they were a group. And then there was me: young, inexperienced in war, with a lifetime of experience in listening to orders without questioning them. It was a very convincing voice that was hard to argue with. *But the Eva of today isn't the one from the past,* I announced to myself silently. *I must atone for my way of life. Mostly for myself, but also for my mother, who I haven't thought of for many days.*

***

The first threat came three days later as I left in the morning for work, a few minutes before eight o'clock. I locked the door, my back to my car. Roy had installed two more locks on the door, so locking up took longer than usual. When I turned around, I saw the writing. On the car, on the driver's side, in black spray paint, were the words, "Beware, dear child."

I went back inside the house and locked all the locks on the door. I sat in the kitchen and couldn't stop shaking. My legs jumped up and down like a machine and the pounding of my heart was deafening. The sound was incessant. I couldn't even get to the telephone—I sat there shaking and terrified for a long time, until it felt possible to get up and call Roy. He promised to come right over. What seemed like an eternity passed until he arrived.

"Eva, I'm begging you—withdraw the complaint," Roy urged me.

I really wanted to please him, but I couldn't. Withdrawing the complaint would be an admission of defeat for me, and I knew I wouldn't be able to look myself in the mirror.

"I can't," I said.

"Of course you can," he said. "You have to understand that they aren't playing. These aren't idle threats. This is a warning. They are capable of much worse."

Roy stooped down in front of me so that my head was a bit higher than his. He tried to catch my gaze.

He began again, this time more aggressively. "Eva, you will withdraw your complaint!"

"No, Roy, I am not withdrawing anything!" I jumped up from the chair, almost knocking Roy over. "You don't understand. You don't understand anything! Ever since I was a little girl I've been like... Like the wind, going wherever I was blown, like air. My father, my idol, turned out to be a fake. Do you know what it's like to find out that someone you idolized was faking it? Can you even try to understand what that feels like? For twenty years it seemed that my father was like all the other fathers, that everything he did was right and just, that stupid little me should follow him blindly.

"I even rejected my own mother because he did—because of him, I didn't have a mother, never felt a mother's hug. Do you see the depth of my loss? I lived like a trained pet, making no decisions, never objecting to anything, just existing—that's it. And I'm angry—so angry at myself! I can't even look myself in the mirror because it shows me just a... nothing. Can you understand my disappointment? My frustration? My desperation?"

The tears were streaming down my face, but I didn't try to stop them. It was the first time I had voiced my disappointment in myself. It was a feeling of disgust, of great contempt. These last discoveries about my father and mother opened a door for me that had been locked with a million locks.

"Roy, if I withdraw my complaint, I will go back to being that nothing Eva. This complaint isn't just a complaint for me. It's defiance, maybe even revenge. Revenge for my life up until now; revenge against my father who cheated me all those years; revenge against myself for just accepting everything. You have to understand that standing up to these Nazis is a stance against my previous life. It is a decision to change it. Do you think I don't know that they're dangerous? Of course I know it, but I am not prepared to go backward."

"Not even if it costs you your life?" he asked all of a sudden.

I thought for a minute before I answered. "Yes. From my point of view, going back to my previous life would be like dying."

Roy was silent. I could see the battle going on inside him. I understood him. He was afraid for me. But I also knew that he understood.

"Roy, if my father were here, he would order me to change my mind. The fact that he's no longer alive makes it easier for me to do something I owe myself."

I couldn't fall asleep that night. I tossed and turned in bed in total restlessness—hot one minute, throwing off the blankets, and cold the next, pulling the covers up to my neck. I looked around the bed for something to hold on to: a book, an album, something. My eyes fell on the guitar I had never played, the textbooks from high school, old pens, pencils, childish pink curtains, a fancy old lampshade hanging from the ceiling. Nothing had changed in my room since I was a child.

Getting up from the bed and peeling the sheets off, I went over to my desk and pulled down the books from the shelves, piling them on the floor until the shelves were completely bare. I ripped the lampshade from the ceiling, took down the pictures on the wall one after another, and finally pulled down the curtains and heaped them onto the pile in the corner of the room. I looked around. The room was bare, with no symbols of personality. I pushed all the things out of the room and left them in the hallway for the next morning.

I sat in the easy chair in the living room and covered myself up with the wool blanket that was always there. That's how I fell asleep—all curled up in the chair that used to be my father's.

The doorbell brought me out of a deep and dreamless sleep. I looked at the watch on my arm. It was seven o'clock a.m. Fear began to trickle inside me. The doorbell rang again and again.

"Eva, open up, it's me," called Donna.

I got up and opened the door.

"What are you doing here?" I asked sleepily.

"Roy told me what happened yesterday," she answered.

Again I noticed that she and Roy had a relationship that had nothing to do with me, and again I felt a slight pinch. This time it hurt even more.

"So, what are you doing here at this hour?" I asked again.

"I want us to drive together to work."

"What?" I was upset.

"I want us to drive together to work," she repeated.

"So, what, now you're going to come over every morning to take me to work?"

"If need be, then yes."

"Donna, I know you are worried about me, but this isn't a solution."

"Eva, I am very worried about you."

"I know," I said gently. "But I need to deal with this."

"How?"

"I still don't know. I need to think about it."

"I have an idea. Why don't we meet today at your house with Roy and put our heads together and come up with a solution. You don't need to be brave, these are dangerous people."

"I know. It's not a matter of being brave. It's a matter of necessity for me. I'm afraid too," I admitted. "But I am not going to stop my life. I have to continue."

"Let's meet here today and think about it, OK?"

I nodded in agreement.

I followed Donna in my car all the way to the office. After returning home, my next job was to get rid of all the things in the hallway. After two hours, the house was neat and the things were piled in the garbage can in the yard. I didn't feel any remorse or regrets. As soon as the lid closed on the garbage can, I was relieved. I said goodbye to a chapter in my life that was weighing heavily on me and preventing me from moving forward. I went into the house feeling a bit victorious.

Roy and Donna came over that evening. We sat in the kitchen and I made them something hot to drink. The air outside was beginning to get warm, but it was still chilly. The house was warm and a cozy feeling filled the air.

"Look, Eva," Donna said. "Roy and I have been talking, and we have an idea, but I'm asking you to not reject it straight off. Think about it first."

"OK."

Roy continued. "Look, it's dangerous for you to stay home alone. You know these people are capable of anything. They won't stop until you withdraw the complaint against George. Therefore, we thought that at least for a short time, I would move in here with you."

"What?" I was shocked.

"Listen, Eva," Donna said, "it's completely logical. I know that it sounds strange to you, but think for a minute. Roy is a police officer. He has a gun."

"So, what, if they come, he would whip out his gun and kill them?"

"Don't exaggerate. The gun provides security. Nobody really intends to use it."

"I won't do it," I cut him off. "I don't want Roy to leave his home and stop his life to watch over me because of my problems. It sounds like a bad idea."

"Donna, will you give us a couple of minutes alone?" Roy surprised me.

Donna looked at him and then at me, got up, went into the living room and turned on the television.

Moving his chair to sit in front of me, he began, "Eva, we've known each other for almost ten years, right?"

At my nod, he continued. "Only yesterday did I realize how complicated your life has been. Even in the two years since the death of your parents I haven't been able to understand everything you and them have been through in depth. I've known you for so long and only yesterday did I see what I should have seen ages ago."

"What are you talking about?"

"When I left here yesterday, I drove around for hours in the car. I couldn't calm down. You are angry at yourself and I am furious at myself."

I tried to stop him and tell him that he has nothing to be angry about, but he asked me to let him continue.

"I am so angry at myself for not seeing. I should have felt what was happening to you. I knew the kind of father you had, but I never dared talk to you about him."

"I'm sure I would have gotten angry at you if you tried to tell me bad things... In any case I wouldn't have believed you," I tried to reassure him.

"Maybe, but I should have tried," he insisted.

"Roy..." I tried to interrupt.

He continued. "I was so caught up in myself, in my feelings..."

I didn't want him to go on. I knew that if he did, we would have to deal with something we've been putting off for a long time. At that moment, I couldn't deal with our feelings for each other. I preferred to ignore them— to live as if what hadn't explicitly been said didn't exist.

He said, "Eva, I want a chance to make it up to you for being dimwitted. I know that you want to be independent and to rid yourself of the strings to your past, but the crisis you are going through right now is very difficult, and I just want to help you through it. For me, mostly. As soon as it's all over, I will go home. But until then, I will be with you, and we'll fight these Nazis together."

I looked in his eyes, and I saw his aggression and his pleading at the same time. Finally, I said, "OK, you can come live here, but only for a short time."

20

Two days later Roy moved in with me. I moved into my parents' bedroom and he made himself comfortable in mine.

It was strange not to be alone any more. I was used to being alone by now. Even so, I got used to his presence in the house rather quickly. It was nice to know that he would be coming home in the evening, that I would be eating with another person, that I could talk and get a human response, and that I no longer needed to be afraid at night. My sleep became much more relaxed.

One evening, about a week after he moved in with me, we were sitting in the living room watching television. We weren't talking much. He was very tired, and his eyes began to close. I didn't mind that he was sleeping next to me; his presence was calming. Since he had moved in, suddenly I had begun enjoying television shows, my appetite had returned, and I had a new sense of vitality.

Roy's head dropped every so often, the movement waking him every time, until finally I leaned him against my shoulder and let him doze there. The house was dark. Only the floor lamp was on in the living room, and the blue light of the television engulfed the room. Suddenly there was the loud sound of breaking glass, then tires squealing, which slowly faded away into complete silence.

Roy jumped right up as soon as he heard the explosion. He grabbed me, shoved me into the space between the table and the sofa, and leaped on top of me to protect me with his body until we heard the sound of the tires leaving.

We looked up, but the window across from us was still in one piece. We went into my bedroom and there, on the floor, was a heavy brick surrounded by glass shards.

"Are you OK?" asked Roy.

I nodded and gave him a look that expressed my thanks for being there with me. We cleaned up the room. There was nothing else to do. It was obvious that this incident was part of their plan to make me withdraw the complaint. It was also obvious to me that this intimidation campaign wasn't over and that there would be more of the same.

We decided to let the episode pass and not to file another complaint. We did our best to stay at home most of the time. We certainly felt safer inside than we did anywhere else. Donna came over once in a while to visit, but she also tried not to wander around outside after dark. For some reason, the bullies didn't harass her, even though they knew that she intended to testify at the trial.

In the meantime, living with Roy became routine. We were together, but we respected each other's living space. Roy never entered my parents' bedroom, and I avoided going into my former room. It was an understanding we came to without having to talk about it. But what happened that weekend undermined the delicate texture of our relationship.

It was Friday evening. Roy had gone shopping on his way home from work; I cooked dinner for us. When I finished cooking, we sat down side by side and enjoyed the aromas of the dishes we had created with our own hands. Roy poured the wine, and we clinked our glasses, smiling at each other. We felt like we were on a desert island with only empty space all around us—no people, no threats, and no danger lurking in the shadows. We were focused on eating and the casual conversation we were having. A light knock on the door, barely perceptible, replaced the serenity with tension. We looked at each other and waited. We heard the knocking again, this time louder. Roy got up and moved closer to the door. He called me to also come near and told me to ask who was there.

"Who is it?" I asked, but no answer was forthcoming.

I cleared my throat and asked again, "Who is it?"

The answer was surprising: "Mickey."

"Mickey?" I repeated in amazement. As I went to unlock the door, Roy caught my arm, surprising me. "Are you sure?" he asked. *Am I sure it is Mickey, or am I sure I want to open the door for him?* Instead of answering, I shook my arm free and opened the locks.

Mickey stood there, wearing a tailored suit with a red tie, looking very handsome. He looked at me, then at Roy, and then back to me with a question in his expression. I looked at him, then at Roy, then back to him. I felt a wave of laughter make its way from the depths of my stomach. *This can't be happening*, I said to myself. *I've been in this exact situation only the opposite.* Embarrassment was written on all of our faces. The laughter burst out of me—I couldn't hold it in any longer. I stood across from Mickey, with Roy by my side, and my stomach jiggled with laughter.

Roy stepped back and Mickey continued to look at me. I think he was trying to decide whether to be insulted and turn around or come inside. Suddenly I saw the corner of his mouth turn up in a tiny smile, which grew wider until he also began to roar with laughter. Roy stood next to me, moving his head like a pendulum—from me to Mickey, back to me and again to Mickey—until he also surrendered to the ridiculousness of the situation. We stood there like three human statues, laughing our heads off. About what? I didn't know. I just knew that laughter was necessary.

Mickey came inside and joined us for dinner. Roy poured him some wine. Mickey raised his glass and, with a nod of his head, emptied the entire glass. He asked Roy to pour him another glass and again emptied it in one gulp. His face turned a bit red, but it looked like he was feeling somewhat more relaxed. I did the same. I drank glass after glass and felt calm begin to replace the embarrassment. The only one not drinking was Roy. He had a smile on his face, but his body language demonstrated his edginess.

I explained to Mickey why Roy was living in my house, but I left out the part about my father's relationship to George and his gang. Roy sat quietly the entire time without taking part in the conversation. Every once in a while, Mickey caressed my face with his hand. He rested his hand on my arm; when he talked, his body and face were turned toward me. Roy played with the fork in his hand, poking holes in the food remaining on his plate. His face was expressionless. His behavior made me uncomfortable. He stood up abruptly, announcing that he was tired and was going to his room. I tried to catch his eye but wasn't successful. He left the kitchen and, after a few minutes, the door to his bedroom slammed shut.

Mickey and I remained alone. My feeling of unease stayed with me even when Mickey said, "I've missed you." He took my face in both his hands and moved his mouth close to mine in a gentle but endless kiss. It felt like electricity was going through my body. His hands continued along my back, and my body responded to him with yearning. On the wall above our heads, the ticking of the clock was constant and annoying. It was both sleep-inducing and stimulating at the same time.

Mickey held my hand and got up from his chair. I also got up, and we walked together to my parents' bedroom, closing the door behind us. Sitting at the end of the bed made me feel like I was floating inside a bubble. My head was dizzy and my vision was blurred. I thought it might be because of the wine. Mickey moved closer and kissed me again. His hands became more and more demanding, and his mouth hovered over my ears and the nape of my neck. The bubble rolled me from side to side like a weightless object, and my hands moved by themselves toward him.

"Mickey," I whispered weakly. No response. "Mickey," I said again. Mickey lifted his head and looked at me; his eyes were glassy and dreamlike. "Enough," I said.

His expression asked why.

"I can't. I'm just a guest here. This is my parents' bedroom—this is their bed, this is the air they breathed. It's not mine."

The alienation I felt in the room didn't fit with the intimacy between us. Mickey lay on the bed next to me. We remained quiet until I heard his breathing fall into a steady rhythm and knew he had fallen asleep. I moved away from his body somewhat and clung to the edge of the bed. My thoughts were foggy from the alcohol, but the feeling of unease I had felt earlier remained.

I fell asleep toward dawn and woke up when I heard sounds coming from the bathroom. Mickey came out with a wet face.

"There's a towel in the bottom drawer," I said.

The house was quiet; no sound could be heard from Roy's bedroom or the kitchen.

"What time is it?" I asked.

"Six," he answered.

"Are you going?"

"I have to be in Chicago by ten," he said. "I'm sorry I pushed you, but I really, really like you."

I smiled back at him. He came over to me, bent down and kissed me. My hands cupped the back of his head and drew it closer to mine. When we pulled apart, he was standing over me with a warm smile on his face. Little wrinkles like stalks of wheat appeared in the corner of his eyes, which radiated real warmth and affection.

"I really like you a lot," he said again and smiled. "And I want you to come over."

I nodded. He kissed me again, turned around and a few seconds later, the front door closed. I could have gone on sleeping, but there was no more sleep in me. I got up and went to the kitchen. Its appearance had changed from last night. The table had been cleared of the remaining dinner and the sink was empty. The door to Roy's bedroom was closed—he was usually awake at this hour. A gentle knock got no answer. I slowly opened the door and peeked inside. The bed was made and the room was empty. The pinch from last night came back, stronger than ever.

At about noon, the telephone on my desk rang. It was Roy. He said that he couldn't come over today, that he had to take a trip for work and would probably have to spend the night out of town. His words undermined my sense of security. *Is it the tone of his voice or the fear of being alone in the house?* I was so used to him being around that his absence reopened the fear and the anxiety, waking up my imagination, which gave me threatening scenarios. *Tonight will be a sleepless night.* On my way home from work, I stopped at one of the newspaper kiosks and bought a bunch of magazines and crossword puzzles. I almost thought of asking Donna to spend the night with me, but immediately ruled out the idea. She would agree without hesitation, but she loved the routine of her life, and I didn't want her to feel obligated to take Roy's place. She had been relieved when Roy agreed to move in with me. *No*, I said to myself, *I will spend the night on my own.*

Evening had already become night. It was dark outside, and all the lights were on in my house. The darkness brought with it fear and bad thoughts, so the light was comforting. But knowing wasn't the same, and I was afraid. I turned on the television. The voices booming out of the set relieved a bit of the loneliness. Sitting in the living room with my pile of magazines, I flipped through them—photographs, gossip columns and boring articles. The pile next to me grew smaller very quickly. I took the last magazine and paged through it. My eyes were tired and were fighting sleep. Every once in a while, my eyelids began to droop and threatened to close, but my mind refused sleep. My hands continued to flip the pages. The colorful pages passed by me like a scarf fluttering in the wind. I felt my consciousness fading and my eyes becoming heavy and closing. And then a loud, jarring noise split the night.

I jumped up and looked around. The house was quiet and lit up like an island in the middle of the ocean. Complete silence, as if no noise had been made beforehand, but surely the explosion I heard was real. I looked toward the kitchen, but it only scoffed at my fear. I got up from the sofa and looked down the hallway. The door to my room was opened only slightly. I pushed it in, stretched my head around like a curious swan, and then continued toward my parents' bedroom.

The open door allowed me a quick peek inside. I saw it right away. On my father's bureau—like a dead body—was the framed picture of the two of us. Him and me.

I picked up the picture, which was lying face down, and shards of glass rained down like parts of a body. I separated the photo from the frame and more glass scattered onto the bureau and the floor. The photo was of little girl and her big father standing side by side. His hand rested on her shoulder, a symbol of ownership, while his other hand, closed in a fist, covered some object whose tip was sticking out a bit. That was a new detail. I drew the photo closer to my eyes and put it under the light. The expression on his face always seemed related to his distance from me. A hugging hand, his body close to mine. A father filled with pride. Only now, looking closer, his figure filled the entire print, and for a moment, his strong presence filled the room. I opened the drawer, threw the picture inside, closed the drawer, and turned my back to it. But something made me turn around again—something that was in the drawer. I opened it again. A bundle of banknotes sat there, and from under them peeked the corner of a dark green box, rectangular in shape and about twelve inches in size.

There were no markings on the box, no clue to its contents. I put the banknotes aside and sat on the bed. Inside the box there was a packet of about thirty letters. The envelopes were torn down the side with a letter opener and were arranged by date received. Most of the letters were from Germany; some were from Italy and others from various places in the United States. I began to read one of the letters. It included descriptions of the organizational structure of the Nazi movement in Germany and answers to letters that came from my father. My eyes raced over the words. Every once in a while, I encountered the phrase "Heil Hitler." There were questions asking my father about one subject or another. I opened another letter, sent about five years ago. The word "homosexual" caught my attention and I began to read.

The deeper I got into the letters, the more I felt shock and intense shame spread through me. I understood from these writings that my father was advising a group of Germans to react violently against homosexual men, even to kill them in the name of purifying humanity. There were descriptions of incidents where men were executed according to his instructions. It looked like the writers of these letters were looking for his approval for their right to exist. This letter implied that the more radical their treatment of the homosexuals, the greater his approval.

In one of the letters, someone from Mississippi wrote about a factory run by blacks that was set on fire by a group of loyal followers of the ideology. A number of workers burned to death and the entire structure was destroyed. There were also descriptions of the abuse of a young black teenage girl who was part of a dance class where most of the participants were white. The description was callous, and for a moment I pictured the writer to look exactly like George. I folded the letter and returned it to the same envelope.

Reading these letters made me nauseous. I stuffed the letters back into the box and closed the lid on them, moving it to the side of the drawer in order to put the bundle of money next to it. But something got in the way—a small brown envelope. I opened it and found various objects inside, some metal and some made out of fabric. There were also old pictures, one of the Führer; others were of my father photographed with some other person I didn't recognize. At the bottom of the envelope was a black metal swastika. I held it in my hand, turned it over, and then I remembered. This was the object my father was holding in his picture with me.

I held the swastika in such a way that one of its points protruded a bit, just like in the photo, and knew that this was the object in my father's fist. Why was it so important for him to hold this while being photographed with me? I didn't want to think about it. What I did understand for sure was that my father was a very prominent figure in the movement. As the drawer shut on my father's secret world, the front doorbell rang, accompanied by the familiar knock. A jingle of hope rang inside me. I got up and went to the door. "Roy?" I whispered.

"It's me," came the answer.

I don't think I had ever opened the locks on the door so fast. I flung the door wide open and jumped into his arms. Roy stayed as still as a statue, waiting for me to calm down and let him out of my embrace. I pulled away and he came inside and locked up the house.

"I'm exhausted," he said. "I'm going to sleep."

Just like that, with no explanation, without giving me a second glance, he turned his back on me, walked into my bedroom, and closed the door behind him.

I stood there with my mouth agape. It was obvious that he was angry. Without thinking, I opened the door and walked in after him.

"Eva," he said in an angry tone.

"Don't 'Eva' me," I said. "I want to know what's going on here."

"I'm tired. I drove for five hours, I just want to go to sleep."

"You will go to sleep after you explain to me what's going on!"

Roy stopped for a minute and sat down on the bed. He propped his head in his hands and sat bent over on the edge of the bed. It looked like he was trying to decide something. He lifted his head for a moment and fixed his eyes on me. His expression was unclear. He looked at me until I began to feel uncomfortable, but I didn't pull my eyes away from his. His face changed right in front of me. The muscles in his face suddenly grew softer, his tightly closed mouth relaxed, and his body flopped back. His eyes were still fixed on me when he said, in the gentlest voice I had ever heard from him, "I love you... That's what happened to me."

My eyes refused to leave his; we continued to look stubbornly at one another. My mind had drifted away, but my body continued to stand. I wanted to run away, but my legs were steadfast on the floor and didn't move an inch. Roy continued in his silence. I didn't feel a thing, didn't know what to say—I only knew that I had to get out of there.

I was finally able to move and left the room with his eyes stabbing me in the back like two nails, making my feet move faster. I went into my parents' room, locked the door behind me, and sat on the bed, my heart beating as loud as drums in a concert hall. My chest rose and fell and then began to cry. Why was I crying? I was flooded with emotions that were unclear. They were all jumbled up and rolling around like a colorful ball whose colors became one—anger, rejection, love, hate, bitterness, friendship, exploitation, desire, longing. All these emotions merged together and created a world that was illogical—I wanted to kick it out, out of my thoughts, out of my life.

I fell asleep in my clothes and woke up in the morning exhausted. When I left the room, Roy was already gone. It was obvious that our relationship had taken an unwanted turn. I wondered what would become of us in the future. *Will he come over this evening, or leave me alone? Will he sever all contact with me? Will he demand some kind of response from me?* I changed my clothes and went to work.

Even at work, I couldn't stop thinking about the future of our relationship. I was ashamed to admit that it was mostly worry about staying home alone. Never for a moment did my feelings for him entire my mind. His soft words continued to echo, but they didn't have the strength to force me to rummage around in my feelings. I decided to wait for the evening and see what transpired. The decision was his and his alone, I convinced myself.

As the hours passed by, my emotions were reduced to just one main feeling: anger that he decided to reveal his feelings for me. Slowly but surely, I convinced myself that he did a selfish thing and that these things should not have been said, certainly not when I was in my current state. The anger continued to grow and my self-assurance also grew. If he came over this evening, I would tell him exactly what I thought. Only my decision didn't coincide with reality. When the door opened, the same familiar Roy stood there, and what had happened yesterday was not evident on his face. We were in the same boat floating safely on calm seas.

"I brought warm rolls and peanut butter," he announced.

Surprise must have been written all over my face, but he completely ignored it.

"Want me to make you one too?"

I nodded. He turned away from me and busied himself preparing dinner. He even began to hum some tune to himself. His movements were assured. He asked me to take out plates from the cupboard and set down the silverware, promising that the food would be ready in a minute. When we sat down at the table, he talked incessantly about work.

"How about you?" he asked suddenly.

"Me?" I was surprised.

"Yes, how was your day at the office?"

"Not any different from other days."

"What does that mean?"

"It means that work is routine. There's nothing exciting about it, no surprises."

"Challenges?"

"Challenges?" I laughed. "No, there aren't any challenges."

"So why do you continue to work at a job that doesn't interest you?" he asked with a serious face.

His question caught me unprepared. "What do you mean?" I asked.

"You've been getting up every day for years now to go to the office and do what's asked of you. You apparently do it well, but you get no satisfaction from it, no interest... Haven't you ever thought about making a change, trying to work somewhere else? A different area?"

He was right. The job bored me. My path had been determined by my father, and I had never once considered straying from it. Roy had put a mirror in front of my face. At that instant, I saw my apathy, my passivity, my lack of self-confidence, my dependence.

"I'm sorry," he said. "I didn't mean to make you sad."

"No, you're right. Totally right. I needed to hear these things, they are completely correct. For years, I've been traveling down a path paved for me in advance, and it's become routine for me to travel down the same path without even realizing I am capable of deviating from it."

The atmosphere suddenly became heavy.

"Coffee?" he asked.

Ignoring his question, I said, "You know, my lack of trust in myself is so enormous that it never occurred to me that I had the power to change something."

"And now?" he asked in a whisper.

I turned my head toward him and was surprised that he was there. Thoughts were muddled up in my head, fighting one another. The emotions were familiar, but there were also some new ones. I felt a strong urge to be alone.

"I'm going to sleep," I announced and got up from my chair. Roy followed me with his eyes until the door of the bedroom closed and separated us.

21

One week later Mickey called and invited me for the weekend again. I hesitated a bit at first, then, in a snap decision, replied that I'd be happy to. When Roy came home that evening, I informed him that he was off-duty this weekend. When he asked why, I replied casually that I was going to Chicago. The name Mickey was not mentioned, even though we both heard it quite clearly.

The scenery on the way to Chicago had become familiar, as well as the roads. The signs on the side of the road became irrelevant, and I could concentrate on my driving and the music playing on the radio. I was in a good mood. It felt like a heavy, frustrating burden had been lifted from my shoulders. This weekend I would clear my head of thoughts and my heart of confusing emotions. I liked Mickey very much and knew that he would do everything in his power to make sure I enjoyed my visit.

He was already waiting for me as I drove into the driveway of his house. His embrace was warm and genuine. As we walked into the house, he put his arm around my waist and his head tipped a bit toward my shoulder. This was how Rivka found us. She was just coming from the kitchen, wiping her hands. She put the towel on her shoulder so she could hug me to her ample chest and said, "I am so happy you came. I've constantly been asking Mickey when you are coming."

I smiled at her warmly. She smelled of the familiar dishes, the smell of home.

"Come, sit in the living room and see what I made for you." She then went into the kitchen and came right back with a glass of cold carrot juice mixed with orange juice. It was exactly what I needed after the long journey. I poured the cold drink down my throat and felt even better than I did before.

"You changed the picture," I said, seeing that the painting previously hanging over the sofa had been replaced.

"Yes," she answered. "Shlomo painted it a few years ago."

I looked at Mickey and we both remembered the painting that had been on the wall at the office, the painting that brought me to his home. We smiled at each other.

She said, "OK, my dear, I'll let you get organized; Mickey will give you a hand and then we will all meet up at dinner."

Mickey helped me carry my light bag upstairs. He set it down on a chair, sat on the bed, and motioned for me to sit next to him.

"I missed you," he said.

"I missed you too."

He kissed me on the lips, and his hand hovered over my hair. I felt tiny pinpricks running up and down my body, and I kissed him back. He smiled at me and stroked my cheek. "We need to do this more often..." he said and kissed me again. His lips caressed my cheeks and over my ears. My whole body was aroused, feeling like the petals of a flower opening, one after the other, until I could no longer control them. Mickey stroked me more and more; his hands were like delicate paintbrushes drawing rapturous lines all over my body. My breathing became faster and my hands broke free on their own to explore his body.

Suddenly everything stopped. Mickey, with a flushed face and a hoarse voice, said, "We should wait a bit. I want you very much, but not like this."

I remained sitting for a while on the bed after he left, trying to control my breathing—we should have continued, without planning and without too much thinking, just letting things develop on their own. I took a shower in order to cool my body down and relax. When the water began to wash over my body in little streams, I promised myself that there wasn't going to be a lot of thinking going on during this visit; I was going to try to relate only to what was happening at that exact moment. With this promise, I got into bed. The cool sheets relaxed me and put me to sleep until a knock on the door urged me to get ready for dinner.

Dinner was good and the atmosphere was terrific. Mickey's older sister arrived with her husband, introducing me to the entire family. I felt very comfortable. Rivka treated me like one of her daughters. She clucked around me to no end and asked if the food was tasty and if it reminded me of home. Mickey was somewhat quiet, but glanced over at me every so often. At the end of the meal, he asked if I wanted to take a brief walk outside. We left the house and only then did I appreciate how big it was. Behind the house was a large garden with fruit trees. There was a cherry tree surrounded by blueberry and blackberry bushes, which formed a necklace around the trunk. Mickey said, "Around July or August, we pick the fruit and my mother makes jam. She freezes the remaining fruit for several months and then makes more."

It was a rather chilly May. The blackberry bush scattered white flowers that would become the sweet ripe fruit. Further on, I saw a large piece of land covered entirely with other fruit trees. There were pear trees, plum, and apple—even peach trees, which Mickey explained were a special kind, the only one able to withstand the cold climate of the area.

The aroma pervaded my nostrils and a chill passed through my body. I took a deep breath of the marvelous scent and was sorry there wasn't still some fruit I could taste. "Toward the summer, we can pick the fruit, and then you can taste every one of them," he promised.

My senses had awoken. A new energy pulsed through me. I asked Mickey many questions and he answered each one patiently. Every so often he would hug me and laugh enthusiastically.

"It's so beautiful here," I said.

We walked back to the house in silence. His sister had already left and his parents had gone up to their room. Only our footsteps could be heard in the empty space.

"Would you like something to drink?" he asked.

"No, I'm completely full," I answered.

Mickey poured himself a glass of cold water from a bottle in the refrigerator.

"What has happened since you found out your mother is Jewish?" he asked suddenly. "Have you researched the subject at all?"

"Let's leave the serious subjects for tomorrow," I said. "Today everything is good and pleasant and simple."

He looked at me for a moment and then he placed the used glass in the sink, turned out the light and gently prodded me to go upstairs. He opened the door to my bedroom and followed me inside. His hand held mine and he led me to the bed at the far end of the room. He held my face between his hands and kissed me. It was a different kiss from that of the afternoon, more demanding, and with the last vestiges of my sense of reality, I knew there was no coming back from it. My hands responded to his and my body to his body. It was a dance we both knew how to perform. First he led, then I did. I was a different Eva than the one I knew. Unburdened Eva, untraceable, without a thought. Just Eva. No strings attached, without a past and no fear of the future.

We woke up in the morning in each other's arms. It was the first time I had ever slept in the nude. I woke up before he did and discovered my head resting in the crook of his arm. I tried to move away slightly, but he caught me and said, "You are not moving away from me."

I liked it there. The rattle of dishes could be heard from the floor below. His mother was busy making breakfast. I didn't want to get up.

"Let's stay in bed and skip breakfast," I said.

He said, "OK, but I don't want to just lie around in bed."

"What do you want to do?" I asked with fake innocence.

"Let me show you."

Lovemaking in the morning was different from that of nighttime. My body seemed to want to finish all that it had missed thus far. We finally fell asleep again in utter fatigue. Nobody bothered us, nobody knocked on the door. We woke up at noon and decided it was time to start the new day.

When we went downstairs, Rivka was watching television and Shlomo was reading the newspaper. Rivka tried her best to avoid my eyes and I was thankful for that. I was embarrassed and went straight into the kitchen. Mickey made us both a cup of hot coffee.

"What are your plans for the day?" she asked.

"I don't know," I answered.

Mickey suggested we take a trip.

"Where to?" I asked.

"We'll see," he answered.

We said goodbye to his parents and Mickey asked them not to wait for us for dinner. When we went outside, Mickey walked over to the car and sat in the passenger's seat.

"Hey, you made a mistake," I cried.

"Nope, no mistake. You drive!" he ordered.

"Me? But I have never driven this kind of car before; it's huge."

"A car is a car. If you know how to drive one, you can drive them all."

"But—" I began.

"No buts. Get in and start it up. I want to watch you for a while. I still don't know your profile that well," he said, smiling mischievously.

I got into the car with trepidation and looked forward in fear. "Mickey," I tried again.

"It will be fine," he said calmly. "Just start the engine and start driving slowly. You'll see that in a short time you'll get used to the size of the car."

"Where are we going?"

"I'll direct you."

Even though I was afraid to drive, another thought entered my mind: *He trusts me; he believes I am capable.* The thought gave me confidence and filled me with gratitude. As time went by, I in fact did feel more confident behind the wheel. My seat became more comfortable, I loosened my grip on the steering wheel to some degree, and the muscles in my body relaxed.

The car glided along the road like a boat on the waves. The shock absorbers floated up and down and created an agreeable atmosphere. Every now and then Mickey would direct me where to go, and once in a while I would catch a glimpse of him staring at me.

"Turn right at the next street and then take an immediate left," he instructed.

"But what are we doing here? This place is locked." I said, recognizing exactly where we were.

"I owe you something," he answered.

I stopped the car near the door. He took out a key and opened the door for me. The room was completely different from the last time I saw it. It was totally exposed. The little cabinet that had held the many index cards— disappeared. The shelves had left their imprint with holes in the wall, and the table where he used to sit had apparently been moved somewhere else. If the dust covering the place was any indication, I would have guessed that no one had visited for quite some time. The room was deserted except for two round wooden chairs and one large familiar painting on the wall.

Before he could begin speaking, I said, "Mickey, there's something you have to know."

He saw the seriousness of my expression and didn't try to change my mind.

"Do you remember when you visited me last time, and I told you that Roy was staying with me to protect me from George and his gang who are trying to get me to withdraw my complaint?"

"I remember," he said.

"Well, besides the fact that George is a vile and disgusting man, he belongs to a group of neo-Nazis operating out of our area—"

"I'm not surprised," Mickey interrupted me. "By your description, this is the perfect type of man to belong to a group like that. These are ignorant thugs who think that a stupid ideology gives them the right to hurt people."

"Mickey—" I tried to stop him, but he kept going.

"These are scum, murderers. There are a few groups like this in Chicago too. They should be outlawed."

"Mickey!" I tried again. Every sentence he uttered sucked up a little more of my courage to tell him about my father.

His face grew red and suddenly he had aged. There were lines of fury etched like veins into his cheeks. The room suddenly became scary. The dark and naked walls, which looked like a bodiless skeleton, began to close in on the compressed and suffocating air. The hard chair hurt my butt and my body turned to stone; I swallowed my fear of this man's wrath.

Suddenly it grew silent. I looked at him. He looked like a runner who had just run a great distance; a runner who has been running and running, the wind and the rain etching inerasable memories in his face. And while he was running, he had turned into an old man. His body was folded over on the chair and his hands rested on his knees like fragile sticks. His breathing was labored and irregular. His father's story was unquestionably his story.

"Let's go," he said suddenly.

"But Mickey—" I tried to speak, but he had already risen and was walking toward the door. I wanted to insist he hear what I had been trying to tell him, but he was hurrying me up, closing the door behind us and locking it with an old lock.

We walked into the alley and this time, he sat behind the steering wheel. Something had made him extremely angry, an anger that couldn't let go of him. Even so, I still hoped to unburden myself from the weight of my father's story. I waited for him to calm down so he would be able to listen to me, but he was silent the entire way back. I tried to rekindle the light mood from before, but he was deep inside his anger, his reaction surprising me to no end.

"Mickey, what's going on?" I asked.

"Nothing is going on, Eva, everything is fine."

"Then what happened earlier, why are you so angry?"

"I'm not angry anymore," he said, avoiding the question.

I decided not to push it; in any event, he wasn't going to give me a straight answer right now. We returned to his home in the suburbs. When we walked in, Rivka joyfully welcomed us back and suggested we set the table because they had been waiting for us for dinner, but Mickey ignored her and went up to the second floor. After a moment, we heard the door to his bedroom slam shut. I didn't know what to do, whether to also go up to my room or stay with his parents. Rivka saw my embarrassment and suggested I go freshen up a bit. She said and she would leave me a covered plate of food in the kitchen for me to eat whenever. I thanked her with a nod of my head and went upstairs, where I sat down on the bed and went over everything that had happened to me since we left the house.

Mickey's easiness during the drive into the city was the complete opposite of his behavior in the little abandoned room. I had never seen him explode like that before. He always seemed so calm and reserved. In the end, I had never told him about my father. I packed up what little stuff I had and went downstairs. Rivka gave me a quizzical look.

"I have to leave," I said.

"Maybe you should wait a little longer. I'm sure Mickey will be down in a few minutes."

"No, Rivka, I really have to go." I kissed her cheek and left the house. The drive home was faster than the trip to Mickey's house. My thoughts gave me no rest. I was surprised at Mickey's reaction, but also angry at myself for not insisting on telling him about my father. *If our relationship is to have any chance, then he has to know everything about me.* These thoughts and more were shaking around my head all the way home. The scenery got on my nerves; the light on the gas tank indicator became nothing more than an insignificant and unimportant glimmer. My foot on the gas pedal didn't change its pressure for a long time and the car continued on its own, in the familiar lane, right up until it drove into my driveway, gasping from thirst.

As soon as I walked into the house, the sight hit me right away. My first thought was that I had entered a stranger's house. The bureau that stood next to the front door was lying upside down on the floor and the vase that sat on it was shattered into amorphous blue shards. The fragments on the floor were just a sign of what had happened in the rest of the house. The living room, which I had left neat and orderly, had turned into a room paved with broken pieces of furniture, with a couch full of holes made by a sharp object, and curtains hanging at the end of their rods. The newly replaced window was shattered and bits of glass littered the seat underneath it. The television was also damaged, shattered to pieces. I was in complete shock. My gaze moved toward the kitchen, where I found a similar sight. The cabinets were wide open, their contents spilled onto the floor; the refrigerator was savagely emptied of the food it had stored; the kitchen table was upside down, one of its legs ripped off. There was not one single object that hadn't been battered. It was a thorough destruction of property that left no room for doubt. Whoever did this did it out of enormous rage. The situation in the bedrooms was the same, save my parents' bedroom.

The destroyer had not gone in there. My hand reached out automatically and dialed Roy's number. He answered on the first ring.

"Yes."

"It's me." Silence. "Can you come over?"

"Where are you?"

"At home."

"I thought you were coming home later tonight or tomorrow."

"No, I came home now."

"So...?"

"Someone came in and turned the house upside down..." My sobs could be heard before the tears even began to flow.

"I'll be right there. Don't touch anything."

Roy was also stunned by the destruction. "There is not one thing they didn't touch," he noted dryly.

When he went through the bedrooms, he saw that my father's room remained intact. He looked over at me and came back toward the kitchen. The policemen arrived half an hour later and began to collect evidence. Roy answered their questions and I went out and sat on the stair outside the front door.

When we were finally left alone, he said, "I don't think you should stay at home."

"I have nowhere to go," I said.

"What about Donna?"

"No, I'm not going anywhere."

"Eva, this is not a game, this—"

"Roy, I am not leaving this house!"

After a brief silence, he said, "Fine. Let's start putting things back in order."

22

We settled back into our routine. He no longer asked me about my trip to Chicago. We were on high alert during those days. It was obvious that the break-in was just one of many incidents yet to come. The trial was set to begin in one month. They were surprised by my stubbornness, but they were convinced they would break my spirit. If I left the house when it was dark out, it was always with someone else. Sarah came over once in a while and begged me not to leave the house, not even to visit her. I wasn't about to tempt fate. I was very scared, but I was also determined not to relent. Roy tried to get home as early as possible. If he had to stay late, he would call me to let me know and stay on the line until he heard the sound of the door locks clicking into place.

It was the middle of the week. Winter was beginning to subside and summer was lightly knocking on the door. Roy called to say he would be home late and asked to hear me locking up the house. About an hour had gone by when he called again and said that he was actually going to make it home early. He was home just half an hour later. We were sitting in the living room, the new television was turned off, and we were relishing the quiet. I was sitting in my father's chair, the only one that remained intact after the devastation. Roy went into the kitchen to make himself something to eat. I thought to myself that I should do some shopping the next day because the refrigerator was almost empty. Hearing the sounds in the kitchen and the dull whistle of the wind outside lent me a feeling of calm. These sounds were common when my parents were alive, but they didn't give me a calm feeling then. At Mickey's house, it was Rivka that filled the house with sounds of life. Shlomo was silent most of the time.

Roy came in with a cheese and tomato sandwich on a plate.

"Want it?" He offered me the plate.

"No," I answered. "I already ate. I'll go shopping tomorrow. I'm sorry there isn't a wider selection in the fridge."

"It's fine," he said. "Should I turn on the TV?"

"No, I like it like this, unless you want to."

"No, I also like it like this, it feels like home."

I looked at him for a minute and smiled.

"I'm thinking of going back to school," I blurted out.

Roy turned his head toward me and his eyes urged me to continue.

"I think it's time for me to go back to college."

"What would you like to study?"

No one had ever asked me that question. *What do I want?*

"I don't know," I whispered. "Maybe something having to do with people..."

"In what manner?"

"I don't really know, but the subject of the soul intrigues me. Why people react in a certain way, how they choose how to deal with incidents..."

Roy didn't say a word, but his eyes stayed with mine and said exactly what I already knew.

"Correct, I'm looking for answers. But it still seems interesting to me."

"So?"

"So what?"

"So, what are you going to do about it?"

I hadn't yet thought of the practical side, but my answer came out clear and concise. "I'm going to go to college and find out."

"Let's turn the television on and see if there's anything interesting on," Roy leaned his back against the sofa, and I thought I saw a shadow of smile at the corner of his mouth.

At eleven o'clock that night, we turned off the television and went to our bedrooms. I was tired and expected to fall right asleep. Suddenly, there was a rustling sound from the front of the room. The hallway outside my door was dark and quiet. I closed my eyes and pulled the blanket closer to my body. Again the sound—this time, for a split second, I saw a shapeless bubble rolling toward the entrance. It was the first bubble in a long time. I shrugged off the blanket and stepped out of bed barefoot. The bubble was gone.

I followed, and looking toward the front door, it seemed the transparent air there was moving around. I moved along the hallway to the basement door, which was ajar. *Funny, I always lock it after myself.* Fear crept like a worm from my feet up to my chest. I walked back to my bedroom and opened the door. Roy was sleeping soundly, his mouth open and his breathing regular. "Roy," I whispered and he woke up immediately.

"What happened?" he asked. He sat up in bed, completely alert.

"I think there is someone in the basement."

"You heard something?"

"No, the door is open and I always lock it behind me."

"Wait here, I'm going to check."

"I'm coming with you."

Roy let out a brief sigh and said, "Follow me quietly."

We reached the door of the basement. It looked to be open even wider than before. Roy cocked his ear toward the basement and gave me the sign to keep quiet. *Really, as if I was going to have a conversation with him at that moment.* We didn't hear a thing. He turned on the light and immediately looked inside, and down. Nothing could be heard, nothing moved. The basement was as silent as the rest of the rooms in the house.

We crept down the stairs slowly. He was first and I followed. Nothing had changed since I was down there the last time. Most of the boxes were lying on the floor, still closed, except for those I left open. Before he could ask, I said that I had been going through them.

"Does everything look normal to you?"

I took another glance around. "Yes, everything seems to be exactly as I left it."

"What brought you down to the basement?" he asked again. "Did you hear something?"

"No. I don't know. I woke up all of the sudden. Maybe I heard something. I don't remember now..." I had no intention of telling him about the ghosts I'd been seeing.

"What did you find in these boxes?"

"All sorts of things. I found toys, dolls, board games—they're all new, still in their original wrapping."

"Why didn't you use them when you were little?"

"Because I didn't know they existed."

"I don't understand."

"I have never seen these things before."

"So whose are they?"

"I don't have a clue. Somebody named Ethel. That's what it says on the box."

"Who's Ethel? Do you know anybody named Ethel?"

"No! Actually, now that I think about it, I've seen that name before, but I don't remember where."

"Try to remember. Maybe it's the answer to the mystery of the boxes."

"I've seen this name, I'm sure of it." My thoughts rambled about, trying to open a box of faraway memories. Now I was sure that name should tell me something, but I couldn't focus on my memory; everything was foggy.

"I know," I said suddenly. The fog had lifted all at once and I recalled the page I found in the kitchen pantry after my mother died.

Roy looked at me inquisitively.

I explained. "After my mother died, I was cleaning the kitchen pantry, and inside one of the boxes I found the birth certificate of someone named Ethel."

"Where's the certificate?"

"I don't remember where I put it. I was in a bad way, and I must have put it somewhere without paying attention."

"It could be that those things belong to someone who lived here before, or maybe your parents let someone store these games in their basement."

"Could be. I'll try to look for the certificate."

"What's in this box?" asked Roy, pointing to a box with the letters sent to my parents from school and were never answered.

"That is an exhaustive description of the involvement of my parents in my life as a student and their worry, their concern..."

Roy heard the sarcasm in my voice and understood. He didn't ask to see the contents of the box.

We opened other boxes. They all contained old objects; some were familiar to me and some were not. There was an old kettle without a spout, a rusty iron, a few old books held together by spider webs. In one of the boxes there was a shower curtain carefully folded, two rugs that looked new, and cups for holding toothpaste and toothbrushes. They all looked like they hadn't been touched by human hands. I turned the box around to see if anything was written on the side, but there were no markings whatsoever on any of the sides. While I was busy with the boxes, Roy strolled around the room. Every once in a while, he would pick up some of the old objects; he showed me an old gramophone and told me he thought it still worked.

"Take it," I said.

"No," he said. "It's really an archeological specimen. I couldn't take it."

"Take it. Anyway, I don't intend to use it, and if it stays here covered in dust and mildew, I'll have to get rid of it in the end."

"OK, you talked me into it."

Roy continued toward the other side of the room and I continued to dig through the boxes. Suddenly he came over to me with a small brown box in his hand. It was a miniature treasure chest. There were two thick parallel metal lines drawn across the lid, which was locked with a tiny key that was still in the keyhole.

"Where did you find this?"

"Under the shelf. It was next to the wall, like someone didn't want it to be found."

I took it from his hands and turned it upside down. There was the rustle of papers coming from inside.

"Let's try and open it. We need a sharp object to break the lock," I said.

Roy took the box from me and gave the lock a sharp tap. It broke right away and fell on the floor.

"It looks like the box has been here a long time," he said.

We lifted the lid. On the inner side of it was a sticker in the shape of a heart with the word "love" written on it in red marker. Inside the box were various slips of paper. Some of them were cut into different shapes—some in the shape of a heart. There was also one letter inside an envelope. It looked like the box belonged to a young girl. I fingered the shreds of paper, knowing they would disintegrate under my fingers. I took one of the notes and read, "My love, our love is eternal." There were tiny stars drawn underneath the writing. On another piece, it said, "I love you so much. Always." I continued to rummage around and caress the little notes—another one had "Annabel Lee," by Edgar Allen Poe, written on it:

Annabel Lee
It was many and many a year ago,
In a kingdom by the sea,
That a maiden there lived whom you may know
By the name of Annabel Lee;
And this maiden she lived with no other thought
Than to love and be loved by me.

I was a child and she was a child,
In this kingdom by the sea,
But we loved with a love that was more than love—
I and my Annabel Lee—
With a love that the winged seraphs of Heaven
Coveted her and me.

And this was the reason that, long ago,
In this kingdom by the sea,
A wind blew out of a cloud, chilling
My beautiful Annabel Lee;
So that her highborn kinsmen came
And bore her away from me,
To shut her up in a sepulcher
In this kingdom by the sea.

The angels, not half so happy in Heaven,
Went envying her and me—
Yes!—that was the reason (as all men know,
In this kingdom by the sea)
That the wind came out of the cloud by night,
Chilling and killing my Annabel Lee.

But our love it was stronger by far than the love
Of those who were older than we—
Of many far wiser than we—
And neither the angels in Heaven above
Nor the demons down under the sea
Can ever dissever my soul from the soul
Of the beautiful Annabel Lee;

For the moon never beams, without bringing me dreams
Of the beautiful Annabel Lee;
And the stars never rise, but I feel the bright eyes
Of the beautiful Annabel Lee;
And so, all the night-tide, I lie down by the side
Of my darling—my darling—my life and my bride,
In her sepulcher there by the sea—
In her tomb by the sounding sea.

Underneath the poem, it said, "In life and in death—together."

When had the tears begun to stream from my eyes? They were dripping onto the paper in my hand. I didn't know whether it was the poem that moved me so much or the sentence written at the end of it. When I lifted my eyes, I saw Roy's incredulous expression. He took the page from me and began to read it. Several minutes went by before he placed the page in my hand. When he spoke, his voice sounded a bit hoarse.

"Would you like to go upstairs?"

"No, let's stay down here a little longer."

Roy sat down next to me, his shoulder touching mine. The chirping of the crickets could be heard outside, but inside, in the stifling basement, there was complete silence, disturbed only by the rustling of papers in my hand.

I picked up another piece of paper with the simple words "I love you" written on it, without drawings or decorations. One sentence in the center of the page, joining other pages that together told the love story between a boy and a girl; a story with an unknown ending.

I reached the bottom of the chest where a single letter rested. The envelope was open. There were brown stains on the sides from years of neglect and mildew. I took the letter out. It was folded into fours. My hands were careful not to tear the old paper as I straightened it out on my knees. It was the only piece of paper in the box that was dated. April 1973.

Nichka, my love,

Your tears are engraved on my shirt like the stains of memory. I caress them with my fingers and kiss them. That way I can feel you, as if you were still with me, next to my body. Don't cry, my love, our love is stronger than any distance. My beautiful Nichka, you know that we have our whole lives ahead of us and what is two years in comparison? Think constantly of the time when we will be together and inseparable. Think about the joy we have experienced together, the laughter. Your marvelous laughter is ringing now in my ears, overcoming the dull hum of the airplane's engines taking me away from you.

If they were to ask me what is unique about your love, my answer would be immediate: your laughter. Don't ever stop laughing—your laughter overcomes anything. I see you with your long hair spread across your shoulders, moving your head from right to left, your laughter filling my heart with happiness and hope. Please guard it well. I promise I will give you many reasons to laugh, love of my life. Have I ever told you that you are the sunrise of my life? That a rainy and gloomy day becomes instantly brighter and full of hope when you are by my side?

I want to tell you so many things, but emotions are overflowing inside me and making it hard for me to get the words out. Two years, my love, they aren't even a test for us. After all, our love is eternal. Go up to our rock every once in a while, the one we carved our love into. Every time you feel sad, go to it, until I return to you and we pick up from the exact point we stopped and these two years will disappear as if they never were.

Take care of yourself, my Annabel, take care of our love, the joy of life within you and I will try to move time forward as fast as I can.

I love you so very, very much,
Your David.

This time I didn't even try to stop the tears. Roy put his hand around my shoulders. We sat next to each other and a sudden sadness enveloped us both. The silence around us was agreeable at that moment. The cricket stopped singing its song, and only the echo of our breathing was heard. A single ray of light suddenly made its way through the window's shutters. Morning had broken. We realized we had spent an entire night in the basement, so full of the house's secrets.

"Shall we go up?" asked Roy.

"Yes."

We went to the kitchen and Roy made us both some tea. It was cold outside and the chill had entered the house. A cup of tea was exactly what we both needed at that moment. Roy made the hot drinks in silence. I didn't want to speak, and I didn't want to hear anything. The letter and the notes in the box affected me in an inexplicable way. It was the first time I had encountered a love so powerful. The old, disintegrating page with its blue faded ink had guarded this special love for all this time; its hiding place couldn't diminish it at all. Even now, with every fiber of my being, I could feel the depth of emotion that arose from the words that were saturated with the sorrow of separation.

The silence in the kitchen continued. Apparently, we both needed time. Finally, I heard Roy say, "How about we stay home today and not go to work?"

For a minute I wanted to resist, but the moment passed. I answered that I thought it was an excellent idea.

"What should we do?"

"How about we get in the car and let it decide where to go?"

I sat back in the seat and closed my eyes. Roy led us out of town. Every once in a while, we'd stop somewhere that looked appealing. We didn't have a plan, and that was what made it so enjoyable. When we began to make our way back, it was already ten o'clock at night. Roy stopped at a gas station. He was a little tired and needed a drink to refresh himself. We sat at the table in desperate need of cleaning. Flies swarmed around us, looking for the crumbs of food left behind by other diners. I cleaned the table with my hand and set down the two bottles of Coca-Cola and the sandwiches we had ordered. All of the sudden Roy asked me the question I had been trying to avoid for many months.

"Eva, how come your father married your mother, a Jew?"

"I really don't know," I said. "Maybe she kept her Jewishness from him too, like she hid it from me."

"Do you think there was a chance though that he knew?"

"If he did, then he was even crazier than I thought."

"You're right, it doesn't make sense," Roy said thoughtfully.

In a momentary flashback, I saw my father's face in front of me, and then I said the following sentence, which had been buried inside me ever since I was a little girl—buried and covered in infinite layers of camouflage. "He hated her!"

Roy lifted his head and looked at me in surprise.

"And she him," I continued.

"I don't understand. If they hated one another, why did they continue to live together? What brought them to such a level of hatred?"

"These are questions I don't have the answers to, Roy. These things are also incomprehensible to me."

"I mean, they could have separated," he said, thinking out loud. "It was in the eighties, people got divorced."

"I really don't know," I said. "I wish I understood more."

The atmosphere became uneasy. "OK, we need to get moving," he said. I finished my drink and got up.

"You know, I would like to know," I said.

Roy nodded and opened the door to the car for me.

23

I came home from the office late the next day after trying to finish the work that had accumulated on my desk. It was seven o'clock in the evening when I got home. Ten minutes later there was a knock on the door—soft at first, but when I didn't answer, they became stronger and more demanding. Finally, I asked who it was.

"Attorney Shapiro." George's lawyer.

"Are you alone?" I asked.

"Yes."

I opened the door. A man about thirty years old, with a round face and rosy cheeks, stood before me. He reached out to shake my hand and introduced himself. His voice was deep, in complete contrast with his baby face. I invited him to sit down and asked if he would like something hot to drink.

"Thank you, I'll settle for a glass of water."

"Are you allowed to be here?" I asked. "As far as I know, according to law, the defendant's lawyer isn't allowed to meet with the plaintiff."

"You're right," he said and his plump body sank into my patched-up sofa. He took a sip of water and continued, ignoring my comment. "You must be wondering what brought me to you two weeks before the trial date."

I nodded.

"Well, I don't know if you're aware of the fact that the trial won't be easy. George and his friends intend to make it as hard as possible for you."

"What do you mean?"

He moved around on the sofa to adjust his bottom and said, "Well, they intend to show up in court en masse and make a lot of noise." I waited for him to continue. "You know George. He's a stubborn man; he won't back down easily."

"What does he have to back down about? I don't understand what you mean."

"He won't let go of the opportunity to show you in a negative light."

"Meaning?"

"He claims that you lured him to your home."

"And how exactly does he say I did that?" I asked. The indifference of my tone covered up the anger that was boiling inside me.

"You asked him to come and fix your window."

"So?"

"He claims you insisted that he be the one to perform the installation."

"What?"

"He claims that he suggested sending one of his employees, but that you asked for him explicitly. He claims you tried to seduce him when he got to your house."

"That I seduced him?"

"Yes."

I couldn't believe what I was hearing. This story was so grossly distorted, and this man was sitting in front of me making it sound like I was the one on trial.

"George claims that you complied with him and that if the neighbor hadn't come in when she did, you would have continued in mutual consent."

"I don't believe it," I mumbled. Dizziness hit me. My mouth was dry, so I got up to get myself a glass of water. *The man is just trying to scare me. Calm down. There's no way the facts could be distorted that much.* Suddenly I was frightened. *What if the judge believed this slanted story? What if the judge himself belongs to this gang?* Disturbing thoughts ran around in my head and made me realize that the trial wasn't going to be simple. *How naïve of me—I have barely met with my own lawyer. He must think the same thing—he hasn't contacted me since our first meeting. He only said that he would work on it, told me there was nothing to worry about, and asked me to leave things for him to handle. Now this man, with his misleading outward appearance, is sitting here. And he has the nerve to threaten me?* I walked out of the kitchen with my glass of water and asked him to leave.

"Don't you want to hear why I'm here?" he asked. He continued to sit on the couch, ignoring my request.

"Not especially," I answered.

"I'm going to tell you anyway. George is prepared, despite the misunderstanding between you, to compensate you with an amount of money decided between the two of you. He is prepared to forget the whole thing. He just wants to go back to his routine and leave this incident behind him. What do you say?"

The lawyer's round face suddenly turned into the face of an animal on the prowl for his prey. His venomous tongue moved smoothly, trying to entice me, the victim, to get closer to his mouth so he could swallow me up.

"I say that you can tell that scum of a creature you are protecting that I don't intend to sign any deal with him. Tell him that the truth is stronger than any of his and his friends' threats and manipulations. And besides, isn't Shapiro a Jewish name?"

Mr. Shapiro got up from the sofa, looked at me with a vague expression, and left the house, slamming the door behind him.

I collapsed onto the sofa. My hands were shaking and an intense nausea hit me. I ran to the bathroom and emptied the contents of my stomach. The mirror above the sink showed me the terror written all over my face. My courage thus far had been phony. *Who am I to fight these grownups when violence is their way of life?* Suddenly the real danger I was in became clear to me. This was like David fighting Goliath. Young, inexperienced in life, naïve to the point of stupidity, with my false show of bravado and adherence to the truth—but the bravado was only a mask that helped me feel worthy and valuable. *What should I do now?*

The threat filled up the entire room and succeeded in undermining my self-confidence. I got into the shower, feeling like I had been raped—like George's attempt had now been completed. The lawyer's words echoed in my ears: "George is prepared to forget the whole thing and return to his routine." *It would be so simple,* I told myself, *to just drop the whole thing, take the compensation and move on. So why not just agree?*

I scrubbed my body with a sponge until my limbs were scratched and red. I had to rid myself of this visit. But instead, when I left the bathroom and sat in the living room in clean clothes, I was still left with the fear.

When I told Roy about what had happened, he lost control. It was the first time I had ever seen him lose it.

"Listen to me," he said. "You have to get out of here. You can't stay in the house alone. As the trial gets closer, they'll increase the pressure on you."

"I don't know what to do," I said. I didn't argue this time. I didn't play the hero.

"I want you to move in with me," he continued.

"What?"

"You have to get out of this house. You can't stay here."

"But Roy, your parents—"

"My parents will handle it."

"I mean, your mother hates me..."

"She doesn't hate you—she's just like that... Not nice."

"Roy..."

"Eva, right now you cannot indulge in 'I won't feel comfortable.' Your life is seriously in danger. These are people who have no boundaries and no conscience, and they will stop at nothing to prevent you from getting to that courtroom. Your life is more important than that."

There was a lot of logic to what he said. Besides, in the state I was in, I was easy to convince.

"I'll come," I said finally.

Roy came up to me and this time hugged me tight. "Don't worry, everything will be fine," he whispered in my ear. "I won't leave you alone."

Somehow his words were calming, and so was being in his arms.

I moved some of my things into his room over the weekend; his mother passed by, muttered a reserved greeting, and went on her way. *These are difficult times*, I thought to myself. Roy moved into the living room and I slept in his bed. He was always there when I got home from work—he didn't leave me alone for one moment. Donna stopped by every once in a while for a visit. She was angry that I didn't come to live with her, but she also looked relieved.

***

The day of the trial arrived. It was hot. The flowers were bowing their heads and the people were moving slowly as if they were carrying the burden of the sun on their shoulders. It was eight o'clock in the morning when Roy and I left for the courthouse. Donna met us there. The courtroom was packed—a few faces were familiar from my encounter with the neo-Nazi group. Above them all was the figure of their speaker, the one that called me "dear child." His eyes searched for mine and he wouldn't relent until our eyes met. My eyes fell first. My lawyer told me he had arranged for me to testify after George. "That's a good thing," he tried to reassure me. "The jury usually remembers the last person to speak." His words did not mollify me. I was terribly tense, and for a moment I was sorry to have gone forward with the whole process. *I should have given in*, I said in my heart; *George is known all over the city, and there's no way they would decide against him.* I imagined him waving hello to one of the jury members and receiving a nod in return.

I sat down on the chair designated for me and my lawyer shook my hand and promised it would be all right. Of course, I didn't believe a word. I looked around. People were coming to see the show. Nobody was really interested in the truth or justice; they wanted a show that would interrupt the routine of their lives, and George provided exactly what they wanted. He got up on the stand with a smile and before he sat down he waved a number of times to his acquaintances. He glanced over at me once, a mocking smile on his face. Every one of his movements testified to his self-confidence, as if he already knew the outcome of the trial.

His lawyer, Mr. Shapiro, with his questions, was able to paint a completely different picture from what really happened. Although at my house he had moved with confidence, here he seemed more tired, maybe even defeated. He approached the witness stand where George was seated and leaned against it like a leaf hanging on to a tree trunk. Every once in a while he would return to his table, sit in his chair, look over one of the sheets of paper on the table, get back up, and return to the witness stand. George wasn't pleased with his behavior and from time to time scrunched up his face in anger. One time he even asked his lawyer if he would like him to go into more detail.

Finally, his testimony was finished and it was my turn. Would my body respond—would I be able to get up from the chair? I heard my name being called, but I remained seated. My attorney squeezed my hand and urged me to go to the witness stand. I turned my head around and caught

Donna's worried expression. Roy sat next to her looking at me and smiled in encouragement. I got up and with hesitant steps, went up to the witness stand.

"Are you Eva Brown, the son of John and Maria Brown?" asked the court bailiff.

"No!"

There was complete silence in the courtroom. I knew every eye was focused on me. The judge leaned forward and asked the bailiff to repeat the question.

"I am the daughter of John Brown and Sonia Schwartz."

The silence was broken all at once. People who didn't know me personally, but knew my parents, thought that perhaps I had lost my mind. I saw George smile and then become serious.

"My dear, you must speak the truth," the judge whispered to me.

"Your honor, my mother's former name was Sonia Schwartz. When she married my father, she changed her name to Maria Brown. I would like to use her former name."

The judge gave the order to the court clerk to write down my words. I looked over to the table where George sat with his lawyer. It appeared to me that the attorney looked a bit smaller. His face suddenly took on a more serious expression and he fidgeted in his chair uncomfortably.

When the words left my mouth, my fear left me. I was no longer afraid of the questions posed to me and I knew exactly what I was going to say. The words came out as if they were written on a sheet of paper in front of me, but they came from my heart. I walked off the witness stand taller by several inches. Roy had a broad smile on his face and an expression in his eyes that had never been there before. More witnesses took the stand after me, among them Donna, whose testimony was concrete and concise. George's lawyer called a number of his friends to talk in his favor.

The turbulence inside of me took on a tangible shape. It was maybe the first time in my life that I felt proud of myself. I hadn't planned my words in advance; they were there waiting for the first opportunity to come to light. I felt as if a huge burden that I had been carrying for a long time had been lifted, and I could now breathe easier.

Roy and Donna greeted me after the testimony phase. The verdict would be given within a week. Roy didn't say a word. He hugged my shoulders with one arm and walked me out of the courtroom. In the car, while driving home, he still didn't speak. But when we arrived, he didn't get out of the car right away. He turned to me and said only four words. "I'm proud of you."

I wanted to go home, but Roy asked me to stay with him until the verdict came down.

Exactly one week after that day, we were called back to the courthouse to hear the jury's decision. When we walked into the courtroom, I walked toward the table where my lawyer was waiting. Mr. Shapiro suddenly approached me, put out his hand to shake mine, and said, "Good luck." He then returned to his table, sat down next to his client, and looked forward toward the center of the room. He and George didn't exchange one word between them.

The judge entered the courtroom and sat down. Murmurs spread throughout the room. A group of skinheads came in and sat down next to George's friends. The judge asked for silence and turned to the jury.

George was found guilty of attempted rape. When he heard the verdict, he pounded the table with his fist and I heard him hiss, "Whores." The judge turned to him and asked him to calm down, but he was already out of his chair and beginning to scream. "Whores, that's what they are, a bunch of whores." His lawyer didn't try to stop him. He continued to sit in his chair and let George yell. The courtroom security guard approached him, but George pushed him away and he fell on his back. The spectators were hysterical. Some were encouraging him and others were gaping in shock while enjoying the scene playing out before them.

The judge pounded his gavel on the table and demanded quiet in the courtroom. George wasn't calming down. He threw everything from the table up in the air, grabbed his chair, and threw it into the center of the room. Suddenly the door opened and policemen rushed inside. They tried to get near him, but it was difficult because George was ranting like a rabid gorilla. His arms were flailing about. He was shuffling around heavily until it looked like he was about to collapse any minute. The policemen were finally able to grab him and, with great effort, handcuff his hands behind his back. George was removed from the courtroom to the sound of repressed chuckling coming from people who had remained in their places to see the humiliation of a man they had recently admired.

Roy again asked me to stay until the sentence was given, but he reluctantly agreed to let me return home. I packed up my few belongings and he followed me to my house. Before the car was even parked, I saw what they had done. On the front of the house the word "Whore" was sprayed in huge red letters. The front door had been broken down. When we got closer to the entrance the strong stench of feces overpowered us. The entrance hall, floor and walls, was covered in some kind of animal feces. The door to the basement was detached from its frame and lying on the stairway. The living room wasn't any better. The powerful stench of urine rose from there, and it was impossible to go inside. I ran from the house, feces from the floor smeared on the soles of my shoes, unable to take the humiliation and the cruelty. I sat on the grass and wailed loudly. The watery tears washed over my face as if they were trying to purify it from defilement. I took my shoes off and threw them far away from me. The stink was still too heavy to take. Everything was contaminated and filthy. The insult stung like poison oak.

Roy was by my side. He stroked my head and said, "I hosed the house down. Everything is wet. I suggest we come back tomorrow and take out the furniture to let it dry. In the meantime, there's nothing we can do"

"Let's go," I said. We made the drive to his house in silence. There was nothing to say. His mother met us at the entrance. Her eyes expressed surprise. I didn't have the energy to deal with her unpleasantness. I walked past her in silence and went into Roy's bedroom, which I had vacated less than two hours earlier.

I tried hard not to give in to despair. My earlier satisfaction and pride had disappeared without a trace. The bold threats had succeeded in deflating me, turning me back into a little girl who wanted her father by her side, who needed his strength to feel safe. That night in bed I spoke to him, asking for his help like a little girl asking to hold his hand when learning to take her first steps. My equilibrium was gone, and all the talk about change, about newfound strength and courage, did me no good now. I needed a grownup—somebody to tell me that everything would be OK, that he would watch over me and protect me. One more abusive action would devastate me completely. Lying on the bed with only underwear on, unable to bear the touch of clothes on my skin, I heard Roy knock softly on the door and came into the room. He sat at the edge of the bed and asked me how I was.

"Depressed," I answered.

"From what?" he asked.

"From what? From not being able to see an end to this," I answered sadly.

"Eva, don't give up. You're holding yourself together heroically. You can't back down now. It will be over soon. The sentence will be given in the next few weeks and then there will be nothing left to do. Be patient, but don't give up on me."

"Oh, Roy, I don't have the energy to be strong anymore." I was on the verge of tears.

"Come here." He pulled me into his chest. As he did so, the blanket slid off, revealing my chest. Roy lowered his head and looked at me. I made no effort to cover myself and remained unmoving in his arms. His eyes looked at my breasts for a moment, then he hugged me to him again as he whispered my name in a hoarse voice. He leaned back and covered me with the blanket. My heart was beating like crazy. Roy looked into my eyes, then bent down and kissed my lips with a tender, almost indiscernible kiss. He got up and gently closed the door behind him.

24

I didn't have time to think about what had happened between Roy and me in the following weeks. I walked around in a daze. The upcoming sentencing was hovering over my head like a butcher's knife. I wanted it to be over already. I was hoping that the court's final decision would put an end to all the threats and scare tactics.

Time has two sides—a devilish side and an angelic side. The devil makes it seem as if time is standing still; the angel gives you the feeling that it's running by too fast. The devil had the upper hand this time. It seemed like time wasn't moving at all. One day followed the next, and every minute felt like an eternity. I preferred not to appear in court. I had already demonstrated my daring and didn't see any need to prove anything to anyone. Roy went to the court session, and I went to the office. It was senseless to wait at home. I had to keep myself busy. He came to the office at noon.

"Come on," he said. "Let's go get a bite to eat."

I refused. "No! First I want to hear what happened."

Roy insisted. "I will tell you everything outside while you eat something."

Before the beginning of the trial, and even before that, I had lost my appetite. Entire days went by where I didn't put a thing in my stomach.

Roy tried to convince me to eat, but my appetite was nowhere to be found. The tension replaced my desire for food and the threats made me want to disappear. I had lost more than thirteen pounds. My clothes hung on me like rags on a scarecrow. I hadn't been wearing any makeup and completely neglected my outward appearance. I only had enough energy for minimal function, and there was nothing left to take care of my other basic needs.

"How long did he get?" I asked as soon as we sat down in the little coffee shop that served sandwiches and soft drinks.

"Start eating and I'll tell you," answered Roy.

Roy ordered a guacamole sandwich and French fries for me. He ordered an egg sandwich and salad for himself. He waited until I took a bite of the sandwich and then he told me that George was sentenced to six months in a Chicago jail. In addition, he was ordered to compensate me and given a warning not to come near me or my house for the next two years.

"I don't want his money," I blurted out.

"I figured that's what you'd say."

"Let him keep his money. I don't want to touch it."

"I have an idea what we can do with the money," he said, hiding a smile.

I lifted my head up and looked at him with indifference. "I don't want that money!" I repeated.

"Don't take the money. You can pass it on to someone else," he said.

"To whom?" My curiosity was piqued.

"Maybe to some charity that provides assistance to Jews or connected somehow to Judaism."

I looked at him incredulously. *What a brilliant idea.*

"That would be sweet revenge on George. What do you think?"

I gave him an enormous smile.

"Sometimes I don't understand where you get such brilliant ideas. I mean, you were such a terrible student," I teased him. Then I became serious. "So, what do you suggest?"

"I suggest we start looking for a charity to donate George's generous contribution."

We agreed to meet the next afternoon at the library. We were hoping to find a list of all the aid organizations involving Jews and choose one that seemed suitable.

Ira the librarian welcomed us with a tired smile. At first, she didn't recognize us, but after several seconds her eyes lit up and she said, "You were here a while ago. Did you find what you were looking for?"

"Yes," we said, nodding.

"I'm glad," she said. "What can I do for you today?"

We explained what we were looking for. She thought for a moment and suggested we go over to the computer on the far side of the room; she gave us a box of microfiche to go over.

"Microfiche?" I looked at Roy in amazement after Ira left and went back to her desk at the front of the library. "Remind me what year it is?"

Roy smiled. "You forget, Eva, that everything that happens in large cities comes to us in delay. If you want, we can go to the Chicago library. I am sure that the twentieth century has reached them."

Time ticked by. The microfiche contained a long list of Jewish organizations throughout the United States. We tried to find one just a few hours from our town so we decided to check by area. We finally found a few organizations. Three in Chicago and another two east of our town.

"We need the Internet," I said.

"Chicago. We're going to Chicago tomorrow."

"Chicago, tomorrow," I agreed.

We both left early from work and were on the road to Chicago by noon. A feeling of optimism washed over me, but I also knew deep inside that my troubles weren't over with the verdict; sweet revenge, however, sweetened the fear of the unknown. I was determined to make sure George knew exactly where his tainted money was being donated. I would make sure that the money would serve a good purpose despite its source.

This thought accompanied me throughout the drive. Roy looked over at me every so often and smiled at the feeling of optimism in the air. We enjoyed pleasant conversation, but the incident from more than a week ago still stood between us. We were careful not to come near it.

We arrived in Chicago as a gray sky heralded the evening of a cold winter day. Strong winds were blowing and the buildings seemed to be swaying. People bundled up in coats, like headless creatures, were hurrying to their homes. The map directed us to the Chicago Public Library. We had chosen it because we heard it was one of the most beautiful libraries in Chicago. However, as someone coming from a small town that still used microfiche and cellphones were only possessed by precious few, we were afraid of getting lost.

The library was revealed to us in all its glory. The building was built from red brick with huge glass windows inviting the sunlight to enter and illuminate the massive reading room. The building's roof was adorned with statues that looked like enormous gods protecting the statue of an owl, the symbol of wisdom.

The inner structure was no less impressive. The high ceiling gave the feeling of infinity. Upstairs, on the ninth floor of the building was a winter garden, a wonderful place covered by a glass roof divided into squares. The residual light from outside and the abundant vegetation created a vast, special space that lent a feeling of intimacy opposite the meticulous and lavish architecture. We had no idea we were going to a place that was much more than just storing books. Touring the building was so appealing to us that we forgot why we had come. It was already six o'clock in the evening when we pulled ourselves together and approached the information desk on the third floor. The pleasant librarian announced that the library was closing in one hour and asked us to hurry. She sent us to a room with several computers and explained how to conduct a quick search.

The hour passed quickly and we still hadn't found what we were looking for. The lights began to flash, signaling to the last visitors that the time had come to leave. Roy and I looked at each other with disappointment that we weren't able to fulfill the goal we had come for.

"What should we do?" I asked.

Roy thought for a minute, and then he said, "There are two options. We could go home and return another time, or stay here overnight and come back tomorrow morning."

"I think we should stay," I answered, after giving it some thought. "It's already too late to drive all the way back in complete darkness, and you must be really tired. And besides, it's important for me to finish this business as quickly as possible. I don't want to take the money until I know what I'm going to do with it."

"OK." Roy nodded his head. "Now we need to find a hotel for the night."

After about an hour of searching, we found a small hotel on one of the side streets in the city with a price that suited our wallets. It was a modest, clean place, and a light breakfast was even included in the price. We entered the room and were surprised to discover that there was one double bed.

"Would you like me to go back to reception and ask about two twin beds?" he asked after he saw my hesitation.

"No, that's not necessary." I tried to hide my embarrassment. That moment in his bedroom surfaced in my mind. Roy tried to keep the atmosphere noncommittal. He proposed that I take a shower and try to fall asleep first so that his snoring wouldn't bother me. He got into bed only after he was sure I was asleep.

I got up before him in the morning. He was asleep on his back, his mouth closed and his sleep calm and quiet. When he woke up, I was already dressed and ready to go. We went down to breakfast on the first floor together and waited for nine o'clock, when the library would reopen its doors.

We were among the first to arrive at the library. The enormous hall was all ours. The woman by the counter recognized us and nodded at us. We sat down in front of the computer we had abandoned the day before and concentrated entirely on the task for which we had come. Here we also encountered a very long list of Jewish organizations, but with the help of the librarian, we were able to trim down the list to just a few that were located a reasonable distance from our hometown.

There were organizations whose purpose was to strengthen the bond between the Jews living in the diaspora and the State of Israel. Others dealt with sending youths to Israel and bringing Israeli youths to meet local Jewish teenagers. One organization provided organized tours to Israel. One association's main goal drew my attention; they conducted conferences and summits in order to raise money to further Jewish education among Jewish youths in the United States. I wrote down the name of that organization and continued to search. Roy scrolled the pages slowly and allowed me to read what was written with my own eyes.

Suddenly, something caught my eye. "Go back," I requested. On the screen, there was a women's organization whose goal is to empower women and assist them through health education, contact with the community, and providing an emergency response service. As I read further, I realized that this was exactly what I was looking for: an association supporting women who have suffered from violence and sexual abuse, allowing them to escape the cycle of violence and realize their potential in order to build an independent and healthy life.

"This is it," I said with confidence. "This is what I want."

Roy nodded in agreement. "Jews and women," he said. "Exactly what I was thinking to myself." He printed the page with the details of the organization. We left the library extremely pleased.

"Hold on to this paper. Don't lose it," I said to Roy.

"Don't worry," he said. "I put it in my pocket next to my gun." He winked at me, and I gave him an affectionate shove.

"Since we're already here, why don't we take the opportunity to see a bit of the city?"

"I think that's a great idea." My mood had improved. I felt that I was moving toward closing another one of the unsuccessful chapters of my life.

"What do you suggest?"

"Since these winds are unbearable, I suggest we go up to the Sears Tower and look out over the city from up high."

"You're right. I don't want to walk around outside and be gone with the wind."

Roy smiled at my buoyant mood. He took my hand in his and pulled me toward the street. We decided to take a taxi and leave the car in the parking lot. The taxi dropped us off at the entrance to Sears Tower, one of the tallest buildings in the world, which towered over all the other buildings in the city. Its black façade separated it from the other structures in the area. When we entered the building, the clerk in the lobby suggested we take one of the pamphlets lying in a pile in front of him; we learned that apparently the building had 130 elevators.

We stood in front of one of the elevator doors that led to the top floor. A number of people stood next to us. Some looked like tourists, like us, and others looked like businessmen. The elevator to our left arrived. It stopped on the number 1 and then came down to the ground floor. The elevator doors opened up and people began to stream out of it. Roy and I stepped aside in order to let them through.

"Eva?" I heard a familiar voice.

I turned my head around and to my great amazement caught Mickey's surprised expression.

"What are you doing here?" he asked.

My surprise was so overwhelming that I couldn't find the words to answer him. I didn't know whether to tell him I was just sightseeing or explain that we had come to find something at the public library.

"Hello, Michael." Roy held out his hand and Mickey turned around toward Roy.

"Roy, you're here too?" He returned Roy's handshake, and his eyes met mine. "What are you doing in Chicago?" he asked.

"We came to the public library; we needed to search for something—"

"We decided to do a little sightseeing," Roy said.

"I see."

I don't understand a thing, I told myself. Someone, somewhere in the universe, is playing a joke on me; I'm like a pawn on a chessboard with an invisible hand determining its path on the board.

"How are you, Eva?" Mickey turned his face toward me and his back to Roy.

"Fine... I'm fine," I stuttered.

"I'm sorry I haven't called. I've had a rough few days, but I meant to call, of course."

"It's OK, Mickey. I know you've been busy," I said diplomatically.

"That's not what I meant," he said. I didn't react.

"Is it possible for you to stay in Chicago tomorrow as well?" He was still completely ignoring Roy's presence.

"I don't think so," I answered.

"We're going home today!" Roy stood beside me. "We only came to see the city from above, and then we're going home."

Mickey heard what Roy said, but he continued to look at me. "I'd like us to get together," he said, ignoring my lack of reaction to what he said before. "I'll call you this week and we'll talk. OK?"

"Fine," I said and looked up at the number showing on the elevator to our left. The doors opened. Roy took my hand and dragged me inside. Mickey and I continued to look at each other until the elevator doors came between us again.

Our bright mood was replaced by the need for the trip to end. The events that had taken place in my life since my last visit with Mickey had created a barrier that prevented me from any thought about our relationship. All of the sudden that barrier collapsed, and I was flooded with fractured images of a relationship that ended before its time.

We reached the top floor and the view was impressive. Chicago was spread out before us like a colorful quilt. Tall towers and short ones, straight roads and curved, quiet traffic that moved by its own rules. A whole life was going on down there in silence. I stood in front of one of the windows and looked out. All of a sudden I felt Roy's arm on mine. He said, "You've been standing in the same place for fifteen minutes. Don't you want to see the city from other directions?"

"Yes," I said, but I didn't make a move.

"Come on."

"No, Roy. I want to go." I saw the hurt look on his face, but I didn't change my mind. My mood had darkened, and all I wanted was to be in the car on our way home.

***

Two weeks went by. Mickey called as promised.

"I'd like to come see you this weekend," he said.

At ten after six that night, I heard a knock on the door. I opened it and he came close and hugged me tight. His mouth sought out mine, but I said, "Not now." I broke free of his embrace. He was carrying a small backpack, and it was obvious he intended to stay at least until tomorrow. He looked really tired to me. Tiny wrinkles created lines on his forehead and cheeks. His hair had turned gray at the temples and was in disarray.

I brought him a cup of coffee and told him that dinner would be ready in one hour. We sat down in the living room. He looked around at the stained furniture and maybe wondered about the smell, but he didn't say anything.

"How are you, Eva?" he asked.

"OK," I answered quietly.

"You must be angry with me."

I thought for a minute before answering. "I don't think I'm angry. I just don't understand what's happening to you—what's happening to us."

Mickey looked down and played with his coffee cup. "What's happening to me has to do with my father," he said finally. "It's also affecting us."

I was silent, so he continued. "I didn't call you because I didn't want my mood to cloud our relationship."

"Why, did something happen?" I asked anxiously.

"I had a conversation with my father, a conversation we have never had before. For the first time, he talked to me about what happened to him there. I'm sure he didn't tell me everything, but he told me things he's never told me before."

His face suddenly hardened. The creases I saw earlier grew deeper and he sat hunched on the sofa. Blood was pumping through the vein on his neck and his face had darkened.

"Would you like a glass of water?" I asked with concern.

He ignored my question and began to speak. "Two weeks ago, my father wasn't feeling well. He had a cold, a cough—nothing out of the ordinary. My mother made him a cup of tea and made sure he ate something. But the cold got worse. His cough became so bad that he could hardly talk. I sat next to his bed and made sure he took his medicine and drank as much as possible. His fever went up and he began to hallucinate. He said things, some that made sense and some that didn't. One day he began to cry very loudly—he was dreaming and his crying had something to do with the dream. He took my hand unexpectedly and began to mumble: 'What have

I done... What have I done?' I tried to wake him up. I even shook him, but he continued to cry. Then he began to talk. At first it seemed he was dreaming out loud again. Little by little what he was saying connected directly to the story he never told me."

Tears began to stream down his cheeks and Mickey's voice grew hoarse. I got up, brought him a glass of water, and urged him to drink. He took a few sips and blew his nose with a handkerchief he pulled out of his pocket.

"Would you like to talk about this later?" I asked.

"No, I have to talk about it now," he answered right away.

"When my father came out of that closet, after they took his parents away, he didn't know what to do. He was just fourteen years old. He wouldn't leave the house, afraid the neighbors would turn him in. Every time he heard footsteps outside the front door, he was sure they were coming to take him, so he would get back in the closet and stay in there for hours—until nighttime when all was quiet. During these weeks, he hardly ate and lost a lot of weight. He used up whatever his parents had left behind. After a number of weeks, he left the house. At first only at night and then, little by little, during the day as well. He was so lonely...he didn't have a soul in the world..." Mickey was muttering to himself, and I felt the intense pain coming from him, making its way to me as well.

"What happened after that?" I asked. I was caught up in his story and curious to hear the rest. "Did he tell you?"

Mickey nodded and continued. "One day he was coming out of the house on his way to the market where he stole food from the stalls. He didn't have a choice. He didn't have even a penny left to spend. That day he wasn't lucky. The merchant noticed him and called the police. They knew immediately that he was a Jew. They took him to the police station, where they beat him until he lost consciousness. The next day they put him on a truck with other Jews and transferred them to the ghetto. He didn't tell me everything he went through, but from what he did say, I could tell these were terrible days, full of so much suffering that he wanted to die. He even tried once to commit suicide, but someone saved him. When he told me this, he cried and mumbled: 'For what? For what?'"

"What does that mean?" I asked. "After all, he was saved in the end, and he raised a family."

"That's right. I didn't understand his reaction either, and I told him so."

"So, what did he say?" I asked.

"Nothing. He cried and fell asleep."

"And that's it?" I asked in disappointment.

Mickey sighed and shook his head. "The next day I spoke with him again. He didn't say much—just that from the day he was saved, he swore to do everything in his power to stay alive."

"What do you think he meant?" I asked.

"I'm not exactly sure, but I get the feeling he's hiding another horrible story that he doesn't want to talk about."

"Did you ask him? Try to encourage him to talk about it?"

"I tried, but it didn't help. He was crying the whole time. I couldn't sit next to him anymore and watch his suffering."

"I'm so sorry," I said, truly sorrowful. Mickey loved and admired his father so much—that was the reason he never left home. *And it's also the reason*, I thought, *that he worked in a business he didn't like and didn't interest him at all.*

Mickey's story stayed with me throughout the coming weeks. Luckily, the transfer of George's money took up most of my free time. I tried to make contact with the organization I had chosen, but it didn't come about. Most of the time, the line was busy, and when they did finally answer, the call would get cut off in the middle.

I decided to go there. I looked up their address and discovered, to my consternation, that Roy and I had not been far from there on our way back home. This organization apparently had a number of branches throughout the United States, and one of them was in a suburb of Chicago. I didn't tell Roy I was going. Ever since we had returned from our trip, a tremendous distance stood between us.

I made the journey without any problems. The weather had grown mild. Light winds were blowing. It was afternoon by the time I stood in front of a building with peeling walls. It was in the process of being restored, so scaffolding covered with green burlap had been constructed up to the center of the building, trying to hide the ugliness of the exposed walls. There was a sign directing pedestrians and another temporary sign, pointing the way to the offices I was looking for. Someone had tried to clean up the entrance to the building, but dust blew in every time the door was opened. The elevator was broken. Fortunately, their office was on the second floor. I rang the bell on the intercom and received an immediate polite answer—the same voice that had answered the phone. I said, "Hello. I came to meet somebody regarding a donation."

"Who are you?"

"My name is Eva Brown."

"Who are you supposed to meet with?" The speaker asked politely but still left me standing outside the door.

"I don't know. That's what I came to find out."

"Please wait."

Several long minutes passed before the door was opened by a young woman wearing a pink pantsuit. Her hair was pulled back and pearl earrings adorned her ears. Her expression was cold and polite.

"Please come in. Mrs. Levine, the branch manager, will see you in a short while."

The secretary returned to her place behind the counter. I sat for half an hour on an old sofa looking through magazines. Suddenly I heard a voice next to me. "Miss Brown?" I lifted my head and saw one of the most beautiful women I had ever seen. Her hair was very short, with shades of white, black and gray mixed together. Her face had no trace of makeup and was flawless, as if each feature had been meticulously placed by a sculptor to create a perfect harmony. She had kind eyes. She leaned toward me and asked again, "Miss Brown?" Her eyes hypnotized me. She held out her hand and helped me up from the sofa. "Come, let's go into my office," she said, and turned around. To the receptionist, she said, "Cathy, could you make us two cups of coffee?"

"Right away," answered Cathy.

Her office was clean and functional. On her mahogany desk were various writing implements and a large calendar. On the right side was her computer and on the left, two framed photographs. On the wall next to her was a bulletin board with notes written by hand. The walls were otherwise free from decorations, save one large picture hanging on the wall across from her. Despite the functionality of the room, it had a cozy feeling to it. The carpet was dark; light penetrated from the window, and her smiling face created an atmosphere that said no matter what is said in this room, it will be received with understanding and help will be offered.

"Well, what can I do for you?" she asked in a warm voice.

"I don't know really where to start," I stammered.

"Start at the beginning," she said, surprising me.

"OK, well, I want to donate money that I'm supposed to receive in the next few days to the organization."

"Perhaps you could tell me a little bit about this money you want to donate?" Her voice was quiet and low. My fear of having to reveal where the money was coming from vanished. Suddenly I felt a real desire to share the horrible experience I went through with her. Somehow, I knew she'd understand. I told her everything. About the first time George came to my house, about the attempted rape, about the threats I received, about the trial, and finally about my decision to donate the filthy money to a Jewish organization.

Mrs. Levine didn't stop me even once. She sat upright in her chair like a queen, her eyes never moving from mine the entire time. When I finished talking, the room was silent. She bowed her head, then lifted it back up and said, "You've been through a very, very difficult experience. How do you feel today?" Her answer caught me off guard. I expected her to talk about the money and explain how to transfer it to the organization. But she ignored the subject entirely and was only interested in me. Her question struck a dormant nerve that suddenly awoke, and my tear ducts turned on the waterworks. I'd been so busy lately just surviving, protecting myself from harm, that I never stopped to examine my true feelings. Now that the question has been asked, I once again became that little girl needing a mother's affection.

Tears were streaming uncontrollably down my face. Mrs. Levine got up from her chair, came around the desk, lifted me up from my chair, and hugged me, which only served to increase my weeping. I couldn't stop the choking sobs that emanated from the depths of my gut or the infinite tears streaming down and staining the blouse of this woman who I had never met until an hour ago.

I couldn't still my crying. My whole body shook. Mrs. Levine led me to the couch at the end of the room and came back with the cup of coffee that had cooled on her desk.

"Take a small sip," she said. "It will help to calm you down."

It took several long minutes before my breathing became regular and the tears began to dry on my cheeks.

"This is the first time you've cried like this," she said.

I nodded in agreement, and she said, "Good, this is the beginning of the path."

I didn't understand what she meant.

"Now I want to ask you another question. Why did you choose our organization? There are so many others that deal with survivors of sexual abuse. Why us specifically, a small, barely recognized organization?"

"A little while ago, I found out that my mother was Jewish."

"And your father?"

"My father was Christian. He was also..." I couldn't say the words. Maybe I was afraid that if I did, she would ask me to leave her office.

"He was what, dear?"

"He was...neo-Nazi..."

She took my chin, raised my head up, and asked, "And how do you feel about that?"

"I'm ashamed," I answered without hesitation.

"And when did you find this out?"

"I found out recently, after he and my mother were killed in a car accident. Until then, I idolized him."

"You've been through a rough time," she said.

The tears were threatening once again to erupt.

"Listen, Eva, I'm glad you came to us, and we would be happy to accept your donation. I think you made a very brave decision, but I want you to let us do something for you."

"What—" I began, but she interrupted me.

"I have been at this organization longer than most. Unfortunately, I have a great deal of experience with what you have been through. A lot of girls and women come to us asking for help and we try to help in any way possible. You also need help. You can't continue on with your life until you've dealt with this horrible experience. I am asking that you let us help you. We have excellent professionals and a lot of love to give."

This was the first time that someone had seen that I needed emotional assistance. Mrs. Levine touched on the exact location of the loose thread in my body, the one that constantly reverberated and threatened to break.

This time I looked straight into her eyes and nodded.

"Wonderful," she said. "I'll set up an appointment for you to meet with one of our therapists and you can continue from there. I want you to know that you can always call us. We have people that are always on call and available to help at any hour in any way. I want you to promise me." Her eyes never strayed from mine until I agreed out loud.

When I left the office to the street outside, it seemed like the sunlight was caressing me more than before. I walked toward the car, thinking about what had happened during the last two hours, and realized that throughout my entire meeting with her, Mrs. Levine had spent very little time on the donation and most of the time on me, Eva, a girl she had never met before but nevertheless made time for.

25

One week later, George's money arrived. I wanted to get rid of it as fast as possible, so I decided to drive to the offices of the organization, hoping to get lucky and find Mrs. Levine in the office again. *What do I want from her? What will I say to her?* I didn't know, but I was hoping to see her.

When I arrived, I went up to Cathy, the receptionist, and asked if Mrs. Levine was in. Cathy answered politely that she wasn't in the office and asked if I'd like to speak with Rachel. Before I could answer, a young woman in her thirties came up to me and said, "Eva?" I nodded in surprise, and, smiling, she invited me to follow her.

We went into a room that was completely different from that of Mrs. Levine. It was brightly lit by two large windows, one of which was open, allowing the sounds of traffic below to filter in with a dull, continuous hum. The table under the window was loaded with objects and papers. It was a total mess. There was a stack of books resting on the sofa across from the table. Strips of various sized papers were stuck to the wall with transparent tape—most likely reminders from years ago. Rachel sat me down on the sofa and moved the books aside to make room for us.

"How did you know I was Eva?" I asked inquisitively.

"I spoke with Hanna Levine. She described you in such detail that the minute you walked into the office, I knew it was you."

I was disappointed that Mrs. Levine was out. I wanted to leave the check and leave. But Rachel had other plans.

"I suspect you wanted to meet with Hanna. She's lovely, isn't she?" Before I could answer, she said, "Hanna deals mostly with managerial issues—she just happened to be here when you came in. She's usually running around the various branches in the country. Although it wasn't chance that you came on a day she was here—I believe that everything happens for a reason." She smiled at me, revealing two rows of white teeth covered by plump pink lips. "Hanna told me your story, but I'd like to hear it from you."

"But I came in to bring the money I'd like to donate to the organization."

"Great! We'll deal with that later. Now I'd like to get to know you."

She stopped speaking and looked at me. I looked back at her, but I didn't know what else to do. I spread my hands and moved restlessly on the sofa.

"Would it be easier if I asked you questions?"

I nodded.

"Well, I know that you experienced an attempted rape; I know that your parents were killed in a car accident; I know that your mother was Jewish and that you only found this out recently; and I know that you are very ashamed of the fact that your father is connected with the neo-Nazi movement, which you found out only after his death." She paused for a moment, and then asked, "How did you feel when you found out your mother was Jewish?"

I had expected her to ask other questions. Why did she, like Mrs. Levine, choose to ask about my feelings?

I contemplated the question briefly. "I'm not sure I know," I answered.

She raised her eyebrows and let me continue. "I was very surprised. I didn't have any connection to Judaism, and knew nothing about it, but suddenly I belonged to that world. It was really strange—it's still strange to me. I don't understand why my mother kept it from me, and I understand even less why she chose to marry my father."

"The subject bothers you," she said.

"Yes," I answered immediately.

"If you were to receive the answers to your questions, do you think you would be more at peace?"

"I suppose so, but I don't really know where to start."

"Let's begin with you telling me everything you know about your mother."

"The truth is that I don't know very much about her."

During the next hour, I found myself talking, and not only about my mother. She asked me questions that I didn't have the answers to, forcing me to deal with them. It was reassuring when she said that not every question has an answer. "Sometimes it's important to simply remain with the question."

The conversation with her had drained me. I felt as exhausted as if I had carried a load weighing several tons.

"You're tired," she said.

"Yes, very much," I said.

"I completely understand. This discussion is not easy for you."

"No, not at all."

"Why?" she asked suddenly.

"Why what?"

"Why is discussing your mother making you so tired?"

"I don't know."

"Try."

"I guess I'm just trying to pack everything I missed out on all my life into a very short time."

"What do you mean?"

"When she was alive, she was like a dead person to me. Now, after her death, I'm trying to bring her back to life. It's really hard. It's hard for me—I want to know who she really was, not just the way she presented herself. But on the other hand, who was she for real? I'm so confused."

"I understand."

"Besides, I have so many questions to ask her. I want to understand why she kept secrets, and why didn't she share them with me when I grew older, when I could have understood."

"Why do you think she acted this way?"

"I don't know. Maybe she knew that she didn't stand a chance, that my father was everything to me."

"And if she had told you everything, what would have happened?"

"I guess I would have been angry. It would have been very frustrating— it would have thrown me off balance."

"And maybe she knew that that's what would happen to you," she said, thinking out loud.

I looked at her face, and without hesitating, I said, "She wanted to protect me."

Rachel looked at me and didn't say a word.

***

The fatigue that took hold of me after my conversation with Rachel continued that whole week. I trudged through my daily routine waiting for the weekend to come so I could rest. Thoughts ran rampant in my head and gave me no respite. Images of my mother passed in front of my eyes. She looked like someone else, someone that was a stranger but somehow familiar to me. One night I woke up in a panic, sat up in bed, and looked around. The house was quiet. *What had awoken me? My dream.* I played the images in reverse and they quickly became a clear and vivid memory.

I was in the living room. Suddenly the door opened and George walked in. His huge frame filled the hallway. His hands were reaching toward me and I was shrinking down into the sofa, sinking low and praying for it to close up on me. I clearly remember trying to scream, but no sound came out of my mouth. As he came closer, it became clear that the body was George's, but the head was Mickey's. I screamed soundlessly, 'Mickey, Mickey,' but he continued coming toward me, his eyes boring into mine. He kept coming, and my body felt his presence with every fiber of my being. His breathing sounded like hammers pounding in my ears. I put my hands over my ears and closed my eyes.

Suddenly, out of the blue, a hand grabbed me and forcibly pulled me out of there. I was dragged by the unseen hand, my body bouncing across the ground. It seemed to take a very long time to move away. The hand finally stopped, drew me close to the body attached to it, and hugged me to its chest. Arms surrounded me, crushing me painfully. I tried to get away from the hug, but the arms continued to press, suffocating me. I thrashed around, trying to break free, and the arms released me all at once. Before I ran away from them, I saw my father's face smiling at me warmly.

And then I woke up.

Donna could tell that something had changed in me and tried to find out what it was, but I didn't want to share it with anyone. I felt like I needed to go through this process alone. It was easier for me to talk with Rachel than with Donna or anybody else among my few acquaintances. My conversations with Rachel shook me up, but also enticed me to talk to her again.

I met with Rachel a number of times. Each appointment began with me carrying a heavy load, and each one ended with me feeling lighter. It was difficult to bring these things up. Rachel didn't take pity on me; she asked me hard questions that sometimes had no answer. She insisted on asking me how I felt, what I wanted to do, what I'd like to say to my mother or my father if they were still alive. Through Rachel, their images came to life, and I talked to them like I never did when they were alive.

During one of the meetings, Rachel wanted me to describe my father's physical appearance. I began, "Well, he was tall and broad. Actually, you know, he wasn't that tall, he was average in height, maybe a bit taller than my mother. Not much taller, though. He wasn't what you would call handsome; he was the kind of man you wouldn't turn your head at if he passed you on the street. He had a narrow face with many furrows of age carved like trails on both his cheeks. When he smiled, and that was a rare occasion, you could see rows of yellow and neglected teeth. Besides that—" All of a sudden I stopped.

"What happened?" asked Rachel.

I felt the tears streaming down my face soundlessly. I didn't know what was happening to me.

"What happened, Eva? What's going on in your head?"

"I... I don't know... It's strange..."

"What's strange?"

"It's the first time I've ever described him like this."

"What do you mean?"

"I always saw him as a big, strong man, with a handsome face, the kind that women turned their heads at. And now, I don't understand what I'm saying. I'm describing the face of a completely different man. This isn't my father. Rachel, who am I describing?"

Rachel was silent a moment, and then she said, "Maybe it's your father as you see him today?"

I was in complete shock. *How could it be that I always saw my father as a giant up until a few years ago, and suddenly he's become a man like all other men? All of a sudden, he is ordinary... Maybe even small.*

"Eva, what's going through your head?"

"That I don't understand what's happening to me."

"What's happening to you?"

"My father was like God to me, and suddenly he is a little man. Rachel... How can it be that I'm describing a completely different person from the one who was almost Superman in my eyes? How can that be?"

Rachel didn't answer; she waited for me to continue.

"To me, he was unqualified justice, he was enormous. He decided my morals for me, he decided what was right or wrong for me, he was my role model, larger than everyone else..."

"And now?"

"Now he is a small man with radical opinions, without morals or sense of justice, violent and abusive..."

"Abusive?"

"He abused my mother..." I was crying and the tears streamed down my face like a raging river. "He abused me..." I said with a broken voice.

Rachel gathered me into her arms and leaned my head against her chest. She stroked my hair and rocked me like a baby in her mother's lap. A gigantic rupture came on the heels of understanding as the curtain was wrenched from my eyes. My blurred vision of the world—what I had believed was the real world—was blown to pieces, disappearing somewhere in the ocean of tears pouring down my face. It was like cleaning a glass window in order to see out. Things became clearer, and I saw them in a different light. A new light, more logical and understandable.

***

It was one of the worst moments of my life. Maybe even worse than the moment I learned of my parents' car accident.

Two weeks following my appointment, Rachel called and asked me to come in again. "I'm a little busy," I answered, trying to put her off. I didn't have the energy to deal with the shattering of another myth. I needed time to recover from the last meeting.

"It's important," she insisted. "This is different."

Two days later I walked into the familiar office. There was something comforting in the chaos of the room. One didn't need to be careful. I could say anything, and the room would absorb my words—acceptance without limitations.

Rachel asked me to sit down next to her on the sofa. She took my hand in hers and began to speak. "Eva, I think I can help you gather information on your mother," she said, to my complete surprise.

"What do you mean?" I asked.

"There are Jewish organizations that deal with locating people. These organizations were founded to help locate people lost during World War II. These are people that spend a great deal of time and effort in this line of work."

"And what does that have to do with me?"

"These good people are trained in exceptional search skills and have connections in places that you can't imagine. They are familiar with libraries, museums, and archives, and they have access to information sources all over the world. Of course, most of their work is done in Europe, but not only there."

"OK, so..."

"I think we can use their skills to find out details about your mother's life."

"And why are you only telling me this now?" I asked bitterly.

"Because you weren't prepared before now." I looked down, and she continued. "First of all, you need to want it, of course. I think that, up until now, you weren't ready to deal with a reality different from the one you're familiar with. You've grown very strong lately, and I think that even if you find out things that are not to your liking, you will be able to handle it."

"What do you think I'll find out?"

"I don't know, but whatever it is, you'll handle it with your eyes wide open."

I thought about her offer and finally said, "Thank you."

Rachel went over to the cabinet, took out a booklet, and gave it to me. "What's this?" I asked.

"This is a list of Jewish organizations in the United States. I want you to go over it at home and call those that you think might be able to help."

I took the booklet, feeling the weight of it in my hands. Back home, I set it down on the coffee table in the living room and promised myself to look through it at the weekend. But the weekend came, and more weekends after that. The booklet sat by itself on the table. Every once in a while, I'd give it a glance and decide that I would sit down and read it later, but something unexpected always came up to keep me busy and make me forget about my decision.

Another weekend arrived. I firmly decided that this time I would sit down and read through it. I made myself some hibiscus tea, put a number of cookies on a plate, and sat down on the couch. I sipped the tea and reached out to the table. The doorbell stopped me halfway there. I opened the door and was surprised to see Roy.

"Can I come in?" he asked.

"Of course," I replied. "Want something to drink?"

"Yes, coffee. Thanks."

The ocean between us was still there. It felt like the soft sounds of the waves were hiding the storm carrying on beneath the surface.

"I haven't seen you for a while," I said, breaking the silence.

"Yes, I've been pretty busy."

"OK," I said laconically. I wasn't satisfied with the answer.

Roy sipped his coffee and still wouldn't meet my eyes.

"What's this?" he asked suddenly, pointing to the booklet on the table.

"It's nothing. Just something someone gave me."

Roy took the book in his hands and paged through it. "A list of Jewish organizations throughout the United States," he muttered to himself. He looked at me inquisitively.

"Never mind. It's really nothing important—it's been sitting here for a few weeks. I just decided to go through it now."

"If you've had it for several weeks, that means that whatever's written in it is meaningful for you, or—" he drew out his words "—something that scares you."

I should have known I wouldn't be able to fool him. He knew me too well. "It's a booklet containing the names of Jewish organizations in the United States that deal in searching for people missing from World War II."

"I see. That's what it says here."

"And that's it," I concluded.

"Eva, talk!"

Clearing my throat in hesitation, I said, "Well, somebody gave me this booklet so I could find an organization that would help me find out details about my mother."

"How?"

"There are organizations whose goal is to locate people who were lost during the war and they have the skills and the know-how to locate people in general."

"I see, and you're interested in this information?"

He knows me so well, I thought to myself.

"I think it's time," I answered. "I think I'm ready."

"OK, I'll help you," he said naturally.

"Roy, please don't be offended, but it's something I want to do by myself. I need to do it alone."

He looked at me for a minute and then nodded. He understood.

"How come you came over?" I asked. To avoid hurting his feelings, I added, "I'm glad you came. I just haven't seen you for such a long time! So I was wondering if you came over for a specific reason."

"The reason I came isn't important any more. I really hope you find what you're looking for."

"Yeah, me too. Although, you know, I'm afraid of what I might find out."

"I know."

For a minute, I thought maybe we had gotten back to the way we once were, but it was just for a moment. We both knew that at some point we would have to have a serious conversation about what had happened between us, but in the meantime, we chose to ignore the subject.

Mickey called the following week. He sounded terrible over the phone and asked if he could come for a visit. Several hours later, I opened the door for him. For a minute, I wasn't even sure it was him. Instead of the guy who took pride in his clothes, there stood before me a sloppy man. Up close I could see that his shirt was stained, and an unpleasant smell emanated from him.

"Mickey?" I asked in alarm. "What happened?"

Instead of answering, he passed by me, sat down on the sofa in the living room, and covered his face with his hands. I didn't know what to do—whether to leave him alone and let him calm down or try to comfort him. Before I could decide how to act, his sobs filled up the room. I was really scared. I sat down next to him and tried to take his hand in mine, but he wouldn't let me. I continued to sit, feeling completely helpless, waiting for his crying to subside. An eternity passed before he began to calm down, and then, without any introduction and without looking at me, he said, "My whole life has been based on a lie."

"What are you talking about?"

"My father, who I admired and loved..." he murmured, then covered his face again with his hands and grew silent, withdrawing inside himself.

His silence continued. "Mickey, what about your father? Did something happen?"

He began, "A few days ago, I was at a business meeting in the city. Every once in a while, I go to these meetings. Not always, but I have a lot of free time now. During the meeting, we were asked to introduce ourselves. I talked about our family business and a little bit about my father. During one of the breaks, an older man came up to me and introduced himself as Yechiel. We talked a bit about business and suddenly he asked my father's name. He then asked if my father was a Holocaust survivor—what camp he was in and when. And I answered. It felt good talking with someone about that period, someone who understood. After he'd heard everything my father had told me, he gave me a strange look and said, 'Your father, damn him, was a murderer.' And then—" His voice broke and turned into a sob. "—and then he spit on me and walked away."

"What?" I was stunned. Mickey continued to cry next to me, his entire body shaking.

I got up from the couch and poured myself a glass of water. It was obvious that there was more to this story. *Mickey knew something terrible about his father—that was obvious. But what could it be?*

He started talking again through the kitchen door. "When I got home that evening, I told him what had happened. He went up to his room and locked the door. But all my life he'd been covering up some secret—it was time for him to talk. I knocked on the door. He yelled, 'Go away.' But I was going to break down the door if he didn't open it. My mother arrived and tried to calm me down, but I sent her downstairs.

"I pushed open the door and went inside. He was sitting on the bed in silence. I told him, 'Tell me once and for all what happened over there,' but he remained silent, the way he usually does. Finally, I grabbed him, stood him on his feet, and began to shake him. He was like a rag doll in my hands. I yelled at him, 'Now, tell me now!'"

Mickey shouted out loud when he told that part of the story, and I'm sure the neighbors heard him. He wasn't really in my house—at that moment, he was in his father's bedroom, reliving the experience of several days ago.

"Mickey, calm down," I begged him. I gently touched his shoulder. He raised his eyes to me. They were expressionless, and to me he looked like a drowning man the second after all the air has left his lungs.

"Mickey," I tried again. Then I heard what had been kept secret all those years.

"He turned in dozens of Jews at the camp in order to stay alive."

"I don't understand," I whispered.

"A group of Jews at the Treblinka camp, where he was—they were planning to break into the camp's armory and steal what was there in order to take revenge on the Germans and try to escape. My father turned the members of the group into the camp authorities and almost all of them were killed... And I always thought he was a hero..."

"Mickey, I'm sorry," I said. But I had to ask the question. "Why did he do it?"

"Why?" he repeated after me. "Because they promised him that if he gave them up, they wouldn't hurt him. And besides, I'm sure they improved his living conditions."

"How old was he then?"

"Almost eighteen," he answered.

The room fell silent. Mickey didn't speak but was still very upset. He got up from the couch and began to walk around the room. I felt like there was still something he wasn't telling me.

Suddenly I knew. The knowledge hit me like a fist.

"He knew some of the people that were killed?" I asked.

"Yes," whispered Mickey. "His own father."

***

A short time afterward, I sat alone in the kitchen trying to comprehend what Mickey had told me. Mickey was asleep in my bed, dirty and smelly. Apparently, after the whole story came out, he left the house and wandered around the streets for three whole days. He slept outside on a bench in one of the parks; then he went back to his car and came to me. I called his mother and reassured her that he was with me. There was a terrible chill in my bones. Even wrapping myself in a sweater didn't get rid of it, so I got up and made myself a hot drink, walking restlessly around the kitchen, feeling an inexplicable anger take hold of me. I couldn't stand to be in Mickey's presence and had to get away from him—to wander around the neighborhood and try to find an explanation for my feelings.

The similarities between us grew sharper. I saw him as a reflection of myself, and the image was unbearable. My blind admiration toward my father, my stupidity, my attitude toward my mother, the biggest mistake of my life—all were playing out before me in the form of Mickey's broken figure.

I returned home and woke him up. I had to shake him to get him to wake; he was in a deep fitful sleep, and when he opened his eyes, he didn't understand for a moment where he was.

"Mickey, I want you to leave," I whispered. "I want you to go," I repeated, louder.

"I don't understand," he said, tears starting.

"It's hard for me having you here. It hurts too much."

"I don't understand what you're talking about," he said.

"Your story is too similar to mine, and it's difficult for me right now. I'm also going through a process of being disillusioned, and it hurts. I can't take your pain as well... I need time for my own." I continued to stand over him without moving.

He got up, looked at me for a minute with red eyes, and left the house, leaving the door wide open. I closed it after him and went back to the empty room. I sat down on my bed and cried.

26

Two weeks had gone by since Mickey left my house. It was an ordinary day. I left the office at the end of the day; on my way home, I stopped at the supermarket to buy some things, stopped at the dry cleaners to pick up a coat, and went to the ATM to withdraw some cash. My heart was heavy without really knowing why—it felt as if a thunderstorm or an avalanche was coming, and the atmosphere was inundated with anticipation. It was a little past seven. As soon as I went inside the house, I turned on the lights in the east wing of the house. Something was bothering me. The answering machine light was flashing, but I ignored it—the message was probably from either Donna or Roy. After putting my grocery bag down in the kitchen and hanging up my coat, I went to take a shower. The running water caressed my body, but didn't calm the vague feeling of unease.

Afterward, on my way to the kitchen, I saw the flashing light of the answering machine again and went over to turn it on. The message interrupted my plans for a quiet evening.

"Eva, this is Rivka. Mickey has been in an accident and I would really like you to come." She stopped for a moment. I could hear her crying in the background, and then she continued, "He's not doing well, and I'm sure he would be happy to see you... Please, come." Again I heard her sobs, and then she hung up.

I continued to stare at the answering machine. Mickey was hurt in an accident. My legs turned to lead and my body slumped to the floor. I knew he was in a bad way. Rivka wouldn't have called if he wasn't in critical condition. I dragged my heavy body off the floor and headed toward my room, where I sat on the edge of the bed and couldn't get up. I knew.

"Mickey," I whispered. "What have you done?"

About an hour later, I was on the main road to Chicago. I didn't see a thing along the way—it was important for me to get there as soon as possible so he wouldn't be alone with his story. *He has to live*, I told myself, pushing hard on the gas pedal. The drive seemed endless, but every journey comes to an end. I knocked on the door of the dark villa. The garden light was turned off, and the house didn't seem as large as I remembered.

The door opened and Shlomo stood in front of me. He'd aged considerably, as if years had gone by instead of the few months since I'd seen him last. His body was hunched over and his hands shook. He didn't look like the man I knew. I almost asked if Shlomo was home.

"Come in," he said and turned away from me.

The house was silent and not a soul was in sight.

"Where is everyone?" I asked.

"At the hospital."

"And you?"

"I'm here. I don't like hospitals."

It was the one of the very few complete sentences I had ever heard from him. Shlomo sat down in the chair he always sat in at the table, but this time, instead of the usual newspaper that always hid his face, he held a prayer book. He looked detached; I thought for a moment he didn't remember that I was there. His lips moved in silent prayer and his body rocked back and forth in tiny movements. I looked at his face. It was gaunt and his cheeks were lost inside the contours.

"Would you like me to fix you something to eat?"

He shook his head no but didn't stop praying. His lips continued to move independently. I went into the kitchen and made a cup of tea. The remains of a pound cake rested on the counter. I sliced a piece of it and placed it next to the cup. He didn't see me or hear a thing. He was in another place, in another country, one that haunted him.

***

It was already one o'clock in the morning when I arrived at the hospital. The nurse took me to his room. Rivka sat at the foot of his bed and his sisters were huddled by the window. They didn't see me. Mickey was hooked up to a million machines. A monitor next to him beeped. His heartbeat was irregular.

"Rivka," I said, putting my hand on her shoulder.

"Oh, Eva, I'm so glad you came!" She got up and gathered me to her chest. Her sobs grew stronger and her tears stained my blouse. His sisters stayed by the window, looking at us from a distance.

"What happened?" I asked after she released me from her embrace.

"It was a mistake. Mickey was cleaning his gun and a bullet accidentally fired and hit him."

"I see," I said, and avoided looking over to the window. "How's he doing?"

Rivka began to cry again. She said, "Not so well. The doctors say the next forty-eight hours are critical. If he makes it through them, he has a chance. Eva, talk to him. I'm sure he can hear—he would be so happy to know that you're here."

Rivka gave me her chair. She called her daughters to leave the room with her. "Talk to him," she said. She went out and left me alone with him.

I didn't know what to do. It was hard to speak to Mickey; he didn't look like a human being, but an extension of a machine. I took his hand, which was lying beside his body, and rubbed it. I wanted to feel the warmth of his body, I wanted to be sure that underneath all these machines there was a person, the first person I made love to. Somebody who spoke to me, who held me and whispered words of love to me.

"Mickey, can you hear me?" I whispered. "I'm so sorry, so very sorry. Please live. We have so much more to say to each other." I squeezed his hand and expected to feel him squeeze in return, but his hand remained limp, like an inanimate object. *What else should I say?* The day's unease suddenly became clear, and now it was growing to enormous proportions. The night he told me about his father burned in my brain. *He can't die*, I told myself. *I have to explain it to him first.*

***

I lived at the hospital that week. Rivka saw me as being faithful and loyal, but if Mickey had been conscious the whole time, he would know the real reason for my dedication. Two days after I arrived, the doctors announced that his condition had improved, but they were careful not to encourage false hope, saying that he needed to be closely monitored. Three more days went by. Every once in a while, I would leave his room and pop over to the villa to shower and eat something, but most of the time I was at his bedside.

Friday night. His sisters had all gone home to sleep; Rivka went with them. I sat on the window sill looking out into the darkness that had fallen over the city. There was something about Friday evenings, something that made them special. I remembered the sacred atmosphere of the Fridays I spent with his family. The aromas of Rivka's cooking, Shlomo in one of his more stylish suits, Rivka covering her face, with her hands over the candles, reciting the prayer, the table decorated with a pure white tablecloth, Shlomo's Friday night prayer, all of us answering "Amen." There was something there I had never encountered before, and my heart opened up to it in anticipation.

"Mom?"

For a second I didn't understand where the voice was coming from. Somebody had disturbed the peacefulness of my Friday.

"Mickey?" I got up from the window and went over to his bed.

"Eva, what are you doing here?"

"Mickey, you woke up," I said in a voice that sounded foreign to me.

"Eva, why are you here?"

"Your mother asked me to come."

He turned his face away from me. I took his chin in my hands and moved his eyes back toward me. "I'm glad that she asked me to come," I added.

"Why?"

"I would never have forgiven myself if..."

"If I had died." He completed my sentence.

"Yes," I whispered.

"So now that you see I'm alive, you can go."

"No, Mickey, I'm staying."

"I don't want you here," he said. He was having trouble talking.

"I know, but I intend to stay anyway."

He turned his gaze away from me once again and for a long time didn't say a word.

After this conversation, we didn't speak at all. I would come to the hospital, and as soon as he saw me, he would turn away from me. Rivka was aware of the tension between us, but didn't mention a thing. She preferred not to deal with what she saw because she believed that my presence contributed to his recuperation.

At the beginning of the second week of my stay there, I felt that it was time to leave. I went up to Rivka and told her that I was going home. She hugged me and said, "Please, Eva, stay a few more days. I know that something happened between you, but despite the way he's acting toward you, I'm sure he wants you here. Sometimes he can be very stubborn and unpleasant, but it only means that he's in pain. It's hard for him to admit it out loud, so he hurts other people. He's very much like his father in that respect."

"Shlomo hurt you?"

My question caught her off guard and I instantly regretted asking her. "I'm sorry, Rivka." I wanted to take it back immediately. "I don't have the right to ask you."

"You know what, Eva? You *do* have the right to ask me. I am, after all, the one who asked you to be a part of what we are all going through, and you agreed right away. I think that you absolutely have the right to ask me this question. Shlomo, as you must have noticed, doesn't speak much. His silence has continued for many years. When we were young, I saw it as an advantage—I thought he was a very wise man, and the things he chose to say seemed in my eyes to be very intelligent. But over time, I've come to realize that my relationship with him has sentenced me to a lonely life. What little communication we had between us turned into short questions with yes or no answers. Shlomo became more and more withdrawn and was a mere shadow in the house, although at work he behaved completely differently. The children were born into this atmosphere and his silence drove them as far away as possible."

"Except for Mickey," I said.

"It was different with Mickey, much more complicated."

"Would you like to tell me about it now?"

"Come, let's put off this conversation to another time... Our souls are heavy enough, no need to add any more."

She wasn't going to talk about what happened. She was quiet, like her husband, but her silence was different than his. Before she could get up from the sofa, I got up and hugged her tightly. At first, she was surprised by the sudden gesture, but then she embraced me and we stayed like that for several long minutes, taking comfort in each other's arms.

"Will you stay?" she asked with a shaky voice.

"Yes," I answered without hesitation. "Let me just call my office and tell them I'm extending my vacation."

My soul has been linked with this family, and my connection to it will remain, irrespective of my relationship with Mickey. Of this I am sure.

***

Slowly but surely, Mickey began to recover. Every day brought new improvement to his condition. He moved his head more easily, his limbs woke up, and the medical team agreed to let him get out of bed and take short walks. He still frowned at me, but he was used to my presence. He let me hold his arm while taking slow steps, agreed to let me help him eat, and sometimes even listened to me giving him a summary of current events, even though he pretended to be asleep.

After a few days, the doctors announced that he was being released from the hospital for the weekend. Mickey reacted with indifference, but Rivka was already planning the dinner she would prepare for him.

When we arrived at the house, Mickey stopped at the entrance and looked around. He scrutinized the house as if it was the first time he'd seen it.

Shlomo was nowhere to be found. I asked Rivka where he was, and she whispered, "It's hard for him."

The Sabbath passed in silence. Mickey barely spoke, answering Rivka's questions with only "yes" or "no." Shlomo closed himself up in his room and came down only for meals. Mickey's sisters called. They said that even though they wanted to come, they couldn't, and that they would try to visit next week. I really wanted to go home, but I couldn't bear Rivka's sadness, so I stayed till the end of the weekend.

Rivka spent most of the time in the kitchen and asked that I sit next to her. I knew she was afraid of the moment when I would leave and she would be left completely alone in a silent world. Our conversations centered on normal topics and we were careful not to touch on any subjects that were too emotionally charged. Mickey chose to spend his time in his bedroom. He refused Rivka's invitation to come downstairs.

On Sunday morning, I went up to his room. When I went inside, he said that he was tired and asked me to leave him alone. I ignored his request and sat down on the edge of the bed.

"Mickey, we have to talk," I said to his back.

"We don't have to do anything," he answered.

I felt my anger raise its head, but I tried my best to keep it in check. I tried again. "Mickey, stop this now. Let's talk."

"It's not important anymore," he answered, his back still a barrier between us.

"It's important to me!" I said loudly. I got up to move to the other side of the bed.

A sigh escaped his lips and he turned around, sat up, and leaned his body against the pillow.

"Eva, I really don't think we have anything to say to each other. You made that perfectly clear the last time we were together."

"I didn't make anything clear," I answered angrily. "You came over with your father's story and expected me to comfort you. You don't understand that I have my own story and my own guilt and I can't share in yours. You're not angry at me, Mickey, you're angry at yourself, like I'm angry at myself. It takes time to deal with the guilt you unjustly took upon yourself."

"I don't know what you're talking about."

"Oh, you understand just fine, but you're not willing to open your eyes to see it, to see the years you've wasted. To understand that the father you loved so much passed the burden of his actions on to you instead of carrying them himself. But now you are a big boy and not so naïve, and you need to shake this load off your back. Enough already, Mickey. No more running. Nobody expects you to continue. You owe it to yourself. Somebody has to release you from the burden of this legacy. It has to be you."

I was distraught and angry. Not at him, at his father—maybe not even at Shlomo. Mickey's situation was also mine. *We both have been victims by choice. For years, he and I have denied what was in front of us and allowed life to pass us by without really touching it. We are both carrying the burden of guilt on our shoulders.*

I was caught up in my thoughts when I heard the sobs. At first they were weak and choked, then the crying grew louder, shaking his emaciated body. Mickey covered his face with his hands. I wanted to go to him and hold him, but I held back. I backed up quietly, opened the door, and left.

I went downstairs wearing my backpack. Rivka was leaning against the table in the kitchen with her back to me. The house was dark except for the light in the kitchen. Her head rested against her arms and her back was slouched forward. I wanted to go to her, to caress her and promise her that everything would be OK, but instead, I opened the front door and left the house, not knowing if I'd ever see them again.

27

Two months passed and I didn't hear a word from Mickey or Rivka. There were days when I debated whether to call them, but I never did. *Mickey will call me when he is stronger—he can have the time he needs.* My blessed routine carried me through intense working days. Donna and I got together at least once a week. Sometimes we'd go out to a movie, and sometimes we would sit at my house and talk. My search for an organization to help me gain information about my mother took up most of my time. Each one I called told me that they didn't search for people not connected to World War II. Except for one—a pleasant man answered the phone and showed real interest in my story. His name was Josh and he informed me that the chances of finding my mother through his office were slim, but he took down my details and promised to contact me if anything should come up.

At some point, I got tired and called Rachel. She was happy to hear my voice and asked how my search was going. She was disappointed to hear that nothing had changed since the last time we met. I was surprised that she didn't offer to help.

I called Roy, but he didn't answer. I waited till evening and called him again. His mother told me he would be back in a week and promised to tell him I had called. It was obvious to me that she wouldn't tell him a thing.

I went to Sarah's house, the only place where I didn't feel the need to protect myself. She accepted me with her usual warmth. After I sipped the tea she made me and tasted the crunchy cake she served, she casually asked how my investigation was going.

"Not very well," I answered.

"Why?"

Instead of answering her question, I turned to her and, with a direct look into her eyes, asked why she made me leave her house when I asked about my mother.

"I didn't make you leave, my dear."

"But—"

She cut me off, saying, "You want answers from me that I can't give you. I came to live in this house about a year after your parents moved in. I didn't know anything about them. Over time, after your mother and I became friends, I realized that their relationship was very complex. Your mother told me very little about what was going on with them. She spoke mostly about you."

"About me?"

"Yes, she loved you very much."

"So how come I never felt that love?"

"I can't answer that for you. I expect she had her reasons."

"What reasons?"

"I'm sure that if you keep searching, you will find the answers to your questions."

A little while later, back at my house, I thought about what Sarah had said. "She knows more than she's telling," I said aloud to myself. "She's pushing me to keep looking." Of that I was sure.

I was determined to go forward with my search. I called one of the organizations I had spoken to before, but this time I presented them with a different story. I told them that my grandfather and grandmother were

Holocaust survivors and would like to know if anyone from their families was still alive.

"Have they applied to us in the past?"

"No," I answered. "Up until now, they have refused to talk about what happened there. Only recently have they begun to tell me about that period."

"I see," answered a man's voice. "Well, I need to know what camp they were in, their previous residence, if they were married during the war, names of any children, the number appearing on their arms—any information they remember. Even something that may seem to you to be unimportant."

"That's a problem," I said. "My grandfather is very old and can't provide hardly any information and my grandmother... Well, she's also confused. Sometimes she says one thing and then she contradicts it with completely different information. The only thing I can say for sure is that they didn't have children at that time and they probably weren't married then either."

The silence on the other end of the line sealed the fate on this attempt as well.

"I'm sorry," he said, and the connection was gone.

I became depressed. I felt a strong need to get out of the house. A new mall had opened up about six months ago, and that's where I was going. I wanted to get lost among the faceless crowds, to be around people without touching them and without them touching me.

I stopped in front of the store windows. My mood improved. Suddenly I found myself in front of a furniture store. I went inside and walked among the aisles. I had the sudden urge to replace my foul-smelling shabby furniture. Its presence in my home was like a monument to George's actions.

"It's about time," I murmured to myself quietly.

An unexpected voice beside me said, "It's about time for what?"

I looked over and found myself looking into eyes as green as a tranquil lake.

"I'm sorry. I didn't mean to startle you." The woman smiled, revealing two rows of snow-white teeth.

"I was talking to myself, wasn't I?" I asked self-consciously.

She answered, "Yes, but only I heard you. How can I help you?"

"I don't really know. The truth is, I was going to buy clothes but found myself in a furniture store."

We smiled at each other, and then she said, "I'll let you wander around on your own. If you need help or advice, I'm Joey. I'll be around if you need me."

The saleswoman walked away and I continued to wander among the furniture. There was a pretty double sofa the color of gold that I decided to come back to after reviewing all the other furniture. Then I saw it. It was standing in the corner of the store, separate from the rest of the furniture. Its crimson color stood out like an island surrounded by an ocean of furniture. Its color seemed to fill the space where it sat. I knew that I was going to buy it. The reclining chair. It was time to replace the old with the new, the past with the future.

I called the saleswoman over and pointed to the chair in the corner. "A wonderful choice," she said with a smile. "Would you like it in this color or a different one?"

"I'd like it exactly as it is."

"You should know that the fabric is unique—it repels liquids, so you don't have to worry about keeping it clean. Have you tried it out yet?"

"No."

"Well then, come on! Sit down and feel how it hugs you."

I sat down in the chair and that's precisely how I felt. "It's exactly what I want."

28

At six o'clock in the evening, there was an unfamiliar knock on the door. I had arrived home from work just a half hour earlier. I had just finished my shower and gone into the kitchen to make myself something to eat. Roy had his own special knock and Donna never knocked on the door, she rang the bell. I asked who it was and a strange voice answered. "My name is Peter. You don't know me—I'd like to talk to you."

"Regarding what?" I was sure he was a salesman, the kind that comes to your house and doesn't leave you alone until they get you to buy whatever product they're selling. "I'm not interested in buying anything right now, thank you."

"I'm not here to sell you anything. I'm looking for John Brown," he said.

Warning bells went off. "Who are you?" Fear began to creep in.

"Look, I just want to talk to him. Are you his wife?"

"No, I'm his daughter."

"Is he in?"

"No."

"Come sit outside, that way you'll feel safer. OK?"

I opened the door. A man of about fifty years old stood there. He had broad shoulders, dark skin, and sunglasses. He held out his hand and we introduced ourselves.

We sat on the steps outside the front door.

"I'm a homicide investigator," he said.

I swallowed hard and all my senses grew sharper. "What do I have to do with homicide?"

"You have nothing to worry about. The case I'm talking about happened more than twenty years ago."

"I don't understand what that has to do with me."

"You're right. I actually want to speak with your father."

"My father's dead," I said.

"Oh, I'm sorry to hear that," he said.

"Why do you need him?"

"We're investigating a homicide, and we have reasonable grounds to believe he is connected with it."

"My father?"

He nodded and I could see sympathy on his face.

"Well, he was killed in a car accident three years ago."

"I see."

"But I would still like to know why you think he has a connection to this murder."

"Are you sure?"

"Yes," I replied emphatically.

"I'll start at the beginning. In Florida, at the end of 1973, there was a car accident. A young man was killed. He was driving the car when the accident occurred. According to the police report, which I recently reviewed, the driver was apparently driving on a narrow, winding road. A truck appeared out of nowhere; the truck driver lost control of his vehicle and crashed into the car. The young man was thrown straight into a fifty-foot ditch. He didn't have a chance. The car caught fire and several weeks passed before they were able to identify the victim. The incident was investigated and eventually filed as a severe car accident. There was no reason to suspect anything else."

"I still don't understand how this story is connected to my father."

"A few months ago, we arrested a sixty-year-old white man on suspicion of murder. During his interrogation, he confessed that he was hired more than twenty years ago to intentionally crash his truck into the car driven by the young man that was killed. He said that he had received a hefty sum of money to fake the accident. He carried out his part of the deal, received the payment promised him, and disappeared from the state."

"And why are you telling me this story?" I began to lose my patience. I wanted him to leave me alone.

"Because the person that paid him to carry out this accident was your father."

I looked at him in complete shock. "What are you talking about? I don't understand."

He emphasized each word. "Eva, your father hired this man and paid him money to kill the young man driving the car."

It felt like my blood was boiling in my veins, like fiery sparks from the sun were burning every inch of my skin. I felt dizzy and stood up to vomit. This was too much. *Who the hell is this man?* I asked myself. *I mean, he hasn't shown me any identification, maybe he's planning to hurt me and is making up stories in the meantime.* I wiped my mouth with the back of my hand and went up to him.

"Can you show me your ID?" I moved away from him as I was asking the question, turning back toward the house. I was prepared to run and lock the door behind me, but the man, Peter, put his hand in his pocket and took out a badge. I looked it over and read, "Peter Jenkins, Investigative Officer." The badge looked authentic.

"Where's your mother?" he asked suddenly.

"She was killed with him."

"I see. Again, I'm sorry."

I nodded and waited. He then turned to me and asked if he could stay in touch with me if the need should arise. I told him he could, and asked, "Could you perhaps give me some information about my father?"

He was surprised, but tried to hide it. "Explain yourself," he said.

"After my parents were killed, I discovered that I don't know anything about them. I don't know anything about their past, their backgrounds, where they came from, if I have other family..."

"They never talked to you about it?"

"No!"

"I don't know if I can help you. What would you like to know?"

"Where did you come from? I mean, are you from the same place where my father lived as a child?"

"I'm from a suburb of Chicago. The case was transferred to us a little over a year ago, but we were only recently able to locate the last residence of your father. The young man who was killed lived in our jurisdiction. As far as I know, your father lived in one of the city's suburbs, a place called Chester."

My hands became clammy and my heart began to race.

Peter noticed my agitation. "Come sit down," he said. "I can see you are upset."

"Do you have a specific address?"

"Not with me, but I can check."

"Please."

"I'll go back to my office and check. If you could call me tomorrow, I'll let you have all the information I can find." He handed me his card.

"Thank you. Thank you very much."

Peter nodded, gave me a little salute, and left. I was alone on the steps and couldn't decide whether I was happy about finding a clue or miserable after learning yet another horrific detail about my father.

A car pulled up in front of the house, a door slammed, and footsteps grew close to me until a shadow darkened my path.

"What are you doing here outside?" asked Roy.

I took a deep breath and said, "Trying to comprehend what I just found out."

Roy waited for me to continue.

"Apparently, besides being a Nazi, my father was also a murderer." I burst out in hysterical laughter.

"Come here," Roy lifted me on to my feet and pulled me into the house. He sat me down on the sofa and went into the kitchen. A few seconds later, he returned with a cup of tea.

"Drink!" he ordered.

"I can't."

"Drink," he said again and sat down next to me. He moved the strands of hair covering my eyes, leaned my body back, and brought the cup to my mouth. "Take a few sips, it will calm you," he said gently. I listened to his voice and took a sip of the sweet tea. "Take a deep breath," he commanded. I did as he asked and slowly began to feel my breathing return to its normal rhythm. Roy got up again and came back with a damp cloth. He placed it on my forehead, and then wiped my cheeks and neck. Then he pulled me close to him, leaned my body onto his chest, and wrapped me in his arms. He didn't say a word and neither did I. We sat like this for a long time.

The hours passed by and nighttime arrived. I must have fallen asleep. I awoke to find myself lying on the sofa, covered by a thin blanket. The living room was dark except for a floor light shining in the corner. Roy was sitting on my newly purchased easy chair, his eyes closed and his breathing steady. I didn't want to wake him, so I got up slowly from the sofa and went into the bathroom to wash my face. I lifted my head and looked at my reflection in the mirror. "So, your father is a murderer. You are the daughter of a murderer." Tears streamed down my face. Quietly. In desperation.

***

From that day on, it was like I was possessed. Thoughts about my father—my idol, the stranger, the monster—wouldn't leave me. I was overwhelmingly restless, periodically leaving the house to walk the streets. Once, when Sarah noticed me and called out for me to come in to her house, the thought of warm cookies and the feeling of family in her home made me crudely refuse her invitation. I didn't deserve to enjoy myself, and certainly not to receive warmth and love. I was the daughter of a monster that fed on my love and blind admiration. My soul was replete with feelings of guilt and endless anger at myself. I couldn't stand moments of enjoyment—couldn't smile, couldn't look at myself in the mirror, couldn't stop hating my stupid self for closing my eyes all those years. I wanted to be a new person.

The decision took hold immediately. I ran home, took out a suitcase, and crammed a load of clothes into it. It was the middle of the day, and Donna was in the office. I called her home and left a message on her answering machine saying that I wouldn't be coming in to work in the near future, adding, "Please don't try to find me, I'll come back when I can."

I got into the car and began to drive, not knowing where, just wanting to put as much distance as possible between myself and the place that only increased my self-hatred—the house I grew up in was a lie. My foot pressed down on the gas pedal and the car drove on and on. After several hours, I stopped at an unfamiliar city. The city welcomed me with indifference. Nobody noticed my arrival and no one tried to make contact with me. I rented a room in an old apartment house that suited my needs. I wanted to be anonymous and assimilate into the human kaleidoscope of the city.

I felt safe after a week. I bought a map and walked around town like a tourist, visiting a different part of the city each day and walking around until my feet screamed for rest, wearing myself out completely. I left each morning as soon as I woke up and returned to the room in the late evening, living mostly on snacks during the day, not eating a real meal for more than a week. As the days went by, this weakened me. The distances I walked grew shorter and my feet dragged.

My vision grew blurry. Sometimes I ran into obstacles and fell. Sometimes people helped me up, but most gave me strange looks, lowering their heads to avoid my eyes and or simply moving away from me. At first I didn't understand why they were acting that way, until one time a shop window showed me my reflection. I was a shadow of myself. That pleased me. *The former Eva has disappeared. In her place, a new Eva will appear, more moral and aware.* I smiled at the shadow in front of me and said goodbye to old Eva in my heart. I leaned my body against the window and tried to walk away, but my feet wouldn't move.

People passed by me and not one of them stopped. *Perhaps I have become invisible. Perhaps I have annihilated her.* I sat down on the sidewalk, leaned my chin against my chest, and fell asleep. When I opened my eyes again, it was dark all around me. My legs were in a strange position and my hands had changed color—now they were purple, and my fingers wouldn't move. My breathing was heavy. A few people passed by on the sidewalk, but none of them looked at me. Somebody threw a coin that landed at my feet.

I am going to die. So, this is what it's like—not so bad. If I stay here all night, I will freeze to death, but I don't care. Apathy replaced the will to live. Passivity took control of me. I closed my eyes and waited for death.

When I opened my eyes again, I found myself in a bed with tubes coming out of my arms and nose. *Is this a hospital?* An old woman was in the bed to my left covered in a white sheet, her breathing labored and wheezy. The bed to the right of me was empty. *This must be the place they put people who are terminal.* When I woke up again, the bed to my left was empty. Someone touched my hand. I turned my head and looked into a pair of nice brown eyes. "How do you feel?" asked Brown Eyes. Without the energy to answer, I just moved my head. "If we hadn't found you, you wouldn't have made it."

"Who are you?" I asked and didn't recognize my voice.

"I am Nurse Rosa and you are in the hospital. You were unconscious when we found you and brought you here. You're going to be OK, but you need to follow our instructions. A doctor will come and examine you later."

I nodded and asked how long I had been there.

"Three days," came the answer. "Do you have any family you would like us to contact for you?"

"I'm not from here," I answered.

"Where are you from, dear?" she asked in a voice as soft as velvet.

I could barely whisper the name of my hometown.

"Who should we call?"

Without a hint of hesitation, I answered, "Roy."

I must have given her the number, since she stopped asking me questions and let me escape into a thoughtless sleep.

They told me I slept two more days. When I opened my eyes, I saw Roy. He was sitting in the chair next to the bed looking at me. His face look tired and several years older than the last time I saw him.

When he saw that I had awoken, he got up, came over to me, took my hand and asked, "How do you feel?"

"Better," I answered.

"What did you do, Eva?" he asked and sat on the edge of the bed.

I didn't have anything to say.

"Why didn't you come to me?"

"I'm sorry," I said.

Tears began to run down his face. He got up and turned away from me.

"I'm sorry," I said to his back.

"It's my fault. I should have known what you were going through."

"How could you? I didn't even know myself."

"I was so worried about you."

"Sorry."

When he turned back toward me, his face was the face I knew again.

"What did the doctor say?" I asked.

"That you need to get stronger, eat nutritious food, drink a lot, and rest."

"Roy, I want to go home."

I went home two days later. The nurse and doctor that took care of me made me promise to eat proper food from a list they gave me, and to drink a lot of liquids. We didn't talk much on the way home. Roy let me take it easy; he didn't ask any questions and didn't ask for promises. When we got home, he helped me inside. I was weak and needed support. He helped me lie down in bed and said he would come back later. After a little more than an hour he returned. I heard him moving objects around in my old bedroom, dragging something. When he came into my parents' room, where I was lying down, I asked him what he was doing in my bedroom.

"I was arranging my things," he answered briefly.

"Your things?" I wondered.

"Yes, I'll be here for now," he declared.

I didn't say a word. Inside I was happy that he took the initiative and reached a decision on his own without consulting me. I needed someone to take care of me. I wanted someone to insist on watching over me, to not listen to me, and Roy fulfilled my silent wish.

The next day, when I woke up, I heard him fiddling with the dishes in the kitchen. The clock said it was nine o'clock in the morning. *What is he doing home? He's usually at work by this time.* I tried to get out of bed, but the moment I got up, a bout of dizziness threw me back into bed and I tightly shut my eyes. A few minutes later, he came into my room with a tray full of all sorts of good things.

"Come on, I'll help you sit up."

"I'm dizzy," I complained.

"We'll do it slowly." He came up to the bed and leaned toward me. His head moved close to mine and I took a deep breath of his cologne, which smelled of wildflowers mixed with sweat. He rearranged the pillows behind my head and leaned me back against them. Then he set down the tray, which held a pot of tea, a glass of orange juice, fragrant cakes, and dollops of tasty jams and butter. The scent of the cakes spread throughout the room and the aroma stimulated my nostrils. I took a deep breath of the smells and felt my chest expand.

"What about you?" I asked.

"I already had something to drink."

"Roy, don't you need to be at work now?"

"Nope, I'm not working today."

"But—"

"Shh," he whispered. "I also deserve a day off."

He sat down on the bed and waited for me to start eating.

"I can't eat with you watching me like that," I said.

"OK, I'll be in the other room. Call me if you need anything."

I devoured everything on the tray. The little cakes were sweet and crunchy, and I swallowed each one, filling my empty body.

Roy came back to take away the tray. He leaned toward me just when I moved to sit up straight. Our heads bashed together and our eyes met. My hands automatically reached out and grasped both his cheeks. I brought his head close to me and kissed him lightly on the lips. "Thanks," I whispered.

He put the tray back down on my knees and took my face in his two hands and kissed me long and passionately. He then pulled back, moved away, and said, "You're welcome."

He took the tray and left the room.

29

A few days later, while I was still recuperating, the telephone rang. I was sitting in the living room with a blanket covering my legs and a cup of tea in my hand. Roy sat next to me, looking over some papers related to his job. The ringing broke the silence and caused us both to look at each other in question. It was nine o'clock in the evening. Roy got up to answer. I heard him say into the receiver, "This is Roy. One moment." He put the receiver down on the table, sat down next to me, and said, "Michael."

I got up slowly, walked toward the telephone holding on to the wall to my left.

"Hi. Mickey. How are you?" I said into the phone, my heart skipping a beat.

"I'm OK. Really OK," he emphasized.

I felt uncomfortable speaking to Mickey with Roy sitting near me, so I turned around so that Roy couldn't hear what I was saying.

"I wanted to know how you are," he continued.

"I'm all right now," I said.

"What happened?"

"I was sick, but now I'm recuperating."

"Something serious?"

"It's a long story, not for the telephone."

"I see," he said. Then he asked, all of a sudden, "Would you like me to come over?"

I hesitated for a second before I answered. "Not yet, Mickey, I want to get well first."

"I want to see you before..." He stopped.

"Before what?" I asked.

"Before I leave."

"Leave?"

"Yes, I'm moving to London."

"What do you mean?"

"I'm going to live in London," he repeated.

"Why?"

There was a long silence, and then he said, "I need to get away from here."

"I understand. You're right."

"I know you understand," he said gently. Then he tossed out a question that left me breathless. "Eva, will you come with me?"

"What?"

"I want you to come with me to London."

"Mickey, I don't understand."

"I love you. I need you. I want you to come with me to London. Eva, are you still there?"

"Yes."

"I'm sorry to surprise you like this. I was actually calling to ask if I could come over. I wanted to talk to you in person. But somehow it just came out. I'm sorry."

Once again there was only silence, and then I said, "I don't know what to say."

"Look, I'm leaving in about a month. Can we get together before then?"

"I think so."

"Can I call you again?"

"Yes."

"I hope you feel better."

Before he hung up, he said again, "Eva, I love you." And then I heard a dial tone.

I found it difficult to turn around and face Roy. I was overcome with guilt. I told myself that I didn't do anything wrong, but still, I felt uncomfortable.

But Roy wasn't in the living room. I saw that the sofa was unoccupied. Only a cold cup of tea remained on the table.

I held on to the wall and shuffled to the living room. I sat down on the new easy chair and stayed there till morning. My thoughts gave me no rest. *Mickey wants me to go with him to London. He said that he needs me. This is the first time anyone ever said that to me.* I had never felt needed by anyone, and that particular sentence had quite a strong influence on my judgement. On the one hand, the temptation to leave everything behind and start afresh in a new life in a different place, far from my personal history, was huge; the possibility of a relationship, something I had never experienced before, both stirred me and terrified me; and finally, the fact that Mickey was Jewish held a strong connection to new feelings growing inside me. On the other hand, leaving everything behind would mean never knowing. All my questions about my parents and my life would remain questions forever. And then there was Roy. It was clear that moving to London would spoil the new connection formed between us. Exhaustion finally took hold. I fell asleep folded into the chair. That's how Roy found me the next morning.

"You slept in the chair?"

"Yes, I fell asleep," I answered drowsily.

"Shall I help you back to your bedroom?"

"Yes, please."

Roy helped me into bed. He made me a sandwich and poured a glass of milk and left them on the side table next to me.

"I have to get to the office," he said. "I'll be in touch." Before he left the room, he looked at me for a good long moment, as if he was going to say something, but turned around and left instead.

I fell back asleep immediately, not awakening until the early afternoon hours. The house was cold. When I sat up in bed, another bout of dizziness rocked me. I waited for it to pass and then got up and ambled toward the kitchen. *I have to get back to my old self. I have some tasks to finish.*

I went into the hallway where I had hung my purse. I took out a note with a telephone number and dialed. A formal voice answered, "Police, how can I help you?"

"I'm looking for Mr. Peter Jenkins," I said.

"With what is this regarding, ma'am?"

"Personal."

"One moment please."

"Peter Jenkins," I heard his deep voice say.

"Hello, this is Eva Brown speaking, I—"

"Eva, I called you several times, but there was no answer."

My heart was pounding like a galloping racehorse.

"I found the address you wanted, the last known address."

The pen in my hand shook. I wrote down the address he gave me and thanked him for his efforts.

"Don't hesitate to call if you need help."

I folded the note and stuffed it into my wallet. I wanted to get up and go there at that very moment, but I didn't have the energy. I decided that I would make the trip alone as soon as my strength returned.

30

A month after my conversation with Officer Peter, I drove to the address he gave me. I put on a sweatshirt and blue jeans, tied a flowery scarf around my neck, and was on my way. I was already in the city by ten o'clock. I stopped at one of the gas stations in order to ask for directions. The friendly man at the station explained that I had to leave the city and drive to one of the neighborhoods in the outskirts.

I arrived in the neighborhood where the houses were old; time had scratched its marks into them. The paint was faded, the yards looked unkempt, and the streets were dirty. Elderly people sat on the stoops.

I went to the address Peter gave me. The yellow paint on the front of the house was stained with signs of age. There was a motionless old rocking chair on the front porch. The house looked neglected. I knocked on the door with a trembling hand. No answer came. I knocked again, and then I heard the sound of legs being dragged. The door opened and in front of me stood a large woman. Her legs, visible under the old dress she wore, were thick like tree trunks, with a network of bulging veins. Her hair was disheveled, and she looked like she had just woken up. She scared me a bit. I took a step backward and spoke to her through the screen door.

"Hello, my name is Eva Brown. I'm looking for information about someone who once lived here. His name is John Brown."

"And what's your connection to him?" she asked, with a thin voice in direct contrast to her physical appearance.

"I'm his daughter."

The woman looked me over with piercing eyes and said, "His daughter, eh?"

I nodded. "Do you know him?" I asked.

"Unfortunately, yes," she answered and my heart skipped a beat. "Come inside."

The inside of the house was completely different from its exterior. The floor was covered with carpets, and in the middle of the room stood a table with a vase of fresh flowers on it, spreading a pleasant, unfamiliar scent. Light-colored curtains hung over the windows and moved gently with occasional gusts of wind. The house was spotless. The hallway leading out of the living room was unadorned with neither photographs nor carpets, but looked sparkling from where I stood.

"Please have a seat."

"Thank you."

"Can I offer you a glass of juice?"

"I would love a glass of water, thank you."

She dragged the weight of her body and returned with a small tray holding two glasses of water. She then sat down on a chair next to the sofa, turned to me and asked, "What made you come here today?"

"I only received the address a few days ago. My parents were killed in a car accident a few years ago."

"I'm sorry to hear that," she said, but her voice sounded uninterested.

"Did you know my father?"

"I lived in this neighborhood with my parents, on the other side of the street. Everyone knew everyone back then. Your father's family kept their distance from the rest of the neighbors. He continued to live in this house after his parents died."

"When did they die?"

"I gather he didn't tell you anything about his family," she said.

I nodded.

"His parents were hardworking people. His father was a construction worker and his mother worked as a cleaning lady. They came home late at night, and until then he and his brother would roam the streets picking on other children. Actually, his younger brother just followed him around, the poor kid; he was a few years younger than your father and was at his mercy. There were times when the adults living on the street got together to try and figure out what to do about their behavior. They also tried to talk to the parents, but nothing helped."

"I didn't know he had a brother."

"Look, you seem like a very nice girl. Are you sure you want to know everything? Sometimes not knowing is better than knowing."

"I want to know all of it!" I said. "That's why I'm here."

"There was a rumor that he killed someone," she said all of a sudden. Maybe she wanted to shock me, but my expression never changed.

"Who?"

"I don't know, but it was a rumor going around the neighborhood. I wouldn't be surprised if it turned out to be true."

"When did you buy the house from him?" I changed the subject.

"I bought it from his brother after your father disappeared, more than twenty years ago."

"And where did he move to?"

"I don't know and I don't care."

The animosity she showed toward my father oozed from every word that came out of her mouth. "Why do you hate him so much?" I asked.

She didn't hesitate for a second. She said, "Because he was a bad man."

"He was a wonderful father," I said. I was surprised by my need to defend him, especially after what I had learned about him recently.

She didn't react.

"What else do you want to know?" she asked.

"Why do you hate him so much?" I repeated my question.

"It doesn't matter. It's something personal."

I decided to leave it alone.

"Do you know where his brother lives?"

"The last time I heard, he was living somewhere in or near the city."

"Do you have his address?"

She hesitated but then got up and went into the hallway. A few moments later she came back and handed me a piece of paper.

"Thanks," I said and got up to shake her hand. "Wait, I don't know your name," I said.

"It doesn't matter," she said and went to open the door for me.

I left the house feeling awful. Something unsaid stood between us throughout the entire conversation—something I decided to place at the bottom of a box and seal away forever. Her hatred toward my father was enormous, of that I was sure.

I stood on the sidewalk across from the house and looked around the street. It was the street where my father lived and where he spent his childhood and teenage years. I tried to imagine him as a teenager, roving the street right there in front of me, going up to one of the kids, hitting him and stealing his backpack. I imagined him sneering at the child's tears as he ran away. The picture was etched into my brain. It seemed so realistic that tears of sorrow, anger, frustration, and pity began to roll down my face and drop onto the sidewalk—the same sidewalk that had borne witness to the painful images of a frustrated teenager whose self-hatred was eating him alive.

I placed my hands on the steering wheel of my car and took a deep breath. I asked myself if I really wanted to know. Maybe it was better to stay in the dark and accept a quiet conscience in return.

The temptation was huge, but so was the need to know. The bullet had left the chamber and there was no way to put it back. I hit the gas pedal and turned my car toward the address in my hand. After a fifteen-minute drive, I reached a quiet street lined with one-story houses. This street was completely different than the one I had just visited. There were elm trees standing on both sides of the street. Their fallen leaves mingled together, generating a cheerful sound with each step. The street cleaner drove along slowly at the curb, gathering the remaining leaves and sand. It was the afternoon. The street was quiet except for the mechanical sound of the vehicle disturbing the peace.

I finally found the house. The name Brown was written on the mailbox in brown lettering. I was smiling, even though my body was as taut as a guitar string. Suddenly I didn't know what to do. *They don't even know me. Maybe they don't even know I exist. What kind of reaction will I get?* The fear pushed me back, made me want to get back into my car and flee. I took one more step forward and reached the green fence in front of the house. On the other side, there was a garden hose in the grass, its nozzle resting in a recently prepared flower bed, with some digging tools and a small rake by its side.

There was an iron knocker on the front door. I knocked with it. My heart was pounding louder than the cleaner's pump on the street. I knocked again, harder.

"Just a minute," said a woman's voice.

The door opened a second later. Before me stood a woman about forty-five years old. Her hair was pulled back into a ponytail and her face had no makeup. I was tongue-tied. I stood there like a statue and didn't know what to say.

The woman looked at me in wonder and finally asked, "How can I help you?"

I wanted to talk, to respond, but no voice was forthcoming.

"Are you OK?" she asked in concern. "Come sit down." She came out of the house and led me to a chair on the porch. "I'll bring you a glass of water." She went inside and came back with a cold glass of water.

"I'm sorry," I said in a voice so low it could hardly be heard.

"It's OK. Would you like me to call someone for you?"

I shook my head no. "I'll be all right in a minute," I promised. I took a sip of the cool water and felt my throat open up and my tongue begin to work again.

"My name is Eva," I was finally able to say.

"Hi, Eva. I'm Michelle."

"Eva Brown," I added, and I saw her face transform. I had piqued her curiosity, although the name Eva by itself didn't mean anything to her. She looked at me and waited for me to continue.

"I'm John Brown's daughter."

She didn't react at first, but then she clenched her lips and I saw her jaw tighten. She got up from the chair and leaned against a wooden banister on the porch, as if she felt the need to put some distance between us.

"I'm sorry I came out of the blue. I only found out today that my father had a brother. I didn't know I had family."

Apparently, it was a mistake to refer to her as my family. Michelle apologized and went into the house. After a few minutes, she came back and said, "Ron will be here soon. You can wait for him here." She went back into the house and left me alone on the porch.

After about a half hour, a car stopped next to the house. I felt my heart about to explode. A broad-shouldered man, shorter than my father, wearing glasses, opened the gate and came up to the porch. I got out of the chair and extended my hand. He ignored it and sat down in the chair across from me. Tears threatened to appear. The insult burned into my soul. I wanted to run away from there and disappear, to never come back, to never again see these people that hated me without even knowing a thing about me. But I stayed seated. When he began to speak, his voice was as cold as an icy mountain.

"What do you want?" he asked.

"Nothing," I answered.

"Then why are you here?"

"I wanted to meet you. I didn't even know you existed until today." I sounded like I was begging.

He must have detected my miserable state, because his voice grew a bit softer as he asked, "Your father never told you about me?"

"No. He never told me about you. He was killed a few years ago in a car accident."

"I know," he said.

I was surprised, but I didn't make a comment.

Suddenly he got up from his chair, turned his back to me, and leaned his body on the porch banister. A moment later, he turned back around and said, "My brother and I haven't been in contact since before he left the city without saying where he was going. One day he just disappeared. No one knew where he was. My parents died, and I lost my only brother."

"Why did he leave?"

"I don't know," he said. He turned his head away from me. "Do you have any brothers or sisters?"

"No, I'm an only child. I also don't have any other family. My father never talked about you or his parents, and my mother never mentioned any family."

"I see. So how did you find me?"

"I met a woman who lived in your parents' old house," I said. "She told me."

"Yes," he sighed. "Mrs. Jacobs."

"She spoke about you with a lot of hatred."

"Yeah," he said, without adding a thing.

There were so many things I didn't know. A myriad of questions swirled around in my head, but I knew this wasn't the time to bring them up.

"What kind of father was he?" he asked suddenly.

I thought about how to answer this complex question and finally said, "Before he died, he was a great father, but after he died, not so much."

He looked at me and then he said, "I'm starving. Come and eat lunch with us. Michelle must be waiting for us."

Lunch was, strangely enough, both tense and relaxed at the same time. We talked about a number of subjects, but carefully did not talk about one: the name of my father was not uttered even once. It was obvious that this family was carrying a lot of baggage with respect to my father. And it was also clear that if I wanted to stay in touch with them, it would take time before we would be able to talk about things. After lunch, I got up and made my apologies, saying that I had to get home. Michelle stayed behind to get the kitchen in order, and Ron walked me to my car.

He said, "You need to understand that I am very angry at John. You don't have anything to do with it, but I need some time to absorb the fact of your existence. I have a lot more questions for you. I want to know everything, but that's enough for today."

He took out a business card and offered it to me, then took out another card and asked for my address and phone number. Before I could sit down in the driver's seat, he grabbed me and briefly hugged me to him, and then, as if his actions had embarrassed him, he ran back toward the house.

I left there feeling strange. *Something huge happened to me today. I have a family. Am I happy or upset? Maybe both. My father had a life besides the one I knew, and I have to get used to that. On the one hand, he was a loving father, and on the other, he was a monster. But they were the same person. The loving and caring father was the fruit of my childish imagination and the unknown. The monster was there the whole time. My mother knew it.*

When I got home, Roy was there. He welcomed me and came into my bedroom—his bedroom.

Ever since that conversation with Mickey, the atmosphere had changed at home. Roy was still concerned about me, but in a different way. He would leave in the morning, after taking care to make me something to eat. When he came back in the late afternoon, he would close himself off in his room. Sometimes I wasn't even sure if he was home at all. It felt like he had become just a roommate, and the distance between us felt enormous. The deep, close connection that had formed between us had all but disappeared.

It was seven o'clock in the morning when I woke up the next day. I got dressed, made myself a sandwich for lunch, and left the house. Roy had left a while earlier. A strange car was parked at the end of my driveway, blocking my way out. A man whose face wasn't visible sat behind the wheel. I debated whether to approach him and ask him to move his car, but recent experience had taught me to be cautious. I stood in place, shading my eyes from the blinding sun. The window rolled down and then I heard him call out, "Eva? It's me, Ron."

"Ron? What are you doing here?" I asked. He opened the car door, got out, and started walking toward me.

"I'm sorry to just show up like this. I didn't sleep all night. I had to see you, to talk to you. I just got in the car without thinking and came."

"I'm on my way to work," I said.

"I know, I know. I just thought... You know what, I'll just hang around until you come back from work and then we can talk." He began to walk back to his car.

"Wait," I said. "Come inside."

"Are you sure?"

"No." I smiled, opening the door and inviting him in. His steps were hesitant, as if he was afraid of something and was ready to bolt any minute.

He needed time to grasp the fact that he was in his brother's house, and it wouldn't be easy for him. He walked into the house in silence and immediately looked right and left. His hand felt along the wall until we reached the living room. I invited him to sit down and asked if he would like something to drink. "A glass of water," he said. He was pale, his throat visibly rising and falling. He removed his glasses and mopped up the sweat that covered his face with a handkerchief he fished out of his pants pocket. He sat down on the couch and looked around the room, as if he wanted to take it all in. I went to the kitchen to get him a glass of water and took my time in order to leave him alone with his private pain, with the memories that must be flooding him. When I turned back to the living room, he lowered his face, resting it on his shaking hands. He was crying—silently and aloud—trying unsuccessfully to choke back his feelings. His whole body shook. He grabbed his face with both hands and let the crying burst forth like a stream. I sat on a chair in the kitchen and let him cry for the both of us.

After he calmed down, I sat down next to him without a sound.

"How old are you?" he asked.

"Almost twenty-four," I answered.

"Tell me about him. What kind of father was he?"

I began to tell him about the father I once had, making an effort to remain a little girl as I described the father I had adored, the one that had medicine for every ailment. Ron wasn't satisfied. He asked direct questions arising from his knowledge of the man we were talking about. Slowly but surely, the fatherly image of my childhood converged with that of the man I came to know after his death.

"That's him," he said finally.

"And there's one more thing," I said making a spontaneous decision.

Ron lifted his eyes to me.

"He was a neo-Nazi!" I blurted out.

His eyes opened as wide as teacups. "What did you say?" he bellowed

"He belonged to a group of neo-Nazis; he was one of their leaders."

Ron got up from the sofa and began to walk around the room.

"Since when?"

"I don't know. I found out about a year ago."

"How did you find out?"

"That's a different story," I said after a while. "It's still hard for me to talk about."

"I see," he said and looked into my eyes. I lowered my head and played nervously with a button on my shirt. After a moment, he whispered, "Did he do something to you? Did he hurt you?"

"Not in the way you're thinking of, but in a lot of other ways, yes."

Ron sat back down next to me and took my nervous hand in his.

"Tell me about him," I said.

"Are you sure you want to hear it?"

"Yes," I answered confidently. "I have to."

"You will learn that the man you knew during his life is different from the one I knew as a youngster," he said. Then I heard him mumble to himself, "Or maybe not..."

"We were born and grew up in the house you visited, the one that Mrs. Jacobs lives in now. John was born three years before me. Our house was not a happy one. Our parents worked in menial jobs in order to support the family. My mother was a cleaning woman and my father worked in construction. They would come home late in the evening, bone tired from a hard day's work. I hardly saw them. When they came in, they were so tired they hardly said a word. They ate, and my father went straight to bed. My mother stayed behind a few minutes, until we went into our rooms, and then she also disappeared until the next evening. That's what our lives were like. A gray, lifeless routine.

"My father was a weak man. He resigned himself to his life and never had any hopes of escaping it. As time passed, John became a teenager eaten away by anger and frustration and took it out on my father. He ridiculed him, called him names, and once, when he couldn't bear the misery of his life, he hit him and injured him. Because of that, he spent a year in a juvenile detention center. When he came home, he had become a bully that people chose to stay away from. During the first years, he looked out for me. He was a role model to me, just like he was for you. I admired him for his strength, and for the fact that people were afraid of him. I tried to be like him in every way. But I was physically weaker than him, so he became my protector. If somebody said a bad word about me, they would feel the might of John's fist.

"John became the neighborhood thug. My parents didn't have any influence over him. The only figure he spared to some extent was my mother. Every once in a while, he would buy her a present with the money he earned doing odd jobs or money he stole. She asked him to stop, but he continued anyway.

"He dropped out of school before he went to the detention center. I continued to study and graduated high school. I was very lonely. My classmates distanced themselves from me. They were afraid to get into trouble with my brother and preferred to stay away from me as well.

"I was sixteen when my father died. He was killed in a work-related accident. The day they notified us of his death, I came home from school and saw two unfamiliar cars parked in front of the house. My mother was sitting in the living room crying. Two unfamiliar people sat next to her. There were noises coming from John's and my bedroom. John was going berserk like he never had before in my life. He was smashing anything and everything. He demolished the desk, ripped the sheets to shreds, upended the beds; nothing in the bedroom remained whole. Minutes later, police sirens approached. Two policemen came in and took him with them. It was the first time I was truly scared to death of him. This guy, my brother, was capable of anything. I left the house and closed myself up in the shed in the backyard. I was a teenager with a scared and terrified little boy inside him.

"Life changed after my father's death. John took my father's small shoes and grew them to enormous proportions. Now they were shoes made of steel with sharp daggers in the toes. His attitude toward my mother changed. He saw her helplessness and couldn't bear it. He would yell at her, insult her, sometimes even push her, and she would withdraw deeper and deeper inside her shell. I tried to stay away from him, but he wouldn't let me. Looking back, I understand that he needed me more than I needed him. I was the only person close to him that really loved him. Yes, I loved him despite his actions. He was my brother.

"My mother died two years later. She had given up on life. She faded away in front of our eyes until she couldn't take the burden of life itself and closed her eyes by choice. John became my only family; the only one I had in the world. Inside I knew that he wasn't good for me, but I thought there was no choice—he was the only one left. It was better to be with him the way he was than to be without him. And his attitude toward me also changed. He would beat me, demand that I do odd errands for him, and would find other ways to abuse me. I became his punching bag.

"If I was late coming home, he locked me in my room for hours without food or water. Sometimes he would rip apart my clothes and school books. Other times he would interrogate me about where I was going and decide whether to let me go or not. He became my warden, and the house was my prison. I wasn't the only one to suffer at his hands; all the children in the neighborhood felt his wrath. He would take things from them, threaten them. Even adults were afraid of him. The kids stopped going out on the street in the afternoon, preferring to spend time in their homes or yards. He strutted around the street like a peacock. But I knew the truth. I knew that hiding inside him was a scared soul that needed someone to give him a feeling of security, and that he acted like a monster so he wouldn't have to deal with the scary demons inside him."

"And how did you leave him in the end?"

"He left me—he disappeared, without leaving a trace or clue as to where he was. But before that a few more things happened. When he left, I breathed easy again, but I also wanted him to come back.

"When I was eighteen, I signed up for college. Considering the state of things, it was a really brave step for me to take. John tried to dissuade me, to get me to forget the whole idea. He said that studying would lead me nowhere. When he saw that I was adamant, he threatened not to give me a penny to pay for my studies. But the small inheritance left by my parents was divided equally between us, by law. He couldn't touch my portion. Despite his threats, I signed up for college not far from our house. I wanted to get away from him, but I didn't have the courage to go too far away. John never forgave me for deciding to go to school. He saw me as being pretentious and superior. He never stopped teasing me. He'd hide my books, and once he even tore up one of my papers. But the more he threatened, the more it became important for me to graduate and succeed. It drove him crazy.

"The lady you met, Mrs. Jacobs, lived in the house across the street from us with her parents and her brother. The boy was a handsome kid that girls flocked to, and the girl, Beth, was very pretty. She loved to laugh. We could hear her laughter from across the street. She was cheerful, always smiling and always willing to help. John despised this family. They served as a reminder of everything he ever wanted and couldn't have. He developed an obsessive hatred for the family. One day he bought binoculars and put them down near the window. Every night he would watch them. When I pointed out once that he was invading their privacy and it was against the law, he slapped me so hard that I never made a comment to him about his behavior ever again.

"Watching the family became part of his routine. When evening came and it was dark, he would sit down, take out the binoculars, and watch the family's house; Beth's room faced the street, and I knew he was focusing mostly on her. Maybe he hoped that one day he would be able to get close to her. And that day came, except it was the worst day I had ever experienced in my life.

"I had come home from classes that day later than usual, after working at the library to finish up an assignment. It must have been around eight o'clock when I got home. John was sitting by the window as usual at this time of the evening. Suddenly he got up, stopped in the kitchen, took something from one of the drawers, and ran out of the house. I watched him go but didn't do anything. I took a shower and sat down to prepare the school assignment—the hours flew by without my looking at the clock.

"The door opened suddenly and he walked into the house. I got up from my desk with the feeling that something had happened. I walked toward him, but he barked at me to get lost and then threatened me with the knife in his hand. I went back to my room and sat down on the bed.

"To this day, I've never forgotten the look on his face. For a split second, I saw the bruises and scratches, but mostly I remember his expression. It was the look of madness. Even now, I see that look in my mind any time I think about him. When Michelle called me yesterday and told me that you were at our house, the image of his bruised face popped up, and the things he said to me echoed in my ears like a thunderous bell.

"He didn't leave the house for two days. He closed himself in his room and only left once. I didn't understand what had happened to him. He was usually awake by noon and came home in the evening, when he would grab something to eat and sit down to watch the Jacobs' house. Suddenly everything changed. He stopped watching Beth's room and would come home after midnight. I didn't know what he was doing.

"One day I came home from college during the evening. The last remnants of light shone outside. Few people were on the street. I got off the bus and started walking toward home. I remember hoping that John wouldn't be there. His actions and irregular behavior made me extremely anxious, and I couldn't concentrate on anything.

"Except I never reached my home that night. I was deep in thought and didn't notice a group of guys coming toward me, holding baseball bats. Before I realized what was happening, they jumped on me and began beating my entire body. For a moment, I thought they wanted to rob me, and I tried to reach my hand into my pocket to throw them my wallet. But they weren't robbers; they were waiting for me to beat me up. Beth's brother was in the mob.

"I knew this was the end and accepted my death calmly. Beth's brother said, 'He ruined my sister's life and I'm going to ruin his.' I closed my eyes and waited for death to come. Suddenly everything stopped. I woke up in the hospital. My whole body was covered in bandages. Evidently, while they were beating me up, a police car happened to drive by and they ran away as soon as they saw the policemen.

"My recuperation took a very long time. I was hospitalized for four months. Apparently, I was close to death. The doctors told me that at some point they almost gave up on me.

"I left the hospital half a man. The doctors had to remove one of my kidneys and my spleen. One of my lungs was injured, and sometimes I have asthma attacks that force me to go to the hospital for a few days. But the worst part is that my ability to father children was damaged. That's the reason Michelle and I don't have any kids."

"And that's the reason Mrs. Jacobs expressed such hatred toward your brother," I said.

"Yes. She never recovered from the incident. I think she even spent time in a psychiatric hospital. She never got married and lives alone to this day."

"She never pressed charges against him with the police?"

"No, she chose not to. I still don't understand why."

"She bought your house and lives in it," I said quietly.

"One day, after John disappeared, I heard a knock on the door. I was still very weak and spent most of my time in bed. My muscles lost their tone and I got very thin, like a skeleton. When I opened the door, she was standing there—Beth. All she said was, 'I want to buy your house from you.' At first I didn't understand what she was talking about—what house? She answered immediately that she wanted this house.

"The more I thought about it, the more it seemed like the best solution for both of us, and I agreed to sell her the house. It was one of the wisest decisions I ever made. We never talked about her reasons for buying the house; she never explained and I never asked. Maybe it was a kind of revenge for what he took from her by force. For me, it was a kind of compensation for the terrible injustice he did her, and also a kind of revenge against my brother."

"You said he disappeared?"

"Yes, when I got out of the hospital, he wasn't home. He had taken a few things and disappeared. From that day forward, I never heard from him until yesterday, when you came to us."

"Did you try to find him?"

"Not at first. I think about a year had passed before I began to try to find him, but I wasn't successful. I also didn't try especially hard. After many years, I even went to your church and asked the priest about him. He told me that John was killed in an accident."

"So that was you?"

He nodded and continued. "With the money from the sale of the house, I bought my current house. I found a job at a bank in the city and married Michelle. I learned to live without him. Every once in a while, there were rumors, but I never paid any attention to them. There were days when he came into my mind, making me wonder what was going on with him, but I chose not to know. Usually my mental image of him had him behind bars. It was clear he would go to prison—he never seemed like a family man."

"Would you like something hot to drink?"

"Yes, please."

I made two cups of coffee and we went out to the front porch. The air was chilly. Ron turned out to be an interesting and intelligent conversationalist. He told me about his work at the bank and offered to help me with the money that remained following my parents' death. I was happy he offered, because I assumed that meant he intended to remain in contact with me, although we did not talk about the future. In the late hours of the afternoon, he got up and said he had to go.

"Can I keep in touch with you?" I asked with trepidation.

"Let's let time take its course," he answered vaguely.

I was disappointed in his answer. But after the story I heard him tell, I realized that it was the best he could give for now.

31

Roy left the house. I was in the kitchen and heard sounds coming from his room. When I went there, I saw him packing.

"Are you going somewhere?"

"I'm leaving."

"Leaving?"

Roy stopped for a minute and asked me to come in and sit down next to him on the bed.

"Eva, I can't go on like this."

"Like what?"

"You know what I'm talking about."

I knew. His feelings were hanging over us and between us the whole time, but I preferred to act as if everything was normal.

"I understand that you're confused, that your situation is problematic, but I have to move on."

I didn't know what moving on meant. I didn't want him to move on— he needed to stay exactly where he had been until now! But our situation was indeed untenable. Finally, I said, "I understand." He was probably hoping for a different answer, but I couldn't tell him what he wanted to hear.

He waited a moment and then got up to continue packing.

"Are you leaving now?"

"Yes."

"I met my father's brother yesterday," I said, hoping it would pique his interest and he would want to hear more and stay. I was a little girl who didn't want to stay home alone, but Roy wasn't the mother who's always available. He just said, "Great, I'm happy for you."

When he finished packing, he planted a light kiss on my lips and left the house. Once again, I was alone with my loneliness, and this time the pain was physical. I was a bundle of nerves as I wandered around the house, finally deciding it was time to visit Sarah. I had run into her on the street the week before and promised I would come over. She didn't pressure me, but said that she would be happy to see me again.

When I entered her house, I was welcomed by the same scents, the same warmth, the same doilies on the armrests of the chairs. Nothing had changed; nothing was out of place. There was a measure of comfort in that. Something about the permanence and predictability had a calming effect on me and gave me a sense of security. That's how I felt with her, given the painful turmoil I had experienced over the last few years. Before I could get over one trauma, something else would occur. Sarah was like an old tree whose roots are deep and long-lasting.

"How are you?" she asked after placing a plate of cookies on the table and sitting down in the chair across from me. I thought I saw tiny wrinkles forming on her cheeks, and her body appeared thinner. When she sat down, she did so slowly, as if every movement took an enormous amount of effort.

"I'm OK. And you?"

"Oh, I'm as old as ever," she chuckled. "Tell me what's been going on with you the last two weeks."

I debated whether to tell her about Ron and decided that she deserved to know. "I found out my father had a brother, Ron. I met him yesterday."

Her curiosity was genuine. "I didn't know he had a brother," she said.

"Yeah, neither did I."

"How did you find out?"

"I met someone who knew him and he told me."

Sarah was wise enough not to ask too many questions. "Tell me about him," she said.

"He's a very nice and smart man. He doesn't have any children, works at a bank, and is married to a woman named Michelle."

"And..."

"And what?"

"Do you want to tell me what he told you about your father?"

"I'm not sure," I said, pondering out loud.

"Is it that bad?" she read my mind.

"Yes," I answered simply.

"Is it that hard for you to talk about?"

"I'm ashamed."

"I understand."

"He was a bad man," I said suddenly. "Did you know he was like that?"

She didn't answer right away. Maybe she was choosing her words carefully so as not to hurt me. Finally, she said, "I know that your mother was not happy."

"Did she talk to you about him?"

"Very rarely."

"What did she say?"

All of a sudden, Sarah got up and asked if I would like a cup of tea. I said no, and she disappeared into the kitchen, returning after a short while holding a cup of tea. She didn't say a word the entire time and then sat back down in the same spot. She took a sip of tea and said, "She didn't tell me, she just led me to understand that her life wasn't simple—what was visible from the outside wasn't necessarily what's really going on."

"But besides the fact that she was Jewish and her name was Sonia, I don't know anything about her. I don't know where else to look."

Sarah didn't say a thing; she just shrugged and made a gesture of helplessness with her hand. Then, like she had last time, she said she had somewhere to go and hurried me out of her house.

32

My sense of loneliness grew deeper. I found myself sitting alone without a single soul to talk to. Even Donna kept her distance from me. She was angry because of my many absences from work, and because I didn't share what was going on in my life with her. And Roy—Roy almost completely broke off all contact. He called once a week, and then it was like he was doing it out of a sense of duty. The conversations were brief. Mickey called once and I asked him for more time. I was back to square one. No parents, no friends, just me, my memories and secrets.

One day, when I was close to losing hope, Mickey called and asked to come over. I agreed hesitantly, and he arrived a little before eight in the evening. I made us both something to eat and we sat in the kitchen. He had changed. His hair was short and he looked younger than his age, but also older. His body language projected a heaviness. He moved slowly, and it looked like every movement was difficult. His speech, which before was to the point, was now weighted, and it seemed like each word was passing through a filter before being spoken.

"Eva, have you thought about what I proposed?"

"I thought about it a lot, but first tell me what's been going on with you these last few weeks."

He took a deep breath and said, "OK." It was clear he wanted a more decisive response from me, but he answered anyway.

"These last few days have been very difficult for me. I've been thinking and replaying my life, and I know I've made a lot of mistakes, but I'm going to fix them now!"

"And what about your father?"

"I don't want to talk about that. It belongs in the past."

He got up from the chair and went into the living room. I followed and sat down next to him.

"How do you feel today, after everything?" I didn't want to say the words.

He said them instead of me. "You mean after my suicide attempt?"

"Yes."

"I don't know. Something is happening to me. Something is changing, but I don't know how to put this something into words. That's why I want to go away. I need time to think, far from the place and the people connected to this story. I need alone time."

"And why do you want me to go with you?"

"Because I love you," he answered immediately.

"Why?"

"Why?" he repeated. "I don't know. I just love you. I want you by my side all the time." He came close to me and took my hand in his. "I love you, Eva," he said. He hungrily pressed his lips to mine. His hands stroked my hair. I responded and felt myself disappearing into his world. A world with an unspeaking father and a mother who has accepted her fate and the fate of her son: guilt.

Our hands roamed all over each other with unrestrained passion. We were the only ones there at that moment, with nothing around us. Inside, we both knew that afterward there would be nothing left to give.

We lay in bed breathing heavily, our bodies close together. His arms embraced my body and I curled up inside them like an infant. This is how we fell asleep—holding each other like two people drowning. Morning arrived, and so did reality and the need for a decision. Mickey kissed my nose and got up from the sofa. He went into the bathroom and stayed there for a long time. When he came back, his face was back to the one I saw the day before, serious and grown up.

An hour later we stood by the front door. Mickey looked at my face and I returned his gaze. There was no need for words. Our lovemaking was the chord of separation. Mickey had some rough days of soul searching ahead. He didn't need me by his side. I would only get in the way of his devoting himself to the process he was about to experience. Besides, I also needed to do some soul searching—to let go of the heavy burden of the past and the difficult memories, alone, without the weight of his guilt added to my own. From the beginning, I knew we didn't have a chance, even though the journey we took to discover it was apparently crucial, at least for me. I gave him a long kiss and closed the door.

33

Several days after Mickey's visit, I decided to visit Donna. It was late afternoon, almost twilight. I didn't announce my visit. She opened the door for me before I could knock. "I saw you coming," she explained.

The last time I was in her house was after the first shocking discovery about my father. I was in such a bad way I never looked around. Now I saw that the house was clean and meticulously organized. The white walls made the apartment feel cold. There was not even one picture on the wall, and no rugs on the floor. I glanced quickly at the kitchen; it looked like it hadn't ever been used. The counter sparkled like crystal, and the chairs were in precise places under the table. Donna suggested we sit out on the balcony. She lingered a few minutes in the house, and then came out with two cups of coffee. With her hair gathered at her neck and her flowery dress, she looked a bit old-fashioned. Her face, clean of any makeup, shone brightly, and her warm smile was a complete contrast to her cold house.

"I met my father's brother," I said.

Her eyebrows raised in astonishment. I told her about my meeting with Ron at my house.

"You'll find a family for yourself yet," she said, her tone sounding somewhat ironic.

"Donna, didn't your foster parents have any family?" I asked. I saw her eyes, which had been shining a minute before, go dark like a candle being extinguished.

"They never mentioned any family, and nobody ever came to visit, except for neighbors living close by. But that's OK," she added quickly. "I'm used to living by myself. I like it this way—not answering to anyone. I used to think I wanted a family, children. But I'm not willing to give up my independence."

"Aren't you lonely sometimes?" I asked.

"Now and then, yes," she answered. "But that's OK too. My loneliness and I are good friends and we accept each other." She chuckled. "And now, enough of this melancholy. How about a good movie? We haven't been to the movie theater in a long time."

"You're right," I said.

"So, get up! We're going!" She stood up, gathered the coffee cups, and went into the house.

"What, now?"

"Now!" she commanded.

I smiled to myself on the way back home. When I imagined a close friend, it never occurred to me it would be someone like Donna. She was surprising—sometimes chilly, but full of warmth. We were so different from one another. She was extremely sure of herself, decisive and direct, while I was insecure, hesitant, and usually afraid to vocalize what was in my heart. The glue that joined us together was the great dissimilarity in our personalities.

"The perfect couple," I said to myself out loud.

**

The next few days passed by in a monotonous routine. I was alone most of the time. The house was quiet, and the nights passed with no extraordinary occurrences. My strong feeling that there was someone in the house watching over me had disappeared as well. Sometimes I wished it would return.

One day Ron called and invited me over for dinner. I gladly accepted the invitation. It was the first friendly voice I had heard in many days. My loneliness seemed to have taken on a shade of detachment and isolation. It went so far as to prevent me from even talking to people at work. I noticed that they kept their distance from me, as if they were afraid my mood might be contagious.

On Friday night, I put on a pair of jeans and a new red shirt, bought the day before on my way home from work. The color went well with my face and my hair, and my reflection in the mirror pleased me. My outward appearance undeniably compensated for what was happening in my gut. I was distraught. So many questions troubled me. *Would there be more meals together? Is this what it will be like from now on? What will I talk to them about? Will they want to know more about my father? My mother? My life?* I went to dinner with serious misgivings.

Michelle opened the door. Her eyes were bright and a warm smile graced her face. I hoped her smile was authentic. Ron was waiting inside and welcomed me with a hug.

"Come, sit down," he invited me. "This is your place."

I wondered if he meant only for dinner or in general.

Ron and Michelle made every effort to make me feel good. They avoided talking about my father, instead asking about my job at the office, about my friends, about my studies. I told them that I was in college up until my parents died, and Ron asked why I didn't go back to school. I told him that I intended to register for the following school year.

"If you need help, in any form, call me," he said. Then, surprisingly, he added, "Even if it's financial help."

I was so surprised that I looked down and didn't answer. His offer touched my heart. It involved so much more than just an offer of financial support. He was saying, in his way, that he wanted to stay in touch with me, that I was family now. It was the most treasured and touching thing anyone had said to me recently. I thanked him. When the meal was over, Michelle brought out dessert from the refrigerator and asked me to help move the dishes out to the porch. "We'll eat dessert out there," she said.

It was a lovely evening. A light breeze swayed the fringes of the tablecloth. Ron sat next to me and Michelle sat across from us.

"Such nice weather," he said.

"Yes," Michelle and I answered at the same time and smiled at each other.

"What was your childhood like?" he asked suddenly.

I asked him what he meant.

"I mean, how did you pass your time as a child? Did you have lots of friends? Where did you hang out? I'm asking because I want to get to know you better."

"I didn't have a lot of friends. I spent my afternoons with him. He insisted on it. He used to bring home boxes of model airplanes, sit with me on the floor, and help me put the pieces together."

"He had good hands," Ron said.

"And friends—didn't you have any?" asked Michelle.

"Not really."

"And your mother, what did she think?"

"I don't know," I said in a soft voice. "She didn't talk very much."

I think Michelle hinted to Ron to stop asking me questions about my mother because suddenly he changed the subject.

"Who gave you the name Eva?" he asked.

"I think he chose the name," I said, sure for some reason that he had chosen it. He loved my name, loved to use it. One time when I was a teenager, I heard him yell, 'Eva, her name is Eva,' before my mother hurried into their bedroom and shut the door. Yes, no question about it; he chose my name.

"You know who Eva Braun was," he said taking for granted that I did.

I saw Michelle stretch back in her chair, trying to catch his gaze. I didn't understand her behavior. When it seemed that he was going to continue speaking, she got up and asked if anyone wanted seconds. Ron said that he was full and so did I.

"So, who was Eva Braun?" I asked.

"Eva, would you like to come help me in the kitchen?" Michelle said suddenly.

I saw Ron send her a questioning look, and then his expression changed. He cleared his throat and said to her, "Here, I'll help you."

Michelle had made quite an effort to stop the conversation. I realized that she was trying to prevent Ron from answering my question. I got up as well, and said, "Wait a minute, Ron, answer my question. Who was Eva Braun?"

Ron looked helplessly at his wife and sat back down in his chair. Michelle remained standing. The breeze from before had stopped, and the air became stifling. The peaks of the trees stood erect, silent and threatening. I felt a crisis coming. My hands began to sweat.

"Ron, who was Eva Braun?" I asked again, but my memory shot the answer to my brain before he could answer.

His answer hammered another nail into the box that was my life.

34

My life had attracted more than a few crises. I imagined my father sitting on a cloud holding a scepter. He waved the scepter from side to side, and every time it leaned toward one side or the other, something happened—something he thought up in his warped little mind. If I had any doubts about the things he did, they had completely disappeared. Now I knew. *My life has been a staged performance designed by a malicious mind. He didn't love me. He wasn't capable of love. Everything he did for me, everything he taught me, every direction he led me, was the result of his vile desires. He never intended to atone for his childhood actions. He never felt guilt for the way he treated his parents and his brother. Did he ever regret raping Beth? I don't think so. There was no place in his soul for a conscience or guilty feelings. Nature created a monster, and that monster was called Father.*

Discovering the connotation of my name was a rough blow. I realized that, for him, I was proof of his loyalty to the group he belonged to. I was a pawn on his chessboard, and he moved me from place to place at his will. But the question of why my mother married him remained a mystery. Something or someone forced her to join her life to his. It was clear she didn't love him—maybe even hated him—but she continued to live with him anyway. Until I discovered the secret to the root of their relationship, I would not rest.

35

Winter arrived and brought with it torrential rains. Tree branches broke off and blocked the sidewalks and streets. There were a number of car accidents, including one that caused the death of a ten-year-old boy. People tried mostly to stay indoors. The radio reported that several homeless people had frozen to death. The residents complained that the city wasn't sufficiently prepared. The sewers weren't capable of dealing with such large volumes of water and the streets flooded. Cars broke down and were creating uncharacteristic traffic jams all over. But in spite of the weather, I was feeling a type of renewal. The emptying of the streets filled me with the desire to wander them. People sought shelter from the wetness and I went out to embrace it.

I wandered around outside, the rain dripping down my body, my clothes getting soaked. The clear water washed away the filth that had stuck to me over the last few years. To be clean—that's all I asked for. I took a deep breath of the fresh scent of the earth, swallowing the water that ran down my face, taking in something natural and pure, and walked and laughed to myself about my silliness, my childishness, my unconventional actions. I shook off all my guilt and felt like I always wanted to feel— released from it all.

During one of those days, I ran into a woman on the sidewalk who had found shelter from the rain under a cardboard box. Her body was obviously wet. I bent down to her and she lifted her eyes to me and wished me well. Her face was filled with wrinkles, but her eyes looked young. Her hair, peeking out from under a wool hat, was a mixture of red and black.

"Come inside my home," she said with a big smile and moved over to make room for me. I got inside and our bodies—hers thick and mine thin—were pressed together. One of her hands reached out and embraced my shoulders.

"What's a beautiful girl like you doing outside on a day like this?" she asked, her smile still showing on her wrinkled face.

"Walking," I answered.

"Great."

"And you?" I asked. "Don't you have anywhere to go?"

"I do."

"So why..."

"I like it like this, in the rain," she said and burst out laughing, revealing two rows of slightly yellowing but beautiful teeth. "It seems strange to you, huh?"

I nodded.

"But you're out in the rain too. Don't you have a home?"

"I do," I answered with a smile.

"So how come you're out here then?"

"I'm getting clean," came my answer.

"Ahh... From what?"

"From life."

"Is it helping?"

"I don't know. Right now, it's helping."

"Great," she said and laughter rolled from her mouth like champagne bubbles.

"Why is that great?"

"Because pleasure is found in the little things—in the rain that wets your hair, a beautiful melody, a nice word to someone, a smile from someone, a kiss you receive from someone important, a beautiful landscape, a trip you took, a meeting with someone interesting on a rainy day..." She opened her mouth laughed again. It was irresistible, and I joined her. There we both sat, laughing, her arm still embracing my shoulders. We laughed harder and harder. I was holding in my stomach—it was about to burst. Tears of merriment rolled down my face and mixed in with the last vestiges of rain that clung to my hair. We sat like that until the rain stopped.

"Go home, child. Look for the simple things that make you happy." Her hand on my back gave me a little push, forcing me to get up. I left her unwillingly, and she turned away from me as if she already had forgotten I existed.

When I got home, I went into the laundry room to take off my wet clothes. Next to the washing machine was a puddle of water. One of the pipes had come loose and was dripping water. I took a rag and shoved my hand under the machine, pulling out the water. A piece of paper floated in it. It was the birth certificate I had found a few days after my mother's death and then completely forgotten. The name Ethel written beside the name of the newborn had gained new meaning since then—Ethel was the name on one of the boxes in the basement, the one with the toys that had never been opened. I held the paper delicately by the corner and left the room. Droplets of water dripped onto the floor of the room and the carpet in the living room. I flattened it out on the table in the kitchen and soaked up the dampness with a dry paper towel. Some of the ink smeared, but it was still possible to read the writing clearly.

Who are you, Ethel? I asked myself. *What are you doing in my house? Why did my mother hide your birth certificate?* The questions kept coming and no answer was in sight. I left the sheet of paper on the table. I was hoping that by acknowledging its daily presence, some sort of hidden compartment would open up inside my head.

The certificate had been lying on the table for several days when one day my eyes suddenly saw something new: tiny letters were printed on the bottom of the page, in the right corner. I moved closer, trying to figure out what was written, but time had taken its toll; some of the letters were faded and some had become smeared in the water. I sat bent over like a withering flower stem, moving the page forward and backward. I could make out the letters m, o, n, p, and n again. But no matter how hard I tried, I couldn't make any meaningful words out of the letters.

I went to my room and brought out a magnifying glass to see the letters more clearly: the first and last words were "printing" and "Chicago." I wrote each letter in the middle word several times, but the word didn't make any sense. I tried again and again to make the lines form into a real word, and finally came up with a strange one: Manonpo. *Manonpo Chicago Printing.* The name had a Chinese or Italian ring to it—perhaps it was the name of the printer providing printing services to the hospital where Ethel Weiss was born in 1974.

I went to my computer and began to look for printers with that name in the Chicago area, but none of them were called Manonpo. I felt like this was a dead end, but I wasn't willing to give up. *Even if the printing company doesn't exist anymore, someone must know where to find the owners.* I assumed the owners of other printing companies knew each other, at least by name. I took the list of printing companies and began to call them in order. The first five claimed they didn't recognize the name and couldn't help me. On the sixth call, a nice man answered and asked me to keep saying the name Manonpo.

"It sounds like a Japanese or Chinese name," he said.

"Yes, to me too."

"It's strange. Are you sure the printer is in this area?"

"Yes, why?"

"Because there has never been a printing company owned by the Chinese," he said.

"Are you sure? Maybe you don't know them?"

He said in a patronizing voice, "Young lady, I know them all. I've been in the printing business since the age of sixteen. There is no printer in the area or outside of it that I don't know." Then he added, "There never were—and there aren't now—any printers owned by Chinese. They are busy in other professions, mostly retail. They don't have any interest or know-how in printing."

His words were very convincing, but if it was true, how would I go on from here?

My desperation must have made its way through the telephone because he asked if I was still on the line.

"Yes," I answered.

"It's important for you to find this printer?"

"Very much."

"May I ask why?"

"It has to do with someone I'm looking for," I said vaguely.

"I see. And you're sure that's the name?"

I wasn't sure of anything anymore. "I have the birth certificate of someone I'm trying to find, and on the bottom of the page is the name of the printing company. I thought I'd find the hospital through this printer."

"Where do you live?"

I told him the name of my town.

"I know where that it," he said. Then he surprised me, saying, "Would you like to come here with the certificate so I could see it? Maybe I can help you."

I didn't hesitate a second. "When can I come?"

"Any time, my dear. I'm here at my printing business every day. My sons run it now. I'd love the company, and maybe you'll even get a cup of the special tea I brew with my secret recipe."

"How can I possibly refuse, sir?"

"Well then, tomorrow?"

"Tomorrow," I promised.

When I set the phone down, I felt renewed energy coursing through my veins. If he'd offered, I would have gotten into my car and sped over to him that very moment. But he suggested tomorrow. So be it.

Time is a dictator. It has its own persistent pace and nobody can convince it to go any faster. Counting the hours one by one didn't make the hands of the clock go any faster. They sneered at me with the condescension of the all-powerful.

Tomorrow finally came. I was so excited I almost forgot to bring the reason I was going in the first place. I had to retrace my steps to pick up the certificate from the kitchen table.

I arrived at the outskirts of Chicago. The nice man's excellent directions brought me to the printers' office well before noon. He was a man of about seventy, with white hair reaching down to his shoulders. His eyes scrutinized me through the eyeglasses perched on his nose. He walked slower than normal, and when I looked closer, I noticed one of his legs was shorter than the other. He saw me looking and said, "The polio epidemic. It broke out in the area when I was five. They didn't know about the vaccination back then, and the ones who contracted it were mostly young children like me. But better to have one leg shorter than one leg missing, right?" He looked at me and winked.

"Yes," I said and returned a smile.

We went into a room that was in fact a large hall filled with old, silent machines. There was chaos everywhere: papers, printing plates, boxes of colored inks, cardboard tubes, trash cans filled to the brim, tables covered with stacks of notebooks. Even the sticky floor gathered useless objects, and years of neglect had filled it with clutter. The old man cleared a path for me and invited me into a small room with no door whose filthy glass windows separated the pandemonium of the room from the hall we had just come from. He made space on a table and set down a kettle and two cups. For a moment, I wanted to refuse his secret formula, but I didn't dare. He was nice. And besides, I wasn't going to do anything to hurt my chances of getting any vital information from him.

Isaacs—that's what he asked me to call him—poured two cups of the steaming drink and asked me to try and guess what the ingredients were. "I recognize cinnamon," I said. He smiled and waited. "Maybe apple? Or orange?" I tried, but he just smiled contentedly and waited for me to continue. After a few unsuccessful attempts, he waved his hand and said with confidence, "You'll never guess."

I gave up and said, "Delicious." He was pleased.

I wanted to hurry up the meeting and get to the reason I had come there. He sensed my agitation and said, "Well, would you like to show me the sheet of paper?" I took the birth certificate out of my purse and handed it to him. He took it, felt the paper with his fingers, moved it away from his eyes toward the naked light bulb in the ceiling and brought it back down. "What's the name you said?"

"Manonpo," I said.

"You must be kidding. Manonpo!" He laughed. "How did you get that weird name?" His laughter began to roll off his tongue, showing his nicotine-stained yellow teeth. "Manonpo," he repeated, his laughter not dying down. His round stomach jiggled with each new attack of laughter. His laughter grew so loud that he began to cough, and I thought he was choking. I handed him his cup of tea, but he refused by shaking his head. Suddenly he got up from his chair, went to the sink blackened with grime, turned on the faucet, and threw water on his face—water that was a disgusting color. After he calmed down a bit, he picked up a moldy rag and wiped his face with it. His laughter began to die down and then he said,

"I'm sorry, but I couldn't stop, I haven't laughed like that in a long time." It looked like he was going to have another bout of laughter, but this time he controlled himself and came back to the chair across from me. "Robert," he said. "Robert printed this page."

"Robert?" I asked.

"Yes, Robert Mahoney. And he hated the Chinese. That's what was so funny to me."

"Can you tell me where I can find his print shop?"

"I can, but it won't help you."

I looked up questioningly. "Robert passed away five years ago. His wife sold the printing business to someone who tore it down and built a large department store in its place."

"So, the printer no longer exists?" I asked in desperation.

"It hasn't existed for a long time," he said. "But you don't need him."

"Why not?"

"Because I know exactly who he worked for. Robert and I were friends. He worked for me as a printer before he decided to open his own printing business. Everyone was sure we would be enemies, because he became a competitor. But we stayed close friends. We sometimes even passed work on to one another. There was room for the both of us. My sons were angry with me because I gave away jobs—they said we would never succeed as long as I kept doing that, but I valued our friendship and didn't let the business come between us.

"It's different today; my sons work without feeling. They only want to earn money and whatever happens along the way... Well, that's not important anymore, only profit and success. And if someone gets hurt, they say that it's part of the game. I don't understand what game they're talking about. Business is a soul, not a game. I don't go into the main hall anymore, the central one. I sit here and remember how much I loved the work. We would work with our hands, get dirty, and go home all black.

The work was done with soul. We would talk and laugh while we worked. That was our life. Today most of the work is done by machines. Everything is 'what did we earn' and 'what did we lose' and 'how can we make more.'

"My sons go home clean. Their hands are white and their fingernails are clipped and manicured. I know they mock me. I also know that one day they'll be where I'm sitting. It's too bad we don't have a telescope that can show us what we'll be like in the future. Maybe then we would act differently. But I'm talking your head off with boring memories and you want an answer from me."

I thought to myself how lonely he must be.

"The Jesuit Hospital for Unwed Mothers."

"What?" I didn't understand what he was talking about.

"Your birth certificate is from the Jesuit Hospital for Unwed Mothers," he repeated.

"Oh!"

"It still exists, and isn't very far from here. You can go over there right now."

I got up and shook his hand. He also got up. He said, "I hope you find what you're looking for." I left the sweet, lonely man, hoping he would find solace and joy in the success of his sons.

After about an hour's drive, I stopped in front of a very old structure with flaking paint. A rickety old sign hung at the entrance. "The Jesuit Hospital for Unwed Mothers of Chicago and the Region." The pungent odor of Lysol welcomed me, forcing me to pinch my nostrils. I followed a sign with the word "Office" written on it. The walls were painted a light, shiny green. Despite its age, the place was clean and neat. Nurses passed me by with small quick steps. I heard the cries of a baby in the background, and a scream suddenly pierced the air. Someone asked the nurse to come over; a few people were standing around the corridors like me, busy among themselves and avoiding any direct eye contact.

I reached the end of the corridor. I knocked on the door and opened it. There were two desks standing across from each other, each with its own clerk. One of them lifted her head toward me, and the other continued to bend over the papers on her desk.

"How can I help you?" the first one asked in a pleasant and inviting voice. I moved closer to her. All of a sudden I didn't know how to describe what I was looking for.

"How can I help you?" she asked again. Then I saw the other clerk lift her head to look at me curiously.

I decided to tell the truth. "A few years ago, I found this birth certificate at my house," I said. I handed her the sheet of paper. "I don't recognize the name, and the name of the mother isn't listed. I thought someone might need the certificate and would be happy to receive it."

She took it from me and studied it. "Strange," she said. "We always write the name of the mother on the birth certificate, but there's nothing written here. I see the year of the birth is 1974. I'll have to look it up in the archives. The computer contains births only from 1980 on. All the previous certificates are located in the archives."

The clerk sitting across from her asked to see the certificate as well. She was a lot older than the one that answered. I passed the sheet to her and she inspected it. Then she opened a drawer in her desk, and took out a magnifying glass. She moved it back and forth, and the sentence she said completely shocked me. "Someone tampered with the name of the mother."

"I don't understand," I said.

"Someone erased the line where the mother's name is written."

"But who would do that?" I asked. I immediately realized I had asked a stupid question.

The secretary looked at me for a long time with untrusting eyes.

"I didn't do it! I didn't even know someone tampered with the certificate."

Both clerks looked at one another, and unspoken words passed between them.

"Where did you get this birth certificate?" asked the older one.

"I found it at home," I answered.

"And you didn't show it to anyone, your parents, for example?"

"My parents were killed in a car accident. I don't have anyone else to show it to."

I thought I saw the expression on the older one's face soften a bit.

"I'll go to the archives and check," she announced. She got up from her chair and left the room with the certificate in her hand.

I didn't know what to do with myself. I stood between the two desks and regretted coming. *I could have kept the certificate in one of the drawers at home and forgotten about it.* The young clerk bent over her papers and pretended to be busy. I knew that she, just like me, was waiting for her friend to solve the mystery that had brought a bit of color to their otherwise gray office.

Twenty minutes went by before the door opened and the older clerk walked back in. She held two pieces of paper in one hand and a cardboard box in the other. She put the papers side by side on the desk, straightened them out with the palm of her hand, and asked me to come closer to the desk.

I bent my head over the pages, looking from one to the other. The page from the archives was almost exactly like the one I had brought from home, except for one detail. Where the name of the mother was missing on my copy, their copy said Nichka Weiss.

"How about an address? Is one listed anywhere?" I asked.

"Sometimes we have an address, although most of the addresses are phony. At that time, they didn't take pains to write down exact information on the patients. The women that came to have babies in this hospital did their best to submit as little information as possible. We required first and last names but no other details. And when they did give details, the information wasn't necessarily correct. This hospital was a shelter for girls who got pregnant out of wedlock, usually without the knowledge of their family. Many of them gave up their babies even before they were delivered—they were put up for immediate adoption or transferred to an orphanage. Things are different today. Each delivery is documented in the computer, and we require the mother to give us correct information. Today, having a child out of wedlock is no big thing—women do it at both public and private hospitals. Those that come to us these days are mostly young girls whose parents don't have the money to pay for hospitalization somewhere else. We only charge a minimal price."

"I see," I murmured. "So you don't have the address for the mother?"

"Hold on," she said and opened the file she brought from the archives. She flipped through it and pulled out a partially printed page. "There's an address here, but like I said, it's very possible that it's fake. It says here that the mother lives at a place called Cypress Beach and there's also the name of a street... I can hardly make out what's written here," she mumbled. "I think it says Main Street." She picked up the glasses that were lying on her desk and placed them on the end of her nose. "Yes, absolutely. It says 16 Main Street, if I'm not mistaken. The number isn't that clear."

I thanked them, took the birth certificate, and left the room. I wrote down the address she gave me on the back of the page and debated whether to go home or drive to the address. It was the noon hour. I was flooded with curiosity and armed with hope. *Perhaps, after such a long time, I might actually find out who this Ethel is, and how she is connected to my house.* I set out toward the address in my hand.

More than an hour later, after getting lost a few times and retracing my steps, I reached the place known as Cypress Beach, located on the southern shore of a cerulean lake. The road I took was wide and circled the lake.

Next to it was a boardwalk, and a few tourists were walking around. The weather was pleasant, even though a chilly wind was blowing. It was a nice day for a walk, but it wasn't warm enough to take a dip in the sea. From my right window, I saw that the sea was stormy. White foam pounded the coast relentlessly. The sky was blue, adorned by feathery clouds, as light as angel wings. I slowed down and took a deep breath of the air outside. The road continued endlessly. To my left, there were restaurants and cafes filled with people.

I stopped on the shoulder of the road to try and determine where I was. A young man walked to my car window and bent his head down, almost touching mine. He said, "Can I help you?" I was so surprised that I recoiled in alarm.

"I didn't mean to scare you. I'm sorry! You looked a little helpless."

"It's OK," I said, and tried to make my voice light and easy. "I do actually need help. I'm looking for Main Street. Do you know how I get there from here?"

"It's obviously the main street of the city," he said and smiled, revealing two rows of teeth as white as the moon.

"Am I on it?"

"Yes, but you are probably on the wrong side. You need to go to the residential area—that's further down. You should just keep driving until you reach a boulevard lined with tall cypress trees. Then you'll know you've reached the residential neighborhood of the city. Would you like me to show you where it is? I'm free and I don't have any plans..." Again he gave me his shiny white smile. I was tempted to open the door for him and let him in the car, but years of not being spontaneous had taken their toll, and that took precedence.

I said, "Thanks, but I'm in a bit of a hurry." I hit the gas pedal and put some distance between me and the chance of an adventure.

I drove to the boulevard, admiring its cypress trees, so tall they must touch the sky. I drove slowly, checking the house numbers every once in a while, and finally stopped in front of number 16, where my heart began to race. As usual, doubts began to toy with me. *What am I going to say? How will I explain the reason I'm showing up? How will I introduce myself?* The house, like all the other houses on the street, was a one-story light gray house. The window frames were painted dark pink, and the lawns in front of the houses were manicured and healthy. Sprinklers were working on both sides of the path. Parallel to the path were flower beds, straight as an arrow, with colorful flowers at the peak of their bloom.

I rang the doorbell and the door was opened immediately by a woman in her forties. She had an apron around her hips and her arms were held high to protect the ball of dough in her hands. It was obvious that she was in the middle of making bread. Even so, she had a nice smile.

"Hello," she said first.

"Hello," I answered weakly, still looking for the right sentence to begin the conversation.

"My name is Eva, and I'm looking for someone by the name of Nichka Weiss. I received this address..."

"Nichka Weiss," she repeated the name. "And she lives at this address? Are you sure?"

She must have seen the disappointment on my face, because she said, "The name sounds familiar, but I'm not sure where I know it from."

I kept quiet, hoping she'd remember. "You know, I think the previous tenants who lived here—their name was Weiss. I've lived here for fifteen years already, from the day I got married, but I remember that during those first years, mail used to arrive with the name Weiss on it."

"Do you still have the letters?"

"No, after a few years, I threw them away. I didn't see any reason to keep them. Nobody came to ask for them."

"I see. Do you know anything about this family?"

"I think the real estate agent told me they left after their son was killed. But I'm not sure that's true."

"Anything else, perhaps?"

"No, I'm sorry. But maybe you should ask the neighbors. I don't know which ones, though. Edith and Paul, who live next door, moved here after I did, so they wouldn't be able to help you, and their house is empty most of the time anyway. The family only comes during the summer for vacations."

The dough began to drip between her fingers. She gave me an apologetic expression.

"Thank you," I said.

"I'm sorry," she replied, and went into the house.

I got in my car and sat behind the steering wheel, frustrated and disappointed. On the way home, I thought about my lack of progress. *Ethel remains a name on a sheet of paper and on a box. Aside from the new information about the name of her mother, I don't know anything else—no address, no connection to my house. Maybe the solution to the mystery is simpler than I'm imagining. Maybe Ethel is the daughter of neighbors that lived nearby, or her family lived at my house before my parents came here.* I decided to leave Ethel alone for now, but fate, it seems, had other plans.

When I got home, there was a message on the answering machine. I pressed the button and listened. "Eva, this is Josh. Call me, I have something for you." It took a few seconds before I remembered that Josh was the nice guy that promised to try and find my mother.

I dialed him immediately and the secretary's voice answered after one ring. "Hello, may I speak with Josh?"

"I'm sorry, he just went out. One minute, one minute—" I heard her call Josh. "Before you go out, answer the phone, it's for you."

"Hello?"

"Josh, this is Eva Brown."

"Eva, how are you?" His voice sounded just as cheerful as I remembered.

"I left you a message this morning."

"Yes, I just heard it and called you right back."

"Well, I have some good news for you. We were able to locate someone by the name of Sonia Schwartz, who once lived in a place called Cypress Beach."

"Are you sure?"

"Yes, why do you ask?"

"I just came from there."

There was a pause. Then he asked, "Did you find her yourself?"

"No, it's complicated. I was looking for someone else and they sent me there. It must be a coincidence. In any case, thank you, Josh. You've been a big help."

"You're welcome," he answered.

***

I plopped down on the sofa. I didn't know what to think. This strange coincidence was beyond imagination. It was disturbing. I was flooded with vague information and unclear feelings.

My fingers dialed the number automatically. His voice answered after two rings. "Roy?"

"Yes, Eva."

It had been a month since we'd spoken last. I had called him once but hung up before he could answer. Being separated from him was hard for me and increased my feeling of loneliness. I was angry that he was able to refrain from calling me for such a long time. I imagined him meeting someone else. The thought drove me crazy, but it also helped me stay angry and not call him again.

"How are you?"

"I'm fine."

"Are you busy?"

"Not especially. Did something happen?"

"Yes and no..."

"I don't understand."

"Can you come over?" I blurted out.

"I'm not sure I should," he said after a moment.

"Are you mad at me?"

"Yes and no," he said, and I thought I heard a smile in his voice. "When should I come?"

"Now?" I tried.

"I'll be right there."

Roy didn't know how to play games, and that was exactly what I loved about him. He was the straightest person I knew. That's why he preferred to cut himself off from me. He knew he couldn't pretend. Suddenly I felt an intense longing for him—for his long face, his warm smile, his familiar knock on the door, his honest concern, everything. When the knock came, I ran to the door, flung it wide open, and jumped straight into his arms.

"What is this?" he asked after I released him from my hug.

"I missed you," I said softly.

I could see he wanted to say something back, but he changed his mind and became businesslike. "What did you want to tell me?"

"Would you like something to drink?"

"No!"

"To eat?"

"Eva..."

"OK, sorry."

I told him about my meeting with Ron, my father's brother. Every once in a while, I stopped to think about what to tell him and what not to, but Roy, who knew me so well, wasn't misled. He said, "Eva, tell me everything." So I told him everything about my despicable father that gave me life and the name he gave me when I was born. I lifted my eyes to his face to see his reaction, but his eyes remained steady and his face didn't show any shock.

"Did you hear what I said? He named me after Hitler's mistress."

"I know."

"You know? How?"

"I just know."

I became despondent. Roy got up, poured us both a glass of water and came back to sit next to me.

"What else, Eva? Did you discover anything else?"

I shook my head, and Roy waited patiently for me to continue.

"I looked for Ethel." Roy raised his eyebrows in surprise.

I told Roy about my recent discoveries. His curiosity was piqued. "Are you saying that your mother and Ethel's family lived on the same street?" he asked.

"Yes."

"That's weird. So, what are you going to do about it now?"

I said, drawing out my words, "I was thinking that maybe you would agree to come with me to the address I received."

Roy let out a long sigh and said, "You've been very busy lately."

I didn't answer, just looked at him with anticipation.

"When would you like to go?" he said.

I was so happy that I threw my arms around his neck and planted a big fat kiss on his lips. Roy was surprised, but snapped out of it quickly. He unwrapped my arms from his neck, took my head in his hands, and kissed me. When he tried to pull away from me, I wouldn't let him. I continued to attach myself to his warm lips. I moved him closer to me so our bodies were pressed together until we became one entity. When we finally separated from each other, he only asked, "Mickey?"

"Over," I answered.

36

The days that followed flew by like a young sparrow on a clear spring day. The horizon, which had always seemed beyond reach, grew closer and seemed more promising.

Roy came over every day now. We spent every free moment together. The question of moving in together hadn't come up yet. It seemed only natural that he would move back to the house, but we decided it wasn't time yet. We needed more time to digest the change in our relationship. We still hadn't slept together either. We were building a new connection based on an old one and it was fantastic. I had more energy, and I smiled more.

I noticed that Donna was sneaking glances at me, although she avoided asking about the change in me. One day at the office, the department head came over and said that I was doing excellent work. I had never been told that before. I had never felt so alive, so awake. The future suddenly seemed brighter, full of hope.

One evening we were sitting in the living room. Roy was reading the newspaper and I was holding a book in my hand. His eyes were stuck on the same word for a long time. Thoughts were running around my head like a dog chasing its tail. I finally said, "I'm going back to school."

Roy looked up from his newspaper. "Where?"

"Here, at the college I studied at before."

"Did you register?"

"Yes."

"Psychology?" he asked.

I nodded.

"Great," he said and got up from the sofa, pulling me up too. We stood facing each other, our separate bodies becoming a whole. "I love you," he whispered into my hair. I leaned my head onto his chest and circled his waist with my arms. I knew he was waiting for me to say it back. But I didn't. I still couldn't.

***

We planned to go to Cypress Beach on Saturday. We packed a small basket of food and decided that after the visit we would have a picnic by the lake.

Mother Nature had summoned wonderful weather for us. The sun warmed the earth, and its warmth penetrated our bodies and heated us as well. We chatted gaily the entire way. Roy said he had never heard me talk so much.

"You're really a chatterbox," he said fondly, and I was beholden to the love in his eyes.

"Somebody needs to do it," I answered and stroked his arm. The journey seemed short for some reason. I was awash with joy and was hoping the ride would take longer, allowing me to luxuriate in my happiness. *Happiness, a word I had never allowed myself to dream about, that had never had any room in my vocabulary. So, this is what it feels like to be in love,* I said in my heart. Everything seemed beautiful suddenly. The landscape rolling by my window looked especially enticing. Every few minutes I suggested we stop a bit by the side of the road to enjoy the sights, but he just hummed and said that if we felt like it we could do it on the way back. Every now and then he looked over at me and smiled.

"What?" I asked, trying to stop myself from laughing out loud.

"Nothing," he said, "I just love looking at you."

We reached the beautiful boulevard, Main Street. For a moment, I thought I recognized the guy who offered to help me the last time I was here. The cypress trees welcomed me with a slight bow. We passed number 16 and I told Roy to keep going a few more yards. We reached number 22, the address given to me by Josh. The house looked exactly like the one I had been in before. The garden was well-kept, but not as nice as the one at number 16.

Roy parked the car in front of the house. We walked up to the front door. We could hear muffled voices coming from inside and knew the tenants were home. Roy signaled me with a nod of his head to knock on the door, but I wanted him to do it. I don't know why, but I was suddenly attacked with a sense of fear. If it weren't for Roy, I would have picked up my heels and run away from the place. Roy looked at me in puzzlement. To the side of the door, on the frame, I recognized the mezuzah, like the one at Mickey's house. A clay pot with fresh red geraniums sat on the step.

Roy knocked on the door, but no one opened it. He knocked again, harder. We heard brisk steps approaching. The door handle turned and the door opened. A woman who looked to be in her seventies stood before us. There were only a few wrinkles on her face, and her eyes were round and green like two sparkling emeralds.

"Yes?" she asked.

"Hello," I said, but I couldn't say any more than that. Roy came to my rescue. "We're looking for someone who may have lived here once—"

"Sonia Schwartz." I completed the sentence. "We're looking for Sonia Schwartz!"

The woman lost her balance for a moment and held on to the door as if it would save her life. Her green eyes changed color, suddenly turning gray. "Yaakov," she screamed excitedly. "Yaakov, come here."

The shuffling of footsteps was heard and a man of roughly the same age as the woman appeared in the doorway. His hair was white, his body bent a bit, and his eyes were sunk deep in their sockets. He stood behind the woman. We expected her to explain the purpose of our visit to him, but she was silent and her body seemed to shrink; I imagined her disappearing altogether. Only the slippers on her feet would remain.

Roy came around first. "Hello," he said. "I'm Roy, and this is Eva. We're looking for someone who perhaps used to live here. Her name is Sonia Schwartz."

Yaakov, like his wife before him, lost his balance for a minute and held on to his wife who was still leaning on the doorframe. The door opened wide, and I caught a glimpse of the inside of the house. It was tidy and warm.

"Who are you?" the man finally asked in a gravelly voice; I noticed a tear dripping under his thick glasses. Roy wanted to answer, but I beat him to it, saying, "Sonia lived in our house once and I found some things that belong to her. I'd like to return them." The woman pulled herself together. She held on to her husband's elbow and pulled him back.

"Come in."

Roy and I exchanged glances and I walked inside, Roy following behind. The living room was large, and, as I had seen in my glance from outside, it was neat and clean. The geraniums, which must have come from her garden outside, were arranged in a small vase on the center of the table. The sofas were adorned with throw pillows. At the far end of the living room stood a large dresser with framed photos on top. The husband shuffled after his wife, who was still holding on to his elbow, as if she were afraid that if she let go he would collapse and fall down. She helped him sit down in a wide armchair at the end of the table and with a wave of her hand invited us to sit down on the couch. She arranged her hair, which had come loose, with her hands and smoothed out her cheeks, like she was trying to get rid of the wrinkles. "Sit, please," she said.

Roy sat down, and I sat close to him. The feeling of fear that had attacked me before remained, and I needed the touch of his body to feel protected. Roy laced his fingers with mine and squeezed them in an attempt to calm me down.

The woman perked up a bit. She left the room briefly and came back with a pitcher of cold lemonade and four glasses. She poured the drink for Roy and me and left the other glasses empty. Afterward, she sat down on the chair next to her husband, turned to us and said, "Now, tell me about this woman you are looking for."

Roy waited for me to begin to speak. He understood that I needed to do it in my own way.

"Roy and I live three hours away by car. As long as I can remember, I have lived there with my parents, Maria and John. They were killed in a car accident about three years ago."

"I'm sorry to hear that," said the woman. Her words sounded sincere.

I nodded and continued. "One day, a short while after their deaths, the telephone rang at my house, and someone asked to speak with Sonia Schwartz."

The woman's body tensed, and she held on to both sides of the chair in an effort to steady herself. Yaakov let out a long sigh and bowed his head to his chest.

I told the elderly couple everything that had happened to me recently. When I got to the part about the bed that was bought for me, the woman interrupted me. "For you? Why for you—what is your connection to her?"

I felt Roy's fingers clenching harder on mine. I lowered my head to them for a moment and then said in a weak but firm voice, "I found out that Sonia Schwartz was also known as Maria Brown."

326 | EINAT LIFSHITZ SHEM-TOV

"I don't understand," said the woman in a shaky voice.

"I knew my mother by the name of Maria, but I found out that before that, her name was Sonia, Sonia Schwartz. And now I'm looking—"

A scream interrupted my dialogue. For a moment, I had no idea where it had come from. Then I saw the woman fall from her chair and realized it had come from her. She sat on the floor with her body folded over her bent legs. Her hands covered her face, and I could hear sporadic sobs. Yaakov tried to get up from the chair, but was unsuccessful. He sat back down and cried. The tears streamed down his face like tiny waterfalls filling the cracks of his wrinkled skin. Roy and I watched the two of them in alarm, stunned by the scene playing out before us. We didn't know whether to leave the house or continue to sit and wait for them to calm down. We felt helpless in the face of the grief pouring out of them.

The woman recovered first. She held on to the side of the table to get off the floor. Surprisingly, she came over to the sofa and sat down next to me. She turned to me so that her wet face was close to mine. Her hands separated mine from Roy's and took them in her own. I felt a chill run down my body like a winter avalanche and froze in my place. The woman pressed my hands and, in a soft and calm voice that was completely contrary to her behavior just minutes before, asked, "What did you say your name was?"

"Eva," I whispered.

"But Sonia's daughter was named Ethel," she said in a quiet voice.

"Ethel?" This time it was Roy's voice.

"Yes, named for my mother, rest her soul."

"But who is your mother? But why would Sonia call—"

"Because I'm her mother."

"Whose?" I asked, not understanding.

"Sonia's. Yaakov and I are Sonia's parents."

My body became weightless air. The knowledge cut off all my airways.

Roy read my situation immediately and forced me to drink some of the lemonade, grown warm in the glass. I heard him say something to the woman but couldn't understand what. After several seconds, someone put a damp cloth on my forehead. Roy was there. I was aware of mumbling next to my ear, but I couldn't interpret a thing. Roy used the wet cloth to cool my face, and slowly I began to feel myself rising from the deep black hole into the light above. The voices and figures became clearer, until finally I was able to stabilize myself and leaned back on the sofa. Roy looked at me with concern.

"I'm OK," I reassured him.

"Can you stand up?" asked the woman next to me.

"Yes."

Roy wrapped his arms around my waist and helped me get up from the sofa. The woman led us to the other side of the room, where a large dresser stood, covered with framed photographs. There were about twenty photos, each with the same girl in them—sometimes by herself, other times with another boy and girl by her side. In one of the pictures, she was being hugged by her parents. One of the pictures showed her with a young man about her age standing behind her, hugging her with his head on her shoulder. The smile on her face was enormous, and her eyes were shining with joy. The woman next to me moved closer to the photo and said sadly, "That's the last picture we have of her."

I asked Roy to let go of me and moved closer to the pictures. I bent forward and scrutinized the last photo. I examined the facial features, the smiling eyes, the posture. The face was that of my mother, but the expression belonged to a stranger, someone I didn't know. I felt dizzy and asked Roy to help me back to the sofa. Yaakov remained sitting, hunched in his armchair. The woman poured him a glass of lemonade and brought it close to his mouth. His lips shook when he took a sip of the drink. His face was stony and his breathing was labored. He didn't take his eyes off me. He followed my every movement while his lips mumbled, "Nichka, Nichka..."

I took a step backward, moving away from where he was sitting and the nonsensical words coming from his mouth. The woman moved toward him, took hold of his shoulders, and whispered words into his ear. Little by little, he appeared to relax, and his glassy eyes became clear again.

Suddenly, like a rock hitting the bottom of a well, I knew the name he was saying. The name rang in my ears so strongly that it felt like the rock had hit me straight on the forehead. *Nichka. He said Nichka.*

"Why did you say Nichka?" I asked. "Who is Nichka?"

"Nichka is Sonia," his wife explained. "That's what we called her, ever since she was a young woman. At first we called her Sonichka and then gradually it became Nichka." She smiled as if she was remembering a happier past experience.

The things I learned in the last hour connected the links in the chain. Each link had been there, but it hadn't been clear how it connected to the one before it. My heart was pounding like a jackhammer, my blood was racing through my veins, and I was hit with a sudden terrible stomachache. It was obvious that the turmoil I was in would decrease only after I received answers. I turned to the woman, whose name was Leah, and asked her, "Nichka... Sonia... Where did she give birth to Ethel—what hospital?"

Leah and Yaakov exchanged a look. She cleared her throat and finally said, "She gave birth to Ethel at the Jesuit Hospital for Unwed Mothers."

"I went to that hospital. I tried to find out who this Ethel was—I had found her birth certificate in a box in the kitchen pantry."

"What did it say on the birth certificate?"

"The name Ethel Weiss was written on it."

"I see," she said and became silent.

"Who is Ethel Weiss?" I asked.

"She is Nichka's daughter."

"And who was her father?"

Again, the two exchanged a look. Then she said, "David, David Weiss. He was killed in a car accident."

"When?" I asked with a fading voice.

"A few months before Nichka gave birth."

A glimmer of understanding sparked in me suddenly. I asked if I could use their phone.

Roy and the elderly couple stared at me in confusion.

"Yes, of course." She led me to the hallway where a telephone hung. I took out Officer Peter Jenkins' card and without hesitation dialed his number. The office told me he was not working, but after I explained that it was an emergency they agreed to give him the phone number written on the base of the telephone on the wall. It wasn't five minutes before the telephone rang. I picked it up immediately.

"Eva, this is Peter Jenkins," said the voice on the other end of the receiver. "How can I help you?"

"Peter, thanks for calling me back. I'm sorry if I scared you, but I need one answer from you."

He waited for me to continue.

"What was the name of the man killed in the phony car accident?"

"David Weiss," he answered right away.

"Thank you," I said. I didn't let Peter ask me anything.

I went back to the living room. The three of them sat in the same position and silence prevailed. Roy tried to read my expression, but it was obvious he couldn't guess what was going on in my head. "We have to go." I turned to Roy and urged him to get up.

From the corner of my eye, I saw Leah's surprised expression. Roy also looked at me questioningly but got up from the sofa. I took his hand and forcibly pulled him from there. At the door, Leah called out to me, "Wait— just a minute, please."

I turned back and yelled, "Thanks for the drink," and quickly left, begging the earth to open its jaws and swallow me whole.

"What happened to you?" Roy let go of my hand, turned toward me and with an angry look on his face waited for me to answer. I ignored him and got into the car. He followed me and sat behind the wheel.

"Go," I begged; I couldn't stay at that place one more minute.

Roy complied. He hit the gas pedal and the car bolted from its spot.

He drove in silence. When we reached the main road that led to my house, I spit out what I had been holding in. "My father murdered David Weiss."

Roy didn't react. I suspected he was trying to make sense of the pieces of information he now possessed.

"Is that what the policeman who came over told you? Is that who you called?"

"Yes."

"I understand. He told you the name of the driver who was killed." He was pondering out loud.

"Yes."

"I'm sorry, Eva."

The rest of the journey was made in quiet.

***

We entered the house. Roy made me a cup of hot chocolate and helped me sit down on the chair in the kitchen. I was functioning like a robot. My head was full and empty at the same time. Thoughts were stopped by the questions I still had not answered—I had left that horrible meeting more confused than before. So many bells were ringing in my head that it had become unbearable. I held my head with both hands and closed my eyes. Roy sat across from me and quietly watched me.

That night, as we were lying in bed, he pulled me to his body. It felt as though he was trying to pass his strength on to me and erase all the horrific feelings of guilt left me by my father.

37

The days that followed were difficult for me. My guilt grew to unbearable proportions. I walked around bent over, carrying a burden too heavy to bear. It seemed that everyone who passed me by knew my father was a murderer. Every look directed at me was accusing. People pointed at me, their eyes glaring. I closed myself off in the house, not leaving from the moment I came home from work. Roy coaxed me to go to the office, because I didn't want to show myself there either. The actions of my father and my own actions became one. I was living like a hunted animal.

I was convinced that someone was looking for me. When they finally caught me, they would hurt me, punish me. I wanted it all to be over, to find peace—death sounded like an excellent solution. But the will to live was stronger. Many days went by in this state of complete numbness, until one evening Roy said "Enough." When I came home from work, he was already home. He usually arrived after me, in the evening, when it was already dark outside. I went inside, threw my keys on the dresser, and hung my coat up on the hanger by the front door.

I ignored Roy's surprising presence and gave him an apathetic hello. Then I went toward the bathroom to see if there was hot water for a shower, but Roy got up, blocked my way and pulled me to the sofa in the living room.

"Sit down!" he ordered me.

"I want to take a shower."

"Sit!" he ordered again.

I sat down where he indicated and leaned back. I was exhausted and as limp as a marionette.

"Eva, this has to stop."

"Roy, I don't have the energy for this now," I said, intending to get up. But he sat me back down.

"Eva, we are going back there and you're going to tell them everything."

"Are you crazy?"

"You have to come back to life, and as long as you keep secrets from them, you won't be able to do that."

"I can't." I was on the verge of tears.

"You can and you must," he said firmly, and I knew that I had no way out. But I didn't think I could look them in the eye and tell them the truth.

"I'll be there with you to help," he urged me.

"Roy, please."

"Listen, my sweetheart, I love you very much. You know that, right?"

I nodded.

"I know that the moment you let these things out, you will feel differently. You have to trust me on this. You're disappearing... I'll help you," he promised again. "We'll go over there tomorrow."

"Tomorrow?"

"Tomorrow," he said in a calm voice.

"No, let's wait a few days."

The stress of anticipation was keeping me awake. Roy fell asleep and his breathing became relaxed. I turned onto my side but couldn't get comfortable. I saw Leah's face and Yaakov's helplessness. I saw their sorrow when they talked about their missing daughter.

"I don't understand," I muttered to myself.

"What don't you understand?" came Roy's voice, suddenly sounding wide awake.

"Roy, everything is all jumbled in my head. Who is this Ethel and where is she? If my mother had another daughter, what did she do with her, and why didn't she ever mention her? Maybe the woman who raised me isn't even my mother. Maybe that is why she was so cold to me."

Roy was silent. His face was expressive as he looked at me. His eyes searched mine and his hands gently held on to my arms. His lips weren't moving, but his expression said something I couldn't understand.

"Roy?"

"Eva, honey, you have to open your eyes." His hands dropped from my arms and held my face in front of his. "You have the whole picture right in front of you. Look closely."

"I don't understand what you're saying," I said, on the verge of tears.

"You didn't need to look for any more answers. They're right in front of you."

"I don't know what you're talking about. What answers? I don't understand a thing!" My voice broke down into intermittent sobs and Roy gathered me to him in a strong embrace.

And then, through a thick film of tears, with my head sunk deep into his chest, I said what I already knew: "Ethel.. is me…"

Roy tightened his embrace and rocked our bodies back and forth. When my crying subsided, he separated us and looked in my eyes again, as if he wanted to see if there was something new in them, that wasn't there before.

"How do you feel?"

"Weird."

"I know."

"I feel like a stranger lives inside my body. Everything I thought about myself isn't true at all; not my name, my parents—nothing. I need to reintroduce myself to myself."

"What would you like to do?"

"What should I do, Roy? What do you think I should do?"

"I will accept whatever you decide."

"I want to go over there."

"When?"

"In the morning."

"Are you sure?"

"Now I am."

***

We went to Cypress Beach the next day. The whole way I urged Roy to press harder on the gas pedal, but he gently reminded me to try and relax. During the ride, I expressed to him my fears that they wouldn't want to open the door for me, especially after my sudden departure from their house. I went from hope to despair due to the uncertainty of what was about to happen. Between life and death, that's how I saw things. Maybe they will accept me or maybe they will ask never to see me again. Roy tried to calm me down, but he was also tense. He was afraid of the ramifications on my future, on our future, that could arise from the meeting. I wanted everything to work out so much, but in real life there are hitches, especially in my life. Although my life was connected to theirs, the fear of disappointment took away my courage to talk about it out loud. One fantasy swirled around in my head: the fantasy of unconditional love.

We reached the street that had now become familiar. I told myself that this may be the last time I see them. Roy stopped the car in front of the house and I went to battle for my life. We crossed the street. The shutters were open and dots of light shone through them. Roy made way for me and let me stand in front of him.

I knocked on the door, lightly at first, and then harder. I took a deep breath and waited. Footsteps could be heard from inside and the door opened. When Leah saw us, the expression on her face changed and she slammed the door shut. We looked at each other and Roy gave me a loving expression that gave me the courage not to give up.

"Leah, please open the door."

"Go away. I don't want to see you," she said.

"Leah, you have to open up. I'm not leaving here until you open this door."

"You can stand there till tomorrow. This door is not open to you."

"Leah, I'm your granddaughter. I'm Sonia's daughter."

Silence from the other side of the door. No answer was forthcoming for many long minutes.

I slipped my hand into my purse and pulled out the sheet of paper I had brought with me and began to read.

> Nichka, my love
>
> Your tears are engraved on my shirt like the stains of memory. I caress them with my fingers and kiss them. That way I can feel you, as if you were still with me, next to my body. Don't cry, my love, our love is stronger than any distance. My beautiful Nichka, you know that we have our whole lives ahead of us and what is two years in comparison. Think constantly of the time when we will be together and inseparable. Think about the joy we have experienced together, the laughter. Your marvelous laughter is ringing now in my ears, overcoming the dull hum of the airplane's engines taking me away from you.

I stopped for a moment. My weeping mixed in with the same sound from the other side of the door.

"If they were to ask me what is unique about your love, my answer would be immediate: your laughter. Don't ever stop laughing, your laughter overcomes anything." The door slowly opened. Leah stood before me, her face furrowed with rivers of tears.

We went inside. Yaakov came out of one of the rooms and sat in the armchair. His face also showed evidence of tears. Leah invited us to sit down. We sat in the same place we sat during our last visit. It felt like we had never parted and were just continuing the conversation from where we left off. Doubt was apparent on her face.

"Why do you think you are our granddaughter?" she asked directly.

I wanted to answer, but Roy intervened. He said, "I think if you tell us Sonia's story, we will get the answers to questions we all have; it will be safer that way."

Nichka's Story

"David, come on already! It's going to be dark soon and we won't be able to see a thing."

"Don't worry, Sonichka, there are still a few hours of light left. What are you laughing at?"

"You look funny."

"Why?"

"What did you just eat?"

"A sandwich with chocolate."

"I thought so." She laughed. "The chocolate is smeared all over your face. Stop using your hands to clean it—you're making a bigger mess. And now your hair is full of chocolate too," she said, and handed him a handkerchief from her pants pocket.

"Where are you running to?"

"Come on, you old man, move those legs."

They reached the forest clearing behind her house, where a puddle the size of a tiny lake had formed after the heavy rain last weekend.

"Did you bring everything we need?" he asked.

"Of course," she said and burst out laughing again.

"What?"

"Can't you hear it?"

"No."

"Listen."

They both stopped talking for a moment and then she began to cavort around him, circling him while hopping and croaking like a toad.

"Enough. Stop it!" he called out.

"I can't," she said and continued to croak.

"Stop, you're annoying."

"Ribbit, ribbit, ribbit."

"I'm leaving, do your work by yourself."

"No, no. Don't go. I'm stopping! Just a bit more and it will stop on its own. Ribbit, ribbit."

It was always like that. She found something funny in everything they did. He was the serious one. He was always threatening not to go with her again, but then he'd forget and go anyway. A day wouldn't go by that they didn't get together, even on weekends.

She was ten years old and he was almost thirteen. In two weeks, they would celebrate his Bar Mitzvah and he would be busy studying the Torah portion he would deliver at the synagogue. Every day after school, the Rabbi would come to his house and teach him about the Torah. Sonichka would sit at home watching the hands of the clock. As soon as she saw it was five o'clock, she'd jump from her seat and run over to the Weiss family house, which was three doors down from hers. She was very excited about the upcoming festivities and made her mother promise to sew her a wonderful dress that would make all her other dresses pale in comparison so that David would see how beautiful she was.

The Bar Mitzvah day came. She was restless. For some reason the event was important to her. She stood in front of the mirror for hours. When she looked at her face and suddenly noticed a small pimple under her nose, her screams pierced through the walls of the house.

Her mother, who came running to the sounds of her screams, found her sitting on the bed crying. She showed her the pimple, which to her was a catastrophe. Her mother made an attempt to conceal the almost imperceptible pimple with makeup.

That's what Nichka was like, full of powerful emotions.

"Mother, what am I going to do if he doesn't like my dress?"

"It's not the dress, it's you... It's you he will love." Her mother tried to console her.

"Ridiculous," she yelled. "You are talking nonsense. He has to love the dress!"

"He will." The mother tried again, but she knew that nothing would help. If she could speed up time, she would have done so right then and there; she was afraid she wouldn't be able to handle her until the evening.

Nichka was beautiful. Her dress, blue like the surface of the sea, emphasized the blue of her eyes. Her immature body was already suggestive of the lean, tall body of a teenager. When she entered the synagogue lobby, where the reception was being held, many heads turned her way. But she only saw one. She followed the movement of his eyes, saw the way his mouth moved, the way his hands became fists. He went up to her and kissed her on both cheeks.

"You're so ugly," he said.

"So are you. My eyes hurt so much from looking at you."

He is so handsome, she thought and looked around at the girls from his class who were staring at him in admiration. *If one of them dares to approach him, I'll kill her, and if he smiles at one of them, I'll kill him.*

When he sang his Torah portion, she thought he had the most beautiful voice she'd ever heard. He read in a steady voice without errors. The women's section saw mostly his back, but she knew what his face looked like without having to see it. She saw his jaw stiffen right before he began his reading; she knew that he took a deep breath so he wouldn't run out of air, and she knew that his hands were gripping the podium where the Torah was lying. He would let go only when he finished his portion. He was very nervous, she thought; his shoulders were shaking. It was clear that no one else saw what she saw so clearly.

Finally, when it was over, everyone went out to the lobby, shook his hand, and complimented him on his reading of the Torah portion. When she reached him, she shook his hand and said, "Awful. It was just awful!" This time he didn't return her banter.

***

Something happened to him after the Bar Mitzvah. He changed. Maybe he believed that the Bar Mitzvah ceremony required him to grow up. They no longer got together as often as they used to. Now he hung out with friends from his class, and sometimes she saw girls showing up. This broke her heart into a million pieces. She secluded herself at home. Her contagious laughter became a rare occurrence.

When she turned twelve, her parents threw her a party in a small reception hall not far from the house. The Weisses were also invited. Her mother sewed her a white dress with delicate lace borders decorated with pearl beads that shone in the light. Her younger sister Didi put very subtle makeup on her face and glamorous lipstick on her full lips. Her body was not quite that of a girl, but not a young woman's either, and it looked like she wasn't quite comfortable with it. Her mother wanted her to wear white high heels, but she insisted on buying flats instead. She didn't want to be taller than him, but she didn't tell anyone the real reason for her insistence.

When she entered the hall, she didn't hear the murmuring or notice the looks being sent her way. Her eyes searched only for him. He stood next to his father. He was fifteen already, a man. His voice had changed not long ago and sounded deep, although every once in a while, a croak would slip out, and she would burst out laughing. He remained serious. Once he even told her that he didn't ever want to see her again, that he was tired of her laughter. Now he looked at her and she didn't recognize the expression on his face. This was the first time she couldn't interpret what was hiding behind his sea-blue eyes. She moved closer to him, and he tilted his head toward her and planted a kiss on her cheek. "Congratulations," he said and smiled a peculiar smile.

Afterward, he went to sit at the table. She saw his back most of the night. He didn't get up from the table, even when the music was playing and everyone got up to dance. She expected him to also get up, but he remained seated, as if he didn't hear a note of the music. The celebration was completely ruined; she didn't enjoy herself one bit; she wanted it to be over already.

What happened to him? she asked herself. *What did I do to make him act this way?* In the days that followed, he continued to distance himself from her. Every so often he would come over, but after a brief time would say he had to go. They no longer laughed together like they did once. He didn't tease her, like before, when she made him laugh. She felt lifeless. Every day was exactly like the previous one. She wanted to grow up already; she thought that when she got older, she would understand why he was acting like this.

One day she went out to the forest behind her house where they used to go when they were younger. There was a big rock there where they would sit and where they had engraved their names side by side. It had rained unexpectedly the day before. The soil was still damp and the surrounding weeds were slippery. She looked around from where she stood. *This is our place,* she said to herself, *even if he's not here.* She went to their rock and began to climb up. Suddenly her feet slipped and there was nothing to hold on to. She slipped down the steep rock with her hands struggling to grasp something to stop her fall. But the weeds around the rock tore off easily and she continued to fall. She landed on the ground and her head hit a sharp stone lying there. For a split second, she thought *No one knows where I am* and then the world disappeared as darkness covered her.

***

"Stupid," he said.

"You're stupid yourself," she answered, and for a moment she didn't recognize her own voice.

She was lying in a hospital bed, covered up to her shoulders. Her head was dizzy and wrapped in bandages. "What are you doing here?"

"Sitting."

"Why?"

"I told you, because you're stupid."

"David, how did I get here?"

"Your parents came over in the evening looking for you. They said that you left the house in the afternoon and hadn't returned. They were sure we were together, but when it got late and you still hadn't come home, they came looking for you at my house."

"And..."

"And I knew exactly where you were. I ran to the rock and found you unconscious."

"You ran?"

"Yes, I ran... Happy?"

"Yes."

"That's all. We brought you here and you slept like a bear in winter."

"Did you try to wake me up?"

"Yes."

"How?"

"What do you mean, how?"

"How did you try to wake me up?"

"Tell me something, are you crazy? What does it matter how I tried to wake you up?"

"Like Snow White or Cinderella?"

"What?"

"Did you kiss me and then I woke up?"

"You are living in a fairy tale."

They both smiled at the same time and knew their crisis was behind them.

Two weeks later, when she was released from the hospital, they met at the rock in the forest.

"I missed you," she said. When he didn't answer, she asked, "And you?"

"And me what?"

She grabbed the end of a weed and began to put it under his shirt. He squirmed and tried to get away from it, but gave in finally and said, "Yes, I missed you too. Now leave me alone."

When she got home, she went into her bedroom, closed the door, and sat on her bed. *He is so beautiful,* she thought. Now she could wear high heels. He was taller than she was by a head and a half. He was already sixteen years old and she had just turned thirteen, but her feelings for him, she knew, would never change, even when she turned one hundred.

On her sixteenth birthday, they surprised her. She had just come home from school and went into the kitchen to fix herself something to eat. She was always starving when she got home from school. Usually her mother was waiting for her and her brother and the meal was already on the table. This time the house was empty. She was very surprised, because usually on her birthday and her brother's, the whole family was home to celebrate together. The answer to her question was found in a note left by her mother on the table. It said, "My darling, Didi had a terrible toothache so we had to take her to the doctor. Dan is at basketball practice, and Dad will be home from work later. I'm sorry, my sweetie. Happy birthday. Love, Mom."

She was disappointed. It was her special day, after all. She opened the refrigerator, hoping to find a birthday cake baked for her, but there was only regular food. She took out some meatballs and set them on the stove to heat. When she went into her room to change clothes, she heard the screech of brakes and the slamming of a car door. The knock on the door came right after. She went downstairs and opened it. An enormous bouquet of flowers hid his face from her. Laughter burst out of her mouth. "You look ridiculous," she called out.

"So do you. Come here."

"Where?"

"Stop asking questions and come."

She went back into the kitchen to turn off the stove and took her flowers from him. When they reached the sidewalk, he opened the door of the car his father had loaned him.

"I'm not sure I should be driving with you," she said.

"If anything happens, it will happen to both of us," he said.

You're right, she said to herself.

They drove in silence, sustained by the closeness between them. It didn't matter to her where he was taking her. What was important to her was that he was with her, within reach of her body.

They finally reached the center of town. He was a terrific driver. With the confidence of an experienced driver, he parked the car next to the curb, then ran around to her side and opened her door for her. "Madam," he said exaggeratedly, holding out his hand to help her out of the car.

"Clean my shoes, please," she said in ladylike tones. "There's a spot of dust on them."

He got down on one knee and spit on her shoes.

"Crazy person!" she screamed at him.

"There, they're clean," he announced. He stood up and held out his hand. She linked her arm with his and they strolled down the street, mock importance on their faces. He stopped in front of a restaurant and opened the door for her. She stepped inside and he followed her. She saw them immediately. Her parents, her brother and sister, and his parents were all sitting around a table waiting for them. When they came closer, they all began to applaud and sing "Happy Birthday" to her. She blushed with joy mixed with embarrassment.

"Did you think we wouldn't celebrate your birthday?" asked her mother.

The meal was great. While they were waiting for dessert, they each gave her their presents. Her younger sister gave her a box with colorful cards and envelopes so she could write letters; her brother surprised her with a baseball, and her parents announced that they had signed her up for the dancing classes she wanted so much. David's parents gave her a beautiful leather purse with a small bag inside for makeup. But the present she wanted the most didn't come. David was happy like everyone else, but he didn't give her a thing.

The atmosphere during the meal was relaxed. They all had shared experiences and mutual friends, and the conversation flowed freely. As long as they sat in the restaurant, she kept hoping he would surprise her and give her something, but the bill had been paid and the families were getting up to leave. Her mother asked if she was joining them in the car, but David answered that he would drive her home.

When they were alone in the car she kept silent.

"Don't you think I deserve a thank you?" he asked.

"For what?"

"For the surprise I made for you. I arranged the whole thing."

"Oh. Thanks."

"You seem to be disappointed. Is something wrong?"

"Everything is fine. It was great," she said. She plastered a smile on her face, but it wasn't very convincing.

She didn't even know what she had expected; she only knew she was disappointed. She was so absorbed in thought that she didn't notice they had driven up to the forest. "Stay here, I'll be right back," he said.

It was already evening, and the pink sky held on to the last rays of sun. He came back and once again opened the door for her. He took her hand and ordered her to close her eyes. When she resisted, he ordered her again to close them.

He steered her along, making sure she didn't bump into any obstacles in their path. He finally made her stop and told her to open her eyes. They were standing next to the rock. Candles were lit in a circle around it, ten of them. When the wind blew, their lights danced to and fro. She gasped. The disappointment she had felt earlier was replaced with excitement. Tears streamed freely down her cheeks. David stood behind her and waited for her to pull herself together. Suddenly she noticed some type of object sitting on top of the rock. She climbed up and sat in her regular place. David sat down next to her. It was an album tied with a green ribbon. She untied the ribbon and opened the album. Inside were pictures of them from the time they were young—some photos in black and white and some in color. Beside each photo were a few words written in humor that only she understood. They sat like this, looking at the album together. David held a candle in his hand to so they could see clearer. On the last page was a single sheet with only three words written on it, the words she had been waiting for all her life, "I love you. David."

The kiss that followed was, for her, the essence of life. Everything she had hoped for came true.

She would never forget this birthday as long as she lived. He had brought her from the world of a child into the adult world. She was in love with this nineteen-year-old boy, she had heard the words 'I love you,' and she had even had her first kiss. She was the happiest girl in the world.

Nothing was missing.

Since that day, they had met every day—they talked, giggled, kissed. Sometimes, if he could, he would pick her up from school or from dance class.

One day, while she was leaving the dance studio, something strange happened to her. David, who studied philosophy and art at the local college, informed her that he wouldn't be picking her up that day, as he usually did. He had a class that evening. He usually studied four times a week and helped his father the other two days at his accounting office, resting only on Saturday, the Sabbath.

That evening, the dance teacher gave a longer lesson than usual. They were practicing for the performance that was to be held on Independence Day. When she left the studio, it was already dark outside. She began to walk toward the bus stop, but suddenly a car stopped beside her.

"Excuse me, how do I reach Main Street?" asked the driver.

She bent down to see him and explained how to drive there.

"I don't suppose you're going there, are you?" he asked.

She nodded.

"Then come on, I'll take you," he offered.

"No, thank you. I'd rather take the bus."

"What, are you afraid?" he asked with a smile.

"No!" she answered. She stood up and continued to walk toward the bus stop. While she was waiting for the bus, she thought she saw the car parked on the other side of the street. From that distance, she couldn't make out if there was anyone in it.

She didn't even tell David about it because she didn't lend the incident any importance. On subsequent occasions when she left the studio, she thought she saw the car, but she convinced herself that it was just her imagination.

***

It was her dreamy gaze that attracted him at first. Over time, he noticed her long legs and the slow way her body moved, like a weightless kite. She didn't notice him at all. To her, he was invisible, transparent. He was angry at her because of it. Once he even bumped into her on purpose. She excused herself as if it was her fault. Despite her frail appearance, he knew she was strong, and that attracted him even more. He believed that their becoming a couple was inevitable—that he only needed to help her realize.

One day, he passed by her house. She was just coming out of the house. She almost ran into him, but her gaze was focused entirely on the boy walking beside her. At that moment, she looked different in his eyes than the dreamy girl he had conjured in his imagination. She walked with confidence, her hand in the boy's and her gaze fixed on his face, oblivious to the world around her. It looked like electricity was passing between the couple, creating a closed circuit where only they existed.

At that moment, he wanted to run toward them, to hit the boy and drag her with him. But he, of course, didn't do that. An unfamiliar feeling took over. A lump was stuck in his throat and tears of anger ran down his face uncontrollably. He had never had to fight for a girl before. The pain that coursed through his gut surprised him and he hated himself for his weakness. For an instant, he hated her as well, for exposing his vulnerability.

***

The performance took place on a stage especially constructed in the center of town. When she came down from the stage, she ran immediately to where David was sitting, a proud smile on his face.

"You were fantastic," he said and kissed her nose.

"Everyone was great," she said to him.

"That may be true, but I only saw you."

When they moved away from the stage someone said hello. She turned to him but didn't recognize the face.

"Hello," she answered with trepidation.

"You don't remember me," he stated.

"No."

"You helped me find my way to Main Street a few weeks ago."

Little by little, she remembered the young man sitting in the car. For some reason, she felt uncomfortable and wanted to get away from there. "Oh—yes. Good night," she mumbled. She held firmly on to David's arm and pushed him to keep on walking.

"Who was that?" he asked.

"I don't really know," she answered. "One day when I was leaving the studio, he stopped next to me and asked how to get to Main Street. I answered him and then he suggested giving me a ride."

"And..."

"And what? I told him no, of course—that I'd rather take the bus."

"Great. Good girl."

Without a word, they turned to each other and rubbed noses. They went the rest of the way in a comfortable silence.

A week after the performance, when she arrived home from school, a bouquet of flowers waited for her on her doorstep. She smiled to herself. David surprised her every once in a while. One time she had discovered a love letter he had slipped into her purse without her noticing; another time she came home from school, went into her bedroom, and found tiny paper hearts spread all over her bed; and one day, when she arrived at the dance studio, the secretary handed her a brown box with a gold lock that looked like a pirate's treasure chest. The box was full of chocolates and an inscription from him. He was a hopeless romantic.

Now, as she looked at the bouquet of flowers on the doorstep, a huge grin broke out on her face. She picked up the flowers and looked for a note among the stems. She finally found a little white note that said, in unfamiliar handwriting, "To the most beautiful dancer." It was signed with three question marks.

That's not typical of David, she said to herself. That evening, when he came over, she asked if he sent her flowers. He was surprised and asked to see the bouquet and the note that was attached.

"It's not from me," he said angrily.

"I know, so who's it from?"

The question remained unanswered and was forgotten as time went on.

***

Winter had come and with it the rainy season. They spent most evenings in her room, now that Nichka had a room of her own. She was seventeen now, a stubborn and opinionated young woman.

One weekend, her parents announced that they were going to Florida to visit her aunts and uncles, and Nichka received their permission to stay in the house and study for her math exam.

After they left, the silence felt strange to her. There was always someone at home, always sounds of life pervading the house: the clatter of pots, Didi's chattering on the telephone, the clicking of her father's calculator, the sound of the refrigerator opening and closing. The lack of noise filled her with a sense of unfamiliar loneliness. She picked up the telephone and called David. He said he'd be over within the hour.

They sat in the kitchen and made themselves dinner. It was one of the few times that they had been alone at home. The air was full of excitement that neither one would admit to. When they finished washing the dishes, they went up to her room. He asked if she wanted to go over the material for the upcoming exam with him, but she said no.

The tension they had felt in the kitchen accompanied them now in the room. David sat on the bed and Nichka began to arrange her desk. She was mumbling to herself and didn't stop walking around the room.

"Nichka," he said in a low voice, "enough."

She stopped, standing with her back to him, and then turned around and sat down next to him on the bed. They gazed in each other's eyes. No words were necessary. He reached out his hand to her and she to him. Their lovemaking was a perfect work of art. She thought she was going to burst with exhilaration. It was a total loss of control. Her body moved on its own until she almost didn't recognize it. The touch of his skin on hers pleasured her to the point of pain. This was exactly what she was waiting for. She had not one ounce of disappointment or regret; everything was perfect. She heard breathing sounds and couldn't determine whether they were hers or his. She felt his breathing combine with her own.

After they had calmed down a bit, as they lay there together, holding each other, he said to her, "Nichka, let's get married."

The answer seemed obvious to her, as if he had asked her to go with him to the movies.

He suggested they get married when she graduated from high school. She nodded and thought to herself that it didn't matter when it happened. To her, they had always been married.

A week later, he told her that he spoke with his parents and announced to them that they intend to get married as soon as she finishes school. He said his parents thought they were too young and that he didn't yet have a profession or the money to take such a decisive step.

"So, what do they suggest?" she asked, and felt a cold wind chill her bones.

"Nonsense. They suggest some nonsense," he said, trying to avoid the question.

"David, what did they suggest?"

"That I go to my uncle in Florida for two years and work with him."

"Doing what?"

"He's in the textile business; he has a factory there. He offered to take me under his wing and teach me the secrets of the trade."

"And what about your studies?"

"My parents said that I can't make any money from philosophy. As soon as I have a profession and am earning money, I can deal with the things I love, but first I have to have a profession."

"And what do you say?"

"What I told them—that I'm not prepared to leave you here."

That's how the conversation ended between them, but the conversation continued in her head. The words were swirling around her head like steam from a boiling pot of water. Eventually she told him they needed to talk. They were in the forest, on their rock, which looked smaller than she remembered. They hadn't been there all winter, and the weeds had grown like wildflowers.

"You need to go."

"What?"

"You have to go, David."

"I'm not going, Nichka."

"David, listen for a minute. Let's say we get married in another year. I don't have a profession, and I also want to study, and you can't earn any money from philosophy. That way, within two years, you'll have learned a profession and at least we'll have an income from something. What's two years compared to a lifetime?"

"Nichka, I can't be so far away from you!" He was practically begging.

"Me either, David, but we don't have a choice. Think about it—after a difficult period we'll be together forever."

"You're so logical," he said with a touch of guilt.

She swallowed before saying it again, "We don't have a choice, David. It has to be this way."

That night, after he left, she couldn't stop crying. She had an unexplainable fear that he would never come back to her, but she tried to push those thoughts down and away.

Two months later, she accompanied him to the airport with his parents. The separation was unbearable. The feeling that she would never see him again wouldn't let go of her even now.

"You didn't forget anything?" She tossed out a mundane question.

"Nichka, just say the word and I'll cancel the whole thing."

"Stop talking nonsense," she said making an effort to smile.

"My Nichka... I'll call every day, just to hear your voice."

She gave him a sad smile and said, "Go! This is too hard."

Before he detached himself from her, he took an envelope out of his pocket and handed it to her.

"What's this?" she asked.

"Read it at home," he answered. Then he bent down, kissed her, and walked away. She wanted to run after him. She still had so many things she wanted to say to him. But the voice of reason left her weeping in her place, while his figure grew distant and faded.

She opened the envelope when she got home. Inside was a sheet of paper with the poem *Annabel Lee* by Edgar Allen Poe written on it. When she read the poem the first time, she was shocked. She didn't understand why he had left her such a sad poem. Then, when she had read it over and over again, she understood what he was trying to say to her. At the bottom of the page, in his familiar handwriting, he wrote, "*In life and in death— together.*"

A week after he left, she began to look for a job. The afternoon hours were the most agonizing. They had always been together during this time.

After several interviews, she was accepted to work at a restaurant on the main street that was open all day. When asked how many days a week she would like to work, she answered with hesitation, "Every day."

She began to work; she arrived home from school at three o'clock, and at five was already at the restaurant. Her parents weren't crazy about the idea, but she was determined and stubbornly dismissed any attempt on their part to dissuade her from her decision.

She learned the job very fast, and the work was intense and kept her busy for the day. But when she got home, the thoughts that filled her head and the longing she felt were painful and upsetting.

One evening, she found herself alone in the restaurant. All the other waiters had gone home already, and the last of the diners had also left, so she helped the cleaner lift the chairs onto the tables. She wasn't in a hurry to go anywhere. Nothing was waiting for her at home. When she finished, she turned out the lights and locked the door after her. It was ten o'clock at night. She rushed to make it to the last bus in time, hurrying her steps, even running, but when she got to the bus stop, she saw the back of the bus driving away. She was alone at the bus stop. A few people were walking on the boardwalk along the beach. The air was heavy, and she felt the sweat break out on her chest and armpits. She debated what to do. *Walk home? That would take more than an hour. Take a taxi? Maybe just ask my father to come pick me up?*

She eventually decided to take a taxi. Suddenly, a car stopped next to her. She continued walking, but the car moved forward slowly next to her until she stopped. The window on the passenger side rolled down and someone asked her if he could offer her a lift. The voice sounded familiar, but she couldn't place it. She shook her head no and continued to walk back toward the restaurant, where she thought it would be easier to find a taxi. But the car stopped and the driver got out of the car and stood in front of her.

"Hi. Remember me?" he asked.

"No," she answered.

It looked like his feelings were hurt, but she didn't care.

"You showed me how to get to Main Street. I offered you a lift, but you preferred to go by bus."

Suddenly she remembered. He was also at the dance performance on Independence Day, and maybe it was even him that sent her the flowers.

"You remember," he said.

"Yes," she answered.

"Maybe now I can drive you. I noticed you missed the bus, and I'm going that way anyway."

At first, she wanted to refuse, but then she decided to accept his offer. She got into the car, which smelled of cigarettes.

"I'm John," the driver introduced himself.

"Sonia," she said.

"What are you doing in the area at this hour?" he asked.

"Working," she answered curtly.

"Where?"

"At the restaurant we just passed."

He shot a quick glance to his right and said, "Do you need money?" When he saw that his question made her angry, he added, "I'm just asking because you look like a student, and usually students don't work during the school year."

"No, I don't work because I need the money. I work because I want to."

They made the rest of the journey in silence. He stopped the car in front of the house. She thanked him, got out of the car and walked to her house without looking back. It never occurred to her to wonder how he knew exactly where to stop the car.

Several days later, she met him again at the same place and he offered to drive her home again.

"What are you doing here?" she wondered.

"I work in the area," he answered.

"Where?"

"At a real estate office. We offer vacation apartments for tourists."

"You work this late too?"

"Sometimes, when it's necessary."

The next time they met, he suggested they have a cup of coffee together, but she refused, and the time after that as well. The third time he asked her and she refused, he asked her why she was refusing and she answered, "I have a boyfriend."

"So, where is he? How come he doesn't come to pick you up from work?"

"Because he's not in the area. He's in Florida."

"Ah."

"But he'll be back in two years—maybe less than two years."

"And you're waiting for him?"

"Of course."

When she got home she felt ill. The conversation about David had brought up such intense pain that she ran to the bathroom and threw up. She couldn't go to school the next day. Her mother said that she was very pale and suggested she be seen by a doctor. The doctor sent her for blood tests, and two days later she sat in front of him once again.

"How old are you?" he began the conversation.

"Almost eighteen."

She didn't understand what he was getting at.

"Are the results of the tests OK?" she asked warily.

"The tests say that you're pregnant."

At first, she was stunned and didn't understand what he was talking about, but the longer the silence stretched, the closer she came to comprehending her situation.

When she got home, she withdrew into her bedroom and sat on her bed, feeling lost. Suddenly her life was a blank page. There was nothing written—no direction, no answers, and no support. She didn't have the slightest idea what she should do. Every solution she came up with seemed horrible to her. *David can never find out about this—at least not in the near future.* It was obvious that if he did hear about it, he'd come back that very day and all their plans would go down the drain. But terminating the pregnancy didn't seem like an option either.

After that day, when she spoke with him on the telephone, there were times where she almost opened up and told him, but she always stopped herself and talked about other things.

One day, toward the end of her shift at work, she felt a severe pain in her stomach. At first she thought it would pass, but the pain only got worse. She could no longer stand on her feet. The shift manager asked her if everything was all right. She nodded and ran to the bathroom. When she pulled down her panties, she saw they were covered in blood. She was terrified—she felt helpless and alone in the world. She got up with great difficulty, put the panties back on, washed her face, and left the bathroom with tiny steps, trying to decrease the space between her legs to prevent the blood from dripping on the floor. The shift manager came up to her and she said with pursed lips that she had to leave. She could barely drag herself out of the restaurant. Every step she took felt like she was climbing a mountain. She walked and stopped, walked and leaned against the fence by the sidewalk. All of the sudden, she heard a voice call her from out of nowhere, "Do you need help?" She lifted her head up and nodded. He helped her into the car and she asked him to take her to the hospital.

They didn't speak the entire way. She was counting the minutes; time seemed to go on forever.

The doctor that examined her told her that she was very lucky; if she had waited any longer, she would have lost the baby. In any event, he suggested she spend the night at the hospital for observation. John waited for her in the corridor. When she left the exam room, he asked how she was feeling, and she told him she needed to stay overnight in the hospital.

"Would you like me to stay with you?"

"No, of course not," she answered without thinking. Then she added in a softer voice, "Thank you. You saved me."

He made a dismissive gesture with his head, then turned around and disappeared.

When she got back into the metal hospital bed, she thought that it was time to tell her parents about the pregnancy. She got down from the bed, slowly walked to the telephone, and informed her mother that she was in the hospital.

After a while, she heard her mother's footsteps in the corridor. She straightened the pillows behind her head and sat up in bed, preparing herself for another battle in her short life.

Her mother came into the room like a storm, her father trailing behind.

She directed them to sit in the white hospital chairs, and then told them straight out that she was pregnant.

"What? I don't understand," her mother said, shocked.

"Leah'aleh, she's pregnant. What's not to understand?" said her father. He asked, "What month are you?"

"Fourth."

"Four! I can't believe you didn't say anything to us."

"Mother, I only just found out a little while ago."

"And what happened tonight?"

"I was bleeding, but the doctor said that everything is fine—I just need to rest."

"That's it, then. You're done with that job." Her mother said to her father, "I told you she didn't need to work. A girl her age! And you said it was OK."

While her parents were surrounding her with their love and concern, they didn't notice the young man pacing up and down the corridor. Every so often, he passed the opening to her room and stole a glance at them.

Their behavior angered him, awakening an emotion he'd rather forget. His mother's shadow passed before him. He saw her thin, frail body and felt her inconsequentiality. He cringed and his muscles stiffened in his familiar contempt for her weakness. She never expressed the concern for him that Sonia's parents were showing now; she never took a stance of any type on any issue. In his eyes, she was like a dead fish carried away by the stream. He felt the desire to burst into the room, to drag them away, to stop the repulsive closeness so he wouldn't have to listen to the words dripping with concern.

***

Nichka didn't go back to work. Instead, she went to the rock every day, because there she felt close to him. She would run her fingers over the names they carved. Sometimes she would lie on her back and imagine him next to her. Not a moment went by that she didn't think of him, that she didn't remember the words he spoke, the conversations they had, the promises they made to each other. Since he left, 3,144 hours had gone by—a little more than four months. In eight more months, he would come for a visit.

She saved the letter he had given her at the airport inside the pretty treasure box. Not a day went by that she didn't read it. She heard his voice reading the words he wrote to her. She had already memorized it; she could recite by heart.

Several days after she returned from the hospital, a knock came on the door. Her father still hadn't come home from work and her mother was out doing some errands; Dan was away at boarding school and Didi was listening to music in her room. She opened the door and John was standing there. He held a bouquet of lilies; he handed them to her, hoping to gain an invitation inside.

"Come in," she invited him, but there was a lack of desire evident in her voice.

They sat in the living room. She was already wishing he would leave.

"How do you feel?" he asked and real concern was in his expression.

She softened a bit. After all, she didn't want to hurt his feelings; he did save her that night.

"Would you like something hot to drink?" she asked.

"I don't want you to make any effort for me," he answered.

"It's no effort at all. How many sugars?"

After they sipped their hot coffee, he asked why he hadn't seen her at the restaurant.

"I quit working there."

"I didn't know."

"I'm pregnant," she blurted out all of a sudden, surprising even herself.

"Ahh. I see."

She saw his fingers clench into fists and his knuckles turn white. She thought she had embarrassed him and apologized.

"I didn't mean to dump that on you like that. I'm sorry."

"It's all right," he reassured her. "I'm just surprised." Then he asked, "Does your boyfriend know?"

"No. I don't want him to know for now."

He took a sip of his coffee again and she had the opportunity to look at him. She never noticed what a handsome man he was. His hair was dark and his skin was fair. He had high cheekbones, and she noticed he clenched his jaw every once in a while. She felt he could be very gentle, but at the same time very rough, maybe even evil. Something in his face told her that he had a great deal of pent-up emotion that could burst forth at any moment, like boiling lava.

In the weeks that followed, he visited her several times. They would sit in the living room or on the porch and talk. He wasn't a very interesting conversationalist, but his visits helped her to pass the difficult afternoon hours. She never invited him to her bedroom or offered to go with him to the forest. These were sacred places, hers and David's alone.

During one of his visits, he suggested they sit outside in the backyard. Her mother brought out a pitcher of iced tea and cookies warm from the oven. Her parents had gotten used to his presence. They treated him politely and kindly, like a distant cousin who had come to visit, but not warmly. It appeared that they too felt this that this young man visiting their home had something too restrained about him, something not sincere. But these feelings had no real clear basis. His behavior toward her and her parents was faultless.

After her mother set down the refreshments, she announced that she was going over to the neighbor's house for a few minutes. When they were alone, he asked her about her plans for the future, since it had been a month already since she finished high school.

"I'd like to continue studying, but right now I can't. I'll wait for David and then we'll decide together."

"Have you told him about the pregnancy?"

"No, but I will soon. I told his parents, and I asked them to wait until I told him myself."

"How come you're putting it off?"

"Because I'm sure that the moment he hears, he'll come home."

"I see," he muttered. "When are you planning to tell him?"

"This week... I'll tell him this week."

"And if he says he's coming home?"

"I'll be happy. As it is, I'm having a hard time."

She noticed the conversation was centered on her, but she didn't care.

John's life didn't interest her at all and therefore she didn't ask him anything; he didn't volunteer anything.

***

The screams could be heard all along the street. They started from far away and grew closer to her house. Her mother went outside to find out what all the commotion was about. Nichka stayed in her room, waiting for her mother to fill her in. But several minutes went by, and her mother didn't come up to her room. She opened the door and heard intermittent sobs. She heard bits of sentences, "We don't know anything... What should we do..." More sobbing. Suddenly, she recognized the voice. It was Berta—David's mother. Her body stiffened. She wanted to run downstairs, but she couldn't move. One hand held on to the doorframe, and the other looked for another anchor to cling to. She didn't want her mother to come upstairs; in fact, she hoped she didn't. All she wanted was to continue sitting on her bed reading. She didn't want to hear crying or screaming. All of a sudden, everything stopped. She sat down on her bed and felt like she was floating inside a bubble. Everything that was happening around her didn't touch her. She closed her eyes and her head rested against the wall. She felt a bitter taste in her mouth and wanted to spit. The door opened slowly and her mother came inside. She intentionally didn't open her eyes. As soon as she opened them, she knew, the bitter reality would penetrate.

"Nichka," she heard a familiar voice far away, "open your eyes. I need to tell you something."

Her head shook from right to left, and her eyes remained shut.

"Nichka," her mother shook her hand, "Nichka, open your eyes. David has disappeared. Nobody knows where he is. He hasn't been to work for two days now."

Her first thought was that it wasn't so bad after all. David would come back—she was sure. He would come back and explain his disappearance. She opened her eyes and looked at her mother. "He'll be back," she said, absently stroking the hand holding hers. Her mother looked at her with an expression full of compassion, but she didn't say a word. She got up and walked toward the bedroom door. Before she reached the door, she took one more look at her daughter and knew that a dark curtain had come down on the horizon.

***

Weeks passed without a word from David; desperation began to seep into her heart like a burrowing gopher. She spent her days on the rock. She would lie on it, pressing her heart and the growing bulge in her stomach against it. Her parents left her alone, but she saw their concerned looks. When the telephone finally rang in their house and her mother came up to her room with the horrible news, she abruptly shook off the hands reaching out to her and ran out of the house.

Hours went by and her mother began to worry. Darkness had fallen on the neighborhood. When her mother reached the forest, she found her on the rock in the position she had been in during the last few weeks. She took hold of her with both hands and pulled her down. Nichka didn't resist. She felt empty of emotions, desires, everything. Her mother carried her home, helped her lie down in her bed and covered her up to her neck, and then sat down at the foot of the bed and spent the night there with her.

The days slipped away and she hadn't spoken a word. She hardly ate or drank. She lost weight to the point where she became almost invisible. One day her mother found her unconscious. She was hospitalized, her frail body hooked up to tubes. The doctor said that if she didn't start eating, her health would continue to deteriorate and there would be no way back.

The world as she knew it no longer existed. She became someone else, someone she didn't recognize and didn't want to know.

One evening, while she was sitting with her parents in the living room, her father cleared his throat and said, "Nichka, we need to think about the baby." She looked at him uncomprehending.

"What did you say?" she wondered.

"I said we need to think about what to do about the baby."

"What's there to think about?"

"You can't raise him on your own. You're only eighteen years old. You haven't even begun to live yet. You need to study, learn a profession."

"What are you trying to say to me?"

He wasn't able to say the words. Her mother completed them instead. "Nichka, you need to put him up for adoption."

"What?"

"I know that it's hard for you to think about it, but there's no alternative. You're still young. Your whole life is ahead of you." Her mother was on the verge of tears.

She looked back and forth at her parents and said, "The baby is mine and will stay with me forever!"

John arrived a few days after that conversation. He was very considerate. They would exchange words every now and then, but most of the time they sat in silence. That's how it was the next day and the day after. She didn't mind him showing up every day; he became part of her routine, and in some way, she even looked forward to his visits.

Her belly was now huge. She noticed the neighbors' looks; malicious gossip was rampant. Once, while she was walking down the street, one of the girls from her class passed her—Laura, who she was friendly with. When they grew closer, Laura suddenly crossed to the other side of the street and ignored her completely. She had similar incidents at least once a week. She had gotten used to it and when she saw someone familiar she just continued walking.

About two weeks before she gave birth, she was sitting with John on the porch; this time he had something to say.

He said, "Sonia, I have a solution to your situation."

"What do you mean?" she asked.

"I know that people are looking at you disapprovingly—an unwed mother and all—and I want to propose something."

He had succeeded in piquing her curiosity. She focused on his lips and waited for him to continue.

"Marry me," he said suddenly.

"Why would you do that for me?" she asked in a steady voice.

It took a while for him to answer. "Because I love you. I know you don't love me—maybe you'll never love me, but it's a convenient arrangement. Your son will have a father and you'll be a married mother."

He wasn't sure it was love, but he had never felt before what he felt for her. She aroused conflicting emotions in him. When he saw her, he saw only her. She filled up the entire space around him; nothing else existed at that moment. But when he was away from her, he felt contempt for her; she represented everything he never had. He felt special contempt for her family. Even if he didn't want to admit it, his family had left deep scars and a hollowness that could never be filled.

Nichka spoke with her parents that evening and told them about his proposal.

"Do you love him?" asked her mother.

"No."

"So..."

"It seems like the best solution for someone in my position."

"But—"

"Mother, nobody else is going to marry me—a single woman with a child. He seems OK to me. He wants to take care of me and the boy, and he didn't ask for anything in return." She lowered her head and withdrew into herself; she tried to hide the tears so as not to hurt her parents.

Her father let out a sigh and his voice broke as he said, "My Nichka, you are in so much pain."

Her mother said, "You can stay here with us..."

"No, Mother. It's time for me to begin my life, even if it's not the life I wanted." And then, in order to convince them that her decision was solid, she added, "The baby will have a father figure and he will grow up in a normal family. It doesn't matter if I love John or not. Nobody can replace David, but I want to give the child a chance."

A week later, she was taken to the Hospital for Unwed Mothers, where she had her daughter, Ethel. Right away she saw David's eyes in the eyes of her baby daughter. Her smooth pale skin was also his. David was back.

***

One month after the birth, they were married. It was a small wedding. John said he didn't have any family, so the few invitees that arrived were all from her side.

At first, they lived in his rented apartment, a fifteen-minute drive from her house. Her mother came over every day to help take care of the baby. But one evening, John came home and announced that he had been fired from his job. He told her that a close relative of his in the next city over had arranged a job for him and that they had to move there. At first, she resisted the idea of moving away from the city she was born in and her supportive parents. But then she agreed. *To keep the family together,* she thought, *for Ethel.*

Ethel was already a year old, a happy, cheerful child who had only just learned to walk. She ran around from one place to the other, touching everything. Sonia followed her everywhere, letting her experiment, but not letting her out of her sight. Ethel was her treasure, the reason she didn't commit suicide and leave this world. Their daughter was her whole world and nothing was more important. She treated her life with John with indifference. They didn't talk much. The relationship they had before didn't change after they were married. Even if he hoped she would develop feelings for him one day, he never spoke about it.

With time, she noticed John growing closer and closer to the girl. He would sit with her on the carpet in the living room, playing games with her that he had bought on his way home from work; the girl was thrilled, curled up in his arms, constantly kissing him.

One day, when she was three years old, Nichka had promised to take her to the playground near their house. The girl was looking forward to it and was very excited. But as they were at the door on their way out, the door opened and John came in. When Ethel saw him, she left her mother's side, ran to him, and jumped into his outstretched arms, begging him to take her to play in the park. Her mother was completely forgotten. John didn't even take off his jacket; they were already out the door, leaving her behind.

As the days went on, she felt the girl slipping away from her. She felt alone in the world. John spent more and more time with Ethel. Sometimes he would come home early from work, take the girl without inviting Nichka to join them, and go to the playground or even just do errands in town. *When did he become this person?* she asked herself. *Why does he want to hurt me so?* He knew that Ethel was her whole world, and at the beginning of their life together, she thought he had come to terms with it. Except now everything had changed. The closer he became to the girl, the further away he became from Nichka. He created a separate world that included only Ethel and him.

One day she asked to speak with him. He kept putting her off until finally she was able to get his attention. They sat in the living room. It was ten o'clock at night and Ethel was asleep in her room. He tried to avoid the conversation, claiming to be tired, and got up from the armchair to go to the bedroom. But she caught his arm and yelled out his name. She didn't care if Ethel woke up. For a moment, it looked like he was going to slap her, but then he sat back down in his armchair and turned his face to her. She stood over him with her head bent toward him, and asked him directly, "Do you hate me?" He was surprised. He apparently was expecting something different. For a second she saw him at his weakest—confused, embarrassed—but it was only for a fleeting moment. He stood up and moved close to her, his face almost touching hers. He asked, "Do you love me?"

It was now her turn to be surprised. He had never asked her about her feelings for him so directly. She thought he knew that love couldn't possibly develop between them. Now she realized that this clarity was only in her mind—he had continued to hope that she would begin to feel something for him. She saw that hope in his eyes, so close to hers. The longer she kept silent, the more his face began to change.

Suddenly his face contorted from one full of hope to a mask of stone with chilling lines of hatred. She tried to hold his hand, to explain to him, to ask him to leave the girl to her, but he forcibly shook off her hand, pushed her away, and disappeared into their bedroom, slamming the door behind him. She would never forget the loathing on his face.

After that meeting, he used every way imaginable to prove to her that he and the girl had no need for her. Her self-worth began to plunge. David had abandoned her, and now their daughter did as well. Every so often, she thought about leaving everything behind; she felt that no one had any use for her.

One day he announced that they were moving to an apartment in another area. When she asked why, he answered that it was none of her concern, and told her to start packing. The look in his eyes when he said this convinced her not to ask any more questions. They left the next day and moved to a city that was a four-hour drive from their previous apartment. When she told him that she needed to inform her parents of the new address, he grabbed her wrist and said, "You aren't telling anyone anything."

"But I have to tell them," she said. Her mouth went dry.

He tightened his grip on her hand. "You aren't telling anyone anything!" he repeated, his lips pursed. "You won't see them or talk to them—either of them, ever!"

When did he become this monster? she asked herself. *He had been so thoughtful and understanding—sympathetic to my grief and tolerant for my pain. I had even begun to like him.*

He didn't know how to explain what he felt toward her. His feelings were confusing. The stronger his love for her, the stronger his hatred grew. He wanted her to feel pain—pain more intense than what she felt when David died.

Despite his threat, Nichka called her parents. She stuttered when she informed them that they had moved to another apartment and that she wouldn't be able to visit any time soon. She asked them not to contact her in the near future.

However, the following week, her mother called, and John answered the telephone. After he put the receiver back in its place, he shot her an evil glance and then looked over to the little girl sitting next to them on the carpet, who didn't notice the drama playing out before her. His eyes turned back to her and said everything his silence did not. Two days later, they packed their belongings and, for the fourth time since they were married, left their home and moved, this time to an old run-down house not far away.

The madness that affected him led him to change her name and that of her child. On his own initiative, he formally changed her name to Maria; Ethel became Eva.

Years later, she made another attempt to contact her parents, but he found out. He took the girl and did not return until the next day. She lost her mind, running around the streets like a crazy person all night long. When she went home, toward dawn, she found them in the living room. The girl was sleeping on the sofa and he was sitting next to her drinking coffee. Ever since that night, she had not tried to contact her parents; their absence became part of her life. They, on their part, tried to find her using any means available to them. They even went to a private investigator, but it was fruitless; Sonia had disappeared as if swallowed up by the earth.

The sky above her and the ground underneath closed in on her. She lived in a box whose sides were so close to each other that any movement was limited. Once a year, she would buy presents that she hid in a box in the basement. On the boxes, she wrote "Ethel"—the name of the daughter born to her, who, for a short time, was hers.

There was one and only one time she was able to get away from the house; she had to do it carefully and quickly. She knew that he had ways of finding out what she was up to. She arrived at the store, bought a bed for the girl, who had now grown, and wrote her former name on the purchase form. It was a small victory for her, a witness to the fact that she still existed. But when the bed arrived at the house, John sawed it into little pieces and threw them in the garbage.

Being alienated from her family tore Nichka's heart apart. She hoped they would find her. Thoughts of death intermingled with her thoughts about the dinner she had to prepare, the marketing, the housecleaning. They became part of her daily routine and were her only source of comfort. But they were only thoughts. She had to endure as long as her daughter was young; she had to remain there to keep watch.

The child idolized John. He was the authoritarian father, and she accepted his words as if they were the pure truth. He loved her in his own way. When she was four, he began to go to his weekly meetings. She would sit close to the door so she could jump into his arms as soon as he returned. Even when she got bigger she did this. It was important to her that he love her; she wanted to be perfect in his eyes.

Over time, Nichka began to understand that as long as John was alive, the child didn't stand a chance—she had no future. The decision began to develop in her heart, and in time it took form. Her love for her child was beyond death, limitless. In her heart, she knew that her daughter would recover—that this way, she was giving her a chance at life. Wherever she was, Nichka would watch over her. Only this time Nichka wouldn't be alone. She would join David, and together they would watch their beloved daughter grow up. Sometimes she would think about killing John and remaining with the child, but she knew that she would live in constant fear. She was also afraid that the child would hate her even more for remaining while John did not.

It was easier than she thought it would be. Cutting the tiny pipes promised the life that came with death. Two days earlier, she informed her daughter that they were invited to an event held by one of his colleagues at work. Nature was on her side when they left the house that evening. For her, it was a sign that the universe was coming together for her. And then, when it happened, for a fraction of a second, she felt pure serenity. Her soul was relaxed and her body sank ever so slowly into a soft sponge that hugged her with everlasting love. One moment before she lost consciousness, his arms embraced her and she knew she had succeeded, that she had done the right thing.

EPILOGUE

It was the middle of the night when Leah stopped talking. They were sitting in the living room and only shadows could be seen on the walls of the house. Roy's arm hugged her and she let the tears flow freely down her cheeks. Leah was exhausted. Her hands slipped down to her sides and swung like pendulums. Suddenly Yaakov stood up from his chair and came over to the sofa where Eva was sitting close to Roy. He held out his hand and she took it cautiously. Tenderly, he pulled her toward him, his eyes never leaving her face. He lifted his hand and stopped at the bridge of her nose, drawing an imaginary line along its shape. Then he traced the contour of her lips with his fingers and finally looked deep into her eyes. "The eyes are David's and the mouth is Nichka's. You have your mother's nose," he said. He turned to his wife, then turned back to her and opened his arms wide, inviting her inside. She had never felt a feeling of acceptance such as this. It was an embrace that reconnected her to the world, that wove together all the frazzled ends into one with a beginning and an end. "We never stopped searching for you," he said, "always hoping."

Leah got up from her chair and joined the embrace. The fissures in her world had been mended, at least for now.

***

When they arrived at home, a strange feeling came over her. It was no longer a house full of vague memories; these were rooms and corners creating new memories: expressions of hatred exchanged when passing each other, the secrets buried in each other's hearts—hers buried so as not to harm her child and his buried to hurt her. His despicable love for his wife grew into a monster that urged him to perform illogical and unconscionable acts. He was a Nazi married to a Jew. Her loyalty to her dead lover sent him into madness and created a monster that could only threaten and frighten—he would never change her feelings for David. Because of these fears, he held on to the innocent child, who he used as an instrument of revenge. His twisted mind invented tools of war, but the war was only in his own head. Obscuring her past made no difference—giving her and her child different names was a change as thin as a blanket full of holes. The truth was there all the time, and he couldn't alter it.

And she, with her strength, responded to his whims and created a world for her and her daughter separate from his. Ethel was to her always Ethel, and David always remained her father. The name Maria was only a thin veil, transparent and weightless, that could be swept aside with a mere breath. The gifts she stored in the box, those that she purchased every year on the girl's birthday, helped her to preserve her sanity. They were a constant reminder of her motherhood.

And her eyes, the same eyes that looked upon David with deep love in her youth, now watched over the fruit of this love. She gave up the child's love for her in order to assure her a feeling of security, the kind that family provides, even a phony family.

***

The day after she returned from Cypress Beach, she decided to visit Sarah. Sarah, who had pushed her to find herself. When she knocked on the door, there was no answer. She tried to open the door, but it was locked. Her neighbor noticed her there and came over to inform her that Sarah had passed away the day before and that her funeral had been held the same day. In a split-second decision, she bent down and took out the key to Sarah's house from under the welcome mat in front of the door. It was the first time she had entered Sarah's house without her. The living room looked the same. She imagined Sarah coming out of the kitchen with a plate of warm cookies. She saw her warm smile and felt her stomach flood with warm feelings and deep sadness. She looked around, stopping at the objects that had become a part of her life—the embroidered doilies on the sofa, the curtains waving in the breeze, the television lying dormant. She caressed the mantel of the fireplace. She walked to the kitchen, hoping to smell the enticing aroma of her cooking, but the kitchen was clean and orderly, as if it had been prepared for her to leave. Suddenly her eyes fell on a white envelope lying on the edge of the table. There was nothing written on it. She took the envelope in her hand and opened it. Inside was a piece of white paper that had yellowed a bit. She straightened it out and read:

Dear Sarah,

I'm leaving and have left my treasure by herself. Watch over her from here and I will do it from over there. I protected her as best I could, and now it's time for me to go and let her grow up without anyone to stop her. I know that eventually she will discover who she is; after all she is David's daughter. Take care of her as best you can and God will bless you for it.

Sonia

Her tears dropped onto the printed words and stained them with all the pain she had carried her whole life. She caressed the letters with her fingers and felt like she was touching her mother. She felt the great love that had been there the whole time, but that she had discovered only recently.

Sarah had fulfilled her duty and left the world.

***

As time went by, she slowly began to absorb everything she had been through these last years. Some of the events were unexplainable, but all of the coincidences seemed to have a guiding hand behind them. The ghost-like forms that moved her around, the raccoon that helped her find the birth certificate, Sarah's death exactly when she had completed the chain of discoveries in her path. She felt that these occurrences were part of a hidden plan that led her to the story of her life. Secretly, deep inside, she knew that they were there, that everything was carried out by them. The triangle had been reconnected, interwoven with love that was beyond the tangible and the obvious.

The next few days were new for her. She drove to Cypress Beach and met her mother's brother and sister and their families. She also met David's mother and his brothers and sisters. His father had passed away from a broken heart two years after David died. They asked her to move closer to them, but she asked for some time. Her ability to absorb everything that had happened to her was limited. First, she needed to learn to replace the father she had known with another; she needed to let go of the guilt that had been the bane of her existence in the last few years; she needed to accept the death of her biological father, who had been killed by the father that raised her; she needed to learn how to exchange one religion for another.

Sometimes she wondered what would have happened if she hadn't begun the random search for Sonia. She thought a lot about her mother, the mother she only now had begun to know. This woman, who had always seemed so weak and spineless, had turned out to be a sturdy rock watching over her all these years. She understood now that this required superhuman strength, and she assumed she would better understand it when she had children of her own.

***

One evening, after they had returned from one of their trips to Cypress Beach, she and Roy were sitting in the living room. The television was on and she lifted her head every now and then to look at the screen. Suddenly, she realized that Roy was watching her. She turned toward him and as sudden as a gushing geyser, the words came out of her mouth: "I love you."

That night, they made love for the first time. She dove deep into the depths of the sea and the motion of the waves swayed her body like a fetus in its mother's womb. Roy was the other half of the whole, but she had needed time to appreciate it. When they finished making love, she felt reborn.

The End

Acknowledgments

To my husband, Yaakov: without you none of this would have happened. Thank you for your love, which gives me the confidence to fulfill every dream in my heart. You are the pillar of my life.

To my Ortal and Reut: you are the motivating energy. With you and because of you, my dream became a reality.

To Shula and Zizi, my beloved sisters: thank you for your unconditional love and for your comments and honest critique given without reserve.

To my dear friend, Iris Senyor: thank you for your unlimited faith.

To Nurit Tamari: thank you for your encouragement and for constantly believing in my strength.

To Iris Rubin and Ayala Gini, and the rest of the Parliament Women— Rachel Natan, Tami Cohen-Ratz, Naomi Fireberger, Marissa Shoah, Meirav Itzikson, Naomi Gilad and Dorit Chen—a huge thank you for being with me throughout the journey, encouraging, believing, showing interest and promising that my dream would come true. I love you all very much.

To Iris Jersy, my dear friend: thank you for your help and always being available.

To Evelyn, from the Steimatzky literary greenhouse: thank you for the opportunity.

To Rotem Raz, my editor: thank you for your endless patience, for your precise notes, and for making room for my emotions, my desires, and my stubbornness. You are a marvelous partner.

And thank you to all those who accompanied me, whether by a word, a comment, or a suggestion.

You are all partners to my dream.

CPSIA information can be obtained
at www.ICGtesting.com
Printed in the USA
LVHW081450030322
712550LV00022B/345

9 781546 784456